MASTER of DRAGONS

ANGELA KNIGHT

BERKLEY SENSATION, NEW YORK

THE BERKLEY PUBLISHING GROUP
Published by the Penguin Group
Penguin Group (USA) Inc.
375 Hudson Street, New York, New York 10014, USA
Penguin Group (Canada), 90 Eglinton Avenue East, Suite 700, Toronto, Ontario M4P 2Y3, Canada
(a division of Pearson Penguin Canada Inc.)
Penguin Books Ltd., 80 Strand, London WC2R 0RL, England
Penguin Group Ireland, 25 St. Stephen's Green, Dublin 2, Ireland (a division of Penguin Books Ltd.)
Penguin Group (Australia), 250 Camberwell Road, Camberwell, Victoria 3124, Australia
(a division of Pearson Australia Group Pty. Ltd.)
Penguin Books India Pvt. Ltd., 11 Community Centre, Panchsheel Park, New Delhi—110 017, India
Penguin Group (NZ), 67 Apollo Drive, Roseland, North Shore 0745, Auckland, New Zealand
(a division of Pearson New Zealand Ltd.)
Penguin Books (South Africa) (Pty.) Ltd., 24 Sturdee Avenue, Rosebank, Johannesburg 2196,
South Africa

Penguin Books Ltd., Registered Offices: 80 Strand, London WC2R 0RL, England

MASTER OF DRAGONS

A Berkley Sensation Book / published by arrangement with the author

Copyright © 2007 by Angela Knight.
Cover illustration by Franco Accornero.
Cover photograph and handlettering by Ron Zinn.
Cover design by George Long.

ISBN-13: 978-0-7394-8325-1

BERKLEY SENSATION®
Berkley Sensation Books are published by The Berkley Publishing Group,
a division of Penguin Group (USA) Inc.,
375 Hudson Street, New York, New York 10014.
BERKLEY SENSATION is a registered trademark of Penguin Group (USA) Inc.
The "B" design is a trademark belonging to Penguin Group (USA) Inc.

PRINTED IN THE UNITED STATES OF AMERICA

There are always many more people than the author involved in the birth of a book.

In the case of *Master of Dragons*, I'd like to thank my editor Cindy Hwang for her unfailing patience and encouragement.

And, as usual, I owe my wonderful critique partner a debt. Diane Whiteside plays an invaluable role in every book I write, helping me past sticky parts and telling me when I screw up.

Then there's Roberta Brown, who is a friend as much as an agent. She, too, was particular help in putting this book in your hands.

On a more personal note, I'd like to thank some new friends for my new life. I had gastric bypass surgery last year—which is one reason Cindy had to give me all that extra time on this book.

Surgeon Dr. Paul Ross did a wonderful job taking care of me at Spartanburg Regional Medical Center, as did his nurses Diane Smith and Norma Gaffney. My personal trainer, Bethany Morton, helped me rebuild my strength after the surgery during the long process of weight loss.

Most of all, I'd like to thank my husband, Michael, who stayed by my side and took such good care of me as I recovered.

I'd also like to thank my parents for encouraging me to consider surgery, and my son, Anthony, for his love and support.

My deepest appreciation to you all.

THE PROPHECY OF SEMIRA

Trapped by the Dark Ones' legions,
preserved by love in steel,
the goddess Semira will yet survive.
Carried in battle by warrior kings
sustained by her Avatars' need,
she will lend her power
to rightful rulers.
Twenty daughters of her blood
will serve her in loyalty
until the last takes up her mantle
to fight beside the blue dragon knight.
Lost and burning in his fire,
shattered and reborn in Semira's power,
the Avatar will free her goddess.
The Dark Ones will be banished,
and the Two Kingdoms liberated
from he who would usurp them.
And the people will live in peace.

PROLOGUE

Dallas, Texas
April 25, 1995

The first time the knight walked in Nineva Morrow's dreams, he was too much for her. Young as she was, he was too male, too tall, too powerful in his midnight blue armor. He made her teenaged heart race with a combination of fear and yearning.

Even his face looked dangerous, hard-edged and fierce. His cheekbones were high and chiseled, his nose narrow, swooping down to a predator's flared nostrils. His mouth was wide and starkly sensual over the tough angular jut of his chin. Long cobalt hair fell straight as silk around the massive shoulders of a man who was no stranger to battle.

"You'll be mine." It seemed she could feel his voice in her very blood. "When you're a woman, you'll feel my touch."

"No." She shook her head against her pillow.

Scarlet eyes narrowed in anger at her denial, then blazed so bright she could see nothing at all.

When the dazzle faded, a great winged figure had replaced his—a dragon, its scales a shimmering blue, its eyes burning crimson. It roared, breathing a thundering gust of flame that poured over Nineva like napalm.

She screamed as the fire raced over her skin, accompanied by a wave of searing pain. Writhing, dying, she fought to escape, to extinguish the fire with her own magic.

A sword appeared before her eyes, its hilt in the sinuous shape of a nude woman. Blindly, she grabbed for it in the desperate hope it would somehow save her.

A woman's face appeared before her agonized eyes, inhumanly beautiful, hair floating in a pale nimbus around her head. Her irises glowed like opals in the moonlight, flecks of magic shining in their depths.

Nineva stretched one shaking, burning hand out to her. "Help me!"

The woman smiled, joy filling those incredible eyes. "Thank you for your sacrifice, child. You've freed me."

She reached for Nineva, who instinctively tried to jerk away. "Don't!"

Too late. The goddess's delicate fingers closed mercilessly around hers.

Nineva couldn't even scream as Semira's magic ripped her apart.

Nineva jolted awake, sweating, her heart pounding. Jerking upright, she threw the covers off and raised her shaking hands. The skin was smooth and whole, unmarred by burns.

As she fell back against her pillow with a gasp of relief, the alarm went off. She groaned and threw both arms across her face.

Time for school. She had a trig test this morning.

Eyes gritty, she rolled out of bed. It was just as well. She'd never have gotten back to sleep anyway.

* * *

Dressed and ready half an hour later, Nineva clattered down the stairs, her book bag slung across one shoulder.

The air smelled of frying bacon and the delicate scent of scrambled eggs. She veered toward the kitchen as her stomach rumbled in interest. The shower had gone a long way toward washing away the last sticky wisps of the dream. She figured she had time to grab something before she went to school.

Like the rest of the rented ranch, the kitchen wasn't large. Its 1970s-era decor could have used some renovation, but there was still something homey and cheerful about its harvest gold appliances and sunny goldenrod wallpaper.

Nineva's mother stood at the stove, dark hair tumbling halfway down her slim back. Sarah Morrow was a lovely woman, despite her running struggle with the ten extra pounds she wanted to lose. Brown eyes dominated the pretty face so much like Nineva's, and her smile made even the grumpiest stranger smile back. Today she was dressed in a pink flannel nightgown and matching bunny slippers. She looked around as Nineva dropped her book bag by her usual place at the table. "Morning, honey. Sleep well?"

"Not really. I had a truly god-awful nightmare." Shaking off the memory of it, Nineva moved around to press a kiss to her father's cheek. "Good morning, Daddy. How was work?" He and her mother worked second shift at the Drayton Textile Mill. Nineva was usually in bed before they got home.

"Fine." Eirnin Morroc hugged her back with one arm, his expression unusually grim. A shaft of morning sunlight blazed in his short-cropped blond hair and pinkened the curve of a pointed ear.

Nineva dropped into her chair, eyeing him with a frown as she reached for the plate of scrambled eggs. "Is anything wrong?"

"Your father had a nightmare, too." Worry flashed across Sarah's face before she forced a smile. She plated the bacon she'd just fried and carried it to the table. "What was your dream about?"

Nineva grabbed a piece of the bacon and crunched. It was perfectly crisp and smoky, the way her mother's always was. "I dreamed I freed the goddess."

Her father looked up and gave her a tight smile. "That doesn't sound like a nightmare to me."

"You know the legend—'Lost and burning in his fire . . . '" She had to busy herself with the plate of eggs before she could bear to meet her mother's worried gaze. "The dragon burned me, and it hurt. A lot."

Sarah sat down across from her. "It was only a dream, honey." She smiled, but the curve of her pretty mouth looked strained. "Hey, I used to dream I went to school naked."

"Yeah, I have those, too." Nineva forked up a bite, then put it down again, unable to eat with her stomach knotted like fishing line. "But what if this one *was* a vision? The prophecy . . ."

"You're the twenty-first Avatar, Nineva," Eirnin interrupted, his tone unusually sharp. "It's your destiny to free the goddess. If there's pain, you'll be more than rewarded for enduring it."

So they'd always taught her. She'd been able to recite the legend from the time she was a very small child. And yet she'd never considered the implications.

. . . *Shattered and reborn*. Didn't "reborn" imply dying? And was it cowardly of her to even worry about that when the goddess had been imprisoned for so many centuries?

Of course, the Sword of Semira was a universe away at the moment. It wasn't as if she had to worry about it now. This morning's trig test was a much more immediate concern.

Nineva shook off the lingering worry to study her father

with a troubled frown. He didn't usually snap at her like that.

Tall and athletic, Eirnin Morroc appeared a good ten years younger than Sarah, though he was actually far older. Like Nineva, his irises were swirls of opalescence; like her, he had to use spells to appear human. He called himself Ernie Morrow, but that was only the most recent of his aliases.

Eirnin had left the Sidhe kingdom sixteen hundred years before, when his murderous cousin became king. Like Nineva, he'd been born with Semira's Mark, which in his case meant he was destined to sire the next Avatar. It also made him a threat to King Ansgar, whom the Morven people considered the usurper of the prophecy.

Eirnin had wandered Mortal Earth ever since, dodging Ansgar's assassins and trying to father the promised daughter on a series of mortal lovers. When he'd met and married Sarah, he finally succeeded.

Nineva believed her father truly loved her and her mother, but she'd never had any delusions. His entire life was devoted to ensuring she fulfilled her destiny: freeing the goddess. As far as he was concerned, that was the reason both of them had been born.

He looked pale and tense today, worry drawing his sweeping brows down over those striking eyes. "What did you dream about, Daddy?"

Eirnin drummed his long fingers restlessly on the table. He hadn't touched his breakfast. "Hopefully, nothing that will come true." Glancing up at the wall clock, he forced a smile. "You'd better get to school, baby. You're going to be late."

He was right. Nineva scooped up a last piece of bacon, pressed kisses on her parents, and headed for the door. She bounded down the steps of their rented brick ranch and ran for the bright red Toyota that had been a surprise seventeenth-birthday gift. Her parents didn't have a lot of money, so they carefully saved every dime they could. She'd been thrilled to get the car, used or not.

Nineva's mind returned to the dream as she backed a little too fast down the driveway. She'd had prophetic dreams before. What if . . .

The car hit something with a soft thump. A canine voice yelped. She slammed on the brakes. "Shit!" Nineva shoved the car door open and jumped out. "Oh, no!"

The neighbor's Irish setter lay sprawled beside their mailbox, whimpering softly in pain. His eyes had already gone dull with encroaching death as she knelt beside him.

She'd killed him. She'd been so wrapped up in worry for herself, she hadn't watched where she was going.

Guilt and horror stabbed her as she touched his shoulder. His red fur felt so soft . . . Her eyes began to sting with tears. She thought of Johnny, their ten-year-old neighbor, who played with the dog every day after school. He was going to be heartbroken.

No.

Nineva knew she wasn't supposed to do it, knew it could be dangerous. But she couldn't let Johnny suffer for her mistake. If she shielded the way her father had taught her, the king wouldn't be able to sense what she was doing. They'd all be safe, and the boy would have his dog.

As her heart began to pound, she cast a quick spell barrier around herself and the setter. It was going to be tricky. Sometimes her magic escaped her control, particularly when her emotions were running this high.

Sometimes being the descendent of a goddess was a pain. Yeah, she had plenty of power, but it was like manning a fire hose. Getting the magic blasting in the right direction could be a bitch.

Laying both hands on the soft, furred head, Nineva sent her power pouring into the animal with all the guilt and determination in her soul. The Goddess Mark grew warm on her breast. She found the broken ribs that had pierced his lungs, and she repaired them, healed the savage punctures, stopped the bleeding.

Abruptly the Mark flared into a white-hot blaze. Before she could rein the magic in, her shield silently exploded in a shower of sparks.

Nineva winced. "Dammit!" She'd blown out the barrier again. Had she given herself away?

The dog jerked under her hands, then leaped up. She looked up, startled, as the setter dashed off, yelping, tail tucked between his legs. His eyes were ringed with white as he stared back at her.

"Well, that's gratitude for you." Nineva lifted her voice and yelled after him, "The least you could do is lick my face!"

The dog kept going.

The burn on her right breast was throbbing now. Hooking the neckline of her pink T-shirt with one finger, she looked down. The Goddess Mark blazed against her skin, a intricate swirl of gold and iridescence that glowed like a flashlight. Hastily, she drew her shirt up to cover it.

"Nineva!" Her father's stern voice rang from the garage. "What did you just do?"

She jumped guiltily and whirled to face him. "I hit Johnny's dog with my car, so I healed him."

"Nineva! How many times have I told you . . ."

"I shielded first," she interrupted hastily, "but then I had this power surge, and the shield blew. I don't understand what I did wrong . . ."

She broke off. Eirnin had gone sheet white as he stared at her, his eyes painfully wide with some horrible realization. He met her mother's gaze as she pushed open the kitchen door. "Sweet Semira, Sarah, this is why. This causes it."

"What? What'd I do?" Nineva's heart started to pound even harder beneath the Mark. "Daddy, the shield just blew for a minute. The king couldn't have sensed it, could he? Do we have to move again?"

"Move?" Eirnin made a choked sound. "No, we don't have to move."

She'd expected anger, not this black despair. "Daddy, I'm sorry! I know I shouldn't have done it, but I couldn't let the dog die! Johnny loves him. *It was my fault!*"

Without answering, he turned and walked back inside, his usually graceful gait stiff and robotic.

"Mom, are we going to have to move again?" Nineva hurried up the drive to her mother. Sometimes she could talk Sarah around when her father wouldn't listen. "I want to graduate with my class. That's in just three weeks."

Her mother looked away, her mouth going tight. "No, moving's not going to help this time. It's too late for that."

Nineva stopped in her tracks. "What do you mean?" The Mark throbbed like a wound, adding to her panic. "Mom, did I just really fuck up?"

"Don't swear, Nineva."

The hopelessness on her mother's face chased every other concern right out of her head. She caught Sarah's wrist. "We can go. Let's just get Dad and run. Right now."

Her mother turned and jerked her into a tight, fierce hug. "Baby, it's not your fault. You remember that, okay? You're a kindhearted, compassionate person, just like we raised you to be. And we love you."

Nineva wrapped both arms around her and clung, cold, sick nausea flooding her stomach. "Momma, I'm sorry! I love you. It's not too late, we've got time . . ."

Her father walked out of the house carrying a duffel bag. Opening the Toyota's door, he tossed it inside. "There're several changes of clothing and six thousand dollars in this bag, money we've been saving for you. It's your rainy-day fund, so use it only when you absolutely have to. You'll need to get a job, which isn't going to be easy without a diploma, but you'll probably be able to obtain a GED later."

She stared at him. "You want me to just drive off and leave you?"

The frozen determination on his face cracked into pain. He walked over and wrapped his arms around her. He felt tall and strong and warm. "You've got to, honey. They're coming now, and we don't have time to argue. Your only chance is if your mother and I can keep them occupied until you have time to get away."

Nineva dug her nails into his broad shoulders. "I'm not leaving. I'm the Avatar, I can help! We'll fight them!"

He pushed her to arm's length and met her gaze with fierce determination. "And we'd lose. Nineva, this is what I dreamed last night. There are twenty Sidhe warriors on the way. If we try to run, we'll be caught. If Ansgar gets his hands on you, he'll kill you to make sure the prophecy doesn't come true. You're a threat to him he can't ignore." A sick horror flashed across his face at whatever fate he saw for her. "I won't allow that. Go. Now."

"Daddy, no!" Tears of guilt and panic rolled down her face. "I'm not going anywhere!"

Eirnin straightened. In that moment, she saw him as the prince he was. "You're the Last Avatar of the Goddess, Nineva Morrow, and I'm not letting you fall into Ansgar's hands." His opalescent gaze narrowed. *"You will go."*

His spell slammed into her mind, buckling her knees. "Daddy!" she moaned.

"Go." His face was implacable, but his eyes glistened with unshed tears. "You must survive to free Semira. It's your destiny. Too many people have waited and dreamed of this moment. You can't die."

Nineva turned, firmly in the grip of the spell, and got in the car. She fought to call on the goddess and make her body obey, but her hand went to the key and started the car.

As she drove off down the street, she managed to look up into the rearview mirror just in time to see her mother go into her father's arms. He buried his face in her hair.

Nineva was crying so hard she could barely see, but her

body, controlled by her father's spell, drove toward the interstate.

Two hours later, she felt the psychic blast of Eirnin's grief when her mother died. An hour after that, the compulsion spell broke.

She knew what that meant. Her father's magic had died with him.

Nineva pulled over, rested her forehead against the wheel, and fought her tears until she could drive again.

She owed her parents that much.

ONE

The city of Avalon
Twelve years later

The vampire attacked in a flurry of muscle and steel, sword swinging, lips stretched in a manic grin. Kel parried and felt the jolt of blade hitting blade all the way to his teeth. Cachamwri's Egg, the vamp was strong.

Kel drove his sword against his opponent's hard enough to send the man flying. The warrior twisted in midair to land in a crouch, his bearded face grim with determination. Roaring a battle cry, he charged.

From the corner of one eye, Kel saw a blazing ball of mystical energy fly at his head. He ducked and sent a blast of his own back at the dark-haired witch who'd thrown it, then parried her partner's swing. Even as he blocked the blow, he spotted an opening and kicked the warrior in the belly. His opponent fell in a clatter of blue armor and a startled whoof of breath. Before he could scramble away, Kel planted a booted foot in the man's chest and lifted his blade. "Yield!"

Daring a glance at the woman, he saw she was down, too, writhing on the ground.

Laughing.

"Dammit, Kel!" she wheezed between breaths as his spell tickled her without mercy. "Call it off!"

"Not until Gawain gives up." He grinned down at his friend's face. "Say it, 'Wain."

As he expected, the knight laughed and surrendered. "You win, you big lizard! Let her go."

Kel took his foot off Gawain's chest and banished the spell. "Love has made you soft."

"That's what you think," Lark said with a wicked little grin, getting up to dust off her armored knees.

Gawain rolled to his feet and moved to sheathe his sword as he smiled at Kel. "You should try it sometime."

"I think I'll pass." Kel watched his friend's blade slide into its scabbard, remembering the way the leather had felt around his own length. For fifteen hundred years, he'd been trapped in a magical blade, mind-linked to Gawain, able to move only slightly in his steel cage. "I like my freedom."

Gawain and Lark had broken the spell that had trapped him in the sword just six months before. Kel's first act had been to kill the dragon who'd imprisoned him—his own uncle, who'd also arranged his mother's murder.

Now Kel had everything he'd dreamed of during all those centuries of being a prisoner. He was respected and powerful. Arthur Pendragon himself had named him a Knight of the Round Table for the centuries he'd spent protecting Gawain and Avalon with his magic. He had all the women he wanted and a challenging, interesting task—keeping humanity from destroying itself. He had avenged himself and his mother.

His life was perfect. Really.

"Hey, don't knock love until you try it." Gawain walked over to his wife and pulled her into a hard, devouring kiss.

She kissed him back as the scent of their rising desire teased Kel's acute senses. Six months ago, that would have been his cue to go to sleep, sinking into the steel of the sword to give them privacy.

The memory made him restless. "I guess this means we're done with practice. Have fun." Kel gave the couple an offhanded wave and strode away, trying to ignore the sting of jealousy. Any dozen women would be delighted to make love to him whenever he wanted, but none of them would give him what Lark and Gawain shared. He could still remember that moment when he'd been linked with them both—the feel of their perfect, shimmering love.

Kel knew he'd never experience that kind of joy first-hand, because he wasn't human. Wasn't even a vampire or witch, like the rest of the Magekind.

And his kind did not mate for life.

Reaching Avalon's central square, he stopped. Around him rose the shining castles, châteaus, and villas of the enchanted city, all brightly lit by Mageverse magic. The moon floated overhead, a bare silver sliver against the brilliant backwash of the starlit night. The sky was much brighter here than it was on the alternate Earth where the mortal humans lived, more crowded with stars. Whenever he traveled to that other world, the air tasted flat, lacking the familiar sizzle of enchantment. He was always delighted to come home and breathe in the sweet taste of magic again.

Tilting his head back, Kel mentally reached for the Mageverse. He let its familiar foaming warmth flood him, first his senses, then his mind. Then his body.

In the blink of an eye, he began to grow, muscle and bone expanding, strength flooding his consciousness with an intoxicating power.

When he opened his eyes again, the city around him had shrunk. An illusion, of course, born of the fact that his head was now a good fifteen feet in the air.

He spread his great wings and bounded upward, unconsciously extending his magic to lift his forty-foot length. Avalon began to drop away from his scaled belly as he flew higher and higher.

Free. He was free.

Even after six months, he never got tired of this. Flying again, after so many centuries of being tiny and trapped in that damn blade.

A dragon once more.

Kel liked assuming human form—he'd shared a human's mind for fifteen centuries, after all. In many ways, he was more human than anything else.

But still, there was something to be said for flying.

He beat his way higher, enjoying the cool wind against his face. Opening his jaws, he breathed out a great plume of magical fire, just for the pleasure of watching it glow.

He swung into a swooping turn over Avalon, admiring the city's marble towers and whimsical shapes, so different from the Dragon Cliffs he'd been raised in. Humans had a way of turning even the simplest things into art. It was one of the things he liked about them.

From the corner of one eye, he spotted something burning fiercely against the night sky.

He glanced idly around—just as it shot toward him, blazing like a comet.

Startled, he drew up, trying to make out what it was. Great wings and a long snaking neck suggested another dragon, but no dragon shone with multicolored light.

Kel . . .

The alien voice echoed in his mind, impossibly deep, though edged in a sibilant hiss. His spines flattened on the back of his neck with superstitious terror.

Kel's first impulse was to flee, but Knights of the Round Table did not run. Instead he held his position and threw up a magical shield as he watched the burning dragon grow closer.

One thing was painfully obvious: this was no creature of flesh and blood. "Cachamwri," he breathed, realizing at last it could be no one else.

Aye, the burning dragon said.

Kel's wings almost failed him in his astonishment. He fell several feet before he caught himself.

Cachamwri, the god of dragons.

I have a task for you, Cachamwri said, as he swooped into a tight, fiery circle around Kel.

You never answered me. Kel hadn't even intended to say the words. They simply erupted on their own, borne on a sudden lava flow of hot rage. *Centuries I prayed to you, and you never answered.* He'd begged the dragon god for his freedom, begged to learn who had trapped him. To no avail.

Cachamwri spread his wings wide and hovered, great head cocked in inquiry. Kel could feel the pounding heat of him. *Would I have allowed your imprisonment if it had not been my will?*

You wanted *me trapped? What had I* done*?*

Why, nothing. Just the reverse—you're one of my fa-vored.

If that was the treatment one of the favored received, he'd hate to be on the god's bad side. *Then why did you al-low it?*

Because while you were in that sword, you learned skills and gained allies you would not have otherwise. And you'll need every one of them now. The god cut a lazy burning circle around him. *I have a quest for you.*

What kind of quest?

Something appropriate for a Knight of the Round Table. Cachamwri smiled a dragon smile in a curve of scales and teeth. *I need you to rescue a fairy princess—and save a goddess.*

*   *   *

Mortal Earth, Charlotte, North Carolina

He came to her as he often did. Even knowing how it would end, she couldn't resist him. Not when he loomed over her on his knees, his cock long, luscious, and rock-hard, curving slightly upward into a rosy heart-shaped head. His chest formed a broad and powerful V down to narrow hips and horseman's thighs. His flesh gleamed with sweat and smelled of alien magic.

He bent over her, bracing his arms on either side of her head, muscle rippling in thick mounds. Her heart began to pound in anticipation of the pleasure.

At the same time, the part of her that knew better screamed in helpless warning.

He kissed her, his tongue thrusting possessively deep into her mouth. She moaned in delight. His broad chest brushed nipples drawn tight with desire. His long cobalt hair tumbled over her shoulders, teasing her with cool silken strands. Her sex grew wet, clenching in anticipation of his first thrust.

"I love your scent," he murmured against her lips. "I love your taste. Magic and cinnamon."

Still kissing her slowly, thoroughly, he braced his body on one elbow and reached between her thighs with his free hand. Long fingers stroked her outer lips tenderly, then found the creaming seam. Her hips rolled upward in yearning. He made a low, triumphant sound and thrust his fingers deep.

"You're ready for me."

"Oh, sweet goddess, yes!"

His smile was slow and triumphant. "Good." He angled his hips so she could feel the hot, eager thrust of his cock. "Because I'm more than ready for you."

He guided that smooth, warm head to her snug opening, then began to press. Nineva caught her breath at the sensation of his thickness sliding inside. Groaning, she wrapped her legs around his muscular ass.

He lowered his head to whisper in her ear. "Mine. You will be mine. We're destined."

She tensed as her every instinct howled a sudden warning. "No!"

Crimson light leaped up in his eyes. When it faded, he was gone from her body.

The dragon loomed over her, massive and terrifying. Great jaws gaped wide. Fire rolled over her, and she shrieked with the agony of her skin bursting into flame, her hair igniting into a blazing nimbus around her head. Before her horrified eyes, the blackened flesh crumbled away from her arms like ash, revealing naked bone.

When she saw the Goddess Sword, she grabbed for it, even knowing what would come next.

Thank you, child, *Semira said as she blazed.*

Being blown apart was a mercy.

Nineva jolted upright on the thin futon, a scream clawing its way out of her throat. For a moment it seemed she could smell burning meat, and she gagged. Leaping up, she ran for the bathroom, barely making it in time.

When the wracking heaves finally ended, she collapsed helplessly on the worn vinyl floor.

Bad sign.

The past twelve years had taught her that whenever she had the dream, her life was about to take a turn for the worse. Invariably she had to call on the Goddess Mark sometime that day.

Yet she'd been having the dream for the past week with no sign of whatever it was she was going to have to do this time. What's more, the dream had never before swung from eroticism to terror like this. The jolting transition from pleasure to agony made it even worse. She could swear she still smelled smoke.

After the first two nights of the dream, she'd been afraid

to sleep, dropping off for only a couple of hours once exhaustion had made it impossible to stay awake any longer.

Oh, Goddess, please don't let this be a true vision. Nineva laid her head on the vinyl floor and closed her gritty, tired eyes.

If her father had been right, she was the twenty-first Avatar of the Goddess, the one destined to free Semira from the sword with the help of the dragon knight. When she'd been a little girl, she'd wanted nothing more than to do just that.

Then she'd had the dream for the first time, and her parents had died. Nineva had learned to dread the thought of the prophecy coming true. It was cowardly of her, she knew, but there it was.

Luckily, it isn't going to come true anytime soon, Nineva thought, bracing a hand on the toilet to lever herself wearily to her feet. *I haven't met the dragon, and I don't have the sword. It's probably in Ansgar's palace somewhere. It could be centuries before I have to worry.*

After all, she was immortal. At least until somebody killed her.

Staggering to the sink, Nineva grabbed her toothbrush and went to work getting the taste out of her mouth.

She was due to play fairy again this afternoon. Might as well get ready for it, since sleep was out of the question.

The wings were delicate expanses of gauzy iridescence that floated in the cold winter air as Nineva got them out of the back of her car. Flicking the switch on the attached plastic harness, she clipped them onto her shoulders. With a low hum, they began to slowly flap like those of a giant butterfly.

Gathering a handful of her diaphanous skirts, she moved around to the aging Honda's trunk. A touch on her key fob popped it open, revealing her prop box and the magic wand that lay on top of it. The wand's bright silver plastic felt cool as Nineva picked it up, the optical fibers at the tip bobbing gently. When she switched it on, the fibers began to glow like a spray of tiny stars, matching the plastic crown perched on her blond curls.

As always, the crown reminded Nineva of her father. A stab of pain shafted through her, but at least it was bearable, unlike the debilitating guilt and grief she'd endured in the years immediately after her parents' deaths.

The only reason she hadn't yielded to the siren calls of drugs or booze—or some faster means of suicide—was the nagging thought that self-destruction would make their sacrifice pointless. She was the Last Avatar, the means of Semira's survival and the symbol of hope to the Morven Sidhe. She didn't have the luxury of self-destruction.

Though dreams like the one she'd had last night could make the idea more than a little tempting.

No. She had a duty, both to Semira and to her parents. She'd been a stupid, softhearted kid with just enough power to get herself in trouble, and she'd saved a dog. The people she loved had paid for that mistake. Nothing she could do would ever change that. She could only make sure the life she lived made their sacrifice worthwhile. That meant following her father's example: making a living and keeping her head down.

And one day, freeing Semira from that sword, no matter what it cost her. Even if it meant burning alive.

Dragging her thoughts away from the dream, Nineva tucked the wand under her arm and hefted out her box of props. A soft meow emerged from its depths. Snowball, her neighbor's Persian kitten, did not care for his temporary quarters.

"Shhh," she whispered, and tapped the top of the box with a fingertip. Snowball obediently settled down.

Satisfied he wouldn't give himself away, Nineva carried the box toward the spacious three-story brick home that presided over an expanse of lawn gone winter brown.

Absently, she glanced upward. The sky was that perfect crystalline shade the locals called Carolina blue, a product of cloudless January afternoons when the air had a bracing bite. Despite her bare arms and thin skirts, Nineva was perfectly comfortable. Thanks to her bloodlines, she didn't need a coat to keep warm.

It was one of the few benefits of being a descendent of the goddess.

The front door swung open before she even reached it, revealing a harried-looking young woman in blue jeans and a leaf green cable-knit sweater. "Boy, I'm glad you're here," Joyce Clark called over the babble of childish voices coming from inside. She pushed back a lock of shoulder-length red hair and rolled her blue eyes. "The natives are getting restless."

Nineva grinned as Joyce stepped back to let her inside. "Kind of a given, when you've got ten eight-year-olds hopped up on cake and ice cream."

"Good point." The woman gave her an admiring look, taking in her pointed ears, wings, and gauzy rose skirts. "Wow, great costume! Those ears look real."

"Thank you." Nineva always dropped her glamour when she was doing her act, letting her pointed ears show. Normally, she hid them with the spell.

Joyce's eyes dropped to the edge of the Mark peeking above the cleavage of the gown. "Wow. Is that paint?"

"Something like that. Where can I set up?"

"I thought maybe the living room. You can get situated while the kids finish off the cake." She led the way across the granite-tiled foyer amid the shouts and laughter of overexcited eight-year-olds. They stepped into a wide, airy room dominated by a stone fireplace, an elegant cream couch, and an impressive plasma television. "This okay?"

Nineva smiled, ignoring a niggle of envy. She'd never known this kind of wealth. " 'Okay' doesn't do it justice."

Joyce smiled back. "Thanks. We . . ." Before she could

get the rest out of her mouth, a particularly shrill chorus of giggles had her craning her neck to see through the kitchen doorway. "No, Carly, that does not go up your nose!" She lunged toward the kitchen.

Shaking her head in amusement, Nineva parked her box on the cream area rug in front of the couch and started unpacking. Snowball took up the bottom compartment of the gilded box—a set of air holes punched in the side made it safe for any furred or feathered costars Nineva cared to use—while her props occupied the middle. She folded the top compartment down into a flat tabletop, then covered it with a length of rose fabric.

By the time the little girls trooped in at Joyce's heels, Nineva had the props for her opening bit arranged and ready. "Wow!" The expected chorus rose with gratifying fervor as the kids caught sight of her costume.

"Are you a fairy?"

Nineva turned from her box and almost lost her smile. Among the pink and healthy kids was a little girl so pale her skin bordered on gray. Her pink party dress almost swallowed her emaciated little body, and her brown eyes took up far too much of a painfully thin face. Perched on the too-bright curls of her blond wig was a gold cardboard crown, decorated with pink glitter that spelled out "Birthday Girl."

This had to be the Brandy she'd been hired to entertain. Joyce hadn't said anything about her daughter being ill.

Knowing she'd probably regret it, Nineva let her gaze slip unfocused until she could look at the child with other senses. A dark shadow seemed to curl around Brandy's small body, draining the normal blue radiance of life into an unhealthy gray. The darkness drew into a thick knot concentrated in her head. She must have some kind of brain cancer.

Giving her magic free rein, Nineva sensed the tumor was inoperable. Judging by all the poisons in her body,

Brandy had been undergoing chemotherapy and radiation treatments for weeks now, but she was succumbing to the treatments faster than the cancer was.

She had, at most, a couple of months to live.

Now what the hell am I supposed to do?

Pasting a smile on her face, Nineva dipped a curtsy and waved her battery-operated wand. "I am Nineva, Princess of the Fairies."

"I'm Brandy." The child nodded eagerly, her eyes almost painfully wide. In their depths shone a flicker of desperate hope.

Sweet Semira, she thinks I'm real. Without letting her smile falter, Nineva turned to the rest of the children, who had arranged themselves breathlessly on the couch. "And who are you?"

As the children babbled out all their names at once, Nineva's mind worked furiously. Curing Brandy would take an act of major magic that could attract Ansgar's attention. As she'd learned years ago, shielding that kind of magic use was difficult at best. It tended to blow right through her best efforts.

She'd done other healings since the Irish setter that had cost her parents' lives, but only dying humans—and nothing this complicated. It was one thing to fix a damaged heart, but between the cancer and the chemo, Brandy's entire body was compromised. There was no guarantee Nineva could heal that much damage. What if the attempt accomplished nothing except to get her killed?

Would she be wasting her parents' sacrifice?

To give herself time to think, Nineva swung into her act. She'd long since learned to restrict herself to the kind of small tricks any mortal magician might work at a child's birthday party. Anything else could draw her cousin's homicidal interest.

For the next forty-five minutes, Nineva did card tricks, pulled coins out of little ears and noses, linked apparently solid rings together, and made a ball float in midair beneath a scarf. By the end of her act, the awestruck little girls imagined her a genuine fairy princess with fantastic powers. Brandy's watching mother probably thought she was skilled with sleight of hand and stage props.

The little girls had it right, a bit of irony Nineva didn't enjoy the way she usually did.

She couldn't take her eyes off Brandy. Every time brown eyes widened or thin, pale cheeks flushed with excitement, a little needle of pain worked its way deeper in her heart. *Some fairy princess I am. Mom would be so ashamed.*

Mom is dead, the ruthless voice of pragmatism retorted. *And I will be, too, if Ansgar senses me work that spell. Which might not even save Brandy anyway.*

Could she really cure a brain tumor? Nineva had stopped a heart attack two years ago when a middle-aged salesman keeled over at the bar where she'd worked. She'd healed him so quickly, he'd thought the attack was only a particularly nasty case of indigestion. In reality, Nineva had likely given him another forty years of life.

Unfortunately, the burst of power had blown out her shields yet again. She'd had to race home, pack all her stuff, and slip out of town that same night.

But it had been worth it. She may have cost her parents their lives, but if she could save others, that had to balance the scales.

So would saving this little girl. *If* Nineva could do it.

Ah, hell. Who was she kidding? She had to try, King Ansgar and his killer Sidhe warriors be damned. Even if they caught her, at least Brandy Clark would be alive. And if she failed and got caught anyway . . .

Well, Ansgar would regret tangling with her. Nineva wouldn't go down without a fight.

She swung into what was usually the act's climax, pulling Snowball out of a ribbon-bedecked hat with much wand-waving and magical gestures. While all the little girls clapped, Nineva sank to her knees in front of Brandy. "Would you like to pet Snowball?"

The child nodded so hard, her crown tipped forward. She pushed it back with one hand and accepted the little animal with the other.

As Brandy petted the purring kitten, Nineva pulled her into her lap, closed her eyes and cupped the thin little face in one hand. And opened herself to the magic.

She shielded hastily as the Mark began to blaze. A buzzing wave of energy flooded her consciousness with such intensity, she felt dazzled, breathless. It was like flying. No, like being a shooting star, all light and exhilaration. God, it had been so long since she'd dared use her full power . . .

Dragging her attention back to business, Nineva sent magic pouring through her fingertip and into Brandy's small head, right into the knot of lethal darkness. Slowly, carefully, she attempted to pick the knot apart. It only tightened protectively.

Nineva drew in more magic and breathed it over the little girl, concentrating fiercely on the malevolent spot. *Heal,* she thought, focusing her will like a laser. *Heal. Heal, heal, heal, HEAL.*

The tumor abruptly yielded. Mutated cells began to return to normal, slowly at first, then faster as the cancer melted away like a snowball in the sun.

Her tired eyes stung. Ruthlessly blinking back the tears, Nineva sent more magic surging through the little girl's body to repair the damage from chemotherapy and radiation. The Mark blazed until her entire right breast throbbed. She set her teeth and strengthened her shields as she worked, wondering all the while if it would be enough to save the child. Nineva was burning a hell of a lot of power, and she suspected it was leaking through the shield.

"Wow, look at the lady's tattoo!" a little girl whispered.

At last, drained and euphoric, she opened her eyes.

Brandy was staring up at her with wonder. "My head doesn't hurt anymore."

Nineva pressed a quick kiss to her forehead. "Good." She lifted the child from her lap and climbed to her feet. Her knees shook under her, and her skirt was as wrinkled as a gunnysack. She'd have to spring for a dry cleaner.

In her current dizzy state of exhaustion and exhilaration, she didn't particularly care.

Brandy's mother was staring at her, puzzlement on her pretty face. Even the other children watched with solemn eyes. Joyce stepped closer and lowered her voice. "Are you okay? You seemed to zone out for a minute there. And what *is* that thing on your chest? How'd you make it glow like that?"

Nineva flashed her a smile and spun her standard line. "It's a special paint. Increased blood flow makes it luminesce. Part of the act." She'd grown very skilled at lying.

"You're really good." Joyce's eyes drifted to her daughter's face, suddenly grown animated as she showed the kitten to her friends. The gray pallor was already beginning to lift. "Brandy does look better." She bit her lip. "I was afraid this party would be too much, but . . ."

It was easy to guess the rest of the sentence: *It might be the last birthday she'll ever have.*

Nineva concealed a secret smile. Brandy would now have many more birthdays to look forward to. Her doctors would be puzzled at her spontaneous remission, and her parents would be overjoyed.

I did it. Happiness sang through her as she went to work packing up her magic box with shaking hands.

Now, if only she could manage to stay out of Ansgar's hands . . .

TWO

The Mark pulsed on her skin, a deeper, harder throb than before. A throb of warning.

Nineva froze as her elation began to give way to dawning terror.

Ansgar. Ansgar was coming. Somehow he'd sensed her spell.

She had to get out of here before her cousin could get a solid fix. She definitely didn't want a death squad showing up at Brandy's party. All these little girls would make inviting targets.

Nineva cautiously extended her magical senses and sensed . . . nothing.

When she'd healed the heart attack victim, she'd detected the king's hungry attention almost at once, which was why she'd fled. This time, though, there was none of that sense of evil. Apparently the Sidhe king was asleep at the switch.

God, she hoped so. After two solid years of work, Nineva was finally beginning to get good bookings as a magician again, and the tips were generous at Carlos's

Cantina, where she worked as a bartender. If she had to run, she'd lose all that. She'd have to start over at square one, struggling to get by on her savings until the money began coming in again.

Should she run anyway, just to be safe?

It was a question she'd become familiar with over the years. One of the ugly ironies of her life was that, despite Eirnin's and Sarah's sacrifices, Ansgar seemed to somehow know they'd had a child.

Eirnin had told her once he feared the king had sensed her birth. She'd slid from her mother's womb with the Mark glowing on her tiny chest, magic blooming around her like a star. Her father had tried to shield her, but he'd always suspected he'd been too late.

And he must have been. Why else would Ansgar have searched for them all so doggedly? Living on Mortal Earth, Eirnin was no threat to Ansgar's throne, but the prophecy said Nineva would overthrow the usurper. Ansgar couldn't afford to ignore the threat she represented.

The thought of what her cousin would do if he got his hands on her had forced Nineva to live her entire life in hiding. If she allowed herself to be captured, not only would she pay the price, but the goddess would remain trapped in the sword.

Frowning in worry, she watched Joyce Clark write a check for her performance. The frown lifted as she thought of what a bargain the woman was getting.

Seventy-five dollars for her child's life.

It was worth it, Nineva told herself fiercely. *No matter what happens next.*

After collecting Snowball and tucking the kitten back in her magic box, she kissed Brandy on the cheek and said her good-byes to the other little girls. As she carried the box to her car, she reached out again with her magical awareness. And caught her breath.

Something was looking back.

* * *

Nineva shot a worried look at the Honda's fuel gauge. The needle was far too close to E. She didn't want to stop, but if she ran out of gas, she really would be screwed.

In theory, of course, she could simply gate wherever she wanted to go. Her father had taught her the technique years ago, but he'd also told her the resulting energy flare would draw Ansgar's attention like a bonfire on a dark night. As a result, she'd never actually conjured a dimensional gate, and the idea of stepping through one gave her the willies.

No, she'd stick to old-fashioned horsepower. The Honda might be a ten-year-old rust bucket, but it wouldn't land her in the middle of a lava field, either. Or, worse, in the homicidal hands of Cousin Ansgar.

Of the two, Nineva would prefer the lava.

She spotted a convenience store and whipped in to park beside one of the pumps. Scooping her purse off the seat, she rooted around for her debit card, then got out to fill up.

After using the card, she plugged the nozzle into the Honda's tank. As gas began whooshing into it, she felt eyes on her. She whipped her head around.

To meet the dark, surprised gaze of a middle-aged black man filling his own tank on the other side of the pump. He was staring at her gauzy skirts, bare arms, and upswept hair. "Aren't you cold?" he asked in a deep, pleasant drawl. "It's got to be in the low forties."

She gave him a controlled smile. "I'm hot-natured."

A younger man might have made a suggestive reply. He only smiled back. "Yeah, my wife wants to sleep with the windows open in the dead of February. She 'bout freezes my backside off. Hot flashes." He pulled the nozzle out and set it back in its cradle. "Have a nice evening."

"You, too." Nineva felt her liar's smile turn into an honest grin as he drove off. Absently, she glanced across the parking lot to the stand of trees beyond. And froze.

A man stood watching her from among the pines. He was tall, well over six feet—six-four or six-five, maybe. Broad-shouldered and muscular, he was dressed in black jeans and a navy blue sweater. He wore a black leather duster and heavy boots that made her think of motorcycles.

Extending her senses cautiously, she detected no overt sense of magic about him, no buzzing tingle of enchantment. That meant nothing, though. She'd learned to shield her own magic from the time she was old enough to walk.

She frowned, staring at him. There was something familiar about that square, tough face with its broad cheekbones and strong chin. His blue gaze was intense, sensual. He looked at her the way a man looks at a woman he wants.

And means to have.

Oh, sweet Semira. As the realization struck, cold flooded over her skin like a wave of icy seawater. *It's the man from my dream.*

She'd seen him so many times over the past week, wearing just that hot, hungry stare. She'd only taken this long to recognize him because he'd changed the color of his shoulder-length hair: plain human brown rather than the exotic cobalt of her dreams. His eyes were different, too—cool blue instead of the glowing, magical crimson she'd come to fear.

But there could be no mistake. She knew that face.

What the hell was he? Sidhe? Enemy? Future lover? Both? The dream certainly implied that he was somehow intimately connected to her destruction.

He was probably Sidhe, and not one of the nice ones. Hell, for all she knew, he was Ansgar himself.

For a moment, Nineva considered yanking the nozzle from the tank, jumping in the Honda, and peeling rubber for home. Instead she forced herself to give him a flirtatious smile, as if she hadn't realized he was anything but human. Then she carefully glanced away, her expression casual despite her pounding heart. Her sweaty hand felt slippery on the nozzle as she tightened her grip on the trigger. *Fill, dammit.* The gas streaming into the tank sounded barely faster than a trickle.

Panic clawed at her. She had to get away from him. Had to think. Decide what to do.

Though she was no longer looking at him, she could still feel him, see him in her mind. His image seemed branded on her retinas.

Nineva stole another look at him from the corner of one eye. She had to admit he was handsome, if not inhumanly beautiful the way her father had been. His face was a bit too angular and uncompromising for that, with those deep-set eyes narrowed under thick brows. His mouth was wide and unsmiling, his jaw a square, aggressive jut. He looked like he meant business.

Years of nightmares screamed that his business was her death.

He started toward her.

Nineva's pounding heart leaped into a full gallop. She met his eyes directly in a cool, challenging stare and dropped her shields a bit. Drawing on the Mark, she let it glow over the neckline of her gown, hoping to bluff him with the threat of her power.

His direct gaze didn't drop, though a flash of sensual interest heated his eyes as they dipped down to her low-cut bodice. One corner of his mouth kicked up in a half-smile, as though he approved of what he saw.

Dangerous. He was so dangerous.

Was he Ansgar? Probably not. Her cousin wasn't the kind to do his own killing. Assassins were more his speed.

Suddenly the hiss of flowing gas turned into the bubbling of a filled tank. Nineva released the trigger and threw the nozzle back onto its cradle, then swung hastily into the car. Fortunately, she'd already swiped her debit card. She started the Honda and sped out of the parking lot, ignoring an SUV's angry horn blast as she barreled into traffic.

She had to get home, return Snowball to her neighbor, and grab that all-important duffel full of cash. If only she'd packed it that afternoon . . . Unfortunately, the violence of her nightmare had shaken her so badly, she hadn't even remembered the duffel until she was halfway to the party.

She only hoped that mistake didn't cost her her life.

Kel shook his head as he watched the fairy princess speed from the parking lot like a bank robber fleeing the scene. "Paranoid much?" he muttered under his breath.

Then again, you weren't paranoid if they really were out to get you. Particularly if "they" were the army of evil Sidhe warriors Cachamwri had described.

Poor kid. He seriously doubted she'd be able to fight off a Boy Scout troop. And what was with the costume, anyway? She looked like she should be telling Dorothy there was no place like home.

Still, she was a surprisingly lush little thing for a Sidhe, with sweetly full breasts that made him contemplate what it would be like to peel her out of that ridiculous dress.

Unfortunately, it didn't seem she was in the mood.

He sighed and strode around the side of the building until he was out of sight of any curious passersby. Shuttering his eyes, he drew on the familiar warm buzz of the Mageverse and wove it into a glamour.

And promptly vanished into thin air—at least as far as the humans were concerned.

Comfortably invisible, he gestured, drawing a shimmering pinpoint in the air. A flick of his fingers expanded it into a rippling doorway that glowed with a milky iridescence. He stepped through the dimensional gate into a dimly lit room. Curious, Kel gazed around.

Well, Nineva Morrow certainly didn't live like a fairy princess. More like someone who expected to have to race from gas stations. The efficiency apartment was clean enough, but the furniture consisted of a relatively new futon, a couple of plastic milk crates full of shabby paperbacks, and a tiny color TV set sitting on a cheap pressed-wood coffee table. The carpet was worn and marked with old stains that probably predated her tenancy. There were no pictures on the walls—no family photos or posters. The whole effect was bleak.

Interesting. Even if she was broke, the princess could have conjured a few things to make her life more comfortable. Unless she was afraid using any magic at all would make it possible for the Sidhe to track her.

She certainly went out of her way to shield herself. If it hadn't been for Cachamwri telling him where to find her, Kel knew he'd still be looking. And Draconian magic was generally stronger than the Sidhe's. Maybe there was more to the princess than met the eye.

Luckily, nobody's magic was stronger than Cachamwri's. You couldn't hide from the Dragon God.

Kel spotted a hardback book on the coffee table and picked it up. His brows rose. "*101 Tricks for Professional Magicians?*"

Nineva took the stairs to her apartment two at a time. She'd dropped Snowball off at her neighbor's even as her stomach knotted at the delay.

Her duffel lay in the closet upstairs. She had to have it before she could leave. Once again, she cursed the string of car break-ins that had forced her to keep the bag in her apartment. She wished she dared conjure it into her hands, but using any kind of magic at all would be like sending up a flare for her pursuers. *Here I am! Come kill me!*

Nineva gritted her teeth, one fist bunched in her pink tulle skirt as she stalked across the landing toward her front door. She needed to change, too. She couldn't run around looking like an escapee from *Swan Lake*. Reaching the door, she started to put the key in the lock.

And froze as her heart suddenly began to pound. What if the dream man was in her apartment, waiting to attack her? Licking suddenly dry lips, she placed her free hand against the door, closed her eyes, and listened with senses other than human.

Nothing. Not even the faintest hum of magic.

Which didn't mean he wasn't inside, heavily wrapped in magical shielding and ready to blast her into next week. *Then again, maybe there isn't anything to sense. Maybe I was wrong about him being the dream man. Maybe he was just some random human.*

Some big, sexy, random human.

Nineva bit her lip, staring at the door, wishing she could look through it. Wishing she dared.

Or you could just stand out here dithering until Ansgar's men show up to kill you. Idiot. Impatient with herself, she took a deep breath, shoved the key in the lock, and turned it. Lifting one hand in preparation to shield or blast, she threw open the door. It banged against the wall.

Nobody was inside.

The apartment stood empty. No towering dream man, no detachment of armored Sidhe warriors, just her own barren, depressing little apartment. Blowing out a breath in relief, she hurried across the living room and down the short hallway to the bedroom she didn't use. The duffel was in the closet, stuffed with money and a few changes of clothes. She should have just enough time to pack her lone suitcase, too.

Nineva flung the closet door open and reached for the battered dark green bag lying on the floor.

A male voice spoke from behind her. "You know, I'm not going to hurt you."

With a strangled shriek, she whirled, both hands instinctively lifted as she conjured a pair of spell blasts. The twin globes surrounded her fingers with a hot blue glow, ready to annihilate her foe at the first wrong move.

The dream man threw his hands up in an *I'm unarmed* gesture she didn't buy for a minute. "Hey, hold up. I'm not your enemy."

"Yeah, right," Nineva snarled, and hurled one of the blasts at his head.

The burning ball of energy splashed harmlessly off the magical shield that surrounded him like an invisible globe. As it hit, his glamour vanished, revealing a swirl of cobalt blue hair falling around those ridiculously broad shoulders. His eyes were the deep, dark red of rubies in his harshly handsome face. She couldn't see his ears, but she knew they must be pointed.

Just the sight of him brought back the dream agony of burning skin, the smell of her own flesh crisping. Fear clawed at her.

Nineva flung another fireball at his handsome face, gritting her teeth in frustration as it splashed harmlessly off his shields. The Goddess Mark on her right breast began to burn. She conjured another pair of blasts, bouncing on her toes, looking for an opening.

"Dammit, Nineva, Cachamwri sent me!" He moved toward her, blocking each and every one of her force spells as she threw them. Wary as a cornered cat, she backed away. "He asked me to protect you."

Nineva retreated into the hallway, drawing more and more power from the Mageverse as she went, flinging each blast the moment it filled her fingers. "Oh, give me a break," she snapped. "Why the hell would the Dragon God be interested in me?" Though, come to think of it, the Cachamwri Sidhe worshipped the Dragon God. Their king, Llyr Galatyn, was Cachamwri's Avatar, just as she was Semira's. "Is Llyr after me, too?"

"Llyr?" The warrior was beginning to look frustrated now. "No, I'm one of Arthur's men. Cachamwri . . ."

"Arthur who?" She frowned. Her father had never mentioned an Arthur. Besides, that was a human name.

"King Arthur. I'm one of his knights. Look, if you'll just listen to me . . ."

Now he was trying to sucker her with fairy tales. The burn of the Mark built to a savage blaze. "Tell Ansgar I'm not that big an idiot."

The Sidhe's eyes widened. "Ansgar? Ansgar's dead. Llyr killed him months ago."

Reacting to her rage, the Mark flared up like a torch, sending energy lancing down her arms and through her fingers. She yelped at the vicious pain . . .

A huge blast of magic shot from her hands and slammed into the warrior's chest like a fiery cannonball. He went flying with a startled roar.

The crash shook the apartment.

Stunned, Nineva stared down the hallway. A man-shaped hole gaped in the rear bedroom wall, revealing broken two-by-fours, shattered Sheetrock, twisted siding, and empty air. She'd blown him all the way through the back wall of the apartment.

Had she killed him?

Before she could think better of it, she raced to the hole and looked down. He lay on the grass two stories below, not moving. Heart in her throat, she scanned him.

Still alive.

She heaved a sigh of relief. He'd scared the crap out of her, but she didn't want his blood on her hands, either.

Maybe because she remembered the dream taste of his mouth . . .

Idiot.

Somewhere a dog barked furiously. A man's voice yelled a profane question in the distance.

"Oh, hell." Her first impulse was to run, but she knew she couldn't leave the building with a gaping hole in the back wall. What if it collapsed and hurt someone? Heart pounding, she stepped back from the hole and cast a spell. Instantly, it was solid again. Another spell dressed her in jeans and a sweater as she ran to grab her duffel. She didn't bother packing anything else.

A moment later, Nineva was clattering down the stairs. At this point, she could probably gate somewhere, but she wasn't sure she trusted her own skills. The car struck her as safer.

She wanted to be far away from here by the time that big Sidhe came to.

Pain throbbed in Kel's skull with a beat he could feel in his teeth. Slowly, he opened his eyes to a blurry vision of darkening sky overhead. He blinked and managed to focus.

Cachamwri's Egg, he couldn't remember the last time he'd been blasted that hard. Maybe when he'd fought his uncle. But since he'd been in dragon form at the time, it was hardly the same.

The Sugarplum Fairy packed one hell of a wallop.

Groaning, he rolled over onto his hands and knees and gave serious thought to throwing up. He could feel the muscles in his arms and legs twitch in reaction to Nineva's magical attack. For a moment, he thought longingly of his own soft bed.

Unfortunately, that wasn't an option. The Dragon God had given him a job, and he damn well wasn't going to fail.

Whether Nineva liked it or not.

Gritting his teeth, he staggered to his feet and almost fell on his face. Hastily bracing a hand against the building, Kel swallowed hard as he blinked the world back into focus.

Okay, Tinkerbell, the kid gloves are off. Let's see how you like dealing with me in dragon form.

Grimly, he went looking for a place to change.

*   *   *

It had been eight months since Diana London Galatyn had last turned into a werewolf, and she was getting grumpy. To make matters worse, her back ached constantly and she hadn't even seen her own feet in three months, though she'd been told her ankles were swollen.

Meanwhile, Prince Dearg Andrew Galatyn was bouncing up and down on her bladder, suggesting a serious case of ADD. She could almost hear the psychic *Wheee!*

Diana splayed her hands over her huge belly and tried to think happy thoughts at her womb. *Three weeks. Just three more weeks, Dearg, honey. Then you get to come out into the big, wide world where there's lots of room for you and your bony little elbows. And everybody will adore you as the first Sidhe prince born in a hundred and seventy years.* She smiled to herself a little grimly. *Best of all, Uncle Ansgar won't be trying to have you killed, because Uncle Ansgar is worm chow.*

Ansgar, her husband's vicious brother, had hated Llyr from the moment he was born. On his deathbed, their father, King Dearg, had made Ansgar king of the Morven Sidhe, and Llyr the king of the Cachamwri.

Unfortunately, that hadn't been good enough for Ansgar, who'd wanted both kingdoms. Over the next sixteen hundred years, he engineered the assassination of Llyr's ten children and four previous wives, but all the attempts on Llyr had missed.

Diana and Llyr had finally slain Ansgar during the last assassination attempt eight months ago. Now Llyr, like his father before him, was king of both the Morven and Cachamwri Sidhe.

And Diana, werewolf and former city administrator of Verdaville, South Carolina, was trying to adjust to life as queen of the Sidhe. Becoming immortal was cool, and God knew marriage to a gorgeous fairy had its perks, but the workload was killer.

The royal couple had spent the first six months of their

reign in the Morven kingdom, trying to repair the damage
Ansgar had done during his rule. This morning, after a
two-month visit to the kingdom of Cachamwri, Llyr had
embarked on a surprise inspection of the Morven palace.

Diana and her ginormous baby belly had gone along,
though at the moment, all she was really interested in was a
place to sit. The scarlet court gown she wore was lovely
with its gold embroidery and gems, but it weighed a ton.
And God knew Prince Dearg was no lightweight. As a result, the small of her back felt like a rabid wolverine was
chewing on a particularly tasty knot of muscles.

Unfortunately, there didn't seem to be a single chair in
the armory. All the vast chamber held was an astonishing
number of weird-looking swords, not to mention spears,
armor, shields, and whatever the thing with all the spikes
was. All of it was arranged on gleaming wooden racks or
hung on the marble walls between elaborate carvings of
battle scenes.

Diana's attention focused on one particular bas-relief.
Were those fairies killing a *dragon*? It was certainly possible. Though this world looked like the Earth she'd been
raised on, it actually occupied a parallel universe where
magic was a natural law. As a result, the humans that had
evolved here were magic-using Sidhe, and the local fauna
included unicorns, Hellhounds, and sapient dragons. The
Sidhe and the dragons had made peace centuries ago, but
at one time, each had hunted the other.

Before she could waddle over for a closer look at the
carving, a low growl drew her attention to her handsome
husband. Well over six feet tall, the king had a long, elegantly boned face, a strong, narrow nose, and large, intelligent opalescent eyes that sparkled with magic. Hair the
color of moonlight fell to his muscular backside, currently
on mouthwatering display in a pair of black hose. His
faintly Elizabethan black velvet doublet emphasized the
impressive width of his shoulders, and tall, gleaming boots

sheathed his brawny calves. Pregnant or not, just looking at him was enough to make her senses hum.

Unfortunately, one look told her he definitely wasn't in the mood for flirtation. A snarl curled the king's regal lips as those incredible eyes went cold and narrow. "Trivag, *where's my sword?*"

Lord Trivag took a step back, his mouth rounding in an O of dismay as he scanned the armory, apparently hoping the offending weapon would magically appear. A lean, distinguished man with waist-length cobalt hair shot with gray, he looked about sixty, which probably made him six thousand or so. The Sidhe aged very, very slowly. "My King, I inspected the armory myself just two days ago. It was here then."

Llyr turned his incandescent displeasure on the three Sidhe currently assigned to guard the armory. "So, did *you* notice anyone strolling out with the Sword of Semira?"

All three guards fell belly-down on the marble floor with a clatter of malachite armor. "No, Your Majesty!"

"It was here when I inspected yesterday," one dared in a strained voice. He was probably the leader of the detachment, judging by the long blue horsehair tail thrusting from his helm.

"Oh, for Cachamwri's sake, get up," Llyr snapped. "I am not Ansgar. I'm not going to have you executed." In his anger, he raked a big hand impatiently through his hip-length blond hair, revealing the sweep of a pointed ear.

As the three men scrambled to their feet with a rattle and clank, Llyr growled, "Organize a search party and find it. I don't want to tell my subjects I lost the goddess's own sword."

Diana's eyebrows flew skyward. "You've got a sword that belongs to a goddess?"

Llyr watched the guards hurry from the room. "Apparently I *had* a sword that belongs to a goddess. And I'm damned well going to get it back."

* * *

Either the dream man was even tougher than he looked, or something new was after her.

Something evil.

A sense of menace filled the air, so thick she could barely breathe. The warrior she'd fought half an hour ago hadn't felt anything like this.

Nineva peered through the Honda's windshield, searching for the nearest exit. Once again, she strengthened the magical barrier around her car. The spell had fooled Ansgar before when he'd gotten a lock on her, but this time it wasn't working.

She had the uncomfortable feeling she'd used too much power on the Sidhe warrior. Her magic wasn't responding as it usually did.

Spotting an exit, she took it at close to fifty miles an hour, fighting to pour still more magic into the spell as she went. As the overpass sloped up and curved around, she slowed to avoid losing control. But when she turned the steering wheel to follow the curve, the Honda kept going.

Straight for the retaining wall.

Oh, God, she'd gone into a skid! She must have hit a patch of black ice . . .

She fought to steer into the skid and pump the brakes as she'd been taught, but the little car kept going. The wall loomed in front of the bumper. Nineva threw up a shield spell to protect herself against the boom of impact . . .

Which never came.

The Honda went airborne, sailing up and over the retaining wall as if launched off a ramp. But that was impossible; the grade wasn't that . . .

Something had her.

Ansgar's assassins, she realized. *They're just going to smash me and the car into the ground.*

THREE

Nineva unlocked her seat belt and lunged for the door, trying to remember the flight spell her father had taught her so many years before. She hauled up on the handle and prepared to launch herself into space . . .

The door didn't even budge.

Frantically, Nineva threw a look out the windshield. The car had slowed, floating toward the grass below as gently as a leaf. Sweet Goddess, the assassins were powerful.

I am so screwed.

Gritting her teeth, Nineva gathered what magic she could and sent a wall of force at the door, trying to blow it open. The spell rebounded into her face like a slap from a giant's hand. Stunned, she tried to shake off the blow, lifting her fingers to her stinging nose. She touched something wet. She was bleeding.

So much for that idea.

Silently cursing, she sank back into her seat to watch the ground approach. With a grim gesture, she transformed her jeans and shirt into armor, then conjured a sword. The length of steel felt familiar and comforting in her hand. It should; her father had started teaching her swordplay when she was barely taller than the blade she used. Despite her youth, he'd drilled her without mercy. After all, he'd told her, she would eventually be expected to fight the Dark Ones. She'd better damn well know what she was doing.

Nineva had kept up with her training after his death. Borderline broke though she always was, she'd sprung for gym memberships and martial arts classes to make sure she didn't forget how to fight.

Now it seemed all that preparation was going to pay off. The minute they let her out of the car—*if* they let her out of the car—she'd have to be ready to defend herself. She was damned if she'd just surrender to the bastards who'd destroyed her family.

The car touched down on an expanse of frost-pale grass beside the highway, rocking on its tires as its weight settled. For a moment, everything went utterly still under the white sliver of the moon. Heart pounding, she looked around, searching for the enemy.

It didn't take long to spot them. Something moved in the utter darkness under the overpass. She caught her breath, eyes straining.

Thirty men on horseback emerged from under the bridge, their armor gleaming dully in the glow of their magic. The horses' eyes shone green and ghostly, like cats'. The icy ground crunched under their massive hooves, and their tack jingled and creaked.

Nineva's jaw dropped. Sidhe warriors. Out here in front of God and the South Carolina Highway Patrol.

Or not. She could sense the bubble of magic that surrounded them all. Probably an invisibility spell.

All four of the Honda's doors flew open with a quadruple thunk. A man's voice rumbled in command. "Princess Nineva, come out."

It had been a long time since she'd heard the language of the Morven Sidhe, but she hadn't forgotten it. Nineva stared out across the hood and considered telling him to go to hell. Reluctantly, she decided against it.

"Do not make me send a man to drag you, Princess." It was the tallest of the men who spoke, a big bruiser on an even bigger horse.

Nineva curled her lip at him, battling impotent rage as hatred threatened to choke her. Shaking with it, she got out of the car.

Squaring her shoulders, she raised her weapon, fell into a fighting stance, and concentrated on looking like royalty. Her enemies might kill her, but she wasn't going to shame her parents. "All right, now what?"

Warily, she studied the warriors as they rode closer, spears, axes, and swords glittering. They and their mounts wore barbaric armor, matte black and jutting with menacing spikes and horns. With a rising masculine murmur, they jostled into a half circle around her. She promptly threw up a magical shield with her free hand, tightened her grip on her sword, and prepared to fight.

Not that she had a chance in hell. The odds well and truly sucked. Nineva curled a lip at her enemies anyway. "I guess I should be flattered, if Ansgar thinks it takes this many warriors to kill me."

"We have no interest in killing you, Princess." The big warrior swung down from his horse and strode toward her. With a creak of leather and the ring and rattle of armor and tack, the others hastily did the same. Yeah, the big guy was the leader, all right. "We mean you no harm at all."

Warily, Nineva studied her foe. She supposed he was handsome, in an Evil Empire kind of way—tall and Terminator-massive in that ornate black armor, a shimmer of peacock iridescence sliding over the scales whenever he moved in the glow of his magic. The visor of his stylized helm suggested a wolf's snarling muzzle. Leather cords bound animal teeth to twin locks of his long black hair. The teeth clicked and rattled whenever he turned his head. She considered telling him he looked like one of the bad guys from *Lord of the Rings.*

Nah, better not. Instead she asked, "So what do you want?"

He spread his empty hands. "Only to talk."

Nineva conjured a fireball to float above her palm. "Then you're out of luck, because I don't want to hear anything you've got to say."

"Don't be so hasty, Your Highness. I have a proposal you'll find very interesting indeed." The warrior reached up and drew off his helm, then tucked it under one brawny arm.

Nineva blinked in involuntary surprise. He was far more than Sidhe handsome—he was the most intensely beautiful man she'd ever seen, with a long, elegantly boned face and thick black hair that contrasted starkly with his pale skin. His dark eyes seemed to glow with seductive promise as they met hers, and his wide mouth curled up in a smile that suggested tangled sheets and hot skin.

She shook off her involuntary reaction and glowered at him. "I said I'm not interested." *Take that, Darth Legolas.*

"Let's find out, shall we?" Without looking away from her, he gestured with a mailed hand.

One of his warriors hurried forward and clanked to his armored knees. The Sidhe bowed his head and extended both hands toward his leader, offering the sword that lay across his palms.

Even before Nineva's gaze dropped to it, the Goddess Mark began to burn and pulse, urgent and demanding. She caught her breath and stared.

The weapon shimmered as moonlight danced along its jeweled scabbard. Its hilt was shaped like a woman, sinuous and nude, her feet balanced on the crosspiece. Her long hair swirled around her body, veiling her nipples and sex in a way that suggested wild power more than modesty. Her delicate triangular face was uplifted, eyes fierce with a kind of warlike joy. Nineva instantly recognized it from a hundred dreams.

The Sword of Semira.

The leader's hand closed around the hilt. Nineva gasped; it seemed she could feel his touch on her own body. Slowly, as if performing a far more erotic act, he drew the sword from its scabbard. Its blade glowed as it emerged from the gem-encrusted sheath, so bright her eyes stung. Around her, the warriors gasped in awe.

"It responds to you," he said, his voice deep. "It knows you. As you know it."

Nineva's heart began to pound beneath the escalating burn of the Goddess Mark. *Oh,* she thought, staring help-lessly at the sword, *I am in such deep shit.*

Diana Galatyn rested her hands on the shelf of her belly and watched her royal husband brood. Even Dearg Andrew was unusually still, although that might be because he was running out of room to move. God knew it felt like he'd shoved all her internal organs as far out of the way as pos-sible.

It was a good thing she had more than human strength, or she'd never be able to get off this chaise without Llyr's help.

Used to discomfort after eight months, Diana ignored it, much more interested in the expression on her husband's face. He sat sprawled in a chair, muscular legs flung wide, his jewel-encrusted doublet accentuating the considerable width of his shoulders. Black lace cuffs frothed around his big hands, and a huge ruby glinted on his right hand. Any other man would have looked effeminate, especially con-sidering the long, silken fall of blond hair he'd pushed behind one pointed ear. Instead, there was a sense of mas-culine power and iron will about him. For the past sixteen hundred years, he'd been a king, and it showed.

Diana loved him so much it hurt.

She'd also tolerated about as much of this as she intended to. "You know, you're the only man I've ever known who can pace without moving. You going to tell me what's going on, or do I have to guess?"

Opalescent eyes met hers with a flicker of guilt. "Everything is fine."

She contemplated him coolly. "I think that may be the only time you've ever looked me straight in the eye and lied."

He winced. "The sword . . ."

"There's more to this than some missing cutlery, Llyr. If you'll tell me what the hell is going on, I may be able to help. I can turn into a seven-foot Dire Wolf, remember?"

Llyr's sensual mouth tightened. "Not at the moment."

He was right, of course. If she tried to transform now, she'd lose the baby. The anatomical change was too radical. She was trapped in human form until Dearg was born.

But that didn't mean she had to back down. "Okay, so maybe I can't get fuzzy right now. I'm still not stupid."

"I have *never* thought you stupid."

"Prove it."

Llyr gave her a restless, brooding look. "There's a rebellion brewing among the Morven Sidhe."

A sensation of cold spread over her. A rebellion . . . Her hand crept to rest on her belly. History had all kinds of nasty examples of what happened to royal offspring when somebody else wanted the throne. "I thought the Morvens had accepted us after we got rid of Ansgar."

"I thought they had, too." Llyr made a sharp gesture. "Unfortunately, certain parties also saw his death as the opportunity they've been looking for. Apparently he'd been fighting a low-level war with something called the Army of Semira—a kind of rebel underground, half-religious, half-political. Now that he's dead and I've assumed the Morven throne, the Semirans think they finally have the chance they've waited for."

Diana lifted her head as she put two and two together. "They're the ones who stole the sword."

"One of my Morven guards was a Semiran mole. He's disappeared, taking the sword with him. Which is a very serious problem." Llyr's expression grew even darker. "That sword has been carried in battle by the kings and queens of the Morven Sidhe for ten thousand years, even before we became immortals. It's the Sidhe's answer to Excalibur, and it's said to grant its bearer fantastic powers. Many Morvens believe only the rightful ruler can wield it."

"You're not exactly chopped liver yourself," Diana pointed out. "You're Cachamwri's Champion." He'd been born with the Dragon God's image on his right arm, signifying his status as the Heir to Heroes. When Dearg was conceived, Cachamwri had predicted their son would be the next Heir.

Llyr shook his head. "The Morven Sidhe do not consider Cachamwri their god. To them, that's Semira, whom they believe is a goddess trapped in the sword."

Nineva winced. "So it's not just a magic blade, it's a religious object."

"Exactly. And I've lost it."

"Your people are going to be pissed."

"That's putting it mildly."

Nineva dragged her eyes away from the Sword of Semira to her captor's inhumanly handsome face. Her heart was pounding, her head buzzing from the sword's proximity, and the metallic taste of panic filled her mouth. There was only one conclusion she could draw. "You're Ansgar."

For an instant, a terrifying rage flared in the warrior's eyes, so hot she took an involuntary step back. Then it disappeared as his lips pulled into an easy smile that was somehow even more chilling. "Oh, no, Princess. Ansgar the Tyrant is dead." He bowed with a flourish. "I am General Arralt, commander of the Army of Semira."

Ansgar really was dead? A little bloom of hope rose, but she found it difficult to believe. "When? Who killed him?" Had the dream man been telling the truth?

There was that flash of fury again, at boiling odds with Arralt's pleasant expression. "His brother, Llyr, who took his throne these eight months past. Luckily, Llyr is a weak fool." He caught her hand in his big armored one, his expression eager. "Princess, this is our chance. Take up the Goddess Sword and free your people from the usurper." He dropped to one knee before her, his expression taking on a fanatic's passion as he gazed up at her. Around them, armor rattled as his men simultaneously knelt. Moonlight silvered raised faces and shone in gleaming eyes. "I pledge my army to help you regain your rightful throne."

Her own conjured blade hanging lax in her hand, she stared down at him with a sense of unreality. Here it was: her father's dream, offered to her all tied up in a pretty bow. Her parents' deaths would no longer be in vain.

Luckily, Eirnin Morroc had taught her more than legends, magic, and swordplay. He'd also instilled a healthy dollop of cynicism that told her Arralt wanted something. She had a pretty good idea what. "And you mean to be my king."

"I will serve you and the goddess in any way you see fit." He lifted her hand and pressed warm lips to her knuckles.

Yeah, right. And yet . . . Her gaze flicked to the Goddess Sword. The Mark pulsed hungrily on her breast. The idea of being queen was ridiculous; she was a part-time bartender and children's magician. Then there was the ugly problem of dethroning Llyr Galatyn, who, according to her father, had never been the kind of bastard his brother had been.

But that sword . . . She wanted that sword. Despite her nightmares, despite her fears, she *had* to free the goddess from her prison. It was literally what she'd been born to do.

When other little girls had been playing with Barbies, she'd been waving plastic light sabers and imagining their battery-operated glow was Semira herself. She'd even owned a stuffed pterodactyl her mother had bought her, a stand-in for the dragon warrior the legend predicted. Nineva could still remember cuddling in her father's lap, listening to his deep voice speaking the ancient Morven words of the prophecy. Dreaming of dragons and glory.

Yes, she'd come to fear the prediction. But Eirnin had also taught her that prophecies could be derailed. What if she came up with a way to free the goddess that didn't involve the dragon and his annihilating breath? If she allied herself with this Arralt, maybe she could free Semira and save herself at the same time.

Surely that wasn't so wrong?

"Take it," Arralt said softly.

Nineva looked up and found him watching her, his black gaze knowing, as if he recognized the hunger and fear in her soul.

Yet still she hesitated. Once her hand closed over that hilt, her life would never be the same. She'd belong to Semira, committed to the freedom of the goddess and the leadership of her people. It was the purpose she'd been raised for, yet a cold metallic tang filled her mouth. *I'm not ready for this. What will it do to me? What if I bring the prophecy about by trying to avoid it? What if Arralt can't be trusted?*

In the depths of her mind, a voice that sounded like her father's sneered. *Coward.* She winced at the sting of it.

Taking a deep breath, she banished her own weapon, then closed her hand around the Sword of Semira's hilt. It felt cold at first, but as her fingers tightened, it instantly began to heat. Nineva heard a gasp and looked up, meeting the gaze of the warrior who still held it across his palms. The Sidhe's eyes were very wide, as though he, too, had felt Semira awaken at her touch. She lifted the sword from his hands.

"You must feed her," Arralt said softly. "Let her taste your blood."

Licking suddenly dry lips, Nineva turned the sword point upward. The Mark blazed on her breast, so bright the sword glowed in its light, iridescence sliding up the blade, hypnotic and bright. She tried to remember everything her father had told her about the sword. "There's a spell," she said hoarsely. "Someone has to chant it while I meld with the sword." It would form the conduit she would use in tapping Semira's energy.

"I know. I'm prepared to cast it."

I'll bet you are. Nineva shot him a wary look, but his expression showed nothing but that fanatical eagerness. She hesitated again, torn between wariness and hope. She'd sensed something evil earlier. What if it had been him?

On the other hand, once she melded with the sword, there wouldn't be much he could do to her. Even if he tried something while casting that spell, she'd be able to break any hold he attempted to establish.

After all, how could a mere Sidhe warrior be stronger than Semira?

The Mark pulsed in time to her heart, a tide of power rolling through her with each beat. Nineva gave him a short, fierce nod. "Then I'm ready."

For just an instant, Arralt's black eyes blazed with triumph. Then he began to chant, the words so ancient she could barely understand them. The Mark throbbed at every syllable, sending alternating waves of heat and cold sizzling through her.

The power of the goddess . . .

A spell banished her gauntlets, leaving her hands bare.

She wrapped both palms around the sword, sucking in a breath as the magic intensified until it felt like needles of fire and ice shooting through her skin. Gritting her teeth, she jerked her palm down the razored blade. Pain sliced her flesh, and a streak of bright red appeared against the steel. Her blood instantly began to glow and smoke.

An image bloomed in her mind. A woman, nude, glowing like the sun, so unspeakably beautiful, the sight made Nineva's heart constrict. Like the carving on the sword's hilt, her hair reached to her ankles. At first glance, it appeared white, but when she moved, streaks of brilliant color shot through it, as if it broke up the light like a prism.

Semira.

The goddess opened her closed eyes, revealing an opalescent glow brighter even than her exquisite skin. Her gaze locked with Nineva's. And slowly, she smiled—a smile that shone with such welcome and joy, Nineva felt the guilt and torment in her spirit melt away.

My child, the goddess said in a voice like faint silver chimes. *At last you've come. I've been so lonely. I've known such hunger . . .*

For an instant, it seemed Nineva was surrounded by cold darkness. Trapped, isolated, far from life and warmth. She shuddered, knowing this was how the goddess had felt for centuries.

I'm here, Nineva told that shining presence, suddenly determined. *Whatever I have is yours.*

She couldn't abandon the goddess to that lonely darkness.

Semira's exquisite mouth started to curve in a smile—only to freeze. Her beautiful eyes widened in horror. *Trickery! Child, beware . . .*

Nineva jerked, opening her own eyes just as Arralt's big hand flashed out and locked just over hers, clamping down as he dragged both their palms down the blade. She gasped as his blood mingled with hers.

An image flashed before her eyes, carried by his blood: a woman, her mouth opened in an airless scream as merciless male hands wrapped around her throat, choking away her life.

Arralt's hands. Arralt's mother.

The mother who'd been raped by Ansgar, who'd raised her son as her means of vengeance. Who'd taught him dark magic and fed him a diet of hate until he despised himself almost as much as his father.

Nineva fought to jerk away, but it was too late. More images poured into her consciousness, fragmented and terrifying. Arralt, using his mother's death to power a spell that had carried him to another world. A world of evil, of death and sacrifice. He could have been killed—should have been killed. Yet one of the aliens of that world had recognized what he was. She'd seen him for the opportunity he presented and introduced him to her Dark One master, Rakatvira. Who had, in turn, made Arralt a tempting offer: the rulership of the Sidhe in return for the conquest of Earth. Arralt, obsessed with becoming king, cared only for the power he could gain.

Other images flashed through Nineva's mind: a Sidhe woman with hair the color of spring grass and yellow eyes that were unimaginably evil. Somehow she knew it was Arralt's alien host in a new form.

Horned, demonic creatures, radiating a lust for death and blood and conquest, surging through a gate in the middle of Times Square. They roared in joy as screaming pedestrians scattered amid the thunderous boom of crashing cars.

Dark Ones, she realized. *Arralt and the alien are in league with the Dark Ones.*

Magic danced and flashed around the alien witch like a lightning storm as she lifted the Sword of Semira over a woman whose belly was swollen in pregnancy. As Nineva mentally recoiled in horror, she sliced open the screaming woman, then reached inside to haul out a naked, limp infant . . .

Nineva jerked backward, trying to tear herself free of Arralt's grip, but magical lines of force suddenly snapped tight around her. Instinctively, she fought to jerk free, but the Sidhe general held tight, crushing her fingers around the sword, grinding the steel into her flesh.

Semira's chiming voice rang over the mental screams from her vision. *He's trying to usurp the meld!*

I know! Snarling, Nineva threw her will against his, fighting to drive him out of the link. Yet his spell only tightened.

Frantically, she tried to draw on the goddess's power and add it to her own. Even as Nineva sent a searing river of magic pouring against Arralt's spell, she realized it wasn't enough.

I've been locked in the sword too long. Semira's chiming voice sounded even more faint, as if being drained by the effort of fighting. *I've had no Avatar to feed my power. And something is reinforcing Arralt.*

The yellow-eyed woman, Nineva realized. No, not a woman. An alien. A *thing.* She could sense the black, roiling stench of the creature's magic entwined with Arralt's. It was winning.

And once it did, it would feed Mortal Earth to the Dark Ones, plunging them all into hell.

Bloody damnation!

Kel beat his dragon wings hard toward the source of the sinister magic he could sense blazing on the horizon. He'd been searching for that idiot girl for the past hour, but she was far too good at shielding herself.

Then, just minutes ago, he'd sensed a storm of power building—power that had rapidly taken on a very dark cast. Something nasty had Nineva, and he wasn't at all sure he'd be able to save her. Whatever it was had a lot of juice.

With his magical senses, Kel could see the fervid glow it cast as he drew closer. He flew faster, tucking his legs in tight to his body and snaking his head forward to reduce drag. His heart pounded as he remembered Nineva's ethereal beauty. She'd have no chance against that swelling malevolence.

At last he threw his wings wide to slow his flight. He could feel the evil just below him, roiling and stinking like a boiling cesspit. Yet when he looked down, he saw nothing but a stretch of frosty grass beside the highway. The girl's attackers had shielded themselves.

Reaching for the Mageverse, Kel breathed a spell downward at the moonlit ground. The illusion of serenity shattered. A group of armored warriors flashed into view, surrounding a small, blazing figure wrapped in glowing crimson bands.

Nineva.

One of the men stood in front of her, the scarlet bands spilling from his chanting mouth. They coiled around her like mating snakes, binding her arms, strangling her magic.

Kel folded his wings and stooped like an eagle. Simultaneously, he dropped his own invisibility spell.

Below him, heads tilted back and mouths opened on shouts as they heard the screaming wind of his fall. The warriors scattered in every direction, bellowing curses and cries of dismay in a language he recognized.

Sidhe. They were Sidhe.

He focused on one particular face, illuminated in the glow of the crimson bands. Nineva, still wrapped tight in the spell, eyes glowing with magic as she fought to escape. Beside her, her captor snarled up at him in rage.

Kel opened his jaws and breathed out a spell, sending another cloud of mystical energy rolling over them. The Sidhe warrior threw up a shield that sparked and glittered as it warred with Kel's magic.

Kel ignored him, his attention focused on Nineva.

Around her, the bands of crimson energy began to thin as the warrior diverted more and more power to fending off Kel's attack.

But the bonds didn't break. Not yet.

Spreading his wings to break his fall, Kel drew harder on the magic of the Mageverse, intensifying his efforts, blowing more and more power over the girl.

He had to get her out of there.

The dragon knight had arrived at last. Nineva stared up at him with a blend of hope and dread as his magical breath rolled over her. She could feel her bonds weakening, eroding in the face of his power. Arralt's spell gave . . .

Brutal hands snatched the Sword of Semira from her grasp.

"No!" Jolted from her paralysis, Nineva conjured another weapon and leaped at the warlord. "Give her back!"

Steel rang on steel as he parried with an insulting, off-hand strength. She snarled and circled him, probing his defenses with a series of thrusts he casually deflected. Her heart sank as she realized he was stronger than she was, more skilled, more experienced. She didn't have a prayer against him.

Frustrated, Nineva conjured a fireball with her free hand and watched for an opening to throw it.

Semira! Where are you? The link had thinned, now that she no longer held the sword.

The dragon! Semira's voice was painfully faint. *You must ally yourself with the dragon . . .*

Nineva dared a glance upward. The great beast hovered over them, his huge wings beating, an expression of what might have been frustration on his alien face. *He can't fire at Arralt without hitting me,* she realized. *So much for help from that quarter.* With a growl, she hurled her fireball, then ducked as Arralt sent one of his own whizzing for her head.

"You can't win, Princess. You know that." He bared his teeth. "You might as well surrender and save yourself the pain."

"Not as long as I'm still breathing, asshole." Using every skill she'd ever learned from her father, she danced around him, alternately pelting him with blasts and attacking him with her blade. He met every attempt with infuriating ease.

She had to kill the son of a bitch before he destroyed them all. *Semira, please! I can't handle this guy on my own!*

I have not the strength. I have been dormant too long—I need an infusion of magic to reach my full power again.

Tell me what to do, and I'll do it! Nineva sidestepped the warlord's slice at her leg, then lunged. He parried and spun away.

The dragon, Semira whispered. *The dragon is the key . . .*

Cold, stark fear rolled across Nineva's mind. Remembering the nightmare, she could almost feel herself begin to burn.

FOUR

Nineva dragged her thoughts away from the dream. She didn't have time for panic. She had to put Arralt down first.

Her battle skills might not be sufficient by themselves, but maybe she could distract him into making a fatal mistake.

"Semira's general, my ass! Do your men know you're really Ansgar's bastard?"

"Oh, they know." Arralt knocked her blade away with an expression of contemptuous amusement. "They've followed me for centuries while he tried to kill me."

"The way you killed your mother?" She drove her sword at his heart.

His mouth twisted as he parried, then tried to catch her blade with his and jerk it from her hand. She barely disengaged in time and retreated from a ferocious swipe of his weapon. "You saw that, did you?"

"Oh, yeah. Just like I saw your alliance with the Dark Ones, traitor!"

"It's you who are the traitor. Afraid of the goddess. Afraid of the dragon." Arralt laughed in her face as he deflected another desperate attack. "You're not the only one who saw visions in the blood. Mine told me you're a coward, Nineva Morrow." Something black and ugly filled his eyes. "My patience is running out, Princess. Surrender or die."

"No, thanks—I think I'd rather kill you." She shot a blast at his gut with everything she had. Even as it splashed off his shields, she lunged, swinging. He parried, then darted a glance skyward and leaped backward.

Nineva charged, but before she could close with him again, something snapped tight around her waist. She looked down.

A massive clawed hand gripped her, talons curled around her body. Before she could even blink in surprise, the ground dropped away from her feet.

"Nice try, kid, but I'm afraid you're out of your league," a rumbling voice told her over the thunderous flap of wings.

It was the dragon.

"He's got the Sword of Semira!" she yelled, kicking futilely. "I have to get it back!"

The dragon muttered an English curse and dove toward Arralt, who flung a magical blast at them. The roiling ball of energy splashed off the dragon's shields even as the huge creature breathed a spell of his own.

Arralt ducked back, gesturing. The shimmer of a dimensional gate formed in the air.

Oh, hell. *Semira!*

The dragon! Take the dragon as your lover. His magic is great . . .

What? Nineva looked down at the huge claws gripping her waist. She must have misunderstood. *Semira, he's a* dragon*!*

Not all the time. Was there a trace of amusement in the goddess's faint voice?

Arralt whirled and plunged for the gate, the sword

glowing in his hand. The dragon snatched for him, but he dove through, hurling another blast as he fled.

Taking Semira with him.

"No!" Nineva cried in despair, thumping her fists on the scaly hand that held her.

The dragon touched down, head jerking to and fro as he looked for another Sidhe to grab. Around them, closing gates vanished, carrying the last of the warriors away. Nineva sensed the rise of magic as the dragon cast yet another spell.

"Bloody hell. Wherever they went, it's heavily shielded. I can't punch through." The dragon sighed and released her, carefully uncurling his talons.

She turned and looked up at him. And up and up and up. He towered over her, looking more like an animated hillside than a living creature. Moonlight shimmered on his scales as ropes of muscle shifted under his skin. His head was as long as her entire body, crowned by curving horns that gleamed under the moon. His eyes blinked at her, each the size of her head, glowing crimson and flashing sparks of magic.

Semira wanted her to make love to *that*?

The memory of the nightmares only made things worse. Particularly with those scarlet eyes looking down at her, just as they'd done every time he'd incinerated her in those damned dreams.

I don't have time for this. Nineva forced the fear away.

She had to concentrate on one thing: he was the dragon warrior the legends had predicted for thousands of years. As Semira had said, he was the key.

Unfortunately, Nineva had let Arralt escape with the sword. Which put him that much further along with his plan to unleash a Dark One invasion on Mortal Earth.

It was sickening. Arralt was right—she was a coward. In trying to avoid her fate, her duty, she'd lost everything. "We've got to get that sword back, or we're all screwed."

"I know." The dragon's eyes flared red. Nineva sensed a burst of magic so intense, she took an involuntary step back and swallowed a scream.

Was he going to burn her now?

But when she blinked away the magical dazzle, he was gone, replaced by a man. His starkly handsome face and broad-shouldered build were instantly familiar. "Oh, hell. *You're* the dragon?"

He gave her a crooked little smile. "Afraid so."

It was the dream man she'd blasted with everything she had, not an hour ago. Nineva winced. "I'm so sorry. I knew something evil was after me, and when you showed up . . ."

His blue brows lifted. "You assumed I was it?"

She felt her cheeks heat. "I couldn't take the chance you weren't."

"Considering what just happened, I guess that's understandable." He gave her a speculative glance. "Impressive firepower, by the way. The last time I got hit that hard, it was by another dragon."

"I should have saved it for Arralt." Sighing, she transformed her armor back into a red T-shirt and jeans. "We might not be in this mess."

Ruby eyes narrowed as he studied her. "Did you know you're glowing? That mark . . ."

She glanced down at the Goddess Mark. It should have been concealed by the fabric. Instead it radiated through like a flashlight beam, even brighter than it usually was after she'd used her powers. Her heart lifted a little at the sight of it. "I'm still linked to Semira. Maybe we can use it to find the sword." If the link had survived, maybe she hadn't failed. Yet, anyway.

And the dragon was human, so making love with him to feed the goddess wasn't impossible. Just damned uncomfortable. How was she going to explain this to him?

As for her nightmares—well, she couldn't afford to let them stop her anymore. If she had to die to prevent the

Dark Ones from invading, so be it. No matter what Arralt thought, she wasn't a coward. She'd do her duty.

"That's an awfully grim expression." The dragon warrior tilted his head as he studied her.

"I'm thinking pretty grim thoughts."

"Don't worry, kid, we'll figure it out." He thrust a big hand out at her. "Let's try this again. Kel, at your service."

She took his hand cautiously. His skin felt warm and smooth and strong—and thoroughly human. "Nineva Morrow. So are you a human who assumes dragon form, or . . ."

"Nope." Kel gave her palm a gentle squeeze before releasing her. "I'm a dragon who prefers being human. Most of the time, anyway. Sometimes it's handy being forty feet long and scaly."

"Yeah, I can see how it would be." Her hand tingled oddly where he'd grasped it.

Nineva watched as he conjured a dimensional gate with a practiced flick of his hand. Suddenly she was intensely aware of him—his height, his broad-shouldered build, the elegance in those long, tapered fingers. *At least seducing him won't be a hardship.* "Where are we going?"

He turned back to look at her. His nostrils flared as if catching her scent. One corner of his mouth quirked up in a knowing half-smile, and his eyes heated. "Avalon. My home."

Alarm jolted her from her need. "But we need to look for the sword now!"

"And Avalon is full of powerful witches who can help us track down your magic butter knife." He gave her a charming smile and laid a hand on her shoulder. "It seems we're going to be partners, Nineva. You'll have to trust me."

She felt her cheeks grow warm as those strong fingers gave her a comforting squeeze. It was obviously intended as a friendly gesture, but her body seemed intent on interpreting it as something else. "Trust isn't my best thing."

"Yeah, I've noticed that about you." He gave her a gentle push toward the gate. "Give it a shot anyway."

Nineva gave him a searching look over one shoulder, trying to ignore the sizzle and burn running through her blood.

Then she stepped through the gate.

Simmering with frustrated rage, Arralt walked through the dimensional doorway into brilliant, shimmering sunlight. He snarled at the glare. He'd almost had the little bitch. If that thrice-cursed dragon hadn't interfered . . .

As his men gated in around him, he stalked to the huge window that ran the length of the level and looked out over the ocean a hundred feet below. He'd chosen these cliffs as the perfect location for his fortress because they lay on the other side of the planet from the Cachamwri and Morven kingdoms.

And he'd chosen well. Ansgar had never been able to find Arralt's rebel stronghold—and his murderous father had definitely looked. Given the strength of the wards that surrounded them, the dragon's luck would be no better.

In stark contrast to the darkness of the mortal hemisphere they'd just left, the sun was well up here, sparkling on the deep blue waves. Looking down at the narrow strip of beach below, he spotted an incautious mermaid sunning herself on the rocks, her bare breasts lifted, her head thrown back, spilling her iridescent hair over the black stone.

Arralt curled his lip. She'd best keep her wits about her. Hunting the Mer was one of his army's favorite sports.

For a moment he considered gating down to take out his frustrated rage on her. His cock hardened at the thought, but he reluctantly decided against it. He needed to report to Varza. She'd be unhappy enough as it was.

As he turned toward the stone passage that led to his

partner's quarters, his gaze fell on a cluster of warriors. They stood with heads together, eyeing him uneasily. Knowing a budding conspiracy when he saw one, Arralt diverted to confront them. "Does someone have something to say?" His voice was low and pleasant, but several of his veterans flinched.

One of the newer recruits, however, did not have the experience to recognize his mood. "My lord, there was a dragon." His tone was earnest, his clear gaze troubled.

"Aye." Arralt leveled his coldest, flattest stare at the puppy.

Who still didn't have the sense to shut up. "The legends say the Avatar of the Goddess and a dragon warrior will free Semira from the sword. Shouldn't we . . ."

"What? Give that reptile the sword?" Arralt pumped contempt into his voice. "Hand our goddess over to Llyr? Because you may be sure that usurper is behind this. He had his 'god' send one of those lizards in an attempt to fool us." He scanned them all with an icy gaze and watched as even the puppy cringed. "The sword of the goddess belongs in the hands of her people, and her people will free her."

"But the legend!" The puppy's voice was very faint. "Semira herself predicted . . ."

"According to whom? It's been thousands of years. The legend probably began with some addled old woman and grew in the telling." In turn, he met the eyes of each warrior, searching for the seeds of rebellion and disbelief. He needed every man he had, but he'd kill without mercy or hesitation if necessary. "Llyr knows of the legend, and he's trying to use it against us. Or perhaps you want to be ruled by that weakling and his werewolf bitch?" The white-faced young warrior made no answer. Arralt roared, "Do you?"

"No, my lord!" The words sounded reassuringly fervent. "You are our rightful king."

"You have our loyalty, my lord." It was one of his

veterans, a scarred, hard-eyed Sidhe who obviously recognized the danger of the moment. He turned toward the others. "Lift your voices for our future king!"

As one, the men roared. "Arralt! Arralt! Arralt!"

The puppy shouted loudest, Arralt noted with grim satisfaction.

Good. It wouldn't be necessary to kill the whelp. His life would be better spent in battle anyway.

Not that Arralt wasn't tempted. Anger still surged in his blood, and he'd like nothing better than to gut the fool where he stood. But one did not waste assets on a whim.

He gave his men a curt nod, then turned and strode away, heading for his quarters. His thoughts slid grimly to the coming confrontation with Varza. He veered up a set of narrow stone steps, his armored boots ringing. Flecks of quartz glittered in the light of torches as he climbed.

The fortress looked like the rough stronghold it was; he saw no reason to waste magic on amenities. They'd dug a warren of rooms and corridors in the black stone of the cliffs: barracks, a kitchen and dining hall, training areas, interrogation rooms. The furnishings were just as rough—handmade wooden chairs and tables, pallets of hay that served as beds. Conjured furniture might be more elegant, but it also tended to vanish when its creator was killed.

Arralt's own rooms lay deep within the cliff. Personally, he'd have preferred a better view, but Varza did not care for sunlight. Reaching the thick wooden door, he swung it wide and stepped inside. Into a haven of opulence.

The light from a magical fire glinted off gold and gems and rich inlaid wood. His lover had a taste for beauty, and saw no reason not to indulge it.

Through the diaphanous curtains around his bed, he saw a figure rise from the thick feather mattress. The curtains blew aside as if from a sudden breeze, revealing a woman—lush and naked, her hair a waterfall of forest green in the torchlight, her body as pale as new snow.

Even now, he found himself enjoying Varza's sense of theater.

Once, her name had been Ceredith, and she'd been an open, laughing beauty who had loved him with all the passion in her uncomplicated soul. He regretted her loss, but sometimes sacrifices had to be made.

The eyes that had once been sapphire blue were now yellow and hard as she studied his face. "You failed."

Arralt stiffened at the fury rising in her eyes. "Cachamwri knew. He sent one of his dragons. The bloody beast took her." He drew the Sword of Semira from the scabbard he'd thrown across his shoulder and tossed it on the bed. "At least I kept her from escaping with the sword."

Varza's yellow eyes narrowed in sudden interest. "This dragon—what did he look like?"

Arralt shrugged. "Blue, of course. Cachamwri knows of that idiot legend. Even my men were ready to hand over the blade to the creature."

To his surprise, a slow, cold grin spread across Varza's face. "It's not an idiot legend, my love. But perhaps it is an opportunity we can use."

Arralt turned to stare at her, appalled. "You don't mean there's any truth to it?" If there was . . .

She laughed, a seductive purr. "Fear not, my general. Even true prophecies can be twisted into a new shape, given enough skill and power."

"What do you have in mind?"

"Oh, a great many things." The light from the fireplace painted the curves of her lush breasts with gold. Her teeth looked very white against her red lips. "But I must think on that a bit longer. In the meantime, about the kidnapping . . ."

"It is not so easy getting enough men into place. Llyr has been foiling assassination plots for centuries, and he is particularly protective of his wolf bitch."

Her smile was darkly seductive. "Why don't you let me take care of that?"

He grinned back. "Why, Varza—whatever do you have in mind?"

"What I do best." A gesture of her hands sent magic spinning over him. In an instant, his armor was gone. His lingering anger and frustration vanished as she reached out a hand and began to stroke him, lust in her unholy yellow eyes.

Nineva gaped as she turned in the center of the huge square, taking in the surrounding châteaus and castles that shone in the night like magical torches. The cobblestone streets were empty, though she thought she could hear laughter and music in the distance. "I don't think we're in Kansas anymore."

"Not exactly, Dorothy." Kel took her elbow in a surprisingly gentle grip. "Come on. I'll introduce you to the wizard."

She eyed his profile as he steered her across the square. "For a forty-foot dragon, you seem to know American pop culture really well."

He grinned, white teeth flashing. "It's part of the job description."

"Of being a dragon?"

"Of being a Knight of the Round Table."

She blinked at him. "Okay, I'm officially confused."

"We affect a lot of people that way." He laughed, the sound rich and masculine.

Something low in her belly tightened with sweet warmth. Seducing him definitely wouldn't be a hardship, though she had no idea how to go about it. What was she going to say? *I realize we're two different species, but my goddess says we need to play a brisk game of leaping lizards.*

But please don't fry me while we're at it.

Oh, yeah, that was going to be a fun conversation. She

swallowed and groped for any topic of conversation. "Where are we? I thought you guys lived in caves." As a child, she'd built a house for her "dragon" out of cardboard boxes.

"We do. This isn't the Dragon Lands—this is Avalon."

Nineva frowned. "Where King Arthur went when he died?" She'd loved reading about the Knights of the Round Table as a child.

"Yeah, only he didn't die. Arthur's pretty tough to kill." Kel smiled grimly. "God knows plenty have tried."

"He's still alive?" That would make him an immortal. "What is he? Sidhe?" Her father hadn't mentioned that. Come to think of it, he'd told her the stories that had fascinated her were only human myths about some Celtic warlord. But then, he'd come to Mortal Earth sixteen centuries before. A lot could have happened since then.

Kel looked down at her, a hint of mischief in the curve of his mouth. "Nope, Arthur's human. Or he was."

"So what is he now?"

Kel tilted his head skyward, as if mulling over what to say. "Complicated."

Nineva snorted. "That's a big help."

"Hey, it'll be a lot more believable after you meet him." His hand shifted to the small of her back as he guided her up the stairs of a big, Romanesque building whose white stone columns reminded her of a temple. His palm felt deliciously hot through the fabric of her T-shirt, as if his skin was warmer than a human's.

So much for the idea of dragons being cold-blooded.

"So do you live here, or do you live in the Dragon Lands?"

His profile went grim. "I haven't lived in the Dragon Lands in fifteen hundred years."

Nineva blinked. "Why not?"

Kel gave her a crooked smile that didn't reach his eyes. "Backstabbing. Betrayal. Friends looking the other way while my mother was murdered. The usual."

Nineva winced. "I'm sorry."

"It was several centuries ago."

"My parents were murdered, too." She hadn't intended to say it. The words simply burst from her in her surprise at finding she had something in common with this creature of myth and nightmare.

His false smile disappeared as he opened one of the building's massive doors. "I didn't mean to bring up bad memories. What happened?"

"I saved a dog."

"I beg your pardon?"

"I hit the neighbor's Irish setter with my car, so I got out and healed him." Nineva slipped past him into the building, not sure why she felt compelled to confess all this. "I knew I wasn't supposed to use my powers, but I did it anyway. King Ansgar had been hunting me since I was born. He sensed my magic and sent his killers. My father forced me to leave while he and my mother distracted the assassins. They . . ." The rest of the words wouldn't come, so she closed her dry mouth and shrugged.

"I'm sorry." He stepped inside and closed the door, compassion clear in his eyes as he studied her. "You must have been very young."

"Seventeen. Old enough to know better."

"Aren't you being a bit hard on yourself? Seventeen *is* young—even by human standards. And you're Sidhe. You're not even a century old yet."

"I'm half human. Besides, do I look like a kid to you?"

The look he gave her in return was thoroughly male—and thoroughly approving. "No, thank Cachamwri."

Not sure how she felt about the warmth in his gaze, Nineva turned and pretended to study their surroundings. Her brows flew upward as it all sank in. "Wow."

They were standing in a grand marble foyer with a ceiling that soared three stories overhead. More marble shone underfoot in alternating black and white tiles, and immense columns stood like gleaming white trees, their tops supporting the ceiling's gilded buttresses.

But what drew her attention was the bronze statue that occupied the center of the atrium. Nineva moved toward it and stopped to stare.

A bearded, long-haired man in crude leather armor knelt before a slender, robed youth and a delicate girl. The contrast between the warrior's massive strength and the couple's slender elegance was striking. So was the awe in the man's expression as he reached a big, scarred hand for the goblet the boy offered to him.

Nineva moved around for a better look at the couple—and gasped. Instead of the bronze eyes she'd expected, their eye sockets were filled with swirls of magic, vast and infinite and glowing. It was hypnotic, like looking into endless space.

"Who are they?" Her voice emerged as a strangled whisper.

"Arthur, Merlin, and Nimue."

She turned to blink at him, astonished. In Arthurian legend, Nimue had been Merlin's witch lover who had imprisoned him in a crystal cave. "I thought Merlin was supposed to be an old guy with a beard."

Kel snorted. "The legends got it wrong—along with about ninety-nine percent of everything else."

She realized the cup they held was glowing. "What's that supposed to be—the Holy Grail?"

"I wouldn't exactly call it 'holy.' It wasn't the Cup of Christ—that's another thing the legends got wrong."

Nineva dragged her attention away from the cup to study his face. "So what was it?"

"Damned if I know."

She found herself grinning at his cheerful tone. "You're a big help."

"I try." He flashed her a teasing male grin. "I can tell you what it did, though."

He's flirting with me. "And what was that?"

"It altered the genetic structure of everyone who earned the right to drink from it."

Nineva's jaw dropped. "In 500 A.D.?"

He shrugged. "Merlin wasn't exactly a sixth-century man."

"What the hell was he, then? Sidhe?"

"Nope. You're close, though. He and Nimue were aliens from somewhere in the Mageverse."

She recoiled. "They were Dark Ones?"

"Different aliens. He and Nimue were members of a race called the Fae . . ."

"Isn't that another word for Sidhe?"

"The Celts got confused." He shrugged. "Two races of magical people. They got 'em mixed up."

"I sympathize." Nineva was more than a little confused herself. "So why did Merlin and Nimue come to Earth?"

Kel turned and studied the statue, hesitating as if searching for the right words. Finally he said, "The Fae had seen a lot of intelligent races commit mass suicide. Seems humanity doesn't have a patent on stupidity. War, self-inflicted environmental disasters, bioengineered disease—there are lots of ways for a species to render itself extinct."

Nineva grimaced. "Gee, and I was hoping we were the only ones with that tendency."

"'Fraid not. Anyway, the Fae want to prevent those kinds of extinctions. They travel from planet to planet creating champions among every intelligent race they encounter. The champions' job is to guide their people to adulthood."

"Why don't the Fae just appear to people and say, 'Don't do stupid stuff'?"

"Apparently they tried that. Didn't work. They decided the best thing to do is give other species the tools to survive and leave the rest up to them."

Nineva thought through the implications as she studied

the grail statue. "So Merlin's cup made Arthur and his people immortal. Probably enabled them to work magic, too,
right?" Normal humans couldn't use mystical forces, because the physics wouldn't allow it. You couldn't work
spells on Mortal Earth unless you drew on the Mageverse
to do it.

"It's a little more complicated than that."

She gave him a dry smile. "Why does that not surprise
me? Okay, I'll bite. How?"

"The women can work spells, as you say. And they're
pretty damned powerful. We call 'em Majae."

"So what about the men?"

He cleared his throat. "Actually, they're vampires."

FIVE

"Vampires?" Nineva stared at him in amazement. He seemed perfectly serious. "You mean, as in undead, blood-sucking demons?"

"What part of 'ninety-nine percent of the legends is bullshit' didn't you get?"

"You didn't say anything about vampires, for God's sake. Why would Merlin make them vamps?"

"Because Merlin was a vampire. His species evolved that way. It's . . ."

" '. . . A little complicated.' Yeah, I get that." She shook her head. "If I didn't know you were the dragon knight, I'd think you were jerking my chain."

Kel's cobalt brows rose. " *'The* dragon knight'?"

"That story'll take longer than yours."

He contemplated that, then shook his head reluctantly. "Then it'll have to wait. Arthur told me to report in when I got you here, and we've taken too much time as it is. Let's go." His long leather coat swinging with every stride, he headed up the corridor.

Nineva admired the width of his shoulders a moment

before hurrying in his wake. He had a fluid, catlike stride that made her silently curse his enveloping coat. She'd have really loved to see his ass.

Hello? Dragon.

Dragon I'm supposed to seduce.

Well, there was that. Nineva contemplated the seduction issue a moment, doubtful. She'd never tried to seduce anyone; she'd generally been the seducee. None of her amorous experiences had been particularly memorable anyway, having been more a product of loneliness than real desire. There'd been times she'd have done anything to connect with someone, even if that someone had been a bouncer, biker, or horny businessman. Two affairs and one dubious one-night stand didn't make for much of a sexual track record. Or bedroom skill, either.

She sighed.

Kel looked back over his shoulder at her. "Problem?"

"Just contemplating my shortcomings."

He gave her a teasing smile. "That shouldn't take long—it's got to be a brief list."

Her spirits lifted at the warmth in his gaze, and she smiled back. "I guess gallantry is part of the whole Knight of the Round Table gig."

"Yep." His gaze warmed further. "But so's honesty."

"Oh, you're *good*."

Now his grin went downright suggestive. "So I'm told."

Before she could come up with another conversational volley, he pushed open a massive wooden door and stood back to let her enter.

"I'm starting to miss the Soviets," a male voice growled as they walked in. "The nice thing about atheists is they don't think they'll go to heaven if they blow up the fucking planet."

A dozen men and women sat on a dais behind an enormous semicircular table. Its polished walnut front was carved with scenes of knights and ladies—fighting, working spells, drinking from the same grail portrayed in the entry-way statue. Overhead hung a huge chandelier, its crystals shaped like swords. A thick wine red carpet deadened their footsteps as Kel led Nineva to one of the few empty seats in the audience.

She tried not to gape as she stared at the group behind the table. In contrast to their rich surroundings, most of the twelve were dressed casually—in jeans, slacks, and knit or cotton shirts—though one woman wore a brilliant scarlet suit that set off her black hair and pale, flawless skin.

Yet Nineva's attention was drawn to the bearded, dark-haired man who'd been speaking when they entered. Though well built, he wasn't the tallest man in the room, nor was he the most handsome, yet something about him was arresting. Oddly, he wore a black T-shirt with an arm-less and legless knight on the front, along with the words "It's only a flesh wound!" He looked familiar . . .

Nineva blinked, finally recognizing him from the statue in the foyer. Leaning over to Kel, she whispered, "King Arthur is a Monty Python fan?"

"Yeah, but for Cachamwri's sake, don't get him started on the Parrot Sketch. He'll segue right into 'I'm a Lumber-jack.' I've got enough emotional scars without the thought of Arthur in drag."

Despite his supposed taste for seventies Brit-coms, Arthur's expression was grim as he turned his attention to a dark-haired man sitting in the front row next to a pretty blonde. "Reece, what kind of progress are you making?"

The man stood and squared his impressive shoulders as if he had bad news he wasn't looking forward to relating. "Remember that al-Qaeda operative I'd recruited?"

Arthur winced. "They caught him spying for us."

"No, the Americans captured him."

"Hell. Tell your CIA buddies to turn him loose."

"Too late. The terrorists know he was taken. Even if I

get him sprung, they'll assume he's been turned. He'd be dead in a week."

"Fuck." Arthur aimed a glower around the table. "We've got to get some traction on this mess, people. We have to infiltrate that crowd."

The elegant blonde at his elbow spoke up. "But even if we break up al-Qaeda, there are dozens of other nutball groups ready to take its place. Until we can get the extremist mullahs to stop preaching murder as a route to paradise, we're never going to make any headway."

Nineva frowned and leaned over to whisper to Kel. "I don't understand—why don't they just cast a spell on the mullahs and tell them to cut it out?"

Arthur lifted a dark brow. "Because Merlin told us not to. Is this your fairy princess, Kel?"

Kel rose to his feet. Nineva, after a heartbeat, did the same as he gestured in her direction. "Nineva Morrow, Princess of the Morven Sidhe."

"Also part-time bartender and magician," she muttered under her breath, trying not to fidget under the interested gazes leveled her way.

"Did you say you're a bartender?" Arthur asked, amusement quirking his lips.

"Vampires have very acute hearing," Kel told her.

Oh, great. "Yes, Your Majesty. I'm sort of—in exile."

Arthur's faint smile became an outright grin. "Drop the 'Your Majesty,' kid. I haven't been king in centuries."

"Don't you believe it," one of the other men murmured. "Arthur'll be king until he cocks up his toes."

Arthur pointedly ignored the smiles that flashed in agreement. "Glad to see your mission was a success, Kel."

"Not . . . entirely." Tersely, he related his rescue of Nineva and the loss of the sword.

His listeners were frowning by the time he finished. "I'd like to know what Grim thinks of this mess. Hey, Grim . . ."

Magic flared at his elbow, a swirl of sparks that coalesced into a massive leather-bound tome. Without anyone touching it, it opened itself with a thump. "You called for me, Liege of the Magekind?" Its voice was deep, edged in a whispering sound like flipping pages.

"Yeah." He made a beckoning gesture toward Nineva. "Come over here, kid. Let's see what Grim can tell us."

Nineva rose reluctantly and followed Kel toward the dais. "Grim?" she whispered.

"Merlin's Grimoire. Merlin left him for us as a kind of magical database."

"Okaaay." She swallowed as she reached the dais and looked down at the book's open pages. It was like looking up into a cloudless night sky—utter blackness swirled with stars. The unexpected glimpse of infinity made her head swim, and she blinked.

Then the pages were simply pages, marked with words in a language she could almost read. Yet the sense of magic about them seemed a physical presence, a kind of psychic weight. "Put your hand on me," the book said in its whispering voice.

Nineva licked her lips and obeyed, then jerked her hand back. Instead of the smooth cool of paper, the page felt like living flesh, warm and yielding. "It's alive!"

"This one's quick," Grim said, amusement edging his voice.

Arthur reached out, caught her wrist, and pressed her palm against the page. "Quit teasing her, Grim."

"As you will." With that, magic poured through her, foaming, tingling, tasting metallic. Like copper and blood. "Power," the book whispered. "She has power. Her goddess bred true in her. She'll burn so bright . . ."

Nineva shuddered.

"But is she good or evil?" Arthur's voice was suddenly cold and unyielding.

"Good, of course. Her father knew his business. She'll give herself to the fire to save us all."

"No," she breathed, as her stomach dropped like a stone. "Please, no."

"Don't fear, child. It won't be so bad as all that."

"What fire?" Kel sounded alarmed.

"Yours."

"What the hell are you talking about?"

"Necessity."

"You're usually not this cryptic, Grim. What's she going to save us from?" Arthur demanded, studying her with narrow-eyed attention.

"The Dark Ones."

"What?" It was a chorus from everyone in the room, some of the voices outraged, others bewildered.

"What about Merlin's wards?" the red-suited woman snapped, her dark brows pulling down into a scowl. "They're supposed to keep those alien bastards out."

"So they are. Our enemies mean to find a way to shatter them."

"When are they going to make their move?" one of the men demanded. "How can we stop them?"

"That is not clear. There are many paths forward. But all of them involve this girl and the Sword of Semira."

"Great," Arthur growled. "Just great." He turned to the red-clad woman. "Pass the word. Find out if anyone has had any visions about this . . ."

"I did," Nineva said quietly.

Kel's head whipped toward her. "What did you see?"

She shrugged. "Demonic-looking horned creatures, stepping through a dimensional gate into Times Square."

"Any indication when?" Arthur demanded.

Nineva frowned, then reluctantly shook her head. "I don't think so."

Arthur rubbed his forehead as if it ached. "We'd better

meet with Llyr about this. He might have some ideas. Anyway, he'll want to talk to you about this sword."

Nineva stiffened in panic. At the last moment, she censored her instinctive *Hell, no!* to "I'd . . . rather not."

Arthur's eyes narrowed dangerously. "That was not a request."

"Sir, the king of the Morven Sidhe murdered my parents. I've spent my entire life running from his assassins. I have no intention of delivering myself into another king's hands now." Athur's handsome face went regal with cold rage, but Nineva refused to let her own gaze drop. He wasn't the only one with royal blood. "If you insist, I'll have to leave."

Arthur bared teeth that had lengthened into fangs. "You're assuming I'll let you. And under the circumstances, there's no way in hell."

Kel wanted to bury his face in his hands and groan as Nineva faced off with Arthur with the same stubborn lack of fear she'd shown him.

"Are you saying I'm your prisoner?" she demanded, her voice as chilly as Arthur's expression.

From the corner of one eye, Kel saw a force globe form around her hand. He snatched her wrist and used his own magic to snuff it. That was all this needed—for her to throw a fireball at Arthur in front of the most powerful witches in the Mageverse. They'd fry her like a mosquito in a bug zapper. "Forgive her, my lieges. She's had a difficult day." He managed a stiff smile and squeezed her hand in warning. "And so have I, since Cachamwri himself instructed me to protect her." *So please don't force me to protect her from you.*

Apparently Arthur recognized the pleading he was trying to convey, because the former high king settled back in his seat with a grunt. For a long moment, he said nothing. "Ansgar was a psychopath, and I hated his ever-loving guts. I cheered when I heard he was dead. Llyr Galatyn, however, is a good king, and he's proven himself an ally of the Magekind. He's not his brother, Nineva, and he's not going to hurt you."

"With all due respect, I'm a rival for his throne. He can't afford to do anything else." A muscle flexed in her delicate jaw.

Arthur went dangerously still. "You planning to lead a coup, Nineva?"

Oh, hell. Kel's gaze flashed to Nineva's face as every muscle tensed. He gave her another warning squeeze. *Don't say anything stupid.*

"Sir, I mean to stay as far away from the Morven rebels as possible. Anyone who'd help the Dark Ones invade is nobody I want anything to do with."

"Sorry, kid, I'm not letting you sidestep the question. Do you mean to take Llyr's throne?"

Nineva raised her chin. "I have no intention of taking it. But if it was offered, I would not refuse."

Arthur laughed. Kel was relieved to hear genuine amusement in it. "An honest answer. And given that you're a princess, I wouldn't have expected anything else."

Morgana Le Fay spoke up, leaning one scarlet-clad elbow on the table. "Unfortunately, this still doesn't resolve the problem at hand. Llyr must be informed of the situation. We owe it to him. And in any case, if we're going to have to fend off a Dark One invasion, we need all the help we can get."

"Informed, yes," Kel pointed out. "But that doesn't mean we have to hand Nineva over—assuming he even asks us to."

"He will," Nineva said shortly.

Morgana cocked her dark head. "And what makes you say that?"

Nineva shrugged and drew down the neckline of her T-shirt to reveal the glowing Mark on her breast. "I'm the

Last Avatar of the Goddess, the first woman born with Semira's Mark in fifteen centuries. Many of the Morven Sidhe will see me as their rightful queen. Llyr can't allow me to go free."

"And Cachamwri wants you safe," Kel said impatiently. "Llyr isn't going to do a damn thing to you, especially if you and this sword of yours are so important in stopping the Dark Ones."

"One way or the other, I'm going to arrange a meeting with Llyr as soon as possible," Arthur told her. "I won't insist you be present, though I would strongly suggest it. Once you meet Llyr, you'll realize your fears are groundless. In any case, we won't allow you to be taken prisoner."

Her face expressionless, she inclined her head. "Thank you, sir."

Kel had the distinct feeling she wasn't convinced. He cleared his throat. "In the meantime, my liege, may I have your permission to help Nineva search for the sword?"

"Of course." Arthur nodded shortly. "I'll see if I can't enlist Llyr's help with that. His resources should shorten the hunt considerably."

Nineva stirred as if about to protest, but evidently thought better of it. Kel decided he'd better get her out of harm's way before her control broke. He gave the council a bow. "Then with your permission, I'll get Nineva settled in. We'll start our search in the morning."

"Go. And feed her, will you?" Arthur flicked a look over Nineva's face. "She's looking a little pale."

"I'll do that." Kel took her elbow and steered her for the door. She went with the air of a woman making a grateful escape.

As they left the council chambers, he considered and discarded a dozen lectures on how best to deal with Arthur Pendragon and his infamous temper. Though, all things considered, his friend had been rather restrained.

Kel flashed a glance at Nineva's delicate profile as they

started down the corridor. She looked so exhausted, he thought better of the lecture. "Arthur's right—you do look pale. Any preferences in the food department?"

"Not really." Then she cast him a cautious look. "What do you have in mind?"

"How about lasagna? You look like you could use the carbs." Watching her blond brows arch, he grinned. "What, you were expecting barbecued virgin?"

"Of course not," she said, a little too quickly.

"Good, because I swore off barbecuing virgins centuries ago. They give me hairballs."

Instead of the laughter he'd expected, Nineva looked away.

"What's wrong?" Abruptly remembering Grim's prediction, he cursed. "You think I'm actually going to breathe fire on you."

"Your own book seems to think so."

"For once, Grim is dead wrong. There's no way in hell I'd ever do anything like that."

"Even to save us from the Dark Ones?"

"Even for that. First off, we don't do human sacrifices—that's their nasty little game. But even if we did, I wouldn't have a damned thing to do with it. I wouldn't use fire on my worst enemy, much less on you."

"Grim said . . ."

"Grim's not sure exactly what's going to happen—you heard him. Seeing the future is a dicey thing at the best of times. People have free will, and they may not choose the route a particular vision suggests."

She didn't answer, but her gaze was so bleak, so miserable, that he reached out and caught her chin. Her skin felt deliciously soft and warm under his fingers, but the fear in his eyes made him ache. He hated the thought of being feared by any woman, especially this delicate fairy princess. "How could you think I'd hurt you?"

"I don't think you're going to have a choice."

"There's always a choice." Bending his head, he took that soft, trembling mouth.

He'd intended the kiss as a gesture of comfort more than seduction, a reassurance that he wasn't the menacing monster she apparently thought.

He wasn't expecting the desire that lanced through him.

Her lips were just as sweetly arousing, tasting of mint toothpaste and magic, tempting him into pulling her close. Her full breasts pillowed against his chest, teasing him with the promise of how they'd fill his hands. Unable to resist, he tunneled his fingers through the pale blond silk of her hair, enjoying the cool sensuality of it. The thought that she feared him made him feel sick at heart.

Determined to reassure her, he deepened the kiss.

Kel's lips moved over hers, hot and skilled. His tongue slipped inside her mouth in a slow, suggestive thrust that tasted of magic and dark, wild things. He seemed to surround her with his broad-shouldered strength, his arms powerful around her back, her waist.

It had been a long, long time since she'd been kissed. Even then, it had never felt anything like this. Despite her instinctive wariness of this not-quite-man and his intentions, despite her fear of Grim's predictions and her own dreams, something about him made her feel safe. Warm.

Alive.

By the time he lifted his head, hers was spinning. Nineva leaned against him and concentrated on breathing. "I didn't know dragons kissed."

His wicked mouth tilted upward at the corners. "Dragons do all kinds of things."

"And very well, too."

His sensual smile widened. "Why, thank you, ma'am."

She was seriously considering pulling his head down

for another demonstration of his talents when he reluctantly let her go and stepped back. "But we'd better get you fed."

Nineva licked her lips, tasting him. His ruby gaze darkened as it followed the path of her tongue. "If you insist."

Kel opened his mouth as if to say something else, then shook his head. "You're a very bad girl, Nineva."

She gave him a slow, teasing smile of her own. Maybe she had a talent for this game after all. "I can be."

His eyes dropped to the rise of her breasts beneath the snug T-shirt before he dragged them away. She watched him swallow.

Yes, she could seduce him. Dragon or not, he felt a man's desire. Despite her lingering fear, she knew that the sooner she got him into bed, the better. Arthur meant to meet with Llyr the next day, which meant she'd have a whole new threat to deal with. She needed to strengthen Semira, and Semira seemed to believe that making love to Kel would do it.

Following Kel toward the exit, she frowned as a new thought occurred to her. What would this magical exchange do to him? Would it weaken him? If Semira was going to draw on his power, that did seem logical. And if so, didn't Nineva have a responsibility to warn him?

But what if he refused? Semira would be screwed, and Nineva could find herself going up against Llyr without the goddess's backing.

If she didn't tell him, and Semira fed on him while they made love, he'd be justifiably furious. Even aside from the moral question of whether she had the right to do such a thing, she needed his help to make the prophecy come true. She couldn't afford to anger him.

The thought of him angry reminded Nineva vividly of the dream. She shoved the knee-jerk fear away. She had to stop the Dark Ones from invading. Period. Nothing else mattered.

Somehow she had to tell him in such a way that he'd agree to help Semira.

Somehow.

Nineva was still wrestling with the problem when they reached a majestic hill on the outskirts of Avalon. A six-hundred-foot cliff of pale white stone formed one face, while trees and flowers bloomed along the terraced slopes of the remaining sides, warmed and fed by magic despite the winter cold.

The rough rock of the cliff smoothed as it neared the bottom, blending with the stone and glass of the human-style residence built into the base of the hill. A still lake curled around it, casting dancing reflections of the night sky. Trees surrounded the outer banks of the lake like ruffles on a woman's skirt. The cool air smelled of magic and roses.

"Home sweet home."

Nineva blinked at the elegant, imposing serenity of the scene. "You *live* here?"

Kel gave her a crooked smile. "I need a lot of room."

Looking closer, she realized the upper section of the cliff was dominated by the mouth of a huge cave, obviously an entrance for Kel's dragon form.

"It can be tough for me to find a place to land," Kel explained, as he led her along a cobblestone walkway that wound around the lake. "This solved the problem."

"It's beautiful." The sense of enchantment around the moonlit hillside was almost strong enough to taste. She breathed in deeply, entranced. "And there's so much magic here." Smiling, she traced a forefinger through the air, watching sparks trail her hand like fireflies. "You could almost get drunk on it."

"I can see how you'd feel that way, after living your entire life on Mortal Earth." He grimaced. "I always feel a lit-

tle suffocated there. There's no magic at all. You have to
haul it in from the Mageverse."

Ahead of them, the house's double doors swung silently
open. Nineva followed Kel inside, eager to see what he'd
done with the rest of the place.

She wasn't disappointed. Just beyond the entrance lay
a sprawling great room with smooth, curving walls that
arched up to meet overhead. It was like standing in the middle of a huge, pale egg. The floor was covered with a thick,
colorful rug depicting a dragon flying against a dazzling
blue sky. Here and there stood couches and chairs in bright
colors and flowing shapes. A fireplace dominated the center of the room, set in a stone column that swelled at the
top and base, as if it had grown from the very stone. At the
other end of the room, majestic chairs upholstered in red
surrounded a massive oak dining table.

Nineva turned in a slow circle, taking in the curving
ceiling two stories overhead and the window that took up
most of the outer wall. "Wow. This is . . ."

"A bit over the top."

She turned to find Kel watching her with a dry smile.
"Actually, I was going to say impressive."

He headed across the room toward an arched doorway
just beyond the dining table. "I spent the past fifteen hundred years trapped in a sword. I'm determined to surround myself with as much elbow room as I can possibly
get."

Interested, Nineva strolled after him, studying the
bronze statues that stood in niches cut in the walls. Not surprisingly, they depicted dragons and knights on horseback.
"Did you say you were trapped in a sword? Like Semira?"
That was one hell of a coincidence.

"Yeah. My uncle got pissed at me for befriending
Gawain, one of Arthur's knights." He led the way into a
spacious kitchen with thoroughly modern appliances that
wouldn't have looked out of place in a restaurant. "To punish

me—and get me out of the way—he turned me into a sword. Took us centuries to figure out how to free me."

She winced, remembering the loneliness she'd seen in Semira's mind. If it had been that bad for a goddess . . . "How did you stay sane?"

Kel's expression turned brooding. "I shared Gawain's consciousness, perceived the world through his senses. Even drew on his life force. I'd have starved otherwise." He paused in mid-step, frowning. "You know, that brings up an interesting point. How has Semira managed to survive for so long?"

Nineva cleared her throat. "Traditionally, she's relied on her Avatars to help sustain her magic. Royal princesses born with her Mark."

He looked up as he collected supplies from the fridge. "Like you?"

"Like me. Thing is, it's been centuries since an Avatar has been born. She's gotten pretty weak. Just before we lost contact, she told me she needs me to help recharge her."

Kel bent to rummage in a cabinet for a couple of bowls. "How are you supposed to do that?"

"By having sex with you."

SIX

Kel almost dropped the bowls. "What?"

Nineva related her conversation with the goddess in blunt, matter-of-fact terms at odds with the blush that rode her high cheekbones. "She said you're very powerful. Apparently, my making love with you is supposed to channel some of that magic to her."

"So she just ordered you to have sex with me?" He frowned, not happy with this turn of events at all. Yeah, he'd be more than happy to get his hands on Nineva's pretty little body, but only if it was her idea as much as his.

"It wasn't an order."

Kel slapped an onion on the cutting board and started slicing it with long, violent strokes of his knife. "Sounds like one to me."

"I'm her Avatar, Kel. It's my duty to help power her in any way I have to. Including sex with you."

"Well, that's flattering," he muttered.

A delicate hand came to rest on his forearm. Her cool touch stilled him. "It's not exactly a hardship," she said softly. Opalescent eyes shimmered up at him from that heart-shaped face. "I don't know about you, but I enjoyed our kiss."

"I did, too." His voice sounded hoarse to his own ears. His jeans were getting distinctly uncomfortable. He cleared his throat and sighed. *What the hell.* "How much magic is she going to need?"

A smile of surprised delight spread over her face, as if she hadn't expected his surrender. Which only went to prove how seriously she underestimated herself. "You'll consider it?"

He shrugged. "It'd be hypocritical of me not to."

Nineva's pale brows lifted in question.

Kel walked across the kitchen and dropped a handful of lasagna noodles into the boiling water. "Sex and blood sustain Magekind vampires. When I was trapped in the sword, Gawain's Majae partners kept both of us alive." He put the spoon aside and turned to her. "Thing is, Gawain didn't need much blood, and the sex didn't weaken his partners. But this goddess of yours isn't a vampire, and I'd like to know how much magic she's going to take."

Her face went so still, Kel knew she was considering lying. Then she blew out a breath. "I don't know. She didn't tell me."

"Is there any way to find out?"

"I'm . . . afraid not. I've lost contact with her. But I don't think it will hurt you."

He moved to the sink to drain the noodles. "No?"

"According to the prophecy, you play a major role in defeating the Dark Ones."

He growled a curse. "Another fricking prophecy. Which one is this?"

Nineva recited it for him as he started assembling the meal. Her lovely face was expressionless with control, and her voice never wavered. When she finished, he said nothing for several minutes as he slid the lasagna into the oven and uncorked a bottle of red wine.

"Hell of a prophecy," Kel said at last, pouring the wine into two glasses. "Especially the part about your burning in my fire and being 'shattered and reborn.'"

"Sounds a lot like Grim's prediction, doesn't it?"

"Which doesn't make it true."

Nineva shrugged and accepted one of the glasses from him. "It came directly from the goddess. You have to assume she knows what she's talking about."

"How do you know you're this Last Avatar?"

She took a sip of the wine. "Dad counted. There were twenty before me."

Hard to argue with that. Kel grimaced as he led the way into the living room while the meal cooked. "So you grew up with this thing hanging over your head?"

"Pretty much."

"No wonder you blasted me the first time you saw me."

Nineva shot him a look as they settled onto the couch together. "I didn't realize you were the dragon warrior. I'd seen your human face in dreams, but I had no idea who you were."

He gave her a deliberately flirtatious smile. "What kind of dreams?"

Her face went expressionless again. "Visions about the prophecy."

That one stark sentence told him enough to have him wincing. "About 'burning in my fire'?"

"Yes."

Staring into her haunted eyes, he cursed. "I said it before, and I'll say it again—I'm not going to hurt you, I don't care what Grim or your goddess or your visions say." Kel reached for her hand and cradled it in his own. Her fingers felt cool and fragile in his. "I don't hurt women. And I'm sure as hell not going to hurt you."

Hope leaped in her eyes before she veiled them with her lids. "It doesn't matter. Stopping the Dark Ones and freeing Semira is the only thing that counts."

Anger stung him. "I'm not lying."

"You also can't control everything that happens."

He didn't intend to say it, but the words burst from him anyway, carried on a wave of frustration. "Don't you get tired of being a martyr?"

Nineva smiled bitterly. "Hell, yes."

She's afraid, he realized suddenly. *She was raised to trust no one and nothing, not even the ally her prophecy predicts.* Looking into those wide opalescent eyes, he had to taste her again. Had to reassure both of them there was another way.

There had to be.

Her mouth opened for him, warm and sweet and flavored gently with wine. Yet she stiffened slightly as he slid his arms around her. Kel could almost feel her armoring herself against him even as she prepared to yield.

Like hell.

By Cachamwri, making love to him was not going to be one more thing she endured. He was going to make her love every second of it as much as he did.

Gently, using every bit of skill he'd learned from centuries of watching Gawain in action, he cupped her chin and drew her close. She felt so delicate against him, so tiny.

His iron fairy.

Kel swirled his tongue into her mouth to taste and stroke. Drawing his fingers through the moonlight tumble of her hair, he savored its cool silken texture, breathed the scent of her magic. He followed one smooth lock down to the rise of a lush breast and cupped her through her cotton T-shirt. She filled his hand so deliciously, he moaned into her mouth.

No, this wasn't going to be a sacrifice for either of them.

Nineva gasped against Kel's mouth as his fingers delicately plucked and stroked her nipple. If it felt that good through layers of bra and T-shirt, she couldn't wait for him to touch bare skin.

He's a dragon, she thought, trying to hold on to some vestige of control.

Her body didn't seem to care. It was too busy going up in flames under those skillful fingers.

He swirled his tongue around hers in a deliciously erotic duel, teasing her with the promise of what else he could do with it. Overwhelmed, her head spinning, she tore her mouth away to gasp for breath.

Kel seized the opportunity to explore the line of her jaw with his lips, stringing delicately biting kisses up to one pointed ear. He paused to bite the delicate lobe, then tease it with his tongue until she squirmed.

While she was focused on that wicked mouth, one hand traveled down her ribs and up under her shirt. A flick of his fingers opened the front clasp of her bra.

The feeling of that big, warm palm covering her made her shudder with blind delight.

She hadn't expected this. How could she? He made her previous partners seem like clumsy boys or drunken louts. And maybe they had been.

It was for damn sure Kel was neither.

When he finally drew back, his eyes were hot and his cheeks were flushed. "I'm not going to take you on the couch."

She swallowed with an effort. "No?"

"No. There's a bed upstairs." His voice dropped to a deliciously sexy growl. "A big bed."

Nineva's mouth felt as dry as a sock. "Sounds good."

He rolled to his feet and loomed for a moment, tall and powerful. Before she could even think of standing herself, he bent and picked her up as if she weighed no more than a doll.

Instinctively, she grabbed for his powerful shoulders as he turned and started across the cavernous living room for a set of broad spiral stairs. "I can walk!"

"Yeah, but I don't intend to let you." He flashed her a wicked grin. "This is a lot more sexy."

Not to mention overwhelming. Disconcerted, she stared at his aggressively male profile as he carried her up the stairs two at a time. He made her feel small and delicate and female.

But that was an illusion, Nineva told herself staunchly. She took care of herself, and she liked it that way. She was the Avatar, and she followed the path that had been laid out for her.

Alone.

Making love with Kel wasn't going to change that. She couldn't afford to forget the roles they were destined to play. She wouldn't be able to endure what was to come if she let herself get sucked into whatever romantic fairy tale he was trying to spin.

He reached the top of the stairs and strode down a broad, carpeted hallway. Double doors flew wide at their approach, and he swept her inside.

The bed that occupied the center of the room looked almost big enough to accommodate Kel's dragon form. He carried her toward it like a medieval conqueror from a romance novel.

Nineva half expected him to toss her onto it, then follow her down. Instead, he stopped at the foot of the massive canopied bed and swooped in for another kiss.

She found herself drowning in the intoxicating delight of his mouth. He tasted of magic and smelled of starlit nights. His shoulders felt solid and warm under her hands. Still kissing her, he carried her around to the side of the bed.

Kel only drew his head back when he lowered her to the mattress. Breathless, she watched him straighten and look down at her, a sensual smile of anticipation on his starkly handsome face.

"Ummm," she said. "I think I smell dinner burning."

He grinned and gestured, sending a spell shooting

downstairs like a star. "Not anymore." Surveying her, he added wickedly, "But something's definitely hot."

Between one blink and the next, Kel was naked. Nineva caught her breath at the sight of him looming over her. His body was beautifully sculpted with muscle, from broad shoulders angling down to narrow hips and long, powerful legs. His eyes seemed to flame like rubies catching the light.

For a long, humming moment, he gazed at her, all that silken hair tumbling around his shoulders. Taking in that amazing body framed by his cobalt mane, she realized she'd never seen anything so intensely masculine in her entire life. Her gaze dropped to his cock, thrusting from a thick blue ruff. It was long, deliciously broad, with a fat crown and a slight upward curve.

He looked just the way he had in that erotic dream.

Before that thought could chill her, he tilted his head to one side, his smile lazy and white. "You seem to have the advantage of me."

Nineva gave him a long, slow blink. "Kel, *nobody* has the advantage of you."

He chuckled, the sound richly male. "I'm flattered, darling, but I was referring to the frustrating fact that you're still dressed." His eyes suddenly took on a hot male glitter as his voice dropped to a growl. "If you don't get rid of those clothes, I'm afraid I'm going to have to start ripping them off."

Her instant's fear vanished, wiped away by the pure hot promise in his eyes. For a wicked moment, Nineva considered letting him strip her. Instead, she lay back on the bed, deliberately arched her back, and slowly dissolved the spell that maintained her jeans and T-shirt.

As her clothes vanished, Kel's eyes widened. His cock jerked upward, hardening still more, giving Nineva a heady sense of power. She'd never felt so sexy in her life. "This any better?" she purred.

Kel's smile faded as the lust in his eyes intensified. "Perfect." His gaze fixed on her, he crawled onto the bed and straddled her on hands and knees, not quite touching her.

Feeling breathless, she looked up at him. And waited. He only watched her, hot-eyed, letting her anticipation build. Her nipples hardened as her mouth went dry. His gaze flicked to the hardening points, and one corner of his mouth kicked up.

"Are you going to do something, or just stare?"

He sat back on his heels, his cock jutting. "What do you want me to do?"

"You could touch me."

He grinned, taunting. "I could."

"Or you could just tease me until I get bored and go elsewhere." She started to swing her legs off the bed.

Ruby eyes flared. Quick as a snake, he grabbed her ankles and flipped her onto her back again. Slowly, deliberately, he lifted her legs in the air and spread them wide. "You're not going *anywhere*."

Braced on her elbows, she licked her lips. "Apparently not."

But though she expected him to pounce, he didn't. Instead he rose to his knees and looked down at her, his exotic eyes tracking from her face down to the full mounds of her breasts, down her abdomen to the softly furred delta between her thighs. There was something deliciously arrogant in his pose, like a barbarian conqueror surveying a captive. It should have pissed her off.

Perversely, it kicked her desire even higher. She could feel herself getting wet.

I shouldn't be doing this. The thought slid through her mind, a knee-jerk protest from her inner good little girl. Being as much her mother's daughter as her father's princess, she usually listened to that voice.

It felt good to ignore it for once.

"That's a sly look. What are you thinking?"

She tried out a Jezebel smile. That felt good, too. "Take a wild guess."

"That sounded like a challenge." Kel sank down onto his heels, then lowered himself over her, covering her. She caught her breath in anticipation. He flashed her a conqueror's grin as he lowered his head. "I love challenges."

He kissed her as their bodies came together, his cock settling against her belly, his chest brushing her nipples, his hips pressing between her thighs. The sensation of all that warm male strength made her moan in delight. He deepened the kiss, nibbling her mouth, suckling at her tongue, thrusting his own deep in wet, hot exploration. His hair fell around them in a dark blue curtain, cool on her skin.

Nineva curved her arms around his narrow waist. His back felt like sun-warmed marble under her hands. His magic seemed to foam its way into her mouth like champagne. "You taste so good," she breathed.

"So do you. And you feel like my hottest fantasies." One big hand came to rest on her breast, cupping it gently. His thumb stirred over her nipple, which tightened into a berry-firm peak. Smiling, Kel plucked it gently, then slowly twisted, sending a sweet swirl of pleasure shuddering through her body.

Nineva lifted her chin, dragging her mouth from his as she panted, feeling as if she were drowning in the waves of pleasure. "Has anybody ever told you . . ." She had to stop and pant. ". . . you have a real talent for that?"

"Someone may have mentioned it." Kel started a chain of delicious little bites along the curve of her jaw. Discovering one pointed ear, he paused to sample it with teasing swirls of his tongue. Nineva gasped, throwing her head back even more.

"You taste exotic, Sidhe girl," he said roughly. "You make me think of magic and dancing naked in the light of the moon."

Nineva smiled, shuttering her lids. "For such a big, bad warrior, you've got a poetic streak." Her fingers explored the hard satin ridges of his ribs.

"We dragons are a poetic people." He paused to taste the hollow of her throat.

She discovered the upper rise of his muscular ass. It felt temptingly compact and delightfully warm as she cupped it. "In between eating the occasional virgin?"

He lifted his head to give her a grin. "We find the taste of virgin very inspiring." Eying her right nipple, he added, "In fact, I'm feeling pretty inspired right now."

"I hate to disappoint you, but I'm not exactly a virgin."

"Well, there are virgins . . ." His tongue flicked over her nipple, making her gasp. "And then there are virgins."

As he settled down to suckle in earnest, she threaded her fingers through his silken hair. "I'll—Oh!—take your word for it."

"You do that." White teeth raked gently across a beaded point, sending a lovely wash of heat through her body. As he shaped and teased her breast with one hand, he reached between her legs with the other. His palm stroked over her soft hair, then a strong finger slipped between the lips of her sex.

They both groaned. "Goddess," she gasped, "you've made me so hot."

He lifted his head. His eyes blazed like twin fires. "And you make me hard as a pike."

His hand pumped, fingers stroking deliciously deep as he flicked and swirled his tongue over her nipples. Nineva threw her head back as sweet delight stormed her every sense. Her fingers curled into involuntary fists in his hair, knuckles going white. He licked and bit, fierce and gentle by turns.

By the time he left her nipples, she was all but writhing. He pressed a kiss between her breasts, then began nibbling his way down her torso. Nineva caught her breath as she realized his intentions. Her hips thrust eagerly. He rewarded her with another long pump of those wicked fingers.

Then his mouth found her most delicate flesh, and his tongue teased her clit with a series of lazy figure eights. Finally he closed his lips over the hard little pearl and suckled.

"Kel!" Pleasure detonated through her body like an erotic bomb, jerking her spine into a tight bow.

Gently, wickedly, he scraped his teeth softly over her thrumming core. Heat pulsed through her, so bright she saw it behind her closed lids. Crying out, she writhed in the cool sheets, spurred on by his deliciously ruthless mouth.

Just as the last waves died, Kel abruptly reared over her, spread her thighs wide, and presented his thick cock to her slick opening.

Dazed, she whimpered as he started working into her, one slick, solid inch at a time. He felt even bigger than he looked. "Oh, God!"

"Mmmm," he purred. Burning ruby eyes focused on her face as he braced a fist on the mattress, leaning in, pressing hard. "Slick, tight . . . Want more?"

"Yes. Oooh, Goddess, yes!" Nineva threw back her head and gritted her teeth as he fed the rest of his shaft into her. His gaze never wavered from her face.

When his heavy balls finally lay against her ass, he started to pump. The strokes were long, deep, searing her tight flesh with delicious friction. She could only grab his broad shoulders and hang on, her breath sobbing.

Nineva wrapped Kel's cock in cream and velvet. Feeling the pressure of the climax building in his balls, he gritted his teeth, trying to fight it down. He wanted to stay in her as long as possible, wanted to watch her come again.

Iridescent fire swirled in Nineva's eyes whenever pleasure overcame her, a sight almost as hypnotic as the feel of her sex gripping him.

She curled one long leg over his ass as he rose over her,

a bare heel pressing hard, demanding as a knight's spur digging into a stallion's side. Setting his teeth, Kel gave her what she asked for, lunging harder, shafting deeper, fighting the climax that boiled closer and closer to the surface with every hot stroke.

Then her tiny inner muscles began to clamp and pulse again, and he lost the fight with a shout. His orgasm jetted up from his balls in waves of sweet heat. Driving his cock to the root, Kel stiffened, losing himself as she writhed around him with soft, strangled cries.

As they stiffened together, something stirred. Kel sensed the distant presence on the horizon of his consciousness, a ghostly touch of something powerful and elemental—and very female.

Nineva's eyes flared wide, meeting his in startled awareness. "Semira!"

But as if their sudden mutual distraction had snapped the link, the presence disappeared.

"Cachamwri's Egg!" With a groan, Kel collapsed over her, panting. "We almost had her."

"Almost."

"Unfortunately, almost is never good enough when it comes to magic." Kel dropped his head on her pretty breast and concentrated on breathing. "We'll have to try again."

Her teeth flashed white in a wicked grin. "The sacrifices I make for mankind."

Kel laughed. "You're a true heroine."

Diana lay listening to Llyr's heart thump, feeling pleasantly damp and sated. She was a little too close to Dearg's delivery to chance conventional intercourse, but that was no deterrent to a couple as creative as they were. They'd taken turns pleasuring each other with hands and mouths, and a lovely time they'd had doing it.

Now, however, Diana could sense Llyr's growing

preoccupation. Being the sort of man he was, he could never let go of a problem for long.

"Worrying about the sword again?" she asked him, toying with a lock of his blond hair. It felt a little sweat-damp in her fingers and smelled deliciously of Sidhe male. They'd both played hard.

"We've been unable to track the man who took it," Llyr admitted. "Which is no surprise. Arralt has done a particularly skilled job in hiding his base of operations. I'm told he has a fortress somewhere in the eastern hemisphere, but I have been unable to locate it."

"Eastern hemisphere? Like Asia?"

"Not exactly. Our Earth does not have the same land masses as yours, so the continents are different."

"Oh, that's right." This world was so much like the one she'd grown up on in some ways. But then there were the alien continents, apparently the result of tectonic forces made just slightly different by magic. Not to mention the really weird differences, like the dragons and unicorns . . .

Suddenly the air filled with several bars of familiar music. Diana lifted her head in surprise. " 'Blue Suede Shoes'?"

"It's Arthur," Llyr said. "And it must be important, if he's calling at this hour." He rolled over and opened a drawer in the bedside table, then fished out a small object that looked a lot like a cell phone.

Once, of course, it had been. Now it was enchanted. Arthur had given him the gadget months ago as a way to communicate through the formidable magical shields of the Sidhe Kingdom and Avalon.

Diana watched as her husband opened the flip phone and put it to one ear. "Greetings, Arthur."

Her keen werewolf hearing had no trouble picking up the reply. "Sorry to bother you at this hour, but we seem to have a mutual problem."

She listened in growing alarm as Arthur related Kel's

conversation with Cachamwri and his subsequent rescue of an exiled Morven Sidhe princess from Arralt.

Her husband went dangerously still as his friend described the general's escape with the Sword of Semira. Worst of all, it was all part of some plot involving the Dark Ones.

"He stole that sword from my armory," Llyr told Arthur. "We learned of its theft only yesterday. And this girl Kel rescued claims to be the Last Avatar?"

"That's what I understand. Seems a decent enough kid, though. Says she wants nothing to do with this Arralt and his rebels."

"That may be, but I'm going to want to talk to her myself. She may be part of this plot."

There was a markedly uncomfortable pause. "I can understand your caution, but Grim says the girl is on the up and up. What's more, she doesn't much want to talk to you. Apparently she's spent her entire life running from that psycho brother of yours, and she's a little jumpy when it comes to Sidhe royalty."

"That," Llyr said in a silky tone, "is too bad."

Arthur's sigh came clearly even over the cell. "Yeah, I figured you'd say that. Trouble is, Cachamwri has told Kel to protect the girl, and that's exactly what Kel is going to do. I'd rather the two of you not get in a magical pissing match over this."

"I'm not going to hurt her." Llyr's expression went hard. "I do, however, need to question her about the threat to my kingdom."

"I can't let you arrest Nineva, Llyr. I gave the kid my word. And if she really is our one hope to stop the invasion . . ."

"I have no intention of arresting her—at this point—but I need to find out for myself if she is indeed the Avatar, and what her intentions are if she is. That girl could trigger a civil war that could rip my kingdom apart."

"Yeah, I get that. Why do you think I'm calling you at oh-dark-thirty in the morning? I know you don't keep vampire hours."

Llyr dragged a frustrated hand through his hair. "I give you my royal oath she'll come to no harm."

"I'll do my damndest to talk her into meeting with you, Llyr." He paused. "Which might be easier if you come here."

"Fine. I'd like to discuss this with you in more detail anyway. Given the situation with the rebellion, I may need your help."

"You'll have it. God knows you helped pull our chestnuts out of the fire with that bastard Geirolf. And if the Dark Ones do invade, we're going to need every Sidhe and Mage to fend them off."

"That's putting it mildly." Llyr paused thoughtfully. "On second thought, let me speak to the girl about our meeting. I'll give her my oath she'll be safe. Perhaps she'll find that more reassuring."

Arthur considered the point. "That's likely. I'll have Gwen open the wards for you."

"Thank you. I'll be bringing a complement of bodyguards, as well as my queen."

Diana could plainly hear the amusement in the vampire's voice. "Don't like letting her out of your sight, huh?"

Llyr snorted. "These days, she's probably safer in your kingdom than mine."

Frowning, Diana listened as the two men said their good-byes. Llyr snapped the phone shut and sat on the edge of the bed, a frown on his handsome face.

"Why didn't Cachamwri tell you about this instead of going to Kel?" she asked quietly.

"Kel's a blue dragon, and the prophecy specifies a blue dragon."

His tone was so grim, she instinctively covered her pregnant belly with both hands. "What prophecy?"

In growing horror, she listened as he recited it. "Oh, shit."

"My thoughts exactly."

"What's this about the Dark Ones?" Cachamwri had killed a bunch of them ten thousand years before with the help of one of Llyr's ancestors. In the process, the dragon had become a god and formed an alliance with Llyr's line. The remaining Dark Ones had fled to Mortal Earth, only to be banished again centuries later by Merlin and Llyr's father.

"Apparently, they're coming back. Though Cachamwri alone knows how—Merlin erected a magical barrier to protect both Earths. They must have figured out a way to break through it—if the prophecy is correct, and if this girl is the Avatar." He sighed. "I'm going to have to attempt to contact Cachamwri and find out what in the name of the Egg is going on. With any luck, he'll decide to be cooperative."

"We can only hope." Cachamwri tended to play by his own inscrutable rules.

"In the meantime, I'm doubling your personal guard."

She groaned. "Jesus, Llyr, I can barely take a step without tripping over one of them as it is."

He got that familiar hard-eyed look Diana had come to recognize. They'd been married less than nine months, but she already knew no argument she could make was going to budge him when he wore that particular expression.

"This is not a topic open to negotiation," Llyr said, his lush mouth pulling into an inflexible line. "I will not give Arralt and his rebels a chance to kill you."

"Llyr, I'm Direkind. Merlin himself created us to be resistant to magic . . ."

"But you're not resistant to decapitation, so none of my enemies are getting anywhere near you." He sighed and laid a large, warm palm against the side of her face. "I've lost four wives, none of whom held my heart like you do.

And none of whom carried the Heir to Heroes. You are not expendable."

Well, there wasn't much she could say to that, except . . . "I love you."

The kiss he gave her had her counting the minutes until Prince Dearg made his appearance—and they could make love without holding back.

Assuming they all survived that long.

SEVEN

Nineva threw her head back, gasping as she rode Kel's narrow hips. His cock felt a yard long in this position, and each thrust rammed shock waves of pleasure through her body. It was damn near too much, yet she loved every minute of it.

Close. She was so close . . .

Suddenly he arched under her, lifting her off the bed with his effortless brawny strength. Shouting in pleasure, he clamped his big hands over her hips, holding her still . . .

Kel's climax triggered her own. She came, screaming, throwing her head back so hard her hair whipped his thighs.

And on the edge of her mind, she sensed the goddess's presence, glowing like a distant star. "Semira!" Nineva gasped out loud.

But the star faded away again.

Nineva collapsed across Kel's muscled chest with a groan of frustration. "Dammit to hell, we've made love three times tonight. What more does she want?" Her entire nervous system was lit up like the Statue of Liberty on the Fourth of July.

"I do think she seemed a little stronger that time, though." Kel wrapped his brawny, sweat-damp arms around her waist.

"Not strong enough," she grumbled into his chest. "We're never going to find her at this rate."

"The poor woman has been slowly starving for centuries. We'll just have to keep trying." His tone was more anticipatory than anything else.

"Here's an idea—we could get the entire Sidhe kingdom together for one big orgy . . ." Whimpering a little, she lifted off him and collapsed over onto her back.

"Not until I get something to eat." Kel arched his back and stretched. "Semira's not the only one who's starving."

Nineva's stomach rumbled loudly. They traded a look and laughed. She was surprised by how good it felt.

Downstairs in the kitchen again, Kel served up plates of magically reheated lasagna and poured two more glasses of wine. They sat down at his dining table to eat.

Nineva forked up a bite and moaned in delight at the blend of cheese, noodles, and spicy sauce. "Oh, God, this is good! Where did you learn to cook?"

"Centuries of hanging around with Gawain. He views cooking as an essential seduction technique." He gave her a devilish little smile. "Though he's always too heavy-handed with the garlic."

She eyed him over the rim of her wine. "A vampire who loves garlic?"

"Well, he doesn't actually eat it—just gives it a taste or two. Besides, the garlic thing is a myth."

Nineva snorted. "What isn't?"

Kel gave her a slow smile. "Not much." Taking a sip of his wine, he studied her. "Speaking of myths, legends, and prophecies—just how did Semira end up in that sword, anyway?"

She tore off a hunk of crusty French bread and bit into it. Like the lasagna, it was delicious—fresh, hot, and crunchy. Chewing in narrow-eyed pleasure, she contemplated the best way to tell the story. "According to my father, Semira first appeared to my people fifteen thousand years ago. The Morven Sidhe were mortal nomads then, struggling to survive. The goddess took Sidhe form to lead us, served by a series of priest kings."

"Interesting," Kel mused. "So she was always a goddess? Cachamwri started out as a dragon. It was only after he killed all those Dark Ones that he became an elemental— a god. Where did Semira come from?"

Nineva shrugged. "No one knows, though my father thought she was an alien. Not a Dark One, obviously, but also not of Sidhe Earth."

He took a bite of lasagna, contemplating the point. "Makes sense."

"Semira lived among the Morven tribes for five thousand years, guiding them to becoming the most advanced Sidhe race on the planet." She took a sip of her wine and shrugged. "Then the Dark Ones invaded."

"And everything went to hell."

The Dark Ones had enslaved and murdered everyone they encountered, even Dragonkind. The demonic creatures fed on the life force of their victims to power their magic. Torture and sacrifice were essential to their spells.

"When the invasion began, Semira led the Morven Sidhe against the Dark Ones with the help of her latest priest king, Idris. But the attack went badly. The Dark Ones were more powerful than she expected, and they killed most of Semira's forces."

Kel grimaced. "I can understand that. We went against a single Dark One last year, and he damned near killed us all."

Nineva jolted in alarm. "One of the Dark Ones was here? Already?"

"He'd always been here—Merlin had imprisoned him on Mageverse Earth. He got loose. We managed to kill him, though." Kel made a dismissing gesture. "Which is yet another long story. Go on."

"Anyway, Semira drained herself badly trying to defeat the aliens, who had them surrounded. Their general attacked her, and she went down . . ."

"His name wasn't Geirolf, was it?"

Nineva frowned. "Actually, I think it was."

"Figures. That's the one I was talking about. He was a powerful bastard."

"Yeah, that sounds like him." She stirred her lasagna with her fork. "Realizing Geirolf was closing in and desperate to save her, Idris transferred her essence into her sword. He was badly wounded at the time, though, and he had to use his own life force to power the spell."

Kel's brows lifted. "Loyal of him."

"More than that, he loved her. They'd even had children together." She sighed and put her fork aside. "The spell worked. Geirolf thought she'd been destroyed with her lover. The victorious Dark Ones quit the field, leaving the flower of the Morven Sidhe to rot in the sun."

"So who retrieved the sword?"

"Semira's youngest daughter—she was only about ten or so—came out onto the battlefield and found it. Young as she was, the child had sensed what had happened. She was the first of the Avatars, and the one who relayed Semira's prophecy."

"So you're a descendent of Semira?"

She shrugged. "Well, yes."

"Damn. No wonder everybody is after you."

"Exactly. A lot of people would be a lot more comfortable if I were dead."

Kel bared his teeth. "Too fuckin' bad."

*   *   *

Pleasantly stuffed, Nineva watched in astonishment as her lover polished off the rest of the lasagna with cheerful greed.

"Where the hell did you put it all?" she demanded, as he gestured, making their dinner dishes vanish, presumably clean, back to their cupboards. "Have you got a hollow leg?"

Kel patted his flat belly with a satisfied grin. "My other car is a dragon. Besides, I have to keep my strength up if I'm going to service your insatiable lusts."

"*My* insatiable lusts?"

"Okay, your goddess's. Six of one, half a dozen of . . ." He broke off to cover a huge yawn with his hand. ". . . the other." Glancing toward the windows, which were going blue with approaching dawn, he added, "Looks like it's time for bed."

"The sun's just coming up!"

"Yeah." Kel caught her elbow and gently tugged her toward the stairs. "One myth that is true is that vampires sleep during the day, so everybody else in Avalon does, too. You'll get used to it."

Actually, she wouldn't mind a little sleep herself. Between battling Arralt and staying up all night talking and making love, she could use the zees. "Umm . . . do you have a guest room?"

One foot on the bottom stair, Kel lifted a cobalt brow. "We just had jungle sex—repeatedly—and you want to sleep in separate beds? No, I *don't* have a guest room, as a matter of fact."

Nineva fought the urge to squirm. "I've never slept with anybody."

"What, you slink out after you're done with them?"

"If you were afraid of assassination attempts, would you want your lover in the cross fire?"

That stopped him. "Good point." Kel studied her, his

expression sympathetic. When he finally spoke again, his voice was very quiet. "How do you sleep at night?"

She shrugged, uncomfortable. "I ward my apartment. I figure the spell will wake me up in time to fight if anybody hostile shows up."

"Well, you don't have to worry about that tonight. This entire city is warded. I doubt a Dark One could get through those shields." The hand on her elbow was very gentle as he urged her up the stairs. "But I'll tell you what—if any killer Sidhe do attack, I'll eat them. How's that?"

Nineva found herself grinning at his cheerfully bared teeth. "You're a true gentleman."

"Hey, I'm a Knight of the Round Table. Comes with the job."

Arms folded on the pillow under his head, Kel lay staring at the darkened ceiling overhead. He was acutely conscious of Nineva's slim, graceful back as she lay on her side as far away from him as the bed would allow.

The sting of that was surprisingly sharp.

Knowing Nineva, there was probably a great deal of truth in her excuse of not wanting to endanger her lovers by sleeping with them. But he suspected a larger factor was that she simply didn't trust anybody. Not even him.

Maybe especially him.

Even when they'd made love, even when he'd driven her body to climax, he'd sensed that part of her was holding back, fighting to remain behind that armored shell she maintained against the world.

It irked him. It wasn't that he didn't understand the fear of betrayal—his own uncle had imprisoned him in three feet of steel for fifteen hundred years. When his mother had tried to discover who'd trapped him, the bastard had manipulated her into challenging another dragon, who'd then killed her.

So yeah, Kel knew about betrayal.

But he'd never been treated as a possible source of it. For centuries, he'd fought alongside Gawain with his magic, embracing imprisonment to keep his friend safe. They'd both known perfectly well that the spell would have freed him instantly if he'd killed Gawain. That was, after all, what his uncle wanted. Yet the thought that Kel might actually do it had never even crossed his friend's mind.

Kel should know. He'd shared the knight's thoughts, just as Gawain had shared his. Each knew the other could be trusted.

When they'd finally found a way to free him by tricking the spell, Arthur had promptly named Kel the first new Knight of the Round Table in four hundred years. The fact that he was actually a dragon hadn't even entered into the equation. Like Gawain, Arthur trusted him without question. So did everyone else in Avalon, including the women he bedded.

Until Nineva, who apparently trusted no one at all.

Hell of a way to live, when he thought about it. He didn't think he'd ever met anyone so utterly alone.

Thing was, he liked the little paranoid. She was sensual and funny and oddly brave for someone who apparently lived in constant fear. She hadn't even hesitated to attack Arralt, who had a good eight inches and a hundred pounds on her. What's more, she'd known how to fight. Evidently, Daddy Dearest had raised her to be quite the little swordswoman—among other things.

It was just as well Eirnin was dead. Kel didn't think he would have liked the bastard much. It took one cold-blooded son of a bitch to brainwash his own daughter into sacrificing herself for a goddess.

It was no wonder the kid's head was a snake pit . . .

A moan. Not a sound of pleasure, either. Kel lifted his head off the pillow and turned to look at Nineva.

She flopped over onto her back, throwing the covers off. Normally, he would have appreciated the view—she really did have gorgeous breasts—but the fear on her pretty face killed any budding arousal. "No. Please, don't!"

"Nineva . . ."

"NO!" She bolted from the bed as if shot from a cannon, backing away, one hand held up as if to ward off an attacker. Her voice lifted into a heartbreaking wail of pain and terror. *"Kel!"*

He rolled off the bed and caught her by those slender shoulders. "Nineva, it's all right! You're just having a bad dream!"

"Don't!" Her hands began to glow.

"Whoa!" He grabbed her wrists and lifted them upward before she could blast him. "Nineva, wake up! It's okay, you're safe!"

Her mouth rounded in another pitiful cry of terror as he pulled her against him. Then consciousness flooded her blank, panicked gaze, and she stiffened, examining his face anxiously. "Kel?"

"Yeah, it's me. You were having a nightmare. You're okay. I won't let anyone hurt you."

She sagged in his arms. The blue fireballs burning around her hands winked out. "It was you." Her voice sounded far too high, almost childlike.

"What was me?" Carefully, he drew her close and wrapped his arms around her. She quivered against him in wracking shivers.

"You burned me. My skin flaked off in ashes. Goddess, it hurt!" She burrowed against him.

"Me?" He cursed softly and raked his hair out of his face. "Between Grim and your goddess, I guess it's not surprising you had a nightmare—but it was only a dream."

"I know." Nineva pulled away from him and knuckled the tears off her cheeks. She was still shaking. "It's just . . ." She broke off and moved to sit down on the bed,

her slim shoulders hunched. She looked so small and vulnerable, he felt his heart turn over in his chest.

"Just what?" Kel dropped to his knees in front of her so
he could see her face.

"It's so vivid!" Almost angrily, she swiped the tears
away again. "I can feel it. Smell my skin burning. Taste the
smoke. I've been dreaming about it for years now, and
every time it gets worse and worse."

He covered one small, clenched fist with his palm.
"Look, like I told you before, *it's not going to happen.*"

Her tear-swollen eyes met his. "What if you have to?
What if it's what we have to do to stop the Dark Ones? We
can't let them invade, Kel. They'd destroy both our Earths
and everyone on them."

"I know." It had taken Cachamwri achieving godhood to
drive the Dark Ones off Mageverse Earth the first time, but
even then, they'd escaped to the mortal world. They'd tortured and abused humanity for thousands of years, passing
themselves off as gods and demons. If not for Merlin and
the Sidhe, they'd still be there.

If they really had found a way to break Merlin's
barrier . . .

Kel shook the fear off and stood, tugging her up and
into his arms. "Listen to me, Nineva. We'll get your sword
back, we'll free your goddess and stop the Dark Ones, *but
I will not hurt you to do it.* You have my oath on that."

"No!" Her hands closed on his arms with such strength,
he blinked in surprise. "Don't give your oath. I'm not important, Kel. Stopping the Dark Ones—that's important."

He looked down into her delicate upturned face, catching her chin in his hand. "You're important to me."

"You don't even know me."

"I know everything I need to know."

Nineva straightened, squaring her shoulders and stepping back. "Look, I'm sorry about this. Sorry I freaked out.
Just forget about it, okay?"

"No, it's not okay." He watched her get back into bed and slide between the covers.

"You're right—it was just a nightmare. People have them all the time. It doesn't mean anything." She lay down and turned her back to him again.

Frustrated, he ground his teeth, his fists propped on his hips. "Don't you ever get tired of martyrdom?"

Slowly, she turned her head and gave him a glare over her shoulder. "For the last time, I'm not playing martyr."

"Yeah, I could tell by that, 'I'm not important, Kel. Fry me like a chicken leg.' Fuck that, Nineva." Thoroughly pissed off, he slid into bed, then ruthlessly hauled her back against him, ignoring the way she stiffened.

"Let's get one thing straight, reptile," she said in an icy voice. "You may have fucked me, but you don't know me. *Let me go.*"

Coolly, deliberately, he tucked her against him, then threw a leg over her hips when she tried to squirm free. "You're right, I don't know you. But then, nobody knows you, because you never let anybody close. Why don't you give it a shot? Try trusting somebody for once. It might not be a complete disaster."

"You," she growled, subsiding sullenly against him, "are a jerk."

He wrapped both arms more snugly around her. "And you're paranoid, but I promise not to hold it against you."

Nineva lay still, intensely aware of the strong body curled against her back. Despite her roiling emotions, he felt deliciously warm and comforting.

He'd gone to sleep with surprising speed, considering how irritated he'd been. Now, listening to his deep breathing in her ear, she found herself gradually relaxing into his arms.

Damn, he'd pissed her off. She wasn't a martyr,

dammit. She was committed to doing her duty, true, but that didn't mean she *wanted* to suffer. Or that she enjoyed the prospect.

Just the reverse.

Nineva shuddered, remembering the blazing agony of the dream, the fear and horror. Nobody, no matter how fanatical, could wish for such a fate.

So why did she feel so safe in Kel's arms? Why did she want to believe him so desperately when he swore he'd protect her, despite his starring role in her nightmares?

She remembered his calm, determined stare. He'd meant every word he'd said.

And yet . . .

What if the nightmare *was* a vision? Both the prophecy and Grim seemed to indicate it was. True, both also predicted she'd survive to aid in the Dark Ones' defeat—but that didn't mean she wouldn't go through hell to do it.

Nineva looked down and realized she was stroking the hard, round biceps of Kel's right arm. She curled tighter against his comforting warmth and stared into the darkness with aching eyes.

She straddled him like a goddess on a racing horse, her head thrown back, long hair whipping his bare thighs as she ground down on his rock-hard cock.

Lost in the pure pleasure of her tight, liquid clasp, he drove up at her, his gaze locked on her exquisite face.

Never had Gamal known such a woman.

Since he'd become one of the king's bodyguards, he'd grown used to women throwing themselves at him, eager to sample his reflected glory. But Naisi was not like the others. She was no hollow-hearted jade out for a night's tup. Though he'd barely known her a fortnight, she'd entranced him with her warm, laughing spirit.

Not to mention her lithe, strong little body. He felt the

rising tension in his balls as her slick sex milked him. Rolling his head back into the pillow, Gamal gazed up at her as she picked up the pace even more, green hair flying as her breasts bounced.

"Cachamwri's Egg, you conquer me!" he groaned.

Naisi gave him a wicked smile, her cheeks flushed pink with arousal and pleasure. "Not yet," she gasped as she rose and fell. "In a moment . . ."

Her tight cunt flexed, pulsed, and he exploded with a shout of raw pleasure.

"Almost, almost . . ." Her yellow eyes turned cool with calculation. "Now!"

She slapped her hand right in the center of his forehead.

It felt as though she'd punched through bone and brain with a lion's claws. Gamal screamed at the tearing agony, his back arching in pain.

Magic rushed through her cold palm like a tsunami, swamping his consciousness in something chill and stinking. Gamal called on his own power in fear and rage, dragging magic from the Mageverse, fighting to shield, to drive out the evil.

Too late.

He felt himself sinking in the black stench, his thoughts going dim. He screamed again, in horror and betrayal, but his lips made no sound.

Then the darkness closed over him, and his helpless mind went colder. Gamal gave one final desperate heave, trying to save himself from the alien thing that had masqueraded as a woman . . .

The endless night rolled over him, and he was gone.

Varza opened Gamal's eyes and sat up, barely in time to catch the green-haired body as it fell sideways. She laid it out on the bed and paused, watching the narrow chest rising and falling as it waited to be possessed again.

Rolling to Gamal's feet, Varza looked down at his now limp, wet penis with some distaste. What a ridiculous appendage.

On the other hand, there were compensations. Varza stretched and bounced on his brawny legs, enjoying the raw strength of this new body. Conjuring a mirror, she studied her own reflection. Gamal was tall and powerful, capable of swinging a sword or axe with equal ease.

A natural killer.

Oh, yes, Varza decided with satisfaction. This would do nicely.

There was only one problem. His hair had turned from platinum silver to verdant green, while his eyes had gone as yellow as a cat's. Something about the possession process always had this effect on Varza's stolen bodies. It hadn't been a problem with her previous form, but it would certainly give her away now.

Varza let the magic spill. Gamal's hair paled back to silver as his eyes returned to their proper shimmering violet. Varza smiled slowly, a dead copy of Gamal's charming grin.

Much better.

She conjured the armor of a palace guard, then covered the female's form with a blanket. Varza arranged its limbs into a more natural sleeping pose, just in case someone should come in and discover it.

She might need the form later if all went badly. Besides, Arralt seemed fond of it.

Now all Varza had to do was await her chance. One way or another, it wouldn't be long in coming.

EIGHT

Nineva woke cocooned in warmth and comfort that surrounded her back and wrapped around her breasts and hips. She opened sleepy eyes and sighed in pleasure.

The instant before she stiffened.

The warmth was a man's body. She jerked her head around—and met Kel's sleepy crimson eyes. "Good morning." His voice was deep and raspy. His cobalt hair lay in tousled disarray around his angular face and spilled across her pillow.

Nineva blinked at him, torn between the need to cuddle closer and the equally powerful urge to roll away. She cleared her throat and managed to do neither. "Morning."

Kel smiled, slow and sexy, and rested his chin on her shoulder. "What would you like for breakfast?"

She was lucky most mornings to score a bowl of cereal and milk that wasn't past its expiration date. "Whatever you'd like. I'm not picky."

"Pancakes and bacon?"

"That sounds good." Her upbringing reared its polite

Southern head. "I can make it, though. After all, you fixed that great dinner last night."

"You cook?"

"Professionally, in fact. Well, at least in the sense that somebody paid me. Between bartending stints, I've worked in assorted greasy spoons." She grimaced a little, remembering how apt that particular phrase had been when applied to some of her jobs. "Though that might not strike you as much of a recommendation."

"Now you've got my curiosity up." Rolling over on his back, he arched his spine, showcasing a fascinating bulge beneath the thin sheet. "Among other things."

Nineva eyed that promising ridge, but before she could throw off the sheet for a closer look, a high, musical chime sounded. As they lifted their heads, a glowing ball of swirling golden light floated into the room, the outline of a dragon swimming in its depths.

"That's a Sidhe communication spell," Kel said, sitting up with a frown. "And that dragon is Llyr's heraldic sign."

"He probably wants me to turn myself in." For a moment Nineva hesitated, trying to decide what would be the proper thing to wear to speak to a king. Finally, with a grunt of disgust, she conjured a pretty pink top and jeans and rolled to her feet. Hell with it—if he meant to arrest her, she was damned if she'd kowtow to him.

Out of the corner of her eye, she saw that Kel had dressed, too, in the jeans and polo shirt that seemed to be something of a Magi uniform. Apparently every day was casual Friday in Avalon.

"Your Majesty, you honor us," Kel said, in the deep courtier's voice he'd used with Arthur the day before.

"Well met, Kel." The globe's swirling gold cleared, revealing a handsome face framed by pale hair and opalescent eyes.

Nineva started. He looked so much like her father, she felt pain stab her heart. She hadn't expected that.

Unable to help herself, she stared at him hungrily. This is how Eirnin would have looked if he'd survived—barely older than thirty, with long, elegant features and a sense of regal power.

Yet despite his kingly looks, Llyr had killed Ansgar. In retrospect, there was a certain satisfaction in the thought that her father's cousin had slain the monster. As though Eirnin had been avenged after all.

Belatedly, Nineva realized the king was watching her with an intensity equal to her own. "Hello, Cousin." His voice was deeper than her father's had been, resonant with power.

But then, he was Cachamwri's Avatar.

She swallowed and gave him her best curtsy, silly though it felt in jeans. She should have worn court garb, dammit. "It is an honor, Your Majesty."

One corner of Llyr's familiar mouth curled. "Is it indeed? I'm told you're reluctant to meet with me."

Nineva stiffened. Despite his resemblance to her father, he was a different man altogether. She couldn't afford to forget that. "Your brother murdered my parents."

His gaze softened fractionally. "Yes, I know. I'm sorry. And I know exactly how you feel, since he also murdered my first four wives and all my children."

She winced. "I wasn't aware of that."

"I killed him." He said it flatly, the words unadorned, without even a hint of boasting.

"Yes, Kel told me. I am . . . grateful."

"Has he told you my new bride is expecting the Heir to Heroes?"

She felt a bead of sweat rolling down her spine. "That . . . he did not mention."

"You understand, then, why I consider it vital we meet. Particularly since you claim to be the Last Avatar."

She managed not to grind her teeth. "It's not just a claim."

Llyr lifted a cool blond brow. "No? Then you should not fear meeting with me. After all, if you are all that stands between my kingdom and the Dark Ones, I would be a fool to hurt you."

"It's said the Last Avatar will free the kingdoms."

"From 'he who would usurp them.' I'm no usurper. Like you, I'm a descendent of the Morven Sidhe royal house. The throne is mine by my grandmother's blood and my grandfather's right of conquest."

"I do not doubt it. You could be my father's brother." She hadn't intended to say that last.

Again, those hard opal eyes softened. For a long moment, they stared at each other. "Come to me, child." He said it softly. "On my royal oath, I'll not hurt you."

Nineva took a deep breath. "Yes, Your Majesty."

Kel watched Nineva stand frozen as the communication globe vanished, an expression of building panic on her face. "He's a good man, Nineva. He'll keep his oath."

"He really does look like my father." She twisted her hands together. "Almost exactly, even though he's just a distant cousin. His grandmother was my grandfather's sister. Llyr's grandfather married her after he conquered my people."

"You look a lot like him, too. Same eyes, same coloring."

"The goddess's blood tends to be dominant." Sighing, she dragged both hands through her hair. "What the hell am I supposed to wear? Jeans aren't going to cut it, but I have no idea . . ."

Kel smiled reluctantly. "Calm down, Nineva. I've seen the Sidhe in full court garb. I'll conjure something for you."

Closing his eyes, he paused, trying to imagine the best costume to set off her pale beauty. When he thought of it, he reached for the magic, then sent it spilling over her.

When the glitter faded, Nineva wore a forest green

velvet gown trimmed in gold and opals. Its train pooled around her delicate gold slippers. She looked down at it and blinked, her expression awed as she gingerly fingered the heavy skirt. "It's beautiful, Kel. Thank you."

"It suits you." Rising to his feet, he conjured his own costume—a green velvet doublet that matched her gown, its sleeves slashed artistically to show the flowing dark blue shirt he wore underneath it. Boots and hose of the same color finished off the ensemble.

Kel looked up to catch an expression of pure feminine appreciation in her eyes. "You look very handsome."

"Poofy shirt notwithstanding?"

As he'd intended, she laughed. "Nobody would ever accuse you of being effeminate." Her gaze dipped, and her lips tilted into a wicked smile. "Not with that ass."

"Flatterer." Moving toward her, he offered her his elbow. "Let's go meet the king."

Taking a deep breath as if to steady herself, she hooked her arm in his. Together, they headed for the door.

As the king of the Sidhe paced down the line of bodyguards, Varza concentrated on being a dead man.

The entire plan hinged on this inspection. She couldn't let Llyr Galatyn catch even the faintest whiff that anything was wrong with his newest captain of the guard, Gamal.

Depending on Galatyn's degree of paranoia, though, Varza should be fairly safe. The king had done a deep magical scan on his guards just the day before, checking for loyalty and spells that didn't belong. It had been an exhausting process, and it was doubtful he'd do such a scan again today.

Yesterday Gamal had mentioned the loyalty test in passing to his pretty green-haired lover. Varza had instantly known this was the moment she'd been waiting for.

Gamal's loose tongue cost him his life.

Now the only trick was to keep the king from suspecting a switch had taken place. Varza had to shield tightly enough to prevent any magical leakage from warning Galatyn.

"Not quite a year ago, a detachment of my own guard tried to kill me," Llyr said, as he stalked down the line of men. With every step he took, power boiled around him—both from his natural talent, and from the magic that was his as the Avatar of Cachamwri, the Dragon God. "I slew all four of them. Just days later, ten of my men gave their lives protecting me from another of my brother's assassins. We all honor their memory."

As one, the guard gave a deep-throated shout, half-agreement, half-vow. "Galatyn! Galatyn! Galatyn!"

Varza was careful to join in.

The king's voice dropped to a rumble of rage. "Yet just last week, another of your number betrayed me. He took the Sword of Semira and gave it to my enemies. I am shamed by this loss—and so are you."

Actually, of course, poor Ilbrech hadn't stolen anything or betrayed anyone. He'd been dead when the sword was stolen, having fallen to Varza's possession just hours before his body walked away with the weapon.

"Now I'm entrusting you with Cachamwri's most precious gift to me and the Sidhe people: my wife, who carries the Heir to Heroes in her womb. Too many times, I have lost wives and children to killers. Let us be clear, my warriors—*I will not lose her.*" The king's voice dropped into a low, icy whisper that managed to communicate his determination more clearly than a shout. "You will fight for her. If necessary, you will die for her. Any man who allows harm to so much as a single hair on her head will face my rage. And you will wish the Dark Ones themselves had you instead. Do you understand?"

"Aye!" Varza led the men in the shout.

"Good." Galatyn reached Varza's end of the line and

stopped. Opalescent eyes bored into Varza, who, braced at attention, did not move or speak. Confronted with Galatyn's boiling power, she scarcely dared breathe.

Blond brows drew down in a faint frown.

Did he sense something?

Finally the king spoke. "Gamal, you're in charge of the queen's safety while we're in Avalon. Don't let her out of your sight. She's not going to like that—she's used to taking care of herself. And usually, she's more than capable of doing just that, but right now, she's vulnerable. I realize you've got a soft spot when it comes to women, but don't let her bully you. Take care of her."

"Aye, sir," Varza said, not letting her triumph show. "I assure you, your wife won't get away from me."

Her arm hooked through Kel's, Nineva walked the cobblestone streets of Avalon. It was bustling tonight, men and women walking briskly to whatever destinations they had on this chilly winter evening. Most of them would have looked at home in any American city, with the same blend of ethnicity and casual clothing, their skin tones ranging from deep chocolate to Celtic pale. Others were dressed as elaborately as she and Kel, while some were garbed in still more exotic costumes.

Nineva watched a tiny Japanese woman take mincing steps in a beautiful kimono, magic trailing her in colorful swirling sparks. A powerfully muscled man walked beside her in equally gorgeous silk robes, a pair of swords thrust through his belt. They seemed to be having an intense argument in musical Japanese.

A wolf whistle brought Nineva's head jerking around as a female voice shouted, "Hey, Kel—nice legs!"

A deep laugh booming, Kel bowed like a medieval courtier, his free arm sweeping as if waving an invisible plumed hat. "My thanks, milady."

"Who's the babe?" the same woman asked, her dark eyes sparkling as she looked them over. A tall bearded man stood beside her, one brawny arm thrown over her shoulders.

Two couples accompanied them, equally attractive, equal affection in their eyes. It was obvious they knew Kel and liked him.

He indicated Nineva with a gesture. "This is Princess Nineva of the Morven Sidhe." Turning to her, he introduced the three couples, who shook hands and gave her friendly smiles.

It turned out the dark-haired woman and her escort were Caroline and Galahad du Lac. The second dark-haired man was Galahad's father, Lancelot, who looked no older than his son. His wife, Grace, was tall, slender, blond, and breathtaking.

But the pair that really captured Nineva's fascinated attention was the towering, strikingly handsome blond man Kel introduced as Gawain and his petite, lovely wife, Lark.

"I've heard a great deal about you," Nineva said, giving Gawain a smile as she offered her hand for his warm clasp.

Gawain's white teeth flashed. "Take it with a grain of salt," he advised, with a sly glance at Kel. "The gecko loves to stretch the truth."

Nineva lifted her brows. "Gecko?"

"The nickname fit him better when he was in the sword," Lark explained dryly.

"Why are you two so dressed up?" Gawain asked his friend.

"We have a meeting with Arthur and Llyr." As if to stave off questions, he added, "Where are you all headed?"

"The MageClub," Caroline replied, hooking her arm through her handsome husband's. "Us girls are going to drink a pitcher of margaritas, and then I'm gonna get Galahad drunk and take advantage of him."

Kel snorted. "Since when do you have to work that hard?"

Galahad grinned and held a finger to his lips. "Shhh."
Nineva laughed at the wicked humor in his blue eyes.

"So what has you girls hitting the tequila, Caroline?"
Kel asked.

She grimaced as Grace explained. "We just got back
from Iraq."

"Ouch," Nineva said.

Curious, she opened her mouth to ask for details, but
Kel closed a gentle hand around her elbow. "We'd better
get moving. We don't want to keep Llyr waiting."

"Join us after you get done," Gawain said, slapping his
friend on one muscled shoulder.

"We'll do our best," Kel agreed. "But given the circumstances, I'm not making any promises."

As they walked away, Nineva dropped her voice, awed.
"That was Lancelot, Gawain, and Galahad!"

Kel smiled at her. "Yeah."

"Wow." She gave him a sly smile. "They're cute."

To her delight, a warning glint lit his eyes. "And very,
very taken. They're all Truebonded."

She listened as he explained the magical psychic bond
Magekind couples formed—a link so strong, they could
feel each other's emotions and communicate telepathically.

It was a surprisingly seductive idea.

Nineva tried to imagine what it would be like. Not only
being in love, but feeling the love of your lover.

Not being alone.

"It sounds . . . tempting," she said finally.

"Yes." A trace of longing appeared in Kel's eyes. "It
does, doesn't it?"

Nineva stepped through the door Kel opened for her. And
tried not to gape like a tourist.

Gorgeous medieval tapestries hung on the walls of the
circular room, depicting unicorns and dragons, ladies and

knights in glittering thread. Yet beautiful as the hangings were, what really dominated the room was the enormous circular table of dark wood, richly carved and massive, surrounded by twelve equally beautiful chairs.

She caught her breath. "Is that . . ."

"The Round Table? Yes." Arthur rose to his feet. Unlike the previous times she'd seen him, he wore formal court garb, a scarlet doublet embroidered in gold and encrusted with gems. A jeweled sword hung from a belt around his waist. Excalibur?

Nineva stared at it, wide-eyed, but not quite able to bring herself to ask. Kel touched her waist, gently bringing her back to herself. She followed him to a place next to Arthur, where Kel pulled one of the exquisite chairs out for her. She seated herself gingerly with awe.

"I expect Llyr any moment," Arthur told them. "Along with his usual complement of bodyguards, poor bastard. You'd think with that brother of his dead, he'd be able to relax. No such luck."

" 'Uneasy lies the head that wears the crown,' " Kel quoted softly.

"Yeah, which is why I don't miss mine." Arthur shot Nineva a look. "You may want to keep that in mind, kid."

"Believe me, I have no delusions on that score." She remembered her last sight of her parents, clinging to each other in despair and grief. "Just being of royal blood has cost me enough as it is." Before she could say more, her instincts began to clamor.

Power was coming. Not simply the sense of magic that surrounded the Majae, but something far more profound. Every hair on the back of her neck rose as it approached, and her heart began to pound.

The door opened, and Llyr Galatyn swept in, followed by a beautiful blonde and a cool, dark woman who was equally lovely. Nineva recognized them as the women she'd seen meeting with Arthur the day before. At their heels strode a heavily armored Sidhe bodyguard with wary eyes.

Nineva rose and dipped into the curtsy her father had taught her so many years before. Out of the corner of her eye, she saw Arthur and Kel exchange bows with Llyr.

"Rise, child," Llyr said in that deep, beautiful voice.

She lifted her head and met those eyes, so painfully familiar. He was dressed in black and silver, the stark colors making his beauty all the more striking. The power that surrounded him left her feeling breathless.

Like her, he was an avatar, if the avatar of an entirely different god. Yet unlike Semira, Cachamwri was no captive, but a being in his full power.

This was what Nineva could be, if she succeeded in freeing her goddess.

Staring at him hungrily, Nineva was scarcely aware when Arthur introduced the women who had escorted Llyr in—Arthur's wife, Guinevere, and his half-sister, Morgana Le Fay. Under normal circumstances, Nineva would have been fascinated by them, but with Llyr in the room, it was difficult to care about anything else.

"I'm told," Llyr said, "that you should have a Mark."

She reached up and tugged the deep V of her bodice aside, revealing the golden swirl of Semira's bloodline. It had begun to glow, as if reacting to the Sidhe king's presence.

Llyr started to reach toward her, then arrested the gesture. "May I?"

As her mouth went dry, she bowed her head. "Yes, Your Majesty."

The tips of his fingers touched the Mark. She felt the sizzle of his power. Over his shoulder, she met the cold, suspicious gaze of Llyr's bodyguard.

Finally, Llyr stepped back and nodded shortly. "Yes, you're the Avatar of Semira." His gaze met hers. "But your goddess seems very weak."

"She's been imprisoned a long time. And I'm the first Avatar born in centuries. I've got to strengthen her before I can track down the sword and free her from it."

Llyr lifted a golden brow. "How do you intend to strengthen her?"

To her mortification, she felt her cheeks heat. With an effort, she kept her eyes from sliding toward Kel.

"Ah." Llyr's tone was knowing, and a half-smile quirked his lips. After a pause, he said, "My court historian tells me Semira was considered a fertility goddess."

She cleared her throat. "It . . . seems so."

"He's also researched your claim. According to his count, you would indeed be the twenty-first Avatar. Which, if the prophecy is correct, would make you the one who will free Semira from the sword and save us from the Dark Ones."

"That's . . . what I've always been taught." The knot of tension loosened in her belly. At least he believed her.

Arthur invited them all to sit, then offered refreshments. Everyone declined politely.

As the first shock of Llyr's familiar features began to fade, Nineva became aware of the cool appraisal in the king's eyes.

He might believe her, but he didn't trust her. Her stomach started coiling into knots again. Despite his resemblance to her father, he wasn't a friend. He could easily decide to move against her. And what the hell would she do then?

Beneath the table, a big, warm hand wrapped around hers, fisted in her lap with anxiety. She looked up to meet Kel's reassuring gaze.

"So," Llyr said, "tell me what you know of this Dark Ones invasion."

Diana London Galatyn sat surrounded by mounds of fragrant flowers in the conservatory—along with five armed and armored guards.

Llyr's paranoid streak was beginning to get on her nerves. He was down the corridor somewhere, meeting with Arthur and the supposed Avatar of Semira. Usually, Diana would be by his side, but he evidently considered this girl such a threat, he didn't want Diana anywhere near her.

It was ridiculous. After all, Diana was a werewolf; any magical attack would simply bounce off. Of course, the fact that she couldn't transform made defending herself a little more complicated. Still, the bodyguards were overkill.

Yet they were also an understandable precaution, considering Llyr's tragic history. Diana was prepared to tolerate them if they made him feel better.

Forcing herself to ignore them, she concentrated on the rows of figures on the laptop computer she'd had Llyr acquire for her. Since she didn't have a lap at the moment, one of her guards had conjured a small writing desk.

When she and Llyr had taken over the Morven Sidhe kingdom, they'd discovered its coffers were far richer than was strictly necessary. Ansgar had been methodically beggaring his people to enrich himself and his favorites.

Diana had promptly suggested a massive tax rebate for part of the money, but she and Llyr were also considering various public projects for the rest. For one thing, the Morven Kingdom was in desperate need of an educational system for the young, since Ansgar had abolished it centuries ago to save money.

Then there was the crown legal system, which was riddled with corruption from top to bottom. Reforming that was going to be a pain in the ass.

The first step to doing any of that, though, was to figure out exactly how much money was really needed to run the Morven Kingdom. Luckily, Diana was no stranger to budgeting, thanks to her years as a small-town administrator. The kingdom was far larger than anything she'd dealt with before, of course, but the basic principles were the same.

She absently looked up from the laptop as she mulled over the figures. Her gaze fell on the captain of the body-guard, a tall, powerfully built man who was generally laid back and cheerful. He was moving around the room, speaking to each of the other guards, his expression uncharacteristically intense and focused. Diana frowned. Was something going on?

Maybe she'd better wander over and find out.

Varza glanced around as the werewolf heaved her massively pregnant body off the bench and headed in her direction. Suppressing a curse, Varza diverted away from the guard she'd been preparing to bespell. The last thing she needed was to arouse the bitch's suspicions.

She swept a low bow and pasted a smile on her face. "Queen Diana, how may I serve you?"

"What's going on?" the werewolf asked, in that blunt human way she had. "I noticed you seem to be working your way around to all the men."

"I am but ensuring they have their orders."

"Uh huh." Her silver eyes were entirely too acute. "What orders are those, exactly?"

Nosy bitch. She pumped more charm into Gamal's smile. "His Majesty wishes us to remain alert for any threat."

"Duh."

Varza blinked, not understanding the phrase. "What?"

"That's your job, Captain. I'd think that would go without saying."

"Perhaps, but I wanted to impress it more firmly."

She snorted. "Somehow I doubt that's all there is to it, but knowing my husband, he's ordered you not to elaborate. That being the case, I'll let you go back to whatever you're doing." To Varza's relief, she turned and glided off with surprising grace, considering her hugely pregnant belly.

Varza watched as she sat down and went back to her work on her mortal gadget, whatever it was. Once she was sure the werewolf was fully occupied again, she moved toward the fourth and final guard.

The man stood looking wary and alert in his malachite armor, his hand riding the hilt of his sword. Gamal's stolen memories said his name was Krinus, a Sidhe of considerable natural power, intelligence, and loyalty to the crown.

Which was why Varza had saved him for last. Taking him would be risky, calling for the expenditure of more power than the others had required. Had Varza attempted him any earlier, one of them might have sensed it and sounded the alarm. Surrounded as they were by Magekind, that could have been disastrous. Varza had no interest in battling a small army of infuriated vampires and witches— not to mention Llyr Galatyn himself, Avatar of the Dragon.

She walked up to the warrior, who was too well-trained to take his his gaze from the werewolf.

Varza grasped his shoulder as if to draw him close for a private word. The spell sliced through the man's armor as if it wasn't there. Krinus's eyes widened in shock as every muscle froze.

But though his body was paralyzed, his mind was powerful. Even as Varza sent the second spell driving into the Sidhe's consciousness, Krinus shielded and fought back, blasting a wave of fire into his attacker's mind. Varza gritted her teeth, shielded, and poured still more magic into the spell. For a moment, Krinus's defenses held stubbornly solid, but abruptly they failed.

Far sooner than they should have.

Even as Varza's magic blasted through, she sensed the man's power explode outward—a psychic howl of warning, designed to alert the king and his werebitch. Krinus had deliberately sacrificed himself.

Desperately, Varza flung out her own magic after Krinus's. For a moment, she thought she was too late.

And then the Sidhe's spell snuffed out like a candle.

Suppressing a grin of triumph, Varza released her be-spelled victim and walked away. Counting Gamal himself, all of the guards were under her control now.

Only one last element left to fall into place. And if her vision was correct, it should do so anytime now.

NINE

Llyr Galatyn was exquisitely polite for a king, but that didn't stop him from grilling her like a television cop interrogating a serial killer. Nineva answered every question with scrupulous honesty, knowing he'd sense it if she didn't.

The king's gaze chilled when Nineva admitted she'd initially accepted the sword and Arralt's offer to help her overthrow "the usurper."

"So you consider me the usurper?" A muscle flexed in his jaw as power began to boil around him with his rising anger.

She refused to flinch from those cold opalescent eyes. "I wanted the Sword of Semira. Your Majesty, I was raised as the Last Avatar. My father taught me it's my duty to free the goddess and fight the Dark Ones . . ."

"Do you believe me the usurper of the prophecy?" He rapped out the words, refusing to be diverted. His big, elegant hands clenched into fists.

"No, I'm convinced that's Arralt. The actual words of the prophecy are 'the Two Kingdoms liberated from he who *would* usurp them.' That implies he makes the attempt and fails. You *are* king."

"I'm relieved you noticed." Thank the Goddess, he sounded more dry than angry now. "Yet you were willing to cooperate with the rebels initially. What changed your mind?"

Nineva related what she saw during Arralt's spell, beginning with his murder of his mother. Llyr grunted, obviously unsurprised.

His expression turned grim when she described the Dark Ones stepping through a dimensional gate into Times Square. But the king went pale when she spoke of the pregnant woman she'd seen screaming in agony and the yellow-eyed Sidhe female threatening the bloody infant. "The Sidhe female lifted the Sword of Semira over the baby." Nineva took a deep breath. "That was when I started trying to break free, so I didn't see any more."

A long, appalled silence ticked by. "Arralt's working with the Dark Ones," Llyr said finally.

"Apparently," Arthur said thoughtfully. "And so is this yellow-eyed Sidhe woman. Does she sound familiar to you, Llyr?"

"I'm not sure." The king frowned, then turned his attention to Nineva again. "Can you provide a more detailed description?"

"I think so." She found a clear memory and reached for her power. The Sidhe's face appeared in the air, three-dimensional and in color, glowing faintly with magic. A snarl twisted the mouth that otherwise might have been pretty, and eyes as feral and yellow as a bobcat's glared at them with hate.

"Miss Congeniality, she ain't," Arthur muttered.

Llyr didn't even crack a smile at the joke. He was too busy studying the image. "I don't know her, but perhaps others will. If you'll permit . . . ?"

Nineva nodded. The image vanished as he absorbed it.

He'd be able to call it up later for distribution among his men.

"Thank you for your cooperation, Nineva," Llyr said at last, after she'd answered a few more questions. He turned to Arthur. "With your permission, I'd like to speak to Lord Kel."

"Of course." Arthur gave Nineva a smile that didn't reach his dark eyes. She suspected he was worrying about the Dark Ones. "Mind excusing us for a minute? This shouldn't take too much longer."

Nineva nodded and got up, managed a credible curtsy, and escaped from the room with a sense of relief. Her back was damp with sweat beneath the velvet gown, and she desperately wanted to step outside for a breath of fresh air.

Gathering her skirts in both fists, she hurried down the marble corridor toward the double doors that led outside. She'd just hang out on the steps until Kel showed up.

All things considered, it had gone better than she'd feared. Llyr obviously considered the Dark Ones a greater threat to his throne than she was. Thank God for that prophecy, or he might be a lot more hostile.

She fidgeted restlessly, wishing there was any practical way she could start searching for the Sword of Semira. If she didn't find it in a hurry, they were all screwed—Sidhe and Magekind alike. Even mortal humans would be in danger, because after the Dark Ones chewed through the magic users, they'd set their satanic sights on even easier prey.

Unfortunately, until she'd strengthened the goddess enough to guide her, she was just spinning her wheels. And that meant having a great deal of sex with Kel. Not that she minded. He was pretty damned good at it, after all.

If only he wouldn't fry her in the process . . .

At Llyr's prompting, Kel described his encounter with Cachamwri and his subsequent efforts to track Nineva down, culminating in the battle with Arralt and his men.

"So what do you think of this girl?" the Sidhe king asked at last.

Kel hesitated, a little surprised by the depth of emotion the question aroused. "She's not interested in your throne," he said at last, that being the simplest answer he could think of. "She's definitely not working with the rebels."

"So she says," Llyr grunted.

"And you can take her at her word. She's obsessed with freeing Semira—it's what she was raised from birth to do. At the same time, this prophecy of hers scares the hell out of her." He frowned. "And since I play a key role in it, she's not too sure about me either."

"Considering the nature of the prophecy, I don't blame her." The king studied him with a faint trace of amusement, his opalescent gaze acute. "You don't like that."

"Not really, no. I'm not used to having beautiful women fear me."

"*Could* you do it?"

"Breathe fire on her?"

"Yes."

Kel felt Arthur, Llyr, the two Majae, and even the king's bodyguard watching him. "Hell, no."

"Not even to save both Earths from the Dark Ones?"

Knowing when he was being tested, Kel didn't hesitate. "I don't believe the prophecy is literal. There's got to be another interpretation. We just haven't figured out what it is yet."

Llyr sighed. "I hope you are right, my friend. I do wish Cachamwri would put in another appearance to one or the other of us. He could probably resolve these questions."

"Unfortunately, the Dragon God is not in the habit of coming when called." Kel's voice sounded dry even to his own ears.

"Gods usually don't," Morgana pointed out. "And until he does, we'd better figure out what to do about Merlin's

Wards so the Dark Ones don't get the opportunity to invade."

"How did the check of the wards go?" Arthur asked the Majae.

"They're still as strong as ever," Guinevere told him.

"Then how the hell do the Dark Ones intend to get through?" His expression frustrated, Arthur sat back in his seat. "And if they know a way to break the wards, why haven't they done it before now?"

"It's got to be related to the Sword of Semira." Llyr ran a thumb over his lower lip as he frowned in concentration. "The fact that it was stolen just before this all started can't be a coincidence. What does Merlin's Grimoire say?"

"Damned little." Arthur drummed his fingers on the table. "Which is unusual. Grim's not generally this . . . vague."

Morgana shrugged. "Remember when he clammed up just before 9/11? Grim knows something he's not telling."

Llyr blinked, startled. "Why would he do that?"

"Something going on that's fated to happen," Guinevere explained. "He only gets obstructionist when he doesn't want us preventing something that must occur in order to prevent something even worse."

"What could have been worse than the destruction of the Twin Towers?" Llyr asked.

Gwen grimaced. "Al-Qaeda getting its hands on a Russian nuke and smuggling it into Washington through lax security. Which would have happened a year later if the Towers hadn't come down. The U.S. would then have nuked Afghanistan. The Russians would have retaliated after the fallout started killing their people." She shrugged. "World War III would have lasted three days and killed half the people on the planet. The rest would have envied the dead."

Llyr looked at her. "Yes, that would have been worse."

"But not worse than a Dark One invasion," Arthur growled. "I've seen those bastards work. I think it's time for our bookish friend to answer a few questions, fate or no fate. Grim!"

Instantly, the Grimoire materialized at his elbow in a swirl of sparks. "Aye, my liege?"

"What's going on with Merlin's Wards? How do the Dark Ones intend to get through them?"

"A spell."

"No shit. What kind of spell?"

"Are they going to attempt to sacrifice my wife and child?" Llyr's voice was very quiet, but the simmering rage in it drew everyone's eyes.

"If they can capture her."

Llyr's hands curled into fists as his jaw flexed in rage. "And if they do not?"

"They will attempt another spell."

"Grim, give us a straight answer." Arthur demanded. *"How do they intend to break through the wards?"*

"The answer is not yet clear, my liege. There are several possibilities."

"Great." He fell back in his seat with a grunt of disgust. "That's just what I wanted to hear."

Nineva was heading down the corridor toward the building's exit when a tall male figure stepped into her path. "Princess Nineva?"

"Yes?" She studied him warily. A brawny Sidhe with hair as purple as a pansy, he wore a suit of gleaming malachite armor. Which would make him a member of the Morven Sidhe palace guard, according to what her father had told her years ago. Nineva tensed and prepared to call her magic. Just in case.

"Her Majesty, Queen Diana, requests the honor of your presence." He gestured toward the set of double doors he'd just emerged from.

Nineva hesitated. What did the queen of the Two Kingdoms want? And where had she been during the interrogation?

"Your Highness?" The guard opened one of the doors and waited.

It seemed ducking the invitation wasn't an option. She stepped through, then stopped short, impressed yet again by Magekind architecture.

The room was obviously a kind of magical conservatory, full of flowers, plants, and green growing things. An enormously pregnant woman sat on an elegant marble bench in the center of the room. She glanced up, her silver gaze curious.

Nineva sucked in a breath as she recognized those striking eyes and sculpted features. The queen of the Sidhe was the woman she'd seen in her vision, the one in labor.

Which meant it had been her bloody infant the yellow-eyed creature had threatened with the sword. *No wonder Llyr looked as if he'd seen a ghost. I just told him his wife and child were going to be victims of an act of death magic.*

The queen lifted her delicate dark brows. "May I help you?"

What the hell should she tell her? Mentally fumbling, Nineva stalled for time. "Your guard said you wanted to see me."

"That's odd." The queen frowned. "I didn't make any such request."

"But I did." The captain drew his sword with a metallic rasp. The six guards around them did the same, surrounding the women with a forest of glittering points. "You're coming with us." He bared his teeth. "Both of you."

The queen's eyes narrowed as they flicked from blade to

blade. Despite her massive belly, she rose easily from the bench. If she could have, Nineva suspected she'd have coiled into a crouch. "Turning traitor, boys?"

"Just switching to the winning side."

Kel! As the Sidhe queen distracted the guards, Nineva had gathered her magic for a psychic cry for help. Now she sent it blasting outward, only to hiss in frustration as it promptly fizzled out.

Dammit, the bastards must have erected some kind of barrier.

There wasn't time for a second try. Conjuring armor and sword, Nineva stepped between those razor points and the queen's pregnant belly. "Your Majesty, behind me . . . !"

But the guard captain snaked forward and grabbed the woman's wrist. Nineva spun to face him, but he warned her off with a flick of his blade. "Drop the armor, girl. We'll take you in pieces if you don't have the sense to surrender."

Captain Gamal's hand tightened painfully on Diana's wrist as he dragged her back from the determined-looking Sidhe girl. "Come, Your Majesty."

"I don't think so, asshole." Diana twisted her wrist and jerked. Werewolf that she was, she was stronger than he expected. Her wrist slipped free of his fingers.

"Bitch!" He grabbed for her again, but she sidestepped, quick as the wolf she was. He stalked her, a faint scent of putrescence wafting from his body. She gagged at the stench as the hair rose on the back of her neck.

She knew that stink. *Evil.* No wonder her instincts had been clamoring. "How'd they get to you, Gamal?"

"I just don't care to serve a werewolf bitch and her whelp. Both of you are better off dead." Gamal's eyes were cold and flat as a snake's. "Take the princess," he added at his men, who had moved to keep the Sidhe girl from coming to Diana's rescue. "But don't kill her. She's . . . needed."

With a rising feral growl, the six guards closed in on their target. The princess leaped back, parrying the first exploratory attack.

Dammit, Diana thought, retreating from the captain's relentless approach. *If I could just transform, I could take these bastards out in five minutes.* They'd be no match for seven feet of fur, claws, and fangs.

Unfortunately, the change would kill her son. She didn't dare.

Gamal lifted one hand as a bright blue globe formed around it. He hurled it at her head like a fastball, magic boiling off it like a comet. Diana tried to dodge, but her belly made her slow. The globe hit her with a flash of heat, then splashed harmlessly away.

"You really are immune to magic, aren't you?" His wide mouth curled into a snarl. "Let's see how you do with a fist."

She ducked, but he was ready for her this time, and he clipped her jaw hard. Stars exploded behind her eyes as she tasted blood. He was faster than she'd thought.

Another blurring blow, this one a stunning backhand. She tried to jerk back, but her belly threw her balance too far forward. She felt herself start to fall. Gamal's mailed hands clamped over her upper arms and jerked her upright. Her fingers curled into fists, nails cutting into her palms.

No, not nails. Claws. Her hands had partially transformed.

Quick as thought, Diana slashed those curving talons down the captain's face, laying open his cheeks in ten parallel furrows. Blood spurted. He reeled back with a roar of surprised pain, groping blindly for the sword he'd sheathed in order to hit her. "You little bitch!"

A metallic rattle, and Diana found herself staring down the gleaming blade. Gamal's bloody face snarled at her over it. "You don't have to be in one piece, either. All I need is the contents of that fat belly."

She flashed her claws at him and bared her teeth. "You're not getting my baby, traitor."

"We'll see." He lunged.

Kel! Llyr! Once again, Nineva tried to force her magical cry past the barrier. Again, she felt her magic hit it and die.

One of the warriors lunged, his sword darting at her heart. She parried and jumped back, simultaneously throwing a quick look at the queen.

The woman might be enormously pregnant, but she was surprisingly agile. She jerked aside from the sword the captain sought to jab into her shoulder, though she staggered a little, off balance from her precious burden.

Luckily, the traitors apparently wanted to take them both alive, but it was only a matter of time before sheer numbers overwhelmed them. Nineva was good with a sword and reasonably powerful with magic, but she couldn't hold off six Sidhe fighters.

She had to get a message through that barrier. It was the only chance they had.

The Mark throbbed on her breast as she reached deep, drawing on all the magic she had, gathering it into one solid blast. If this failed, she was finished. And the queen wouldn't have a prayer.

KEL! We're under attack! She felt the barrier shatter as her spell punched through it.

The captain whirled, his lips pulling back from his teeth in a grimace of pure rage. "She got through! Kill them!"

Oh, hell.

Kel fought the urge to fidget as the Grimoire droned on through an explanation of the physics of Merlin's Wards. Now that Llyr had finished questioning him, he wanted to find Nineva before she got into trouble. Which, God knew, she was more than capable of—

Kel! . . . under attack! The mental voice was faint and garbled, but the raw fear in it was unmistakable.

"Nineva!" Kel jolted out of his chair and headed for the door at a dead run. "Something's wrong!" Between one step and the next, he was armored.

Magic flared behind him, and the others rose to chase at his heels. He didn't even glance back as he threw open the door and charged into the corridor. The steps of those behind him grew loud and rattling as they conjured armor of their own. *Nineva?*

Nothing. Kel stopped short in frustration, his sword naked in his hand as he scanned the empty hallway. There were literally dozens of rooms she could be in. "Where the hell *is* she?"

Behind him, Llyr cursed like a dockworker. "I'm not sensing Diana either. She was in the conservatory." The king shoved past with a flash of iridescent plate as he broke into a run. Kel shot after him, his heart pounding, his mouth brassy with an unaccustomed taste: fear.

Fear for a girl he barely knew.

In the depths of his mind, Creag tried to fight the spell that held him. His body remained stubbornly paralyzed, though he could hear his king racing down the corridor outside. In his fear for his queen, Llyr hadn't even realized that his bodyguard hadn't followed him. Neither had any of the others.

Yet Creag knew he should be leading the way, protecting Llyr Galatyn. Doing his duty.

If it hadn't been for that bastard Gamal . . . Creag had suspected nothing when the captain called him aside before they'd left the palace. The man's hand had landed on his shoulder, and evil had poured into his mind like a waterfall of sewage, drowning him in stinking darkness, stealing his will.

And where had Gamal gotten such power?

Now that evil rolled from Creag in a wave of dark magic. He cast his will outward, trying to erect a mystical barrier to absorb it.

Nothing happened.

Instead, the blast of evil slammed into the book that lay open on the table. The Grimoire made a strangled sound of protest before slamming shut.

In the depths of his mind, Creag cursed in despair and rage as his body walked over to pick it up. He heard himself speak, his voice so rasping he barely recognized it. "Open the wards, Grimoire."

He sensed the city's great barrier thin directly over his head. A dimensional gateway opened before his eyes, growing in a heartbeat from a tiny point to a rippling oval. With a mental howl of hopelessness, Creag stepped through.

He found himself in a stone room lined with torches where warriors in barbaric black armor waited for him. A man whose dark hair was tied with animal fangs stepped forward and took the book from his hands. He gave Creag a vicious grin. "Kill him."

When one of the fighters swung an axe at his head, Creag couldn't even duck.

As they ran for the conservatory's doors, Llyr flung both hands wide. Kel felt the sizzle of his magic, but the doors remained stubbornly closed.

"Blocked. Some kind of spell." The Dragon's Mark appeared on the iridescent surface of Llyr's armor, tail lashing in rage as it swam over his body. He swung his sword like a baseball bat. The blade thundered against the thick wood, but the door didn't even vibrate. Llyr growled a desperate Sidhe curse.

Kel reached for his own magic, and his sword became a massive battleaxe in his hands. He sent his power blazing into the weapon and chopped at the door with all his strength.

Axe and sword hit at the same time, both glowing as if from a god's forge. The doors didn't so much open as disintegrate, caught between the opposing magical forces of the blades and the enemy's shield. Kel flung himself through the opening as the spell barrier vanished.

Nineva was surrounded by warriors in the malachite armor of Llyr's bodyguard. Two lay at her feet, dead in a lake of blood. Her sword flashed as she wheeled and chopped, trying to fight her way through to Diana Galatyn. The queen was backed into a corner by a man in the horsehair crest of a captain of the guard.

"Gamal!" Llyr roared.

The man glanced at the charging king and lunged, driving his sword straight into Diana's belly. She gasped in pain as she stared down at the blade, buried halfway to the hilt.

Llyr's scream of anguish made the hair stand on Kel's neck. The king swung his sword as his wife went down. The captain's head went flying.

Roaring in fury, Kel shot into the group of men that had surrounded Nineva. One man fell before his axe, cut in two. Arthur drove Excalibur through the chest of a second, while a third died shrieking, incinerated by one of Morgana's spells.

Nineva rammed her blade into the final bodyguard's chest and left it there as she raced to Diana's side.

"Change!" Llyr cradled his wife's bleeding body. His voice was broken with tears he didn't seem to notice. "You can heal yourself!"

"Not yet," Diana panted, writhing in agony. "C-section! Save the baby!"

"Let me heal her!" Nineva laid her hands on the queen's swollen, bloody belly. "I can save them."

"Werewolf," Diana gasped. "I'm . . . resistant to magic. You've got to . . . get the baby out! Then you can heal him . . . and I can change . . ."

Nineva looked up at Llyr, her eyes painfully wide. "I don't know how to do a C-section!"

"I do." Guinevere conjured a dagger. "Hold her, Llyr. And pray."

Varza opened her eyes and cursed in disgust. It was a good thing she'd had the foresight to leave her former body in Gamal's bed. If she hadn't had it to retreat to, everything could have been lost.

She flung the covers aside and sat up, naked. A gesture clothed her in the appropriate court garb, and she rolled to her slippered feet. Careful to keep her gait casual and un-hurried despite her screaming anxiety, she strolled from the room and headed down the jeweled marble corridor of the Morven palace.

She needed to leave the palace, and quickly. Once she was beyond its heavy wards, she could gate back to the fortress unnoticed.

If she tried to simply punch through them, Llyr would realize she'd been involved in the attempt on his wife. He might not be able to prevent her escape, but a few well-placed spells would tell him entirely too much about what he was dealing with.

As it was, Llyr would believe his palace guard was rid-dled with treason. There might be a way she could use that assumption later.

A female Sidhe nodded her head, and Varza gave her a sunny smile despite her simmering anger.

She'd thoroughly underestimated the Avatar and the wolf bitch. The princess was considerably more powerful than she'd believed possible, considering Semira's weakness.

Then there was the werewolf. Varza had known she couldn't transform without killing the baby, but she hadn't realized the bitch could still create claws.

Well, it doesn't matter now, Varza thought in grim pleasure. *At least I cost her the brat.*

Unfortunately, that meant the sacrifice she'd had in mind was off the table. But as long as Creag had escaped with Merlin's Grimoire, there was always the alternate plan.

The baby was dying. The captain's thrust had pierced his tiny side, just over one hip.

His mother whined, a high-pitched canine sound of distress. She'd assumed wolf form the moment Gwen had pulled her son from her body, thus healing the wounds that otherwise would have killed her.

Nineva rested a comforting arm on her furry back as Llyr cradled the little body in his big hands. His face went fierce with concentration as he sent his magic pouring into his son.

Unlike his mother, the baby was not resistant to spells. Llyr had said he wouldn't gain that immunity until he became a werewolf at puberty.

As Nineva, Kel, and the Magekind watched, breath held, the edges of the horrific injury began to spark, then knit closed. The tiny prince jerked convulsively, then sucked in a breath.

And began to wail, a healthy, full-bodied cry of pure wrath.

Llyr looked up, tears in his opalescent eyes as he looked at the wolf. His relieved smile trembled. "He's got his mother's temper."

Nineva sensed magic foam through the wolf. The next

instant, the queen sat beside her, whole again, though her dress still showed the bloody rent across its full skirts. Like her husband, she had unashamed tears running down her cheeks as she reached for her son. With a gesture, Llyr banished the blood from the small, naked body and handed him to his wife.

"Hello, Prince Dearg Andrew," she breathed, cuddling him against her chest. The baby waved his fists, crying lustily. He might be a month premature, but it barely showed. He'd have been a very big baby if he'd gone to term.

A sizzle of power drew Nineva's attention to one of his tiny biceps. A small, intricate dragon glowed against the smooth skin there. Cachamwri's Mark.

She'd helped save the Heir to Heroes.

TEN

The queen cooed to her son, cupping his tiny, dark-haired head in one hand. He calmed, his tears ceasing as he stared up at her. Her lovely face shone with joy. "You look just like your daddy, Dearg Andrew. Yes, you do."

"Dearg Andrew?" Guinevere asked.

The queen looked up and gave her a small smile. "We named him for his grandfathers, Dearg Galatyn and Andrew London."

The baby gazed around at the circle of faces that surrounded him, his huge eyes already milky with opalescence and flecked with magic. His ears formed tiny, delicate points. Nineva thought she saw his father in the shape of his nose and chin, his mother in the bow of his mouth. "He's beautiful," she whispered.

"Thank you." The queen looked up at her, tears brightening that silver gaze. "Thank you for everything." To Llyr, she added, "The princess fought to rescue me the entire time. Six guards trying to cut her down, and she was more worried about me than herself."

The smile Llyr turned on her made Nineva's heart ache,

it reminded her so much of her father's. "You have the gratitude of the Two Kingdoms, Princess Nineva. Anything in my power to give you, you need only ask."

"I . . . ," she began, only to discover speaking was beyond her. Finally she choked out, "Thank you."

The queen reached out and took Guinevere's hand. "And thank you, Gwen. I know it couldn't have been easy cutting me like that, but if you hadn't, I don't know how long I would have been able to keep from transforming." Her eyes went bleak. "And if I'd transformed, we'd have lost Dearg Andrew."

"You wouldn't have transformed. Even if you'd died." Llyr's voice cracked on the last word. Clearing his throat, he looked around at Arthur, Morgana, Kel, Guinevere, and Nineva. "We owe you everything. And we will not forget."

But the spirit of delighted relief shattered ten minutes later when Llyr suddenly remembered his final bodyguard. The man wasn't with them, nor was he among the fallen.

When Llyr and Arthur hurried back to the Round Table chamber, they found that the man had disappeared.

Worse, so had Merlin's Grimoire. Arthur summoned Grim over and over, but the book didn't respond. In desperation, he called on every vampire and witch in Avalon to search by eye and magic, but the book was nowhere to be found.

There was only one possible conclusion.

"We were suckered!" Arthur said grimly. "They diverted us with the attack while the bastard took Grim."

He assigned a complement of Knights of the Round Table and a pair of witches to guard Diana, Llyr, and their son as they returned to their kingdom. Morgana volunteered to go along and help with the investigation into how the rebels had gotten to the palace guard.

Nineva suspected it must have galled Llyr to accept

outside help, but he didn't hesitate. His family obviously meant far more to him than his pride.

Llyr told them he planned another deep and ruthless magical scan on the guards of all his palaces to ensure there were no more traitors among them. Once that was taken care of, he planned to help the Magekind conduct another search for both the Sword of Semira and Merlin's Grimoire.

Nineva's role in all this, everyone agreed, was to do whatever was necessary to strengthen Semira. It was obvious that wherever the sword was, Grim wouldn't be far.

"We've got to find that book," Arthur told Kel and Nineva. "I don't know what those bastards intend to do with him, but I'd just as soon not find out."

Kel glanced at Nineva. "We'll do our best."

"You'd better," Arthur said.

Exhausted, Nineva and Kel trudged back to his hillside home. "I really need a long, hot soak," she told him, rolling her aching shoulders. Even after removing the blood and sweat of combat with a spell, she felt grimy and dispirited.

The enemy had won yet again.

Quiet compassion lit Kel's eyes as he studied her face. "I think we can manage a bath."

He was as good as his word. As soon as they walked into the house, he guided her down a hallway that led to a set of winding stairs.

Emerging through an arched stone doorway, Nineva gazed around, her brows lifted. "You *bathe* in here?" The sprawling stone chamber was big enough to echo, easily five stories of arching limestone walls supported by thick pillars carved with dragons.

"Well, yeah." Kel shrugged his shoulders. "I use it in dragon form, too, so it has to be big."

In the center of the space lay a vast pool, surrounded by

a jungle's worth of plants—ferns, orchids, and towering palms that thrived in the humid, magical air. Tendrils of steam curled from the water's surface, which danced and roiled from the waterfall that spilled into the pool's center from somewhere overhead.

Glancing up the length of tumbling water, Nineva spotted the first blue light of dawn streaming through a cavernous skylight. Probably the entrance Kel used in dragon form. "Damn. You never do anything halfway, do you?"

"Now, what would be the fun in that?" He gave her a wicked little smile, all teeth and dishonorable intentions. "Want to get naked?"

"Actually, yeah." The steaming water looked like just the thing for her aching muscles and sweaty flesh.

Warm air brushed her nipples. Nineva looked down and realized her armor had vanished, leaving her body pale and naked. Her blond hair caressed her bare shoulders as she turned to look at him. "Thanks." Her glance became an appreciative stare.

His armor had disappeared, too. He stood in the streaming dawn light like a dream of a god, shadows pooling beneath firm muscle, his cock hardening under her gaze. His eyes gleamed like a pair of rubies caught in a spotlight as his smile flashed white. "My pleasure."

Nineva was contemplating that luscious cock when he caught her by the hand and gently tugged her toward the water. "Come on. There's some stairs down into the pool over here."

The stone floor felt surprisingly warm and smooth underfoot as they crossed to the pool, and the humid air smelled of orchids and even more exotic Mageverse flora. Beneath that was a trace of something faintly musky and magical that struck her as oddly familiar. After a moment, Nineva identified it: the lingering scent of Kel's dragon form.

He eyed her as he guided her down the steps into the pool. "You're frowning."

Water closed around her ankles, frothing gently from the waterfall. "It's nothing." But it was disconcerting to realize that no matter what he looked like, he wasn't really human.

It was equally disconcerting to realize she cared. After all, his Draconian nature was the reason they were together. It wasn't as if there could be anything more between them than magical sex.

Nineva thought of the love in Llyr's eyes as he gazed at his wife and baby. Something about the memory sent a little jab of pain through her. She pulled her hand from Kel's. "I'm going to swim."

He watched Nineva throw herself forward in a long, flat dive. His cock twitched in appreciation as her lithe little body disappeared underwater with a neat splash. She surfaced a moment later, long legs kicking, smooth, pale backside working as her graceful arms cut through the water in fast, hard strokes.

Kel's mind flashed back to the instant he'd seen her surrounded by warriors, her expression grim and determined as she fought to save the queen. If he and Llyr had been a moment later, they'd have lost them both.

His heart squeezed painfully at the thought—and not because the Dark One invasion would have become a virtual certainty. The idea of Nineva, helpless and surrounded by enemies . . .

The intensity of his reaction was vaguely alarming. *Get a grip, Kel. You're not having a romance here. This is business.*

Nineva picked up the pace, swimming even faster. As if she was trying to get away from him.

And dammit, that hurt, too.

With an impatient growl at himself, he dove into the water and began to swim for the opposite side of the pool.

What the hell was he getting wrapped around the axle

about? She was only using him for sex to power her precious goddess. It was very good sex, true—maybe the best he'd ever had, though only Cachamwri knew why. He'd certainly had more experienced lovers.

Though none of them had ever touched him the way she had. Why else had he panicked when he'd realized she was under attack?

Yeah, she'd gotten to him, all right.

You're setting yourself up for a fall, Kel thought grimly, lengthening his strokes, propelling himself through the warm water with hard kicks. *You're going to convince yourself you're in love with that girl, and she's going to dump your scaly ass the minute she gets her goddess out of that sword. Then she's going to marry some Sidhe prince and live happily ever after while you eat your heart out.*

Anyway, the whole thing was ridiculous. Dragons didn't mate for life. Hell, they barely mated for a single season—just long enough to fertilize the female's eggs.

True, a dragon couple could get pretty passionate for that season, but it didn't last. Unlike with humans, love wasn't a survival mechanism for dragons, since a Draconian female was fully capable of providing for her fledglings by herself. She didn't need a male to do the hunting for her while she devoted all her time to rearing their young.

Up until Gawain had fallen for Lark, Kel had half-suspected love was a mass human delusion—an invention of poets and romance novelists. Then his best friend had formed a Truebond with the woman he loved, and for one shining moment, Kel had shared their psychic link.

And it had been incredible. Far more intense than the comfortable link he and Gawain had shared for so many centuries.

The two had Truebonded so Lark could keep Gawain alive while another knight ran him through with Kel's sword form. At the time, it had been the only way to free Kel from the blade and rescue Arthur.

Kel had experienced their love in all its pure, shining intensity, but there'd been no place for him in it. He'd had to leave the link while Lark fought to save her lover.

For the first time in centuries, he'd been truly alone. Ever since, he'd been haunted by that taste of perfect love. Love he knew he'd never experience firsthand.

Reaching the shallows on the opposite side of the pool, Kel braced his feet on the bottom and stood, swiping strands of wet cobalt hair from his face.

When he turned, he saw Nineva floating on her back at the other end of the pool. Her lovely bare breasts broke the surface, nipples pink and beaded by the cool air. He stared, watching the slow, lazy kick of her long legs. His cock hardened again in a fierce rush.

He could have her now. He could swim over there, and she'd let him take that lush, tempting body of hers in the name of her goddess. He could fuck her in every way he wanted.

But that was the most he'd get from her. There'd be no Truebond union of hearts and souls, no end to the loneliness that had dogged him. There never would be.

His lips tightened, and he hit the water again, stroking hard toward her. If all he could have of her—of anyone—was sex . . . Well, so be it. He'd take what he could get.

Nineva heard the pool churning with his approach. She lowered her feet to tread water and started to pivot to face him.

Big hands caught her arms before she could turn, pulling her around and into those brawny arms. His body felt deliciously hard, his cock rigid against her belly as his mouth came down over hers, wet and hungry and demanding.

It was a ravishing kiss, a kiss that took and gave no quarter. A kiss that stole the breath from her lungs in one ruthless draw. Her heart leaped in her chest as he pumped his tongue deep into her mouth in long, suggestive strokes.

One hand cupped her bare ass, pulling her tight against the beefy rigidity of his cock. The long fingers of the other sought out her breast, thumbing and teasing her nipple until sweet fire ran through her blood.

Nineva gasped against his possessive lips. He made a low growling sound and angled his head to press slow, burning kisses along her jaw and down her throat. It felt so deliciously overwhelming, her wary heart whispered a protest. Surely some quick, anonymous sex would be so much safer. "Kel! What're you . . . what are you doing?"

"What do you think?" He lifted her, bending her backward over his arm as he nibbled and bit his way lower and lower. "Feeding your goddess."

Gasping, Nineva wrapped both hands in the wet silk of his hair. His teeth scraped skillfully over her nipple. Pleasure curled through her in such luscious throbs, she lost the will to protest. "Sweet Semira . . . ," she moaned, as he licked and swirled and tasted.

"Like that?"

She could only moan.

He laughed, throaty and deep. "Yeah, you like it." The hand under her ass shifted, probed; slipped between her soft lips and into her rapidly dampening core. A finger circled her clit, then eased deep into her sex. "You like that, too?"

"God, yeah!" Nineva threw back her head and gasped as he pumped the finger in, then out. Slow and teasing.

"Of course you do—I'm good." A hard note entered Kel's deep voice. "Remember that. I may not be human, or Sidhe, or whatever the hell it is you think you want, but I know what you need."

Then, as if she weighed no more than a rag doll in his arms, he started toward the edge of the pool. He stepped out of the water like Neptune rising from the sea, as water streamed from them. Panting, Nineva clung to his shoulders, looking into those crimson eyes of his. They looked feral, hungry, maybe a little pissed. *What the hell did I do to set him off?*

And can I do it more often?

Kel lowered her to her bare feet, then grabbed her by the shoulders and turned her roughly around. One hand closed over the back of her neck and started pushing her down to her knees. "What now?"

"Guess." It was a rumbling growl. Turning her head, she saw him hit his knees behind her even as he forced her head lower.

Angling her ass in the air.

Nineva shivered as helpless arousal pulsed deep in her sex. Semira help her, she'd never been so turned on in her life. She knew she shouldn't be—she should be outraged at the way he was handling her—but her body didn't care. It craved this—his rough, demanding hands, his big hard body, the urgent upward curve of that big cock.

His hands closed around her hips and lifted her butt, forcing her to brace her hands on the ground. The grass felt cool under her fingers.

Then his mouth covered her cunt from behind. Nineva jerked with a startled cry as his tongue thrust between her lips and licked in one long swipe that made her writhe at the instant kick of pleasure. She felt him settle back on his heels, dragging her up and back, supporting her in a way no human could have as she hung head-down.

Nineva planted her palms on his muscled thighs to support her torso as he ate her like a plum. Gentle bites and nibbles, long licks, teasing circles of his tongue around her clit. She could feel the orgasm pulsing as it built like a storm, low in her tensing belly.

Bite. Nibble. Lick. A sudden hard thrust of his tongue went right into her core. She shuddered and clamped her eyes closed against the tight, merciless spiral of pleasure. "Kel! God, Kel . . ."

He growled back at her, feral as a tiger at a meal. His teeth scraped gently over the hard nubbin of her clit.

She screamed and convulsed, her body lashing in his arms as he held her against his mouth. Still licking.

The hot fire of her orgasm pulsed on, wave after wave as he ate her.

Nineva's long blond hair whipped Kel's thighs as she tossed her head, writhing in his hold. He held her still anyway, enjoying her helpless, high-pitched cries of pleasure.

His cock throbbed and jerked. He ignored it, intent on dragging one more delighted scream out of her mouth. Intent on the sea-foam taste of her sex. Bathing in her.

Finally she collapsed in his arms, limp and panting in the aftermath. He lowered her to the grass with a raw grin of conquest, then flipped her faceup.

Let's see your fairy prince give you that.

Kel surveyed her pale beauty as she sprawled on the ground, dazed and panting. A smile of satisfaction curled his mouth even as his cock jerked in demand. He thought about spreading those pretty legs wide and driving inside, then decided, reluctantly, against it.

He wasn't done with her yet. He wanted more. He wanted to stamp himself on her soul and her body. He wanted to make damn sure she never forgot him.

His gaze locked on the round, lovely globes of her breasts. Her nipples looked deliciously pink and hard, like little cherry gumdrops.

Kel instantly decided he wanted a bite.

Grabbing her hips, he pulled her closer, then covered her body with his. She moaned, half in protest, half in anticipation. Kel smiled a pirate's smile and lowered his head.

The nipple he'd targeted hardened even more against his tongue as he suckled her. She tasted of magic and springwater and lush, helpless arousal. He suckled more deeply, loving the taste.

Her hands came up weakly and tangled in his hair. She moaned. "Kel, oh, Goddess—you're driving me insane."

"Good." He swirled his tongue around the hard little peak, then gave it a taunting nibble.

He loved the way her small, lithe body felt against his, all satin skin and velvet curves. He loved the way she tasted, loved the lush scent of her arousal. Loved her complete boneless surrender. She was his.

At least for the moment.

Later . . .

The thought of what would happen in that "later" made his temper heat again. He growled against the satin slope of her breast and pulled away.

So maybe he wasn't her kind. So maybe she saw him as an animal. He'd show her what an animal could do.

He flipped her onto her belly again and dragged her butt up, high into the air.

"Kel . . . ," she whimpered.

He ignored the pleading sound, aiming his cock at the tempting rosy entrance to her cunt. One hard, deep thrust seated him to the balls. Kel gasped at the tight, liquid delight. For a moment, he didn't dare move, knowing he'd come if he did.

Finally, carefully, he began to thrust.

Kel felt huge inside her, a thick, rock-hard velvet club. He should have hurt, yet he'd done such a good job arousing her that all she felt was staggering delight.

Every thrust seemed edged in sweet fire. Panting, Nineva could only grab fistfuls of grass in her hands and hang on for dear life as he lunged against her. Each long dig coiled her building orgasm tighter.

She felt his wet hips slapping hers, jolting her forward.

Her nipples dragged back and forth across the cool grass, adding another fillip of delight to an already searing moment.

Then he started circling his hips, pressing hard, screwing into her. Grinding. Incapable of speech, she could only throw back her head and keen.

Her climax was abrupt, blinding—and endless.

Kel growled in satisfaction as he felt her coming around him, her tight little cunt pulsing, milking his long shaft with every thrust. He let go and began to drive hard, jolting her forward with every ruthless thrust. His balls drew into tight, hot knots between his thighs as his climax began to claw for release.

Abruptly it burst free. He came with a howl as heat spurted from his cock in long, delicious jets. And . . .

Fire!

The goddess touched him, alien and female and hungry. Hungry for his warmth. Hungry for his power. Her touch sent another desperate spurt of raw lust through him, and he pumped even harder in Nineva's depths as he convulsed helplessly.

Dimly, he heard her scream of delight and surrender. For a moment, he touched her mind—felt her writhing in the hot, sweet fire he'd inflicted. That searing instant drove his own pleasure higher. He howled . . .

Yes! The goddess breathed. *That's it. That's what I need. More!*

Unable to stop—not even wanting to—he came. And came. And *came.* And felt Nineva doing the same, her pleasure spiking his even higher.

Until at last they both collapsed on the grass, panting and spent.

In the distance, he could feel the goddess's pleasure.

Slowly, like a dying ember, it faded away. That wasn't good—they needed her—but there was nothing his exhausted body could do about it. He simply didn't have the strength.

Nineva lay in the loose clasp of Kel's muscled arms, listening to the desperate bellows huff of his breathing. She was panting just as hard, and not only from the amazing pleasure.

For a moment, she'd been linked with Semira again. They hadn't been able to sustain it, but she knew they'd strengthened the goddess.

They were on the right track.

Which was no surprise, really. Kel had broken over her like an erotic storm, flooding her mind with arousal and pleasure in turn. She'd never experienced anything so intense.

No wonder the goddess had reacted.

Wearily, Nineva lifted her head. He lay draped over her back like a hot male blanket, his softening cock slipping from her sex. His breathing had deepened, and his eyes had closed. Between the two of them, she and Semira had wiped him out.

There was a certain wicked satisfaction in that thought.

Of course, he'd wiped her out, too. She yawned in a jaw-popping stretch and nestled back against his chest. He felt wonderful against her, so big and warm, water droplets seemed to steam off his powerful body.

Drained, she relaxed. In moments, she, too, was asleep.

He moved against her, rolling his narrow hips, his long cock delving deep. Nineva threw her head back as pleasure shafted through her in time to his delicious strokes. Her eyes fell closed as she savored the hot sensation of Kel making love to her. Her hands caught his muscled forearms. She frowned. His skin felt odd . . .

She opened her eyes.

And cried out in horror. His muscular body was covered in scales, and his handsome face had become a snarling muzzle. His tail whipped like a crocodile's with every ruthless thrust of his inhuman cock.

"Kel!" Desperate, she fought to struggle free, but his clawed hands dug into her butt and held her helpless.

His crimson eyes watched her helplessness with reptilian pleasure. "You can't get away from me. You can't escape your fate."

Kel opened his jaws, revealing teeth like stilettoes. In the depths of his throat, she could see a hot red point appear, growing into a boiling ball. Flame shot from his mouth . . .

Screaming, Nineva began to burn.

Hard arms caught her as she tried to flee the agony and stark terror. She howled like a trapped thing and struck out, sending a fireball whizzing at her captor.

"Nineva!" Kel shouted, deflecting her blast. "You're dreaming again. It's all right, you're safe!"

Conjuring a light, she stared at him wildly. His skin was smooth and human, and his eyes were soft with concern. "You hurt me!"

"No," he insisted. "It was only a dream."

And it had been, she realized, coming fully awake at last. With a groan of mingled relief and shame, she collapsed into his arms. "Sorry." Her voice sounded hoarse. She cleared her throat and tried again. "Sorry I went off on you."

"Hey, it's okay." He rubbed her back in a silent offer of comfort. "The burning dream again?"

"Yeah." She rested her cheek against his chest and

wrapped her arms around him. "I don't know why. You saved my life today. If it hadn't been for you, they'd have taken me and the queen. And then it all would have been over."

He tightened his hold into a hug. "You can't control your dreams, Nineva."

"Maybe not, but I wish I could control this one."

Slave . . .

With a soundless curse, Varza jolted upright, her stolen heart pounding as she stared around herself for the source of the voice. All appeared well, with Arralt sprawled naked and sleeping next to her. But that was an illusion.

Her master was calling.

She rolled out of bed and padded silently into the next room. There, a golden orb hovered over the black stone altar on which lay Merlin's Grimoire and the Sword of Semira.

At least she'd have something to appease the bastard.

Slave . . . The orb pulsed with dark, swirling colors, blood red and purple and a putrid green. Her master had probably had to work death magic to push a message through Merlin's Wards and reach her here on Sidhe Earth. She wondered which of his slaves he'd killed.

She pushed her stolen hair back from her face. "Aye, Master?"

What progress?

"We've captured Merlin's Grimoire and the Sword of Semira." She coiled her fists in her lap as anxiety twisted her gut.

What of the sacrifices?

Varza winced. "We were unable to take them. Llyr Galatyn and Arthur have them guarded too well."

Unacceptable. Her master's rumble of rage made the orb vibrate. *Our forces are ready to begin the invasion.*

Merlin's Wards must be broken if we are to begin our conquest.

"We have an alternate plan," Varza said quickly. "We only need one more element to begin work, and we're in the process of acquiring it."

Then I suggest you work fast, slave. The orb's rumble grew still more menacing. *And quickly. Or you'll pay the price.*

She bowed instinctively, though she knew he couldn't see her. "We mean to have it very soon, Master. You'll be able to claim your conquest within the week."

The orb rumbled once more, then went dark. Varza slumped in relief.

The Dark Ones had ruled Varza's home world of Odra for thousands of years, feeding on pain and death as they destroyed whatever culture had existed before their arrival. Varza herself knew no other life but fear and the ruthless determination to survive.

Then Arralt had decided to learn the Dark Ones' magic as a means to overthrow his father and his equally hated uncle, Llyr Galatyn. He'd transported himself to the nearest Dark One–ruled planet with a gate powered by his own mother's murder.

Varza, luckily, had found them first, there in her master's capital city. Given the chance, her rival slaves would have slain them all, but she'd had more foresight. Instead, she'd defended Arralt and his Sidhe entourage—collecting more than a few injuries in the process—and escaped back to her lair with them.

There, she'd started her investigation into exactly who the aliens were and where they'd come from.

At first, she'd thought only to claim credit for discovering a new planet for the Dark Ones to overrun. Unfortunately, her probe soon revealed that Sidhe Earth was protected by yet another of the Fae's cursed ward shields. The Dark Ones' rival race had been warding every world they discovered, a gambit that was slowly strangling the growth of the empire.

Disgusted, Varza had handed the Sidhe over to her master, Rakatvira. She'd expected the Dark One to sacrifice them on the spot, but he'd surprised her.

It seemed Sidhe Earth was a very rare and valuable planet indeed—one of the few that had a twin in another universe. Centuries before, Rakatvira and the other Dark Ones had occupied both worlds. Now, however, he had conceived a new plan: they could use the alternate Earth as a launching point to invade the surrounding universe. True, they'd have to draw on magic from their own, but that was no problem at all.

Best of all, the plan would allow them to sidestep the Fae's interference. The empire could begin to grow again, fueled by a new supply of slaves.

Unfortunately, there was still the problem of destroying the Fae's wards, which could only be done from within. Arralt was willing to cooperate in exchange for being allowed to rule the Sidhe as king, but Rakatvira did not entirely trust him.

He did, however, trust Varza, who knew better than to betray him. While she was too alien to pass for Sidhe, she was skilled in possession spells, and Arralt's entourage included the perfect victim.

So Varza had promptly seized the body of Arralt's lover, Ceredith, slaying her spirit with death magic. The general hadn't uttered a word of protest, though she'd seen the ghost of regret in his eyes.

Varza had been a bit regretful herself. The plan meant leaving her own body in Rakatvira's less-than-tender hands, but there was no help for it.

Luckily, the scheme had worked. The Fae wards had not recognized her as a servant of the Dark Ones, encased as she was in a Sidhe's flesh.

Varza had been well-repaid for her sacrifices. For the

first time in her life, she tasted true freedom as she'd worked by Arralt's side. She'd have been tempted to double-cross her master, but she knew Rakatvira would have promptly slain her body, which would have killed her on the spot.

The only glitch had been the failure to capture Nineva and the werewolf. If the alternate plan didn't work, Varza had the ugly feeling she'd be her master's next sacrifice.

ELEVEN

Somewhat to Nineva's surprise, she found the next week to be the most idyllic she'd ever known. She and Kel spent the time making love, eating, and sleeping in each other's arms. In between bouts of passion, they talked about their lives. Kel had a seemingly endless collection of war stories about his adventures with Gawain that alternated between hysterical and hair-raising. She'd never spent so much time with a man in her life, or enjoyed it as much.

Which might explain why she'd never realized how lonely she'd been.

The lone blight on her budding happiness was guilt, born of the knowledge that everyone else was engaged in a desperate search for Grim and the sword. Magekind and Sidhe teams questioned Morvenian civilians or scouted the planet, seeking any clue to the location of the rebel strong-hold. Unfortunately, they'd had absolutely no luck.

When she mentioned her guilt to Kel, he pointed out that the two of them were doing something that might well pay off faster than anyone else's efforts. And he had a point. Semira seemed to grow stronger each time they made love, though Nineva still hadn't managed to determine where she was being held.

The other problem was that Nineva was still having nightmares about Kel. After a particularly violent one woke her one night, he decided they both needed a change of pace.

The long, low brick building seemed to glow with magic and vibrate with music. Blue neon formed a pointed wizard's hat over the doorway, with the name "MageClub" spelled out in flashing red beneath it.

Nineva lifted her brows and hooked both hands through Kel's elbow. "This looks familiar."

He glanced down at her. "Oh?"

"Yeah. I've worked at a dozen places just like this."

Kel grinned. "Oh, I doubt you've worked anywhere like the MageClub."

Still, she felt right at home when they stepped inside. A massive brass and mahogany bar took up one end of the long room, surrounded by small round tables and a few booths, all crowded with laughing, jostling people. The rest of the space was dominated by an impressive dance floor on which a number of couples spun and gyrated to a throbbing rock beat.

"Pretty good crowd," Kel commented. "Probably blowing off steam from the search."

"Oh?"

He shrugged. "I've seen it before. The Magekind can spend only so much time beating their collective heads against a brick wall before they have to get drunk and start something."

"Well, that doesn't sound very mature."

"Hey, they may be immortal ass-kickers, but they're still only human."

Catching her hand, he drew her through the crowd to the bar. Nineva ordered a rum and Coke while Kel asked for a draft beer. She watched with professional interest as the bartender produced them, admiring his brisk, unflappable skill despite the flurry of orders coming at him from all directions. "Nice work," she told him as he flipped a cherry into her drink and handed it over.

"It's a nice change from killing terrorists." The man gave her a wink. He was, of course, disgustingly handsome.

"Kel!" A female voice shouted in her ear. It was high and giggly with an unmistakable note of intoxication Nineva recognized from professional experience. "There you are!"

Somebody jostled her elbow. Barely saving her drink, Nineva turned to find that a well-endowed blonde had wrapped herself around Kel like a fur stole. The woman's red dress hugged every lush curve, while its brief hemline displayed about a mile of leg. Her heart-shaped face was a match for that stunning body, with big blue eyes and a centerfold's mouth.

"Hello, Clare." Discomfort obvious in his eyes, he met Nineva's astonished gaze and tried to peel the blonde's arms from around his neck. "Nice to . . . uh . . . see you."

"I've been looking for you everywhere," the woman burbled, clinging more tightly. She grinned up at him tipsily. "I'm in the mood for a little lizard lovin'."

"Ah." Kel finally succeeded in unwrapping her and set her back on her red stiletto heels. "Clare, this is my new partner, Princess Nineva. Nineva, Clare Amatto."

"Partner?" Not at all discomfitted, Clare gave her a merry smile, big blue eyes sparkling and friendly. Apparently she wasn't the jealous type. "Lucky girl. Has he shown you what he can do with his tongue?" Her grin widened. "Once you've had forked, you'll never go back."

Nineva's eyes widened. "Forked?"

"Oh, yeah. Combine that with the looooong dragon di—"

"Clare," Kel interrupted desperately, "I need to show Nineva around. Be a good girl and—"

"But I've missed you." Clare pouted, her lush mouth exactly matching the scarlet of her dress. "Your little friend won't mind sharing. Right?" She shot Nineva a pleading look.

Nineva managed not to bare her teeth. "Actually, I do." And she did mind, she realized. Violently.

"But there's plenty of him to go around," Clare said, with the earnestness of the truly drunk. She gave Kel an amorous grin. "Plenty. Lots and lots and *lots*."

Nineva felt her hands curl into claws, then made an effort to relax them. What the hell was wrong with her? It wasn't as if they were dating, for God's sake. They might be sleeping together, but it was only to power the goddess, find the sword, and stop the Dark Ones. Hell, half the time he gave her screaming nightmares.

So why did she want to scratch this horny little witch bald-headed?

To fight the temptation, she folded her arms and watched Kel struggle to convince Clare they really weren't interested in a threesome.

"Since your friend is busy," a male voice purred in her ear, "perhaps you'd like to dance?"

Nineva turned to find one of the most handsome men she'd ever seen watching her with dark, soulful eyes. Tousled black hair fell over his forehead, and his mouth looked deliciously sensual. His face was chiseled in a way that reminded her vaguely of some actor, though she couldn't put her finger on just who. He was three or four inches shorter than Kel, but that only made his shoulders look broader in his white silk shirt. Black slacks hugged muscled thighs and fell around narrow, booted feet.

"Dominic Bonhomme," he told her, with a courtier's bow of that gleaming dark head.

"But Kellll," Clare cooed behind her, "I've missed you so! And I'm so . . ."

In no mood to hear the rest, she said between her teeth, "I'm Nineva Morrow. And I'd love to dance."

Just as Kel hit the limits of his patience, Tristan appeared from the crowd with that sense of perfect timing that made him such a superb warrior. "Clare, darlin', I think I should take you home and put you to bed." Taking her by the upper arm, he helped Kel peel her off.

"Tristan!" Clare's smile was sunny and oblivious. "Would *you* like a threesome?"

"Sorry, he's not my type." He brushed a thumb across her cheek and turned her toward the door. "But you are. Come on, love. In the morning, I'll feed you a nice hangover remedy and keep you from dying of embarrassment— though if you're really lucky, you won't remember a damned thing."

"You're so sweet!"

"Not really, but I am willing to pretend." He led her away.

Kel blew out a breath in relief and made a mental note that he owed his brother knight a rescue. "Sorry about that, Nineva . . ." He turned.

She was heading for the dance floor with Dominic Bonhomme, Court Seducer of Avalon. Her back was straight and stiff with indignation. Dominic looked back over his shoulder and gave Kel an unrepentant wink.

That smarmy little . . . Kel took a long step forward.

A hand landed on his shoulder. "Let's talk." Gawain hauled him toward one of the booths that surrounded the dance floor.

"After I kick Dominic's ass."

"No. Now. Besides, it wouldn't be any fun. Dominic's nowhere near your weight class."

Kel snorted. "I'm a forty-foot dragon. *Nobody* in Avalon is anywhere near my weight class."

"My point exactly."

Gawain's lovely dark-haired wife looked up from her drink as he pushed Kel down into a seat. "Hi, Kel."

"Hi, Lark."

The growl in his voice sent her brows up. "Is this going to be one of those man-to-dragon conversations?"

"Probably," Gawain said.

Lark followed Kel's gaze to the dance floor, where Dominic was spinning Nineva into a practiced turn. "Ahh. Well, in that case, I'll give you two some privacy." She rose and glided away, her emerald dress swirling around her long thighs.

Kel barely noticed, too busy glowering at Dominic and Nineva. "Fair fight or not, Bonhomme needs his teeth knocked in."

"Uh huh." Gawain hooked a brawny arm across the back of the booth. "You do realize you're breathing smoke?"

He was right. Twin sparkling plumes of pure rage streamed from Kel's nostrils. He made an effort to regain control before he did something he'd regret.

Enjoy, but regret. "I never liked that son of a bitch."

Bonhomme caught Nineva's hand and pulled her close.

"He does love to stir up trouble when he sees an opportunity." Gawain's green eyes were cool and curious on his face. "I'm just surprised he sees one in you. You've never gotten bent out of shape about a woman before."

"She's not a woman," Kel growled. "She's a princess of the Sidhe, a professional martyr, and the only hope we've got of stopping the Dark Ones."

"A *professional* martyr?"

Kel rubbed a thumb between his aching brows as Dominic swooped Nineva into a dip. She was laughing. "Yeah." He ground his teeth and fought the impulse to stalk onto the dance floor and jerk her away from the too-handsome vampire. "There's this prophecy. It's not helping."

"What kind of prophecy?"

"The kind that says I'm going to incinerate her."

"*What?*"

Grimly, Kel related the story. "Nineva's been having nightmares about it for years," he concluded. "In fact, she had one earlier tonight, which is why I brought her here to begin with. I was hoping to distract her." He watched her cling to Bonhomme, giggling as the vampire tangoed her around the dance floor with professional skill. "It seems to be working."

"Sounds like you should cut your losses and join Tristan and Clare for that threesome."

Kel snorted. "As somebody's already noted, Tristan's not my type. Besides, I've still got to power Nineva's goddess for her."

"Who died and made you the Energizer Bunny?"

Kel's explanation made him whistle. "So basically," Gawain said when he finished, "you've got a licence to have all the sex you want. And she couldn't go home with Bonhomme if she wanted to, because he's not a dragon."

"Somehow I don't find that comforting." Nineva and Dominic had segued into something slow and seductive, with plenty of pelvic contact. The vampire seemed to be whispering something in her ear.

"Yeah, you've got it bad." Gawain watched him with equal parts amusement and sympathy.

Kel shrugged, pretending unconcern. "So I've got a little crush. It's not as if dragons mate for life. I doubt I'm even capable of love."

"That's the biggest pile of horseshit I've ever heard."

He blinked, startled by his friend's savage tone.

"We were linked for fifteen centuries, Gecko," Gawain said roughly. "I know exactly what you're capable of."

"She doesn't trust me, 'Wain." The words came out more naked than he'd intended.

"She will." Gawain's smile was knowing. "You're a trustworthy kind of guy."

* * *

Dominic Bonhomme was handsome, charming, and seductive, with warm dark eyes and a sexy Italian accent that
gave his vowels a faint slur. He danced with an offhand
skill, hips rolling to the sensual beat of the music.

But Nineva's gaze kept straying to Kel's strong profile
as he talked to Gawain, his expression intense.

"Am I boring you?" Dominic breathed in her ear. Nuz-
zling her neck, he added, "I certainly hope not. You smell
delicious."

Given that he was a vampire, Nineva wondered if he
meant that literally. She braced her hands against his
shoulders and pushed him back to a more comfortable
distance. "Ah—thanks."

"I've always wanted to taste a pretty Sidhe girl," he
purred. "Would you like to go home with me?"

Nineva stiffened. "No, I would not."

"But just think how jealous it would make your dragon."

"He's not my dragon. And even if he was, I don't play
games like that."

He lifted a dark brow. "You did agree to dance with
me."

"And I shouldn't have."

"No." Dominic flashed white fangs. "You really shouldn't
have."

She glowered at him. "He pissed me off."

"I know. Which is interesting, don't you think? Considering he was hardly to blame for Clare's tipsy behavior. You're
a bit touchy about a man you've barely known for a week."
Correctly interpreting her surprise, his smile widened.
"Word spreads fast in Avalon."

Nineva stared, realizing he'd been playing her to make a
point. "You manipulated me."

He laughed. "Darling, it's what I do." His fingers

brushed her cheek, cool and taunting. "And I'm very good at what I do."

"Kiss off." She turned her back on him and stalked from the dance floor. Her gaze fell on Kel, who still sat sprawled in the booth with Gawain. A trace of smoke drifted from his nose, and his gaze was brooding as he swigged his beer.

Shame made Nineva wince. She'd acted just like every jealous woman who'd ever made a fool of herself in every bar where Nineva had ever worked. She'd always harbored a certain contempt for those women. Finding herself guilty of the same behavior was galling.

She knew she owed Kel an apology—but not just yet. She wasn't up to facing him right now.

Instead, Nineva veered away and headed for one of the French doors that led outside, knowing she was being cowardly even as she pushed it open.

The air was cold and bracing, cooling the sweat on her skin and the heat on her cheeks. She walked across the brick porch to lean on the wrought iron railing that encircled it.

Brooding, Nineva stared out into the starlit night. A Scottish castle rose over the trees, moonlight painting its stone battlements. Magic flared inside one of its gothic windows, multicolored sparks in the darkness.

She wasn't used to feeling petty. Probably because nobody had ever touched her deeply enough to inspire that kind of behavior.

"You look like you could use a margarita." A petite brunette appeared at her elbow and handed her a glass rimmed in salt.

Recognizing Gawain's wife, Nineva gave her a smile. "Thanks, Lark."

The Maja toasted her with her own icy drink. "My pleasure." She took a sip. "By the way, just for the record—if you hurt Kel, I'm going to break both your legs."

Nineva blinked at her over the glass, startled. Though Lark's tone was deceptively pleasant, the hard glint in her eyes revealed she meant every word of the threat. "I have no intention of hurting Kel."

"Good." The Maja licked at the rim of salt. "He's a good friend and a hero, and he deserves better than to get his heart handed to him by some fairy who doesn't give a damn."

Nineva ground her teeth. After Dominic Bonhomme, she was *not* in the mood for this. "Where the hell do you get off?"

"I watched him watch you dance with Dominic. I don't like seeing that kind of pain in a friend's eyes."

"You're imagining things. We've barely known each other a week."

Lark laughed. "With people who live on the edge like we do, a week is just enough time to get somebody seriously hurt."

"I have no intention of hurting anybody." Nineva tossed her glass over the rail and stalked away as it shattered against a tree trunk. The witch was lucky she wasn't wearing it. "Anyway, Kel's a lot more likely to do the hurting."

The Maja shook her head. "If you think that, you really are an idiot."

Kel spotted Nineva crossing the dance floor like an infuriated queen. He rose to stride after her, but before he could catch up, a delicate hand grabbed his arm.

"Let her go," Lark said, sounding a bit self-satisfied. "I told her a couple of home truths she needed to hear, and she needs time to digest."

Kel glowered at her. "Why the hell did you stick your oar in this?"

"Because you're my friend, dammit, and I hate to see you this miserable." She sighed. "Okay, maybe I should have kept my mouth shut, but she pissed me off. Anyway, I don't think she's good enough for you."

"Lark, she saved Llyr's queen and baby—and risked her own life to do it."

"So she's got guts. She still has her head up her butt."

"Lark, drop it," Gawain said, walking up behind them. "He's a big dragon. He can take care of himself."

"Glad you noticed." Kel rubbed his brow and decided, reluctantly, that Lark was probably right on at least one point: it would be smart to give Nineva time to cool down. Besides, after watching her dance with Bonhomme, he wasn't exactly in the mood to chase her. "I need another beer." He headed for the bar.

Nineva's high heels clicked on the cobblestones in a furious staccato. The really infuriating thing was that she was more angry at herself than Lark.

So Clare had hit on Kel. He hadn't encouraged her— he'd seemed more embarrassed by her drunken attentions than anything else. It wasn't as if he and Nineva had some kind of romance going. It was sex, pure and simple. And not even sex born of personal attraction. They were doing what the goddess required. That was all.

She'd simply had no business getting jealous and flouncing off with another man. Dominic was right about that, much as it galled her to admit it.

Mixed with Nineva's anger was a curious hint of envy. She'd never had a friend willing to go to bat for her the way Lark had for Kel. Even Dominic had been defending him in a backhanded way, at least judging from his parting shot before she'd walked off.

But then, nobody had ever known her well enough to know or care if she was in pain.

Except Kel. She remembered the expression on his face when he'd held her after her nightmare—the tenderness, the sympathy. Remembered the worry on his face when he'd charged Llyr's traitorous bodyguards to rescue her. He'd been afraid for her.

And she also remembered the disappointment in his eyes when he'd looked across the dance floor and seen her with Dominic. Lark was right—she'd hurt him. Though they'd only been together a little more than a week, somehow they'd gotten closer than they had any business getting. Not considering the prophecy.

This was going to be hard enough as it was without them complicating it any more. Neither of them would be able to do what they had to do if their mutual attraction got any stronger. Somehow she had to gain them both a little distance.

If only the goddess would draw the magic faster, they could avoid getting in any deeper. Unfortunately, it seemed Semira was taking her sweet time about it.

Nineva frowned and stopped in her tracks, watching as something shot past overhead, leaving a sparkling trail of magic in its wake.

What she needed was a spell. Her eyes narrowed thoughtfully as she watched the trail fade away. She needed something that would feed their united magic to Semira in one tight burst. It wouldn't even have to be particularly complicated. She could probably whip just the thing up in under an hour.

Suddenly determined, Nineva started toward Kel's hill in long strides. She had work to do.

Piaras circled the clearing, his great wings beating as he watched the men who waited below in the bright sunlight of this hemisphere. He saw no sign of weapons, sensed no indication of any kind of magical trap, but he felt cautious.

You couldn't trust humans. Not even Sidhe, no matter what Cachamwri said.

Still, it was a remarkable offer their leader had made in that series of magical messages. The elimination of Avalon in exchange for certain assistance in killing Llyr Galatyn? Tempting. Very tempting.

But what assistance did this Sidhe general have in mind? It might be worth considering, if Piaras wasn't expected to do anything his people could trace back to him. It was taboo to involve oneself in human affairs, after all.

Piaras had begun to think that particular taboo was one that should be flaunted. The fiasco with Lord Tegid had established beyond all doubt that Avalon was a threat they could no longer afford to ignore. The Avalonian humans and their alien ways needed to be eliminated before the Dragonkind were corrupted as Tegid had been. And if the Sidhe were indeed willing to do the work with minimal involvement on Piaras's part, so much the better.

Deciding it was safe to land, the golden dragon set down in the clearing with his usual skill. "I have considered your offer," he announced without preamble as the general strode forward to meet him. "But as I said, I have further questions."

Arralt looked up at him. "Worry not, Lord Piaras. Everything will soon be very clear indeed."

Kel flew through the night, drinking in the wind that blew cold in his face. The city spread out below him in all its glory, its magical lights shining like diamonds in the dark.

He'd left the bar half an hour before, after drinking three more beers and dancing with two women who hadn't interested him at all. He'd known he needed to fly. Needed to clear his head, drive out the anger and frustration. Remember that he was a dragon.

Cachamwri knew, nobody else seemed to forget. Particularly not Nineva.

Over the past eight months, he'd done everything he

could to become human. He'd turned his back on Dragon-kind and embraced human ways. Yet it was time to face the fact that he wasn't human and never would be, no matter what form he assumed. Even with all his magic, he couldn't change his own basic nature.

Just as he couldn't make Nineva feel anything for him except distrust. Oh, she desired him sexually. She was a sensual woman, and he was very good at human sex, thanks to his centuries observing Gawain at work. But she'd spent too many years having nightmares, too many years hiding from those who wanted to kill her. Maybe one day she'd want to reach out to a man, learn to love. But it sure as hell wouldn't be him.

Maybe he'd made a mistake turning away from Drag-onkind. Yes, they were bigoted when it came to humans, and yes, they'd turned their collective backs on him when he'd needed them most. True, they did view any new idea with deep suspicion, especially if it came from him. But they were still his people. They knew what it was to soar against the sky and breathe magic in long, glowing plumes, to mate in midair and watch the small miracle of a dragon egg hatching.

Maybe it was time he went home.

But not yet. Kel sighed, knowing he still had responsi-bilities to Arthur, Nineva, and the Magekind. They needed to find Grim and the Sword of Semira, so he had to build the goddess's power until Nineva could make contact. Which meant having sex until her bond with Semira strengthened.

But Kel didn't have to keep wishing for something he wasn't going to get. He didn't have to set himself up for more pain.

So he was infatuated with Nineva. It wasn't the end of the world. He'd get over her. All he had to do was keep re-minding himself that theirs was a purely practical partner-ship. *Fuck her and forget her.*

After all, that's what dragons did.

Spotting his hill, Kel narrowed his eyes with sudden determination. He might as well get started now.

He spiraled downward toward the cave opening he'd created for his dragon form, spread his wings to brake, and came in for a neat landing. His claws scraped on the stone, and the rustle of his wings folding seemed to fill the landing cavern.

Otherwise it was dark. Empty.

Which only made sense—did he expect her to wait for him in a diaphanous nightie?

With a snort of disgust at himself, Kel summoned his magic and shifted form. Human again, he rolled his shoulders and headed for the human-sized doorway that led to the human-sized stairs. He always felt so much *less* in the first few minutes of a shift.

Maybe there was a lesson there.

His boots clattered on the stone steps as he made for the second floor and his room. He hoped she was there. And not, say, off with Dominic Bonhomme.

But no. Dominic couldn't power the goddess, and if there was one thing he could say about Nineva, she did her duty. No matter what it might cost her.

Kel frowned, hoping she wasn't asleep and having another one of those nightmares. The look in her eyes in those last seconds before she fully woke wrung his heart every time. He hated to think of her experiencing that kind of fear without him there to comfort her.

Which only goes to prove I'm an idiot.

Despite that thought, his heart beat a little faster when he reached the door to his room. He swung it open . . .

She was waiting.

TWELVE

Nineva held up a hand for silence as she murmured a chant in some Sidhe language he didn't recognize. Kel stopped in surprise.

She was dressed in a long gown of thin scarlet silk split down both sides. Only a golden belt held it together. As she paced, each step she took bared the full length of her gently muscled legs. Her blond hair fell around her shoulders like a gleaming curtain. Candles circled her, their golden glow making her pale skin look almost luminous in the dim light.

She looked like a goddess herself.

Feeling almost hypnotized, Kel drew closer to watch her slow, gliding progress. She'd drawn some kind of intricate circle on the stone floor in glowing lines of blue, gold, and red, marked with glyphs he couldn't read. Each of the candles occupied swirls in the mystical pattern. They radiated magic the way a bonfire radiates heat.

Kel frowned, examining the design as he tried to determine its intent. Though he couldn't read the glyphs, he could feel the eroticism that seemed to vibrate through the magic.

She's working a sex spell to power Semira, he realized. *Damn, I should have thought of that myself.*

The spell would speed things up considerably. Which was, he told himself, a good thing. The sooner they got this over with, the better.

Still chanting liquid Sidhe words in her purring, sensual voice, Nineva pointed down at a gap in the twenty-foot outer ring. It led into a maze formed by the swirling lines of the spell.

Knowing what she wanted, Kel banished his clothing and stepped naked through the gap in the ring. Instinctively keeping his steps long and slow, he began to follow the path drawn into the spell. With each step, the magic grew stronger, dancing over his skin like the stroke of invisible female fingers.

His cock swelled under that enchanted touch, growing hard, thick. His gaze locked on Nineva as she stood across the ring from him. Her nipples rose under the thin fabric of the red gown, clearly visible. Kel lifted his eyes to meet hers—and took a deep breath at the sensual need he saw in those opalescent eyes. Her stare was direct and hungry, even as her voice rose and fell in its musical, incomprehensible chant.

Maybe this was about more than duty after all.

Nineva had to struggle to concentrate on her magic as Kel walked naked through the spell. He moved with a liquid strength, his broad shoulders rolling, muscle rippling up and down his sculpted torso and long legs. His cock rose hard and thick, bobbing slightly above the tight, furred sac of his balls. Just looking at him made her mouth go dry. She barely managed not to stutter as she chanted the ancient words that were designed to bind the spell to Semira.

Under his steady stare, she felt herself grow wet.

By the time he stepped into the center of the circle,

Nineva was aching. She finished the spell in a voice gone hoarse with need. For a moment, they stared at each other, heat swimming between them in waves she could almost see.

Deep within her mind, Nineva heard a purr of approval in a familiar voice. *Yesssss. More, my child!*

"The spell worked," she managed. "We've got a connection to Semira. It's fragile, but it's there."

Kel smiled slowly, his glowing eyes heavy-lidded with desire. "Then let's make the best of it." He leaned down and took her mouth with that knee-weakening skill she knew so well. His lips tasted of desire, masculinity, and a smoky hint of something she recognized as dragon. His broad palms slid up her arms, and his fingers found the thin straps of her silk gown. He pushed them down until the dress slid over her hips and puddled around her feet.

His gaze dropped to her hard nipples, and he covered her breasts with his hands. "So pretty," he said, his voice deliciously deep. "So soft."

Nineva closed her eyes at the feeling of his fingers stroking, squeezing the sensitive flesh. The pleasure made her shiver.

But even as she started to lean into him, she remembered Semira. "Lie down." Her voice was hoarse. "I've got to work the rest of the spell."

Kel looked at her, and the corner of his mouth quirked in a lazy half-smile. "Well, since you ask so nicely." He stepped back. His cock stood high and proud, drawing her longing attention. His smile broadened, as if he read the depth of her hunger. He moved to the center of the spell circle and dropped onto his back, graceful as a cat. His heavy erection fell against his belly, so long it stretched past his belly button. Nineva eyed the tempting width, the thickly veined underside, the flushed and swollen head. She dropped to her knees at his side and reached for her magic. Softly, she began to chant.

The power gathered, thrumming through her body, tingling in the tips of her fingers. Making her grow even wetter.

She reached for him. Touched the satin surface of his mouth, traced the arrogant angle of his cheekbones down his jaw to the round jut of his chin. He watched her, his gaze hot, intent as a predator's.

Nineva continued to chant, though her voice sounded increasingly rough. Still spinning the spell, she traced her fingers down his body, feeling the nodes of power beneath his velvet skin. Her fingers circled his nipples in an intricate, lacy pattern, drawing his magic closer to the surface. Kel groaned in delight, his back arching as if in involuntary reaction. The movement made his shaft bounce against his belly.

Nineva had to swallow and lick her dry lips before she could continue the spell.

Kel could feel his own pulse in his cock. It seemed to strain longingly toward her clever hand. He wanted to howl like a wolf at the sensation of those delicate fingers drawing patterns of energy over his aching flesh. He wanted to beg.

At least she wanted him just as badly. He could smell the salt and musk of her desire as her body readied for his. He gritted his teeth, dying to reach between those long legs and touch her tight, slick flesh.

She reached his cock at last, but she didn't touch it. At least not at first. Instead her fingers circled it, swirling paths of magic, building the spell higher even as she built his desire.

Kel wondered how much more of this he could take before he lunged for her. *Not yet.* He clenched his hands into fists. *I've got to let her finish the spell.*

But it wasn't going to be easy. Her fingertips ghosted up the underside of his shaft now, making it harden even more. Closing her other hand around the base of the organ, she angled it upward so she could continue painting the spell over his skin.

It was all he could do not to writhe.

The magic rose even higher, as if stoked by his growing lust. Nineva reached the head of his shaft and danced her fingers over it, drawing lines of power and lust.

Then she took her hand away. It felt as if she'd attached a hot, glowing string to the head of his cock that vibrated with the force of her magic, sending burning little jolts of delight up his spine. He groaned as his hips rolled upward, helplessly pleading.

"Now," Nineva breathed. "The spell is ready."

"And so am I." It was a growl so deep, it surprised even Kel. He hadn't thought his human vocal cords were capable of that register.

Nineva gave him a wicked little smile. "Good." Her opalescent eyes met his and locked as she slowly lowered her head.

Toward the cock she still held angled upward. Involuntarily, every muscle in his abdomen tightened in anticipation.

Her pink tongue extended toward the blushing, swollen head. He caught his breath and waited. It felt as if his entire nervous system thrummed.

The tip of that hot tongue flicked over the ruddy cap of his cock, collecting a bead of pre-come. Kel shuddered at the stab of delight.

She licked him again, the kind of long, luscious stroke you'd give an ice cream cone. He gasped.

"How's that?" Nineva asked, with that siren's smile.

He laughed, the sound strangled. "Can't you tell by the way my eyes are rolling back in my head?"

"Mmmmm." Another lick, this one ending in a slow, torturous little swirl. She leaned in and nibbled the shaft gently, right under the head, where the flesh was most sensitive.

"Cachamwri's Egg!"

Kel watched, his muscles straining, as she widened her mouth and swooped down, sucking him into wet, snug heat. Slowly, she lowered her head, taking more and more of the thick shaft as her hands stroked the rest. She pulled up, then plunged downward, taking still more of him down that sweet throat. The spell reverberated hungrily as his body jerked.

Her gaze flicked to his. "Don't come."

"Ride me!"

"Not yet." Her grin was blatantly taunting. She sucked him in again and drew so hard, his spine arched as he fought to control the heat building in his balls.

Nineva pulled off him, then plunged down again for another deliciously agonizing suck that lasted a sweet eternity.

Finally he knew he could take no more. "Enough!"

She lifted her head to consider his face. "No, I don't think so." And swooped down over him again.

Kel's control snapped. He grabbed those slender shoulders and rolled her ruthlessly beneath him. Nineva gasped in involuntary surprise, and he groaned at the hot satin of her skin pressing against his. He sat back, grabbed one of her lovely legs behind the knee, and draped it over his shoulder. Seizing the other's slender ankle, he dragged her wide, aimed his cock with his free hand, and drove deep.

Her gasp of startled lust made his balls jerk tight.

Kel's shaft felt a mile long as he sank endlessly inside her in a delicious invasion that sent tight curls of sensation spiraling up her spine. His gaze intent, he braced his powerful arms beside her shoulders and began to thrust, rolling his muscular butt and powerful thighs.

"You feel so slick. So tight. So good." His long cobalt hair fell around her face, rippling every time he pushed inside. He lowered his head and took her lips in a hard kiss of pure masculine conquest, his tongue swirling inside her gasping mouth. Even as he kissed her, he continued to thrust, slow and hard, twisting his hips so his cock seemed to corkscrew inside her.

Nineva could do nothing but cling to his powerful shoulders. He bit her lips just shy of pain, then nuzzled under her jaw, forcing her head up, tasting the pounding pulse in her throat.

Her climax was gathering deep in her sex, beginning to throb in hunger. He felt so damn huge. So deliciously heavy and so incredibly male.

One big hand found her breast. Thumb and forefinger closed over her desperately tight nipple. Squeezed. Twisted with exquisite care. Forced another whimper from her mouth.

"How's that?" It was a deliberate mocking echo of her earlier question, but she didn't care.

Nineva couldn't even manage speech, only a desperate nod. *God, please don't stop . . .*

Another shattering, burning thrust. She curled her leg tighter over his shoulder, bearing down, trying to force him that last fraction she needed to come. Distantly, she was aware of the spell, still thrumming between them. Feeding the goddess.

Kel found her other nipple, stroked, teased. Maddened, she rolled up at him, harder, fighting to grind her way into climax. He chuckled, deep and satisfied. "Never tease a dragon, Nineva."

"Fine, dammit!" she growled. "Fuck me!"

Kel laughed and gave her what she needed, picking up the pace, plunging in and out in sweet, searing thrusts that tore a scream from her lips. She writhed as her orgasm built and built and built . . .

And exploded.

Nineva screamed, unconsciously digging her nails into

the thick brawn of his biceps. She heard Kel roar and stiffen, driving his cock all the way to the root. Holding it there, pulsing.

The spell pulsed in echo. Harder, harder. Growing into a deep thrum she felt in her very bones. She met Kel's startled gaze . . .

Detonation.

Magic roared through them like a second orgasm, ferocious and hungry, blazing with power.

The world went white, then black. Black and flecked with glittering sparks, like a night sky . . .

No, it was *the sky. She could see the moon, riding full against a spill of brilliant stars.*

A moon suddenly obscured by great wings. Must be Kel, flying through the night . . .

No. There were too many wings, too many dragons. A thundering storm of them, filling the sky with blasts of magical fire. Armored warriors rode them, swords or axes or glowing globes of power in their hands as they swooped downward toward an army of mounted Sidhe.

"Nineva?" Kel's deep voice sounded worried.

She opened her eyes to find herself cuddled against him, his arms gone tender now. "What . . . ?" Her voice sounded far too weak. She cleared her throat and tried again. "What happened?"

"We came, and then you collapsed." He studied her, concern evident in his eyes. "Are you all right?"

She licked her dry lips, letting her head fall against his shoulder. "I had a vision. Semira sent me a vision. Dragons."

His gaze went guarded. "Another burning dream?"

"No, not that. I saw Magekind, or maybe they were Sidhe. But they were mounted on a squadron of dragons. Hundreds of them. Fighting the rebels and an army of Dark Ones."

Kel frowned. "Are you sure? My people don't like humans. They're not likely to form an alliance with them, much less carry them into battle."

She lifted her head. It was starting to pound. "Even to fight the Dark Ones? I thought your people suffered as badly as the Sidhe during that first invasion."

He snorted. "We did, but that won't mean anything to the Dragonkind. Bigotry is not the most rational of emotions. Quite frankly, they wouldn't believe it if we told them."

Nineva frowned. "Well, we're going to have to make them believe. We need them, Kel. The goddess wouldn't have sent me that vision otherwise."

Kel closed his eyes with an expression of pain and sighed. After a moment, he opened his eyes again. "Okay. Convincing them is going to be a big, hairy pain in the ass, but okay. What about finding Semira?"

Nineva frowned and reached out, searching for the goddess. The intensity she'd felt during the spell had faded, but she could still sense a faint presence, ghostly and glowing. *Semira?*

Yes, child?

Thank the Goddess, the link had held this time, though it was still painfully weak. *Can you help us find you?*

She sensed Semira's sigh. *I don't know where I am. That witch Varza has encased me in a containment spell. It is all I can do to reach you, even after everything you have done to build my power. Until I'm free again, my strength will be limited.*

We'll have to try the spell again. Do you want us to do that first, or go to the Dragon Lands?

Go to the Dragon Lands. They must join the fight.

Kel said he doesn't think they'll believe us.

You will convince them, child. You must.

Semira's presence faded, leaving her alone. Nineva dropped her head back against the floor. "The spell wasn't enough. Somebody named Varza has the goddess contained."

Kel gave her a seductive smile and started to reach for her. "We'll just have to try again."

She lifted a hand, and he stopped in mid-gesture. "Not yet. First we've got to go to the Dragon Lands."

He sighed and sat back on his heels, watching her scramble to her bare feet. "I'd rather make love. Believe me, it'd be a lot more fun."

Nineva gave him a warm smile. "Oh, I don't doubt that. But unfortunately, Semira was pretty definite. Dragons first, then sex."

"Figures." He gestured, clothing himself in jeans and a black cotton T-shirt. "Well, if we're leaving Avalon, I've got to check in with Arthur. He needs to know about this latest vision."

"Good idea. I'll come with you. Maybe they've learned something about the sword."

"Maybe. But we'd better hurry. It's almost dawn."

As they hurried along the cobblestone street toward the capitol building, Nineva remembered another piece of unfinished business. She cleared her throat. "I think I owe you an apology."

Kel snorted. "Yeah, those screaming orgasms really make my throat hurt."

"I'm serious. Going off with Dominic like that was really juvenile." She shook her head. "I was so damned jealous, I couldn't see straight."

His crimson eyes widened, and he stopped to stare at her. "You were jealous?"

"That's news? You must have been the only one in the bar who didn't know, then." She grimaced. "Thing is, I hate women who do shit like that. I've seen more fights started by bimbos acting like twelve-year-olds. So naturally, I do the same damn thing."

He studied her face. "You know, Clare would be the first to tell you we were never serious about each other."

"Yeah, I figured that. She wouldn't have suggested a threesome if you had been. Women in love do not like to share." Nineva blinked, as if suddenly realizing the implications of that statement. "I mean . . ."

A long silence ticked by before Kel volunteered, "I *was* pretty pissed about Dominic. He's the Court Seducer, so he romances women for a living. I didn't enjoy watching him hone his technique on you."

Nineva blinked. "That's an actual job description?"

"Oh, yeah. See, Dominic's job is giving Latents their powers."

"Latents?"

"Descendents of the Magekind who carry Merlin's spell in their genes. By having sex with one of them at least three times, a Magus can trigger the spell, making her a full Maja. Trouble is, most Latents have been raised as mortals, and they know nothing about the Magekind or their own potential. Dominic has to seduce them into it. And he's really good at seduction."

"Sounds kind of like a gigolo." She wrinkled her nose.

"Pretty much." He looked almost smug at having spiked his rival's guns.

Apparently he didn't want to share either.

The two found Arthur still at work in the Round Table chamber, coordinating the search for Merlin's Grimoire. He listened as Nineva described her vision. When she finished, he exchanged a look with Kel. "Well, your dragon friends are going to love that."

"Yeah, but we're going to have to get them onboard anyway. It would help if they all weren't so blind stupid." He drummed his fingers restlessly on the table. "Any news about Grim?"

"We've looked everywhere, but we haven't seen or sensed a damn thing." Arthur raked his hand through his dark beard, his expression glum. "There is some good news, though. Gwen says Merlin's shields are still up and just as powerful as ever. Trouble is, she's afraid that Grim is the chink in our planetary armor."

Nineva frowned as she sank into one of the massive chairs that surrounded the table. "How?"

"Well, as Grim himself told us, Merlin used Mageverse Earth's ley lines to power the spell." Ley lines were lines of magical force that cut through the planet, rather like Mortal Earth's magnetic lines of force.

Nineva considered the idea. "Makes sense. Using the ley lines would be the only real way to provide that much power to a spell over so many centuries."

"But you'd need some kind of control key—something that contained the actual spell," Kel said, leaning back in his seat with a frown.

"Which is where Grim comes into it," Arthur told him.

"Oh, fuck." Nineva stared at him in horror. "If they destroy that book . . ."

"Exactly. Fortunately, that's easier said than done. Grim isn't really a physical object. He's a magical construct, and he draws his power from the ley lines."

Kel frowned. "So how the hell did the rebels manage to steal him?"

"Gwen thinks they're somehow interfering with Grim's connection to the ley lines. It would be like pulling the plug on a computer."

"Can they break the connection altogether?" Nineva asked, working through the implications. "Because if they did . . ."

". . . That would destroy Grim." A muscle jerked in Arthur's square jaw. "Theoretically, it's possible, but Gwen thinks it would take one hell of a spell."

"Using, say, the Sword of Semira?" Kel suggested.

"There's not enough power in the sword to power a spell like that," Nineva protested. "Semira's just not strong enough. Not right now."

"Depends on the spell," Arthur pointed out.

"Maybe they're going to supplement the sword with something else." Kel rubbed his chin. "A human sacrifice, maybe?"

"I don't think even that would give them enough charge to overcome the planet's ley lines," Nineva said, absently tracing a finger through a carving of the Grail set in the Round Table's gleaming surface. "You're talking about a hell of a lot of power."

"Whatever they're planning, we're going to have to figure it out—and fast," Arthur said. "Because if we don't, we don't have a prayer of stopping it—and we're going to be up to our necks in Dark Ones."

The sun was rising as Nineva straddled Kel's powerful body, acutely aware of the play of massive muscle under smooth, scaled skin and the thunderous beat of his wings. He'd conjured a harness around her to make sure she didn't fall during any aerial maneuvers he might have to do. Bound so securely to him, she felt safe. She tilted her face into the cold wind and let herself enjoy the ride.

It was strange to think that just a couple of hours ago, she'd been making love to this huge, magnificent being. Stranger still to think this was his true form. He seemed so thoroughly human most of the time. As if he were nothing more than a man.

A deliciously sexy, courageous, occasionally maddening man. A man who fought for her, held her tenderly in the aftermath of nightmares. Made the sweetest love she'd ever experienced.

They'd only been together for such a short time, yet she couldn't recall ever feeling so strongly about a lover. But then, they'd spent those days making love and fighting Sidhe rebels to the death. You learned a lot about a guy when he was willing to risk his life for you.

Kel had even managed to banish her fear of him. Nineva wasn't entirely sure when it had happened, but somehow he'd simply eroded her distrust out of existence. Now she found it impossible to believe he would hurt her, regardless of the provocation. Nightmares and prophecies notwithstanding, he simply wasn't capable of it.

Look at the harness he'd created. It had to be humiliating for him to wear a set of straps like some kind of horse. Yet to assure her comfort and safety, he'd done just that.

Kel was right—she'd misinterpreted the prophecy. Semira's predictions must be a metaphor for something else, some union of power they'd share. As for her dreams, they were nothing more than nightmares, inspired by too many years of listening to her father's grim stories.

Nineva lifted her head to watch the sun sliding over the horizon, spilling crimson and gold over the purpling sky. Below Kel's beating wings, the trees of Mageverse Earth looked like exotic toys, while rivers were silver ribbons snaking along the green ground.

Ahead of them lay the mountains of the Dragon Lands, their tree-clad lower slopes yielding to high, rocky cliffs painted orange by the rising sun.

"It's beautiful!" Nineva shouted over the wind.

"Yes," Kel rumbled back. "It does look that way." His voice sounded surprisingly grim.

Kel sensed them coming long before his eyes picked out the distant specks of their forms. He recognized the psychic impression of their magic, though it had been centuries since he'd seen them.

The welcome wagon, Kel thought. *Or rather, the unwelcome wagon.*

Good thing he'd harnessed Nineva in. He'd never bothered with such a rig for Gawain, knowing the vampire had more than enough strength to hold on. Besides, he refused to rig himself out like a pack animal.

For Nineva, though, he was willing to do it, even knowing he was going to catch hell. Those approaching would be only the first to mock him.

Too bad. They'd lost the right to influence him when they'd stood by and let his mother die.

At the moment, though, he had a more immediate problem. Just ahead lay the magical wards designed to protect the Dragon Lands from invaders. They'd been strengthened since his last visit. Not surprising, considering what had happened with his uncle.

Kel sent out the spell that would act as a password, opening the wards for his entry. The shield stayed stubbornly solid.

"Well." He spread his wings to avoid slamming into the barrier, and veered off, snaking his head around to study the shield as he flew.

"What's wrong?" Nineva shouted over the wind.

"Apparently I'm not welcome," Kel told her. "They've changed the magical combination on the Dragon Lands' wards."

THIRTEEN

Nineva swore at the news. "What are we going to do?"

"Don't panic, sweet." Kel sent a tendril of magic toward the shield, probed it delicately. "As usual, they underestimate me."

His years among the Magekind had taught him subtleties of spellcraft his own people didn't know. Dragon magic tended toward raw power rather than intricacy. If you could only pair the two, you ended up with the best of both worlds.

And Kel had learned to do just that.

He analyzed the patterns in the spell shield as Morgana Le Fay had taught him centuries ago, looking for weaknesses. It was so strong, he suspected the entire council of Dragon Lords had created it.

The trouble with that trick was that so many sources of magic could never blend smoothly. There were always seams, places where the spell wasn't quite . . .

There.

Kel found the fissure he was looking for and sent a jolt of power into it, forcing it wider, then wider still. Until, with a triumphant flick of his tail, he winged right through. He paused only long enough to seal the fissure again, then flew onward toward the cliffs. "We're in, Nineva."

He felt her weight shift, as if she was sitting back against the harness. "Thank Semira!" A moment later she shouted, "That was a nice bit of magic, Kel, the way you read that shield and pulled it apart. Do you think you could teach me?"

"I don't see why not. You've got the intelligence and will for it, and Cachamwri knows you've got the power. Not quite to dragon standards, maybe, but you've got more juice than many of the Majae I know."

She smiled, visibly pleased. "Thanks. That's high praise, coming from you."

Though he would have liked to reply to that compliment, Kel realized they'd just run out of time for pleasantries. Up ahead, their formerly invisible welcome wagon had become winged specks that were growing larger with every second. They'd picked up the pace, as if sensing that Kel had penetrated the wards.

"Brace yourself, Nineva," Kel called back. "Things are about to get a little lively."

"I was afraid those weren't birds, not with that kind of power. Are we about to have a fight on our hands?"

"Looks that way. Keep your head down and hang on."

"Do you know who they are?"

"Yes. It's my brothers."

Kel refused to run, so the two dragons caught up easily enough. They swooped and circled around him like a pair of territorial crows, eyeing Nineva with a malicious intensity that made her shift uneasily in her harness.

The blue was the bolder of the two, circling so recklessly close, Kel had to veer to avoid tangling their wings.

"So you're back again, bringing dishonor on the Bloodstone Clan." Irial sneered, his hatred as familiar and galling as a pair of old, too-tight shoes. Their mother had favored firstborn Kel, and Irial had always resented it. It seemed centuries of separation hadn't made his heart any fonder.

"Tegid is the one who dishonored the clan, not me," Kel growled, aware of Nineva's death grip on his harness. He dared a glance back at her and found her sitting pale and hunched. Her opalescent eyes were far too wide. Brave as she normally was, the dragons triggered all her worst fears. "He's the one who engineered our mother's murder and allied himself with the spawn of the Dark Ones. I simply challenged the bastard and killed him. Which is what you should have done, if you'd been any kind of son at all."

"You drove him to his crimes with your unnatural acts," Gruagh whined, circling well clear of them both, green wings flashing. Kel wasn't surprised to see him; he'd always been Irial's tagalong, following their brother's bullying lead. "If you'd stayed away from the humans, none of this would have happened. Everyone says so."

"Then everyone lacks the sense of an eggshell," Kel snapped back. "Tegid was vile and power-hungry from the day he was hatched."

"And you're a toady to humans." Irial sneered. "Look at you, harnessed like one of their burden beasts. Is that ape on your back this Gewin of yours?"

Kel laughed in genuine amusement. "His name is Gawain, and no. This is a woman, you ignorant egg-sucker. Princess Nineva of the Morven Sidhe. Cachamwri sent me to protect her."

Irial's red eyes narrowed in jealousy and suspicion. "You lie! Why would the Dragon God appear to the likes of you?"

"Because he knows he can trust me not to make a botch of things. Now get out of my air. We have words of importance for the Dragon Lords."

Gruagh hissed in contempt, looping around Kel and

Nineva as Irial circled in the opposite direction. It was, Kel knew, a potential attack pattern. "They'll not allow some filthy ape to sully their presence. You might as well go back where you came from."

Kel growled in frustration. He was wasting his time arguing with them, but he strongly suspected he wasn't going to get past them without a fight. "Nineva, armor up," he said in English. "We're going to have to make a run for it."

"What's their problem?" Her voice was just slightly too high as her weight increased. He knew without looking around that she'd conjured her armor and weapons.

"Basically, they're assholes." Seeing an opening in the pattern they'd created, Kel darted forward, pouring on the speed with a burst of magic. He shot between the startled dragons, who roared and beat after him.

Over the thunder of the wind, he heard Irial bellow, "Kill the human! We can at least keep him from trying to foist more of his perversion on the Dragon Lords."

Her heart in her throat, Nineva crouched against Kel's neck, trying to make herself as small a target as possible as the blue dragon roared toward them from behind. *Oh, God,* she thought as her belly knotted, *was this what I saw in my vision? Have I been afraid of the wrong dragon?*

Staring over her shoulder, she watched their foe beating his wings furiously as he fought to catch up. He gaped his jaws wide in the movement she'd seen so many times in her nightmares. A gout of flame shot out, right toward her horrified face . . .

Only to splash harmlessly away as it hit Kel's shield. The dragon roared, crimson eyes wild with rage. Eyes so like Kel's, but missing the kindness that filled her lover's gaze even in dragon form.

His brother shot closer, stretching out his talons, obviously meaning to shred her where she sat. Kel's shield might stop a magical attack, but it wouldn't do a damn thing against claws that would put Excalibur to shame.

Every drop of spit left Nineva's mouth as those huge talons drew closer. She conjured a spear and crouched low over Kel's back as she considered possible targets. One of those big red eyes might do. Punch the spear through into his brain, and . . .

Jaws gaped wide again, revealing jagged teeth the length of her forearm, barely a yard from her head. "Now, you little ape," the dragon hissed, its tone triumphant, "let's see how you taste . . ."

The world spun around her. She screamed in terror and clung desperately to her spear.

And realized she was hanging upside down from her harness. Kel had rolled like a jet fighter. Draconian voices roared, accompanied by the thunder of flame. There was a horrible grating sound of claws on scale. One of them shrieked, she couldn't tell which. Blood arced overhead, then fell to the ground in a rain of scarlet drops.

"She is mine!" Kel snarled, her spell translating his words. He rolled upright again, and Nineva clung to the harness as the blood left her head. "You touch her, Irial, and you'll die for it!"

The blue dragon hissed in pain from somewhere below them. "Perverted, unnatural *thing!*"

"At least I didn't stand by and let our mother die in a duel she had no business fighting. You could have stood for her, you coward!"

Cautiously, Nineva looked down. Blood ribboned from Irial's wing as he half-flapped, half-fell to the ground be-low like a huge, wounded bird. The green dragon spiraled after him to land anxiously by his side.

"Irial talks a good game, but fortunately he's never had the skill or the balls for a real fight," Kel told her. "I knew he'd try for you, the gutless little bully. And the minute he did, I had him."

Suddenly his attitude toward his fellow dragons made a lot more sense. "Are they all like that?"

"No. Some of them have the courage to back up their hate." He sounded grim. "Those are the ones we're going to have to watch out for."

They flew on in silence for several minutes while Nineva's racing heart slowed. Despite her frequent backward glances, no blue dragon reappeared, ready to burn her from the saddle or snatch her up like a greedy boy grabbing a cupcake. Gradually her shaking hands stilled.

"Why do they despise humans?" she asked, relaxing at last. And why didn't Kel share that bigotry? "I know you said dragons and Sidhe used to hunt each other, but that was thousands of years ago."

"When you live as long as we do, 'thousands of years ago' was your grandfather's time. Anyway, that was never the real issue."

"No?"

"Like a lot of immortals, the Dragonkind fear any kind of change. When I befriended Gawain fifteen hundred years ago, some of the younger ones got interested in going to Avalon, too. Their elders were afraid I was going to corrupt them with alien ways. Tegid tried to bully me into renouncing the humans, but I was far too stubborn for that."

"So he turned you into a sword."

"Exactly. He structured the spell so that my only escape was to kill Gawain. He figured that would make sure Arthur and company would turn on me. But Gawain had once saved me from a pack of Hellhounds when I was wounded, and I was damned if I'd repay him with death."

"You'd rather remain a prisoner for fifteen centuries."

"Exactly. But when I got free, I punched Uncle Tegid's ticket and sent him straight to hell." His voice rang with satisfaction.

Nineva winced. "We really are going to have our hands full convincing these lunatics to help us."

"Afraid so."

Anxiety knotted Nineva's stomach into more tangles than a fishing line as Kel soared toward the Dragon Cliffs. They looked as though someone had sliced the face off the mountain—a sheer expanse of ruddy stone, jagged and pockmarked with caves. Huge boulders lay at the foot of the mountain, and a great river meandered around it, gleaming bright in the sunlight.

Dragons were everywhere. Lazing in the sun like enormous sprawled cats, circling on vast spread wings, huge heads thrust from the mouths of caves. Their bodies shimmered like iridescent jewels as the sun gleamed on scales and horns and wings: gold, green, blue, red, and white.

And every one of them grew tense with alarm and hostility when they got a good look at Kel and realized who he was. They swooped toward one another like birds, gathered in hissing little knots as they watched him sail past.

Nineva crouched in her harness, her hand wet with sweat around her spear, and fought sick waves of fear. They could parboil her with fiery breath, snatch her from Kel's back with huge claws, crunch her like a crouton between sword teeth.

Kel turned his head to look at her. "I'm not going to let them hurt you."

"You're a little outnumbered at the moment." Yet the rock-solid certainty in his voice made Nineva feel a bit better. She knew he'd fight for her to his last breath. And a pissed-off Kel was nothing to sneeze at. Her fear abated slightly.

A green dragon darted up at them, making her tighten her hold on the spear. The translation spell Nineva had cast on herself when Kel's brothers attacked rendered his hissing into speech. "What are you doing here? I thought you'd thrown your lot in with the humans."

"Hey, Kel—you're bleeding," a red dragon called mockingly from one of the cliff's jutting ledges. "Been fighting already?"

"Yes, actually. And I won. Care to be next?" He actually sounded bored.

The green dragon veered hastily off.

They're afraid of him, Nineva realized. The thought was comforting. If the dragons feared him even when the odds were so obviously in their favor, they must have reason for it.

Then she frowned, processing what the red dragon had said. "You're hurt?"

"Irial caught me across the belly with his claws. It's nothing. Don't worry—I can still defend you."

Stung, she glowered at his horns, the only part of his face she could see. "I know you may not believe this, but I'm actually more worried about you. If you'll land, I can heal the injury."

"I'm fine." His voice was clipped.

"Yeah, right." She snorted. "Men."

He laughed, or perhaps it was a snort—it was hard to tell. "I'm not exactly a man."

"Oh, you're a man, no matter what form you're in." She eyed one of the circling dragons that looked as though it was working up the courage to fly closer. "Your head could be hanging half off and you'd say, 'It's nothing. I don't need to go to the doctor.' Or the Maja, or shaman, or fairy king, or whatever the hell the local equivalent is. Arrogant, bullheaded . . ."

"*I'm* bullheaded? Who insisted we come here, even when Arthur and I told you—"

"That was different." She wondered if she could hit that red dragon with her spear at this distance, then reluctantly decided against it. "You can't argue with a vision."

A deep male voice rumbled from behind them, startling her so badly she almost dropped the spear. "Kel, what in the name of the Egg are you doing here?"

Kel looked around calmly as Nineva tried to get her weapon pointed in the right direction. "Looking for you. Nineva, banish the toothpick. This is Soren, the dragon we came to see. He's the ambassador to Avalon."

Oh, sweet Semira, Nineva thought, getting a good look at the great beast who followed them, *not another blue dragon.*

He was a huge creature, even bigger than Kel, though his scales were paler than Kel's deep cobalt, with just a tinge of purple. Black horns jutted from his head, matching the spines that marched down his long body all the way to his tail.

"Perhaps we'd better adjourn to my cave, then," Soren said in a voice so deep, she could feel it in her breastbone. "Somehow I have the feeling this is not a conversation we want overheard."

He flew past, and Kel followed, his wings beating in long, unhurried strokes. Nineva hunkered down against his neck and tried to ignore all the hostile eyes she could feel boring holes in her back.

Two sets of multiple gashes ran the length of Kel's belly where the scales were silvery pale, framing a vicious bite mark wider than Nineva's shoulders. The wounds were deeper than the length of her fingers, and blood ran down his chest as he lay on his side. If he hadn't rolled during the fight, deliberately taking Irial's strike, she had no doubt she'd be dead.

Nineva took a deep breath and laid both hands over the bite. The Goddess Mark burned fiercely on her breast as she sent her magic pouring into the injuries. Dragon physiology was different from what she was used to, so she had to concentrate even harder than usual to sense how his body should heal. Distantly, she felt the wounds begin to knit under her spread fingers as the bleeding slowed and stopped.

"I'll say one thing for her, she's got power," Soren said. "I don't know many Majae who could have healed a set of wounds like that."

"She *is* the descendent of a goddess." Kel sounded re- markably like a proud lover.

"And Cachamwri told you to protect her?"

"Insisted on it. *And* told me to help her find this sword of hers."

The blue dragon grunted as he sat back on his haunches, the tip of his tail flicking restlessly. "And Grim's missing, too. That's bad. Very bad. Arthur must be snorting fire by now."

Finished at last, Nineva stepped back. Her knees wob- bled under her. Usually a healing made her feel exhila- rated, but there'd been an awful lot of Kel to heal.

"For Cachamwri's sake, sit down before you fall on your face," he growled. "I told you to let me take care of those. I've certainly healed worse."

"Yeah, well, I wanted to do it." Nineva looked around to see he'd conjured an armchair in the middle of Soren's cave. She collapsed into it. "Healing's what I do." Lately it seemed the only thing she had any success at. Goddess knew she'd been a bust at finding the sword.

"Tell me about this vision you had." Soren settled onto his belly as Kel sat up to wrap his tail around himself like a cat.

Nineva rubbed her aching forehead. The dragon's cave was lit with a green light that reminded her of the view through night-vision goggles on CNN. The sourceless emer- ald glow illuminated craggy walls and the ceiling that soared two hundred feet overhead. Here and there stood thick columns, marked with deep grooves that looked suspiciously like claw marks. Apparently Soren climbed them to reach the second level, which ran around the sides of the cave like a balcony.

"Nineva?" Kel prompted gently, reclaiming her wandering attention.

She cleared her throat and related what she'd seen—the Sidhe and Magekind, riding dragons into battle against the rebels and their Dark One allies.

"Cachamwri's Egg." It was a soft groan. Soren covered his muzzle with a clawed hand, his eyes closed in pain. "They'll never do it, Kel. Let humans *ride* them? They'd rather be tortured by Dark Ones."

"Getting tortured by Dark Ones is exactly what it's going to come to if those bastards invade." The tip of Kel's tail flicked restlessly.

"Perhaps, but the Dragon Lords will never believe it. I've served on that council for centuries now, and I've never been able to get them to even consider things a lot less humiliating than that."

Nineva frowned, remembering how they'd mocked Kel for letting her ride him. The idea of dragon-mounted warriors hadn't seemed so far-fetched—until the past couple of hours had taught her otherwise. "But Semira sent me that vision. It's going to happen."

Soren lowered his head until he was eye to eye with her. She managed not to shrink back in her chair, though his head was taller than her entire body. "Semira is not our goddess, Nineva. And even if she was, they'd never believe a half-breed Sidhe."

"Soren," Kel growled, his voice rumbling with warning.

"You know that's how they'll see her. At least we have some history with the Sidhe—Cachamwri proclaimed them our allies. But you can smell the human blood in this one. And that, to our people, will make her safe to hate."

Nineva rose restlessly from her chair and began to pace in front of the two towering dragons. "I don't doubt you're right—and frankly, the thought of confronting a bunch of bigoted dragons makes my stomach hurt. But the rebels have Grim and the sword, and they're working on breaking the planetary wards. We can't afford to sit by and let that happen without doing something to stop it."

"I'm not sure if she's got courage or a suicidal streak," Soren said to Kel.

"Oh, it's about seventy percent courage." His muzzle stretched into something that looked like the dragon version of a dry smile. "The rest is pure, unadulterated bull-headedness."

Before Nineva could formulate a suitable retort, the beat of huge wings drew her wary attention to the mouth of the cave.

A white dragon rustled inside, eyes huge with excitement, tail lashing. "Soren, is it true? Is Kel here?"

Soren laughed, a deep rumble. "Yes, Eithne, Kel is back." To his guests, he added, "Eithne is my protégée. she's fascinated by all things human, and hopes to be allowed to visit Avalon—once she can talk her clan into allowing it, anyway."

"They are so . . . blind." Nineva's translation spell rendered the dragon's voice as breathy, female, and a bit young. It reminded her of a college coed—and sounded really strange coming from a creature who had to be a good thirty feet long. "I'm not a fledgling anymore, but you'd think I just escaped my egg, the way they take on."

Nineva stepped warily aside as Eithne crossed the cave to Kel. Big as she was, she looked almost dainty next to his massive strength. There was a certain elegance of line to the shape of her head, and her neck was graceful and long, putting Nineva in mind of a swan. Instead of the males' black horns, a pair of fan-shaped frills stood on either side of her head like an exotic hat. Her tail flicked eagerly as she stared up at Kel with what looked uncomfortably like hero worship. "Soren's told me much of your adventures among the humans," she said in that coed voice. "I saw you fight your uncle when you were last here, but you left before I could speak to you. I was very impressed."

Kel looked taken aback, as if he wasn't sure how to deal with the sudden acquisition of a dragon groupie. "I'm . . . sorry I missed you."

I'll just bet you are. Nineva's eyes widened as the implications of her waspish thought registered. *Wait a minute—am I jealous of a thirty-foot lizard?*

Kel gestured at her. "This is Princess Nineva of the Morven Sidhe. She's here to address the Dragon Lords."

Eithne's head swung quickly, following his pointing claw. Her eyes widened as she spotted Nineva. "That's a human? I didn't get a good look at the ones who were with you before." She rustled closer, dipping her great head until they were almost eye to eye. Pride wouldn't let Nineva retreat, despite her clamoring instincts. "But it's so . . . small! The way everyone talks, I assumed they'd be much bigger."

"Hello," Nineva said stiffly. Her translation spell turned her words into what she hoped was the appropriate hiss.

"It talks!" The she-dragon laughed with delight, almost blowing Nineva back on her heels.

"Of course she talks," Kel said, giving Nineva a nervous look. "Among other things."

"Many other things," Nineva growled. The spell gave the sentence a gratifying rumble.

Eithne drew her head up in surprise. "Oh. Well." She blinked huge round eyes. "Perhaps you can tell me about life among your people." She spoke slowly, raising her voice slightly, as one might to someone of dubious intelligence. "I hear your ways are very . . . different from ours."

Nineva bared her teeth. "That's a safe bet."

Soren produced a sound the translator rendered as a strangled snort of laughter. He cleared his throat. "Well,

Eithne, it might be best if you run along. I'm going to have to summon the Dragon Lords and attempt to arrange an audience for Kel and Nineva."

The white dragon swung her head toward him and gave him a limpid look. "I'd be happy to entertain your guests while you're occupied, Soren." Her tail flicked eagerly, then stole over to touch the tip of Kel's. He looked around at it, startled. "I would much enjoy hearing Kel speak of his centuries in Avalon."

"I don't think your clan mothers would approve of my leaving you alone with our guests just now, Eithne. Perhaps later." Soren gave her shoulder a nudge with his nose. "Off with you, then. We'll talk later."

"But Soren . . ."

"Eithne."

"Oh, very well." The white dragon moved toward the cave entrance. "But only because I don't want my brothers to jump Kel." She gave him a downright flirtatious look over one shoulder. "He'd probably hurt them."

With that, she launched herself out of the cave with a lithe spring, like a cat leaping onto a countertop.

"Unfortunately, I doubt it would be quite that easy," Soren told Kel. "She has a great many brothers."

"Red Rock Clan, right?"

"That's the one."

"They do produce beautiful females."

"And touchy, bloodthirsty males, a fact you should keep in mind." Soren gave Nineva a look. "Besides, I have the distinct impression you've got your hands full as it is." He headed for the entrance, forcing Nineva to step aside for his enormous tail. "I'll go summon the Lords, though you probably shouldn't expect me back too soon. It's going to take me time to talk them into seeing you."

"Good luck, Soren," Kel told him. "And thank you, whichever way it goes."

The blue dragon grunted and threw himself into the air.

Nineva waited until she thought he'd flown out of earshot. "What's the Draconian word for 'jailbait'?"

"Nineva, she's eight hundred years old." Magic flared around Kel, and he was human again, dressed in his familiar jeans and black T-shirt. A knot of tension deep inside her immediately loosened.

"Which is what? The equivalent of sixteen in human years?"

He sauntered over, giving her a wicked grin. "More like twenty-five. Are you jealous, Nineva?"

"Why would I be jealous of a giant reptile?" She folded her arms and glowered. "I just don't like being talked about as if I'm a somewhat dim toy poodle. 'Oh, it's so tiny! And it talks!' Bite me, jailbait."

Kel laughed and pulled her into his arms. "That would hurt. A lot."

Nineva sniffed. "I could take her."

"I don't doubt it." His handsome mouth curled up into a smile. "You certainly took me."

Then he dipped his head and found her mouth with his.

FOURTEEN

Nineva's lips felt like rose petals and tasted of mint. They opened against Kel's, welcoming his questing tongue. She melted into him, her soft breasts pillowing against his chest, her arms tightening around his waist.

It was a good thing she hadn't known Eithne was coming into season. That was why the white dragon had been so sexually aggressive, and why her brothers wouldn't have wanted her coming anywhere near Kel.

Yet the truly amazing thing was that even with Eithne pumping dragon pheromones into the air, all he'd been able to think about was Nineva. He'd been preoccupied with the fear in her scent, the way she struggled to hide it and show a brave face to the huge, threatening creatures that surrounded her. When he'd sensed her growing jealousy, it had actually been a relief. At least jealousy was better than fear.

Not to mention oddly gratifying.

Yeah, he thought, still kissing her hungrily, *I've got it bad. But she's not immune to me either.*

Hunger infused her scent now, teasing his own growing

arousal. "I've got to touch you." She banished her armor to stand against him in jeans and a lacy camisole, as if not quite brave enough for nudity. He reached down and cupped her toned little backside in one hand. She responded by hooking one long leg over his hip and boosting herself up, climbing him like a tree. Something about the raw desire in the act sent lust stabbing through him. "Cachamwri's Egg, Nineva," he gasped against her mouth.

"Can we do this?" she murmured back, wrapping her legs more tightly around his waist. "Do we have time?"

"They'll argue and bitch for the next hour at least." Kel nuzzled beneath her chin, bit gently. "And in the meantime . . ." He reached for his magic and surrounded them with an invisibility spell.

She responded with a moan, fisting both hands in his T-shirt, hauling it upward. They both groaned as she found bare skin with those small, soft hands. "We really shouldn't be doing this, making love in your friend's cave. It's tacky."

"Tacky is a human concept." He shuttered his eyes as she found his small male nipples with her clever fingers. He returned the favor, slipping one hand under the hem of her camisole.

She hadn't conjured a bra. Her round, soft breast filled his palm with warmth and sweet femininity. He lifted her higher and found its rosy tip with his mouth. Savored her groan as he savored her taste. Magic and sex.

He danced his tongue over the hard peak, gave it a gentle, teasing nibble. Closed his mouth to suckle. She threw back her head, and the silk of her hair danced over his bare arm as he supported her bottom.

"Am I too heavy?" she gasped.

"You've got to be kidding." His shape-shifted Draconian muscle barely felt her weight at all.

Responsibility reared its head, made him frown. "Should you cast that spell again?"

"If you think I'm going to stop and spend an hour drawing Sidhe power patterns on the floor, you're out of your mind." She ground against him and bit her lower lip. "Besides, I want this time to be for us. Just us."

"Just us," he repeated, and banished their clothing. The sensation of his rock-hard erection pressing against her down-soft belly made heat flood his balls. "Nineva," he whispered hoarsely.

She ground against him again as her eyes met his, bright and laughing. "I gave serious thought to scratching that lizard's eyes out."

He laughed. "You couldn't reach them."

"I'm resourceful. I'd have found a way." Nineva kissed him, slowly, thoroughly, tangling her hands in his long cobalt hair.

He held her like that, loving the satin warmth of her, loving the delicious, teasing anticipation of that tight, wet sex so close to his aching cock. Loving the mint and magic of her mouth.

When they finally came up for air, they were both panting. She clung to him, looking up into his eyes. The opalescent swirl of her gaze was dizzying, as if he was staring into infinity. "What are we?" She brushed a lock of his hair back, as if to see his face better. "What are we to each other?"

He went still. There was something in her face, something he hadn't expected to see. Something beyond duty or desire or even friendship. His heart began to pound with something more than arousal. "What do you want to be?"

"I think . . ." She stopped and swallowed. His eyes focused helplessly on her mouth. "I think I'm falling in love with you."

He stared at her, stunned to stillness.

"Is that stupid? Tell me if it's stupid."

"I thought you were afraid of me."

She smiled, a bare twitch of the lips. "Now, *that* was

stupid." Her grip on his neck tightened convulsively, as with sudden anxiety. "You haven't answered."

"I'm in love with you." He didn't bother with a hedging *I think*. He knew. He'd known for days.

"But you're a dragon, and I'm . . ." She didn't finish, but the complex emotion in her gaze made him wonder what she had in mind. Sidhe? Semira's Avatar? *Doomed?*

"I don't care." Fiercely. His hands tightened on her bottom, and he lifted her, poised her over his hard cock. "It's what we are together that matters."

He rolled his hips up and brought her down, and hilted himself in one breathtaking plunge.

Nineva threw back her head and screamed in a blend of shock and delight. It was almost too much, that sudden impalement, yet at the same time it was deliciously arousing in its very ruthlessness.

Kel cupped both hands around her backside and lifted her to the perfect height, then started to grind in and out. Helpless, she clung to his brawny, sweating shoulders, glorying in their mutual need.

Even in this position, his torso was longer than hers, and she had to look up to see his face. His crimson eyes were wide, wild, intent, and a muscle flexed furiously in his jaw with the effort of his sawing thrusts. His sensual mouth was folded in a tight line.

Every time he drove himself into her, her sex clenched at the sweetly brutal pounding. She writhed against him, not sure whether she wanted to protest or beg for more.

Then he did something, some clever roll of the hips, and suddenly he started hitting exactly the right spot. Each thrust became a spike of delight that wound her building orgasm tighter and tighter in a creamy ball of heat.

She threw back her head with a shout and started grinding against him, arching back in his strong arms, trying to get that last little bit of friction that would shoot her over the edge. Yet it remained frustratingly out of reach . . .

Until suddenly he changed his grip on her ass and traced a finger between her lips. And made contact.

The detonation of her orgasm was silent and blinding, a white-hot blast that tore a scream of raw pleasure from her mouth. As she convulsed, her entire body clamping, he stiffened and roared. Deep inside her body, she felt the hot jets of his pleasure.

And somewhere in the distance, she sensed the goddess's power flare bright. *"Ah, yessss . . ."*

Nineva sprawled across Kel's panting chest and concentrated on breathing. He'd conjured an enormous feather tick a moment ago and dumped them both onto it as if his muscles had suddenly given out.

For a long moment, she thought nothing at all, her mind deliciously blanked by pleasure. She felt boneless, euphoric. At peace, despite the Dark Ones' imminent invasion, despite the need to convince xenophobic Dragon Lords to help. As if she and Kel were up to any challenge, as long as they were together. Too many years of being her father's daughter told her that was a dangerous delusion, yet she didn't care. Not when she could hear his heartbeat against her chest, solid and strong.

Nineva wondered exactly when she'd fallen for him. Love seemed to have crept up on her while she'd been busy doing other things. He'd built it bit by bit from steamy passion and comforting touches, from his willingness to believe the unbelievable, from the rage in his eyes whenever anyone threatened her. He'd shed blood for her without a second thought, taken blows that would have killed her. Who wouldn't love him?

The only question was, why did he love her? Oh, by human standards, she was pretty enough, but Nineva suspected Eithne was the Draconian equivalent of a raving beauty, at least judging by the startled look in Kel's eyes when she'd flown in. And Eithne had the added advantage of being the right species.

Yet against all logic, Kel loved Nineva anyway. She didn't even question that. It had been there in his eyes when he'd said the words, unmistakable as a shout.

Kel, Dragon Knight of the Round Table, loved her. She, who'd never been loved by any man because she'd never let any man get that close.

But then, Kel hadn't exactly asked permission.

A big, warm hand came up and cupped her cheek, tilted her head until she met his eyes. "Are you okay?"

She gave him what she suspected was a catlike smile. "Oh, I'm *much* better than merely okay."

A faint frown formed between his cobalt brows. "Are you sure? I was a little rough there at the end. I got carried away. I'm sorry."

"Don't be." She rolled over and stretched, smiling in sated pleasure. "It was wonderful."

"Good." He smiled, but there was something a little troubled in his eyes.

"What's wrong?"

"Did you mean it?" He searched her gaze.

She didn't have to ask what. "Yes, I meant it." She brushed his hair back. "I love you, Kel. I don't know what's going to happen between us, I don't know if we're going to get some kind of happily-ever-after, but I know how I feel now. And it's something I've never felt before."

He searched her gaze a moment before his crimson eyes lit with such joy, she had to smile back. "You mean it."

"Oh, yeah."

His smile warmed her to the bone. "I love you, too."

"Good, because feeling this way alone would really suck."

Kel's laughter boomed through the cave.

* * *

Knowing they were running out of time, Nineva conjured her armor again. From the sound of it, she needed all the protection she could get before meeting with the Dragon Lords. Kel returned to dragon form while she tried not to wish he could remain human. It was painfully apparent that wouldn't be politically wise.

Even so, she thought his expression softened as he looked down at her from his Draconian height. "I won't let anything happen to you, Nineva."

She forced a smile. "I know you won't."

The thunder of wings drew their attention to the mouth of the cave. "Are you decent?" Soren called from somewhere outside.

Nineva shot Kel a mischievous glance. " 'Decent' doesn't do it justice."

"Bad girl," he murmured, then lifted his voice. "Yes, we're ready."

"Good." Soren touched down in the cave mouth, though he kept his wings spread for takeoff. "I talked them into meeting with you by invoking Cachamwri's name, but we don't want to keep them waiting. I don't know how long their patience is going to hold."

Kel crouched and boosted Nineva astride across his back with a clawed forelimb. "I thought it best not to wear a harness this time," he murmured for her ears only. "Can you manage bareback?"

"I'll give it my best shot." She settled herself into place at the base of his neck, hooking her legs over his shoulders and wrapping both hands around one of the spines that jutted from her neck. Her heart started pounding as he moved toward the cave entrance. By an effort of sheer will, she managed not to scream as he threw himself from the cave and dropped like a stone into the bright morning sunlight. Just as her stomach stuffed her mouth, his spread wings finally caught the air. They soared upward, borne on thermals and magic.

They didn't go far, spiraling upward a thousand feet or so before following Soren into another cave mouth. This one was even wider than his own, as though created to allow multiple dragons to take off and land.

It was dark inside the cave after the sunlit flight upward, and Nineva couldn't see a damn thing as she clung nervously to Kel's warm back. When her vision finally cleared, she realized they were moving down a long tunnel lit by that dim green light the dragons seemed to favor. Like Soren's cave, the tunnel was obviously artificial, with smooth rounded sides that made it look as if it had been cut by a huge drill bit. It sloped gradually downward, curving off into the dim green light. The Dragon Lords must meet deep inside the mountain.

Neither dragon spoke as they walked, their claws clicking on the stone, their breathing deep. Nineva could hear the faint whisper of scale rubbing on stone as they moved. Something about that sound made her sharply aware of being a mammal alone among huge reptiles. She was grateful all over again for Kel's solid, comforting presence.

He wouldn't let anything happen to her.

They rounded a bend, and a light appeared at the end of the tunnel. Draconian voices rose in argument.

". . . could this creature possibly have to say that would be worth hearing?"

"At least it should be entertaining."

"If Cachamwri told Kel to guard this female, we would be ill-advised to refuse to listen to her."

"I'm not convinced the god said any such thing. Kel's probably lying."

Kel growled at that, a deep rippling rumble of rage.

"Why would he do that?"

"Probably out of some worm-witted desire to force us to have contact with those disgusting pets of his."

"Oh, yeah," Nineva murmured to Kel in dry sarcasm. "This is going to be a piece of cake."

"Better put her down," Soren whispered before Kel could reply. "I don't think it's a good idea for her to ride you into the chambers."

"Good point." Kel hunkered down and lifted a foreleg. She gingerly planted her foot in his clawed hand and dismounted. When she stood on her booted feet again, she took a deep breath and squared her shoulders, aware of Kel's worried gaze. "You ready?" he asked.

"Yeah." It was a lie, but she forced a smile anyway and strode into the chamber beyond. Kel and Soren followed, looming at her back like a pair of dragon bookends.

It was one of her better attempts at bravado, but she almost ruined it with a gasp as she got a good look at the chamber.

It was even vaster than she'd expected, an echoing egg-shaped space the size of a football stadium. Twelve dragons in shades of gold, red, blue, and green lay on a curving stone ledge that took up the other end of the chamber. Their eyes gleamed like cats'.

In the center of the ledge lay a huge, glowing egg. It radiated magic in waves that seemed to thrum against Nineva's senses. "What the hell is that?" she whispered to Kel.

"Cachamwri's Egg," he whispered back.

"You mean it actually exists?" She gaped at him. "I thought it was a figure of speech!"

"Oh, it's a lot more than that. It's the embodiment of the Dragon God's power among us."

While they'd been talking, Soren slipped forward and made a complicated snaking dip of his long neck in the Egg's direction. Then he turned and climbed the ledge to settle his great body into the one empty spot among his fellow Dragon Lords.

The dragon who sat closest to the Egg lifted his golden head. "Kel of the Bloodstone Clan would address the Dragon Lords?"

"Stay here," Kel murmured to Nineva, then rustled over

to repeat Soren's neck dip to the Egg before drawing himself to his full height. "I come accompanied by Nineva Morroc, Princess of the Morven Sidhe and Last Avatar of the Goddess Semira." He looked back at her, and she hurried forward, her mouth dry.

Unsure what to do about the Egg—after all, Cachamwri wasn't *her* god—she dipped a full court curtsy, her armor clanking. "My thanks for your willingness to hear my petition, Dragon Lords."

The golden dragon grunted, then turned to address Kel. "You claim Cachamwri instructed you to protect this creature?"

"Yes, Lord Piaras. He approached me wearing a guise of flame and told me to find the princess and the Sword of Semira."

"Sword of . . . ? I have never heard of this." Piaras reared back, looking down his long nose at Kel in arrogant disbelief.

"There's no reason you should have," Nineva said. "It's a holy object of the Morven Sidhe people that is inhabited by our goddess, Semira."

"This is absurd," a red dragon snapped. "Why should Cachamwri care about some foreign goddess? This is some plot of yours, Kel, intended to embarrass the Dragon Lords again. Like that business with the Dark Ones' spawn."

"That was Tegid's plot, not mine," Kel grated. "I make no plots. I only serve Cachamwri as my duty demands."

"The sword has been stolen by rebels in league with the Dark Ones," Nineva said hastily. "Along with Merlin's Grimoire. It's our belief the rebels intend to use the two objects to crack the planetary wards that keep the Dark Ones from invading. If that were to happen, all our people—Sidhe, Dragonkind, and human—would be at their mercy."

"Lies," the red dragon snarled. "The wards are just as they've always been. You are attempting to trick us into some involvement with your ape ways."

A rumble of agreement rose from the other dragons, who stared at them with anger and suspicion.

"What would I gain from such a deception?" she demanded. "As to the wards being solid—that's because the rebels haven't broken them yet. If you wait until they're destroyed, it will be too late for us all."

"The wards draw their power from the Earth itself," another of the dragons said. "It would be impossible for a gang of Sidhe rebels to break them. And with such pitiful weapons—a sword and some alien book? Preposterous."

"If Cachamwri indeed wished us to take some action, he would tell us so." Piaras gestured at the Egg. "We have the very manifestation of his power right here. He would not send some ape with such a vital message."

"Aye," Draconian voices rumbled. "It's so!"

"The creature surely lies. Kel brought her here because he wishes to shame us again."

Kel and Nineva exchanged a hooded glance. He'd been right, she realized. This was an utter waste of time.

An hour later, she and Kel walked from the chamber, leaving Soren to continue arguing their case.

"They're not going to listen to him, either." Nineva scraped her hair back from her face, feeling battered with discouragement. The three of them had tried every argument they could think of, but the Dragon Lords greeted each one with ridicule.

"No." Kel sounded as exhausted as she felt. "They're too afraid of looking weak or stupid to the clans they lead. Among the Dragonkind, that sort of thing can get you killed, since a weak leader will soon find himself challenged by someone younger and more ambitious."

"I gather we're not talking about an electoral challenge?" Nineva asked drily.

"More like a battle to the death. In fact, *I* could have taken Tegid's seat on the Lords after I killed him."

"Why didn't you? No taste for Draconian politics?"

"That, and no desire whatsoever to live among the Dragonkind."

Nineva snorted. "After what I've seen the last couple of hours, I can understand that."

Kel boosted her astride his back, walked to the cave mouth, and leaped out into a long, swooping dive. Nineva was too dispirited to flinch, despite the sickening drop.

The cliffs were lined with dragons, watching them with hostility and suspicion. Some of them hurled catcalls. She fought to ignore them. "For the first time, I'm glad my father's dead."

Kel glanced back at her, a Draconian frown on his muzzle. "What the hell do you mean by that?"

"The only thing I was born to do, and I keep fucking it up." She knotted her hands into frustrated fists and beat them against one of his spines. "I lost the sword, I can't power the goddess, I can't even *find* either of them. Now Merlin's Grimoire is gone, too, and *the fucking Dragonkind won't listen to us.*" That last was a snarl of raw rage. "Nothing I do is working, Kel."

"So what you're saying is, *I'm* a fuckup."

"What—you? No, I meant—"

"But we're partners, right? Cachamwri told me to protect you and recover the sword. I haven't, so by your reasoning . . ."

"You and I both know Arthur Pendragon would not make a fuckup a Knight of the Round Table."

"And I assure you, a Knight of the Round Table would not let himself be partnered with one, either." He aimed a glare at a male dragon who darted too close. The other immediately lost his courage and veered off. Kel continued, "If I thought you were that kind of liability, I would pat you on your little head and leave you back at Avalon with lots of my friends to keep an eye on you. Then I'd go off to find your goddess. Since I have not done that, you are obviously not a liability."

He spread his wings and came in for a landing in Soren's cave, his muscled legs bending to absorb the impact. Nineva was already scrambling down from his neck. "Then why the hell do we keep failing?"

"A lack of instant success does not make you a failure, Nineva. Quitting makes you a failure, and I know you too well to think you're going to quit."

"Fine. It's not over till it's over. Insert stirring speech here, rah rah." She stalked into the cave. "But that still doesn't answer the question of what the hell do we do now? The Dragon Lords don't believe us, they're not going to help us, and the Dark Ones are going to invade. We have to do something."

He followed, his expression thoughtful. "Maybe not."

"What, we wait to become Purina Demon Chow?"

Kel sighed and sat back on his haunches, flipping his tail around his feet. "Sweet, I've been at this a long time, and I've found that when you've done all you can and it doesn't work, it's because your timing is bad. Sometimes when you wait and try again, the opportunity you need falls into your hands."

"But what if it doesn't, Kel?"

"It will." He shrugged. "Or we're screwed. At this point, those are our only two options."

FIFTEEN

Nineva still looked so unconvinced—and thoroughly miserable with it—that he was about to try comforting her in human form when a soft voice interrupted. "Kel? Are you in there?"

He grimaced. Just what he didn't need with Nineva in meltdown—an amorous young dragon honing her skills at flirtation. Unfortunately, females in season were prone toward flights of melodrama, and he knew trying to get rid of Eithne would probably just set her off. "Yes, we're here, Eithne."

She came in for a featherlight landing that spoke of both youth and agility. Her large blue eyes scanned the cave anxiously as her tail lashed like an agitated cat's. "Are we alone?"

Kel managed not to sigh. "Nineva's here." Maybe Eithne would display a little sensitivity.

She made a dismissive gesture. "As long as Soren's not, I don't care."

Standing by his side, Nineva rolled her eyes. "Just pretend I'm not here."

Kel gave the toe of her boot a brush with his tail tip, a gesture meant to comfort. *Patience, darling.* "What do you want, Eithne?"

She moved toward him, her white scales almost glowing in the light of the cave. "I want to go with you, Kel. To Avalon." Seeing him open his mouth to explain just how impossible that was, she stretched out a foreleg in a pleading gesture. "I can't bear it here any longer. I feel as if I'm suffocating under endless layers of expectation and tradition."

"Eithne, you know I wouldn't be allowed to take you with me, even if I thought it was a good idea. Your clan is just not going to permit it."

"But all the females talk about is their eggs and their young and trying to teach their young to fly and hunt and cast spells." Passion lit her great blue eyes. "I don't care about any of that! I want to see Avalon. I want to meet humans and have adventures!"

"Yeah, well, sometimes adventures suck," Nineva muttered.

Eithne looked down at her. Hostility flared in that pretty blue gaze before she returned her attention to Kel. "They say you mate with her. Is it true?"

"And you think this is your business why?" Nineva growled, glowering.

Eithne just growled, apparently reading her answer in his face. "It *is* true." She wheeled away with an angry flick of her tail. "I cannot believe this! I am one of your own kind. I'm in season! And you reject me for this . . . ape!"

Nineva's eyes narrowed. "In season? As in . . ."

"Hormones," Kel snapped. To the dragon he added, "I'm not rejecting you, Eithne. I simply know it won't work. Your clan . . ."

"And mating with this creature *would* work? She's not even our kind!"

Nineva folded her arms and looked up at Kel. "You know, for somebody so enlightened when it comes to interspecies relationships, her bigoted streak is awfully close to the surface."

Eithne curled her lip and took a menacing step toward her small rival. "It's not bigoted to know when something's unnatural!"

Kel decided he'd had enough. "Eithne, get out."

"Kel . . ."

"Now!" It was a full-throated roar.

Eithne gave him a wounded look, then whirled to fling herself from the cave. Kel and Nineva stood silent, listening to the angry beat of her wings.

"You think she's got a point?" Nineva's voice was very quiet.

Kel snorted. "She's full of shit."

"But look at us!" She turned to face him. "I barely come to your elbow."

"At the moment. I could change that in five seconds flat."

"But that's just magic."

"No, it's reality. And we're damn lucky we can change it to accommodate how we feel." He made a hissing sound of pure frustration. "Look, you said you loved me. Did you mean it?"

She spread her hands in a gesture of helplessness. "Of course, but it's not that easy. For one thing, we've only known each other for one high-pressure week, which we spent either fighting for our lives or fucking like bunnies. How do we know this is real?"

"Nineva, I'm almost two thousand years old. I know how I feel. And I know that this"—he thrust out a scaled claw—"doesn't mean shit. Most of my life, I was a piece of metal, but I was still me. I'm me when I'm a dragon, and I'm me when I'm human. And I know exactly what I want. You're it. Now the only real question is—what do *you* want?"

* * *

Nineva stared up into his magnificent, alien face. And realized he was right. It didn't really matter what form he wore. "I want you."

"Good. Remember that."

"Kel? Nineva?" The question sounded over the heavy thump of a big body landing. Soren walked in, looking dispirited and shaking his head.

Nineva wasn't even surprised. "So what now?"

"I keep working on them. Maybe sheer persistence will wear them down." The big dragon flung himself down on his back and extended his wings as though trying to rid them of a cramp. They stretched from one cave wall to the other. "It would probably be best if you and Kel headed back to Avalon and continued . . . whatever it is your goddess needs you to do."

Kel nodded. "We've certainly done all we can do here." He cut a wary glance toward the cave entrance. Three or four dragons circled just beyond it, peering inside with obvious hostility. "And frankly, I think we've pushed our welcome just about as far as we can. We need to get the hell out of here before one of those idiots starts something I have to finish."

So they thanked Soren for his efforts, mounted up, and flew off, both trying to ignore the cold, hostile dragon eyes that watched them leave.

Nineva was glad of her armor.

Some time later, Kel's voice broke the silence that had fallen dismally between them. "We're through the Dragon Lands' wards now. I could gate the rest of the way back to Avalon, but I'd like to fly a little longer. Burn off some frustration. Unless you'd rather . . . ?"

"No, that's fine. It feels good up here." And it did, with the afternoon sun just warm enough on her armored shoulders. Far below them, the ground spread out in a rolling quilt of winter-bare trees and half-frozen rivers, looking like a Christmas miniature at this altitude.

It was pleasant having nothing to do, particularly given that she knew the moment they arrived home, they'd be plunged back into the frantic race to find Grim, Semira, and the sword.

And Nineva was so damned tired. She'd adjusted to Avalon's vampire hours, and her body insisted she should have been in bed long ago. "I'm wrecked," she groaned.

"So get some sleep."

"I'll fall."

Kel snorted. "Give me a break."

Nineva smiled slightly, knowing what he meant: he'd never *let* her fall. So she slumped in her sun-warmed armor and let her eyes drift shut. A moment later, she felt the ghostly touch of a spell taking hold, holding her upright in the harness he'd earlier conjured for her. Comforted, she allowed herself to drift down into sleep.

Her dreams were jumbled, chaotic with images of angry dragons and Dark Ones rampaging through Times Square. She woke barely half an hour later with a pounding heart and palms gone sweat-damp inside her gauntlets.

Peering around as they flew, she gradually began to relax. Everything looked at peace. Below them was a majestic canyon cut by the snaking silver blade of a river. The water foamed white in rapids as it crashed over great boulders, sending up sprays of droplets that glinted in the sunlight. Trees crowded the river edge or jutted from the canyon walls at strange angles.

A bald eagle cut slow circles in an updraft, scanning for its next meal. Without warning, it stooped, shooting downward like an arrow, then arcing skyward again. Silver scales flashed as a fish lashed helplessly in its talons.

A smile of pure pleasure curled Nineva's mouth. "Kel, did you see—"

"Traitor!" The blast of malevolent satisfaction brought

her jerking around so fast, she'd have fallen if not for her harness. The blue dragon appeared out of thin air, his jaws opening, a plume of magical flame shooting right at her face.

Nineva's shield popped into place without conscious thought. The deadly blast boiled over it, only to roll off like water. Kel twisted beneath her, his wings spreading wide as he braked and spun away.

"Irial!" Rage rumbled in his voice. "I told you what I'd do if you tried to hurt her again!"

"You should have thought of that before you stole the Egg!" Irial shot after him, his jaws snapping a fraction from the tip of Kel's tail. "You've done it now, brother! You'll be hunted down like the blasphemer you are. I'll be only the first to spill your blood . . ."

"What the hell is he talking about?" Nineva clung dizzily to her harness as Kel twisted and bit at Irial as he sped by. The other dragon roared in pain.

"Looks like I'm the one who spilled the blood." Kel lunged for his brother's throat.

A sensation of massing power dragged Nineva's eyes skyward just in time to see six more dragons appear. They'd apparently worn some kind of invisibility spell. "Kel! There are more of them!" She conjured a fireball and sent it shooting at the newcomers, but it went wide as Kel closed with Irial for another raking pass.

Blood splashed across Nineva's face, blinding and sticky. She scrubbed it from her eyes. "Kel, dammit, *look up!*"

"Shit!" Kel snarled, finally spotting their attackers. He folded his wings and fell toward the river below, stooping just as the eagle had.

The six dragons shot after them, their wings beating the air in thunderous flaps, their eyes wild with fury. Almost at Kel's tail, Irial dove in pursuit, talons reaching. Nineva fired off another blast and had the satisfaction of seeing it hit him. Irial yelped, tossing his head at the pain. "Ape, you're going to pay for that!"

"*I'm not an ape!*" The Goddess Mark began to burn as Nineva's power rose. The fireball she conjured this time was so hot, she felt it even through her gauntlets. She shot it at him, forcing him to jerk aside. He lost control and tumbled.

But the rest of the dragons were gaining, growing ever closer to Kel's whipping tail. "Speed it up!" Nineva cried, conjuring another fireball and shooting it at the nearest pursuer. "We're about to get toasted!"

The leader, a big gold, opened his jaws. Something began to glow white hot down in the darkness of his maw. Nineva threw up a shield . . .

Suddenly she was hanging head-down in her harness. She swallowed a scream, realizing Kel had dived into a loop. The dragons shot past even as he came up behind them—and gave them a furious rolling blast of magical fire. Several cried out, startled, but they didn't burn. They didn't even look hurt.

"That was a warning shot," Kel called in a battleground roar. "What maggot lie has my brother fed you to make you attack us?"

"It's no lie." The leader banked and shot toward them again. "What have you done with the Egg, thief?"

"What egg?" Kel sounded as bewildered as Nineva felt.

"Don't bother playing innocent, Kel." The gold's eyes narrowed as he and Kel circled each other. "Cachamwri's Egg. I don't feel it on you—you must have hidden it. Where? Tell us now, and perhaps we'll let you live."

Nineva's jaw dropped in horror. "Oh, sweet Semira—the rebels must have stolen it!" Remembering the raw power she'd felt in the mystical object, she went cold. Between it, the sword, and the Grimoire, the rebels would have everything they'd need to break the planet's wards.

Kel shot her an equally horrified look. He snapped his head around and roared, "You idiots! The Egg goes missing, and you automatically chase me while the real thieves get away? How blind stupid can you be? If you don't sense the Egg, *it's because I don't have it!*"

The gold dragon looked taken aback, as if the very vehemence of Kel's protest had made him doubt.

"He's lying." Irial whipped in close to the leader as the whole group swirled in a frenzy around Kel and Nineva. "He and the ape hid it somewhere. Let's kill them, and we'll hunt the Egg at our leisure."

"Be silent," the gold snapped. To Kel he added, "You'd better confess. All of Dragonkind is right behind us. If you tell us how to find the Egg, it will go easier for you."

"We don't have the Egg!" Kel flew in close to pace the leader. The snap of Irial's teeth forced him to twist away. "Think—why would we have hidden it, then gone sailing along where we could be easily caught? We'd have gated off with it, exactly as the true thief did!"

"The other ape must have it—that Gawain of his," another dragon cried. "Kel and this one are decoys, assigned to trick us!"

A great roar dragged Nineva's attention away from the surrounding pack toward the mouth of the canyon. Her eyes widened. "Holy hell!"

Dragons. A huge writhing cloud of them, flooding along the canyon like a river of multicolored scales, growing larger with every beat of their wings.

Her heart climbed into her throat. They'd rip her and Kel apart. And if past attitudes were any indication, there was no way to talk sense into them. The mob would discover the truth only after the two of them were dead.

Automatically, Nineva started to cast a gate, only to hear one of the dragons howl in rage. "They're trying to escape!" The circling six darted in. Plumes of fire splashed against the magical shield Kel erected. Nineva ignored the flames and concentrated on creating the gate back to Avalon.

The familiar silver point of a doorway appeared—but failed to grow. Nineva swore in frustration. "They're blocking me!" She could feel it, the collective magic of the dragons pressing in against her own, smothering it.

Beginning to panic, she looked around at the six creatures circling them. They must have been a delaying force, young and fast enough to find her and Kel and slow them down until the rest of the mob could catch up.

Suddenly the surrounding dragons darted away like sparrows. Even Irial flew off, giving his brother a vicious Draconian smirk as he went.

Giving the mob a clear line of fire.

"Kel!" Nineva cried, staring at the oncoming dragon horde. They were less than two hundred yards away now and closing fast. She conjured a crossbow and the flaming magical quarrels to go with it. The bow would give her blasts greater range. "Any ideas?"

"Go down fighting," Kel growled back. "I'm not going to cower to these bastards." He lifted his voice. "We didn't steal the Egg, you fools! We're innocent! The real thieves—"

"Lies!" Irial howled. "Kill them! Burn them down!"

"Kill them!" A chant rose up from thousands of Draconian throats, making Nineva's ears ring and her chest vibrate like a drum.

She hunkered down against Kel's broad back, staring at the seething mass of scales and wings and claws. Fighting her fear, she aimed the crossbow at the nearest dragon and prepared to fire.

"Wait!" A blue figure dropped into view between them and the mass of furious dragons. Soren. "They did nothing! It was Piaras!"

Dragon voices rose in confusion and anger as the great beasts darted back and forth. Yet they hesitated, either because they believed Soren or they were afraid to catch him in their fire.

"Why do you lie for these thieves, Soren?" one of the mob demanded. "Get out of the way, or die with them!"

"Use your senses—they don't have the Egg!" Soren used his magic to hover in front of Nineva and Kel, shielding them with his own big body. "I personally saw Piaras take the Egg through a dimensional gate. I tracked him as far as I could, but something blocked my spell before he reached his destination. I do know I landed somewhere in the great mountains of the eastern continent, because it was full dark there. But when I flew around the area, I could find nothing. The rebel stronghold is too well shielded."

"Don't be absurd," a red dragon protested, sounding offended. "Piaras would never have committed such blasphemy!"

Kel suddenly spoke up. "Then where *is* Lord Piaras? I don't see him among you, though all the other Dragon Lords jostle to be the first to incinerate us. Why isn't your leader among them?"

Heads turned in confusion. "Piaras?" the red dragon called. "Lord Piaras?"

"He's right—everyone else joined the chase," Soren said. "Down to the youngest fledgling. So why would Piaras be missing—unless he was the one who took the Egg?"

Voices rose in confused murmurs.

At last, a mocking voice called, *the dawning light of reason.*

Nineva jerked her head up just as a flaming figure materialized in midair before the mob. Some of them almost dropped out of the sky in surprise as a shocked mass gasp rose.

"Cachamwri," Kel breathed.

Yes, Cachamwri. Fire boiled around the dragon's flaming body. *And I have had more than enough of this!* The Dragon God's mental voice was icy as he thundered at the mob. *Why do you attack my champion and the princess of the Sidhe while a thief makes off with my Egg?*

"He really is your champion?" Irial's voice rose over the abrupt silence, sounding a little sick.

Have I not said so? The Dragon God wheeled in a furious circle, sparks shooting from his flaming wings. *Pah! I send him to you to give you fair warning, but you are too blinded by old hatreds to listen. Fools! You do not deserve my Egg!*

"What would you have us do?" the red dragon asked in a small, humble voice.

You will assist the humans and Sidhe in recovering my Egg, the sword, and the book, Cachamwri growled. *I care not if it gags you to touch them. They will ride you into battle like the stupid beasts you are, and you will help them turn back the Dark Ones. Fail in this, and you will deserve what you'll reap from your conquerors!*

None of the dragons dared so much as murmur a protest. "It will be as you wish, Cachamwri," the red Dragon Lord said. "We beg your forgiveness for allowing the theft."

As well you should. Now get out of my sight. I wish to talk to my champion and his allies.

Nineva watched, feeling dazed, as the entire mob turned and flew away. None of them made a single sound beyond the beat of their wings.

"My thanks, Burning One," Kel said quietly when they were alone. To Soren, he added, "And to you, too, Lord Soren. They'd have killed us if you hadn't interfered."

Cachamwri sighed in disgust. *Aye. Fools.*

"But I don't understand," Soren said quietly. "Why did you allow Piaras to take the Egg to begin with? You could have prevented it."

The god shot him a look. *The theft had to take place, or none of the rest would follow.*

Soren shook his head. "I don't understand."

Of course not. You are not a god. Cachamwri turned his attention to Kel. *Gather Arthur and his allies, and tell them to prepare for war. Our people will meet them outside the city.* His expression went grim. *It will not be long now.*

With that, he vanished, leaving behind only a fading sparkle.

"But where the hell is the rebel stronghold?" Kel growled, frustrated. "Until we know that, we're screwed."

Soren shook his head as he flew in a wide loop around them. "I saw a vast mountain range under the moonlight, and the sea roaring beside it. But I sensed nothing."

"If their wards were strong enough, that could be why," Nineva pointed out. "Could you take us back there?"

"Oh, of course. But searching those mountains would take days, even assuming they were Piaras's final destination. He could easily have landed there to confuse me, then gated on."

Semira? Nineva thought as the two dragons circled each other. *If I got close enough, would you be able to guide me to you?*

There was a long pause before the goddess finally spoke. *I believe so. But you should work another strengthening spell before you make the attempt. I suspect we both will need it.*

All right. "Semira may be able to guide us the rest of the way in, but Kel and I need to work another spell first. She said she'll need the power."

"At least it's a chance," Soren said. "In the meantime, we'll meet with Arthur and Llyr and start working out the details of the attack."

Kel nodded. "And pray the rebels are somewhere in those mountains you saw."

"Nineva's at work on the final spell to power Semira now," Kel told Arthur, Llyr, his queen, and both councils of the Magekind. They'd met in the council chambers as soon as the sun set and the vampires woke. "It's a complicated piece of magic."

"The question is, will it be enough? And will you be finished before Arralt and his rebels complete whatever they're going to do to the wards?" Morgana asked grimly.

He shrugged. "I don't know. It's going to be a race."

"One way or another, we'd better have everybody in place and ready to go as quickly as we can," Arthur said. "Kel, you really think your people are going to cooperate with us?"

"After the dressing down Cachamwri gave them?" Kel snorted. "They wouldn't dare do anything else. He can be pretty damned terrifying when it suits him."

"Which would be gratifying, if only we had a little more time to practice this," Llyr said. "I am not pleased with the idea of taking all these different forces into battle without having drilled them together first."

"Unfortunately, we're going to have to take what we can get," Arthur told him. "And pray it's enough."

Diana spoke up from her seat as she cuddled her sleeping infant against her breast. "I've been talking to the Direkind Council of Clans. We'll be able to count on at least a couple hundred Dire Wolves. They've already started gathering—we just need to gate them in."

"Two hundred magically resistant seven-foot-tall werewolves." Morgana sat back in her seat and smiled like a cat. "That should scare a few rebels."

"It'll scare them a lot more if they don't have Dark Ones for backup," Arthur growled. "Otherwise, we're going to need every dragon, vampire, witch, wolf, and fairy we can muster."

Kel rose from his seat. "And on that note, I'd better get back to Nineva. If she's on schedule—and I'm sure she is—she should be ready for me by now." He left them to their strategy session and strode out into the corridor, trying to ignore the way his stomach was coiling itself into a sick knot. This time, the spell had better work.

* * *

They stood in vast rows. Thousands of them, grim-faced and ready in their black armor, swords and axes hanging from sheaths.

Ready to fight and die to make Arralt ruler of the Two Kingdoms.

He paced along their ranks, stopping here and there to bark critiques of the state of one's sword or the tightness of another's cuirass. To his satisfaction, Arralt saw no doubt in the eyes of any of them, only a fanatical devotion.

For centuries, he'd been recruiting his army, building it man by man from those who'd suffered at his father's hand. Ansgar being Ansgar, there'd been no lack of recruits.

He only wished it were his father he'd meet in battle tonight, his father who'd fall to his sword. Llyr Galatyn would be a poor substitute.

Still, watching the life bleed from the king's eyes would be sweetly satisfying. Galatyn had, after all, stolen the revenge that should have been his.

How his mother had railed at him when Llyr slew Ansgar. "You've failed me! I carried you in my womb for nine months, you rapist's spawn, built your power all these centuries, taught you forbidden magicks—and you waited too long! That monster was to die at your hands! Yours!"

"So I'll slay Galatyn. I'll still take the throne."

Her still-lovely face had twisted in contempt. "Llyr is Cachamwri's Champion now, you fool. He can draw on the power of the Dragon God himself. You have no hope against him. He'll take you apart, even with your army."

Galling as it was to acknowledge it, Arralt had known the bitch was right. He would have to build his power another way.

He'd found the means in his mother's ancient, forbidden books—books written by the Dark Ones' collaborators centuries before the aliens were driven from Sidhe Earth.

Arralt quickly realized the only means he had of gaining

the power to defeat Galatyn was an alliance with his people's former conquerors. It had been an idea breathtaking in its risk. The Dark Ones could easily destroy him. Indeed, given their vicious nature, the odds favored his death.

Yet not to take the chance meant the death of his dream. Worse the death of his revenge.

He'd chosen to take the chance, even though it had meant he had to murder his own mother. Just any slaying wouldn't have powered a gate that far. It had to be the utter betrayal of the very person who gave him life.

Of course, killing the little bitch had been no real hardship. In her determination to turn him into the weapon of her revenge, she'd tormented him from the day he was born.

Now Arralt would finally discover whether his gamble would pay off—or destroy him completely. Would his army defeat Galatyn's? Even if he won, would the Dark Ones keep their agreement and let him claim his throne? It could go either way.

Looking out across the ranks of his men now, he knew that many of them would be dead before dawn. He, too, might well be dead, or a shamed captive in chains.

Or king.

Arralt felt his lips curve up in a grin of pure exhilaration.

Evegnii watched General Arralt stand looking over the army with that gut-chilling smile. And wondered, not for the first time, what the hell he himself was doing here.

Joining the rebellion had seemed like such a heroic adventure five years ago—a noble effort to overthrow Ansgar the Tyrant, who'd ordered the torture of Evegnii's father for acts of sedition.

Sedition. His father had gotten drunk and bitched about Ansgar's taxes in a tavern, not knowing one of the king's toadies lurked in the taproom crowd. He'd died in the torturer's hands.

At first, joining the Army of Semira had promised everything Evegnii hoped. He'd enjoyed the camaraderie of his fellow rebels and the challenge of mastering the art of combat. Surrounded by so many veteran warriors, he'd learned much.

Then Llyr had killed Ansgar. Soon afterward, the general's mother had died under mysterious circumstances, and Arralt himself had vanished for months. When he returned, it was amid rumors that he'd found a chilling ally: the Dark Ones.

Evegnii began to realize he'd made a horrible mistake. Llyr was said to be a good king—and everyone knew what the Dark Ones were. He was tempted to desert on the spot.

He thought better of it after seeing the public execution of one captured deserter. Evegnii had no desire to be gutted and used to power some act of death magic.

Death magic, for Semira's sweet sake.

Soon, if the rumors were correct, they'd all ride into battle by the Dark Ones' side. Evegnii's sergeant had already warned the entire unit that he'd kill any man who fought with anything less than courage.

Cursed. No matter what he did, Evegnii knew he was cursed. His one hope was to fight like a berserker and pray the general hadn't lied when he'd sworn to reward his men for winning his throne for him.

If only Evegnii didn't have the sinking feeling that his own children would curse his name for this night, no matter what riches Arralt might heap on his head.

Not that it mattered. He had only one choice.

Fight or die.

SIXTEEN

Kel found Nineva where he'd known he would: standing beside the great bed, just beyond the pattern of runes she'd painted on the floor. He could feel the magic hanging in the air, waiting for them to provide the fuel that would ignite it.

Which, he suspected, would require very little effort on his part. Just looking at her was enough to make his libido burst into flame.

In contrast to the sexy crimson negligee she'd worn the last time, she was dressed in a white lace gown that spilled over her sleek curves all the way to her bare feet. A circlet of red roses rode her blond curls, worn loose around her slender shoulders. The Mark of Semira glowed gold on her breast, burning brighter than he'd ever seen it, a silent testimony to the power in the room.

"You look like a bride on her wedding night," Kel said. His voice sounded hoarse to his own ears. His heart had drawn into an hard, aching knot.

She moved toward him. The lacy train of her skirt dragged on the floor, reminding him again of a wedding gown. At least until she got close enough for him to see the shadows of pink nipples peeking through the lace. "I want this time to be about more than the spell." Small, cool hands came to rest on his chest as she lifted her gaze to his. "I want it to be for us, too."

Kel knew what she was thinking. If they died in battle tonight, this might be the last time they ever touched. He brushed the rise of her fragile cheek with a thumb and gave her his best slow, seductive smile. He'd used it a thousand times on countless women, but it had never set up painful echoes in his own chest before. "I'll do my best."

Nineva smiled back, but hers was genuine and warm. "Oh, I know. You've never failed me yet."

He kissed her. It was openmouthed, fierce, just the way she needed it. He broke it only long enough to scoop her into his arms and carry her to the bed. Magic bubbled on her skin as they crossed the boundaries of the spell, then danced down her back as he lay her on the mattress. When she looked away from his handsome face, she saw the interlocking globes of glowing runes orbiting the bed. The Goddess Mark throbbed in answer, hotter than she'd ever felt it. Which was no surprise: Semira herself had guided her in working the spell this time, and the power of it seethed like a building storm.

Then Kel came down over her, covering her with that big, hard body of his, and she forgot about everything else. For once, he'd abandoned his usual casual clothing in favor of a flowing white shirt open to the waist of tight black trousers that were, in turn, tucked into boots.

She smiled into his eyes, trailing her fingers down the muscle revealed by the open V of the shirt. "You look like you just escaped from the cover of a romance novel."

He grinned, but the humor didn't reach his somber eyes. "Hey, I figure if it's good enough for Fabio, it's good enough for me."

Nineva wrinkled her nose at him. "You do realize I was

about ten years old the last time Fabio was on the cover of a romance?"

"That's right, make me feel old."

"You *are* old. You're also immortal, so it doesn't count."

His forced smile faded. "Are we trying too hard?"

"I was just thinking that."

"That's the problem." He brushed his knuckles across the rise of her cheek. "We're both thinking too much. We're going to ruin it." She knew he wasn't talking about the spell.

The kiss he gave her this time wasn't the practiced seducer's version, but one that spoke of need and heart. She looped her arms around his neck and gave herself up to his mouth, savoring the slow stroke of his tongue.

By the time he drew back, they were both breathing hard. For a moment, neither spoke as they stared into each other's eyes. The hard, guarded look was gone from his, replaced by tenderness. He looked down her body, his gaze lingering on her lacy bodice. "You know, the more I look at this nightgown, the more I like it."

She gave him a deliberately saucy smile. "I thought you would."

Rolling onto his side and bracing on one elbow, he trailed his fingers over the lace in a featherlight touch. Her nipples beaded under the thin fabric. His eyes flicked up to her face, and one corner of his mouth curled up in a wicked half-smile. He lowered his head. She watched as he extended his tongue and gave the tight point a slow lick through the lace. A little sizzle of pleasure darted through her at the delicate touch.

Next came a nibble, followed by a gentle rake of the teeth that managed to drag the lace across the point, teasing it even harder. Nineva hummed in pleasure.

"Soooo," she purred, a sudden memory making her grin. "What's this I hear about forked tongues?"

His eyes flashed up at her. "Don't start."

"Oh, come on . . ."

He closed his lips around her nipple and gave her a hot, strong suckle, swirling his tongue over her through the lace. She instantly lost interest in teasing.

Kel's free hand grew busy with the full skirt of her gown, gathering the fabric up until he could find his way beneath. When his warm palm found the smooth skin of her thigh, she sighed in pleasure, arching against him in anticipation.

He was still suckling her through the lace, making the fabric wet from his mouth. Yet the lack of full contact with that skillful tongue was maddening, and she squirmed.

Hungry to touch him, she reached for the deep V of his shirt again, sliding a hand beneath the soft, skin-warm fabric. She teased his nipple and had the pleasure of his groan.

As if in retaliation, he cupped her sex through the lace of her panties. Nineva rolled her hips in a shameless plea for more, and he traced a finger along the seam of her satin-covered lips. She could feel hot cream flood her.

Still stroking that finger back and forth, he gave her nipple another slow swirling suckle, then switched his attention to the other one. Hunger rising, she lifted one hand, on the verge of banishing their clothes.

"No," he breathed, his gaze colliding with her in hot command. "I want to undress you."

She licked her suddenly dry lips, caught by his predatory stare. "Okay." Her voice sounded embarrassingly weak.

Kel sat up and flipped her full skirt up over her hips, baring her slender legs and the tiny lace panties that just barely covered her sex. Approval lit his ruby gaze, and he wrapped a big hand in the thin lace at her waist. One ruthless tug ripped the panties in two. He tilted his head as he tossed the scraps aside, his gaze locked on her most delicate flesh.

In contrast to his cavalier disposal of her panties, the

fingers that touched her blond curls were oddly reverent. "You're so pretty here." He inhaled, his lids lowering over those vivid eyes. "And you smell so sweet."

Nineva watched, almost quivering with the intensity of her need, as he settled between her legs. Big hands cupped her knees, spreading them wide as he lowered his head. She braced up on her elbows to watch as he kissed her on her pale curls.

Then he gave her one lingering lick, right over the seam. Not pushing inside. Just teasing.

Nineva threw her head back and groaned. "Kel, you're driving me crazy!"

"Good." Another lick, just a fraction deeper. Tasting, but stopping well short of touching her aching center. His hands moved up her sides to cup her breasts through the gown.

Kel licked her again, deeper, longer, as his thumbs played over the lace-covered tips of her breasts. She squirmed helplessly.

From the corner of one eye, she saw something flare bright. Automatically, she glanced over. It was the spell globe, glowing hotter, revolving faster, as if their mutual need fed it.

For a moment the thought of the spell—and the battle to follow—almost jolted her out of the mood. But then Kel's clever tongue thrust deep, raking right over her clit, and the wave of pleasure made her throw back her head and cry out.

He ate at her slowly, with swirls and thrusts of that wicked tongue and slow, tugging nibbles of her lips. At the same time, he caught the soft lace of her bodice in his fingers and raked it back and forth over her nipples, teasing them deliciously.

Nineva fisted both hands in his hair and held on for dear life as he taunted her. Teeth. Tongue. Fingers. All working to spill molten pleasure along her every nerve ending until she writhed like a cat.

Around them, the spell was glowing with a hot red light.

*   *   *

She tasted like a midnight sea, of magic and wild, elemental femininity. The slow, unconscious roll of her hips against his mouth was driving him insane. His cock was as hard as a sword blade, aching where it pressed into the mattress. Kel wasn't sure how much longer he could hold out against the driving need to take her, but he was determined to bring her to orgasm with his mouth first.

When she finally stiffened against him with a scream of helpless pleasure, it was all he could do not to moan in relief.

The next moment, her beautiful gown fell prey to his impatient hands as he ripped it in two like a child attacking a Christmas gift. He sat up, his cock jerking as it throbbed in time to his heart. He wanted to fall on her like a barbarian, but somehow he held onto his self-control.

He had to brand the memory of her moment of perfect pleasure on his very soul. He knew he'd need it later.

She looked down her slender body at him, her opalescent eyes dazed with pleasure, her lips swollen, her blond hair tumbled in disarray around her face. Her breasts rose and fell in hard, panting breaths, topped by sweet pink nipples as full and swollen as cherries. Those beautiful legs of hers were spread wide, and the golden curls between them were wet from his mouth and her own desire.

With a growl, he caught her hips, angled them upward, and aimed his aching cock for her tight opening.

The first thrust was blinding. Her sweet flesh clamped around his cock, lusciously wet and tighter than a fist. Kel shuddered at the delicious perfection and wondered how the hell he'd ever last.

He'd just have to find a way. He wasn't giving this up an instant before he had to.

Teeth clenched, he lowered himself over Nineva, braced his fists beside her shoulders and began to slowly thrust.

She groaned and wrapped both endless legs around his waist.

Each slide of his cock into her slick flesh was a taste of paradise—and an exercise in delightful torture as he tried not to come. Clawing for control, he looked down into her lovely face. Which was a serious miscalculation, because there was nothing as arousing as the sight of Nineva lost in pleasure, opalescent eyes sparking with magic. Her soft lips shaped sensual moans in time to every entry.

"Nineva," he groaned. "Cachamwri's Egg, Nineva . . ."

"You feel so good," she gasped back, digging her fingers into his shoulders. Her nails pricked his skin like little spurs, and he ground his teeth. "More. Goddess, more. Faster . . ." Tiny inner muscles tightened around him, rippling.

And he lost control.

He began to lunge, giving her what she begged for, harder, faster, shuttling his cock in and out. Nineva writhed under him, her eyes dazed with the rise of her orgasm. "Kel!"

Kel felt huge, his cock thick and impossibly arousing, impossibly delicious.

Nineva was distantly aware of the Goddess Mark throbbing on her breast in time to her heart. The spell was revolving around them so fast now, it was impossible to make out the individual runes. There was nothing but a blur of red and the foaming dance of magic across her skin.

Kel's muscular shoulders felt sweat-slick under her hands, and his taut backside worked within the clasp of her legs as she gripped him. Each thrust sent another burning spike of delight up her spine.

Until he rammed to his full length and stiffened there with a shout. The sensation of being filled so full was enough to tip her over the edge. She cried out as the sweet pulses started.

Deep inside her magic flooded her with his come. The spell globe imploded in utter silence. They both screamed as the runes sank into their skin like hot snowflakes.

Yes! Semira's voice rang in Nineva's mind, but it wasn't weak anymore. The presence that had been a distant thing suddenly filled her consciousness with ancient power and alien magic.

Nineva caught her breath in awe. *Are you free?*

Not yet. Not quite. The goddess's mental voice seemed to ring in her very bones. *The spell needs one last thing.*

And Nineva, knowing exactly what, felt her blood run cold.

"Kel?" His lover's voice sounded strangled.

He lifted his head from her chest in alarm. "What? What's wrong?"

Her face was pale as milk, and her eyes were huge. "Semira said you're going to have to do it if we're going to complete the spell. Now."

His stomach clenched in sudden alarm. "Do what?"

Her lips trembled. "Fulfill the prophecy."

He stared. "You mean fry you."

"Yes."

"What part of 'Hell, no' eludes her? I thought I'd made my stance on that topic pretty damned clear." Kel rolled off her, unable to lie still with his temper boiling.

Damned goddess. Hadn't they jumped through enough hoops for her?

Nineva sat back on her heels, lush and naked despite the anguish in her beautiful eyes. "But Semira says it's necessary to complete the spell. And we've got to free her, Kel. You know that. It's the only way any of us have a prayer."

"And how do we know it will actually accomplish a damn thing? She said if we had sex, it would strengthen her enough that she'd be able to lead us to her. We've fucked like bunnies, and she still doesn't have a clue."

"Don't use that tone when you talk about Semira," Nineva snapped. "She is my goddess, just as Cachamwri is your god."

"And I'm sick of getting jerked around by gods. They know what's going on, but they won't lift a finger to stop any of it. Instead they expect us to do all the bleeding. Screw that."

Nineva sprang from the bed, anger and desperation in her snapping eyes. "So we're just going to let the Dark Ones invade because we think the gods aren't pulling their weight?"

"No," Kel snarled through gritted teeth. "We're going to stop them. But I'm damned if I'm going to incinerate the woman I love just because some so-called 'goddess' says so. We're going to gate the army to that mountain Soren found, and then we're going to hunt the bastards down and kill them. And *you* are going to be in one big, non-crispy piece when we do it."

"And what if we fail?" Nineva shouted. "What if Dark Ones destroy the wards and we don't have the power to stop them because . . . we didn't have the guts?"

He stared at her coldly. "You mean because *I* didn't have the guts."

Nineva sat back down on the bed and buried her face in her hands. Finally she lifted her head and sighed. "Kel, this is what I was raised to do."

"No, this is what your daddy *brainwashed* you to do. There's a difference."

"You leave my father out of this!"

"Why? This is all about him. You think sacrificing yourself on Semira's altar will somehow make up for his getting himself killed when you were a kid."

"He didn't get himself killed, Kel. *I* got him killed."

"*You saved a fucking dog.* He could have run, Nineva.

He could have taken your mother and gone in the opposite direction from wherever he sent you. Instead, he decided to die a martyr, and sacrifice your mother in the process. Well, I'm not helping you follow in Daddy's footsteps."

Nineva curled her lip at him. "Fine. You want to be bull-headed and stupid, fine. But when the Dark Ones swarm us like locusts, don't say I didn't warn you."

Silence lay between them like a huge icy weight as they prepared to gate to the outskirts of Avalon.

Did he really think she *wanted* to burn, Nineva thought, so angry she couldn't even speak. After all the times she'd woken up sweating and crying, how could he think dying in flames had any appeal to her? She had no desire to be a martyr, no matter what he thought.

But if it meant saving both Earths from the Dark Ones, she was willing to do it. Hell, those bastards would make her suffer just as much if they won anyway. It made more sense to make sure nobody else had to go down with her.

But noooo. Kel was convinced he was right. Besides, he didn't want to deal with the guilt of having to hurt her.

Why she was so in love with the man was a total mystery. He was an idiot. A romantic, softhearted, arrogant idiot.

And she wished he wouldn't keep giving her those icy, aloof looks. They made her crazy.

The moment he gestured the gate into being, Nineva stepped through, having no desire to be alone with him any longer.

She emerged onto a hill overlooking Avalon. The city sprawled white and serene in the light of the moon, like a sleeping goddess. In no mood to appreciate the view, Nineva stepped aside so that Kel could gate in, the grass crackling with frost beneath her feet.

There were dragons everywhere she looked. Eyes

glowed in the moonlight, scales glinted, wings furled or stirred restlessly. And even more astonishing, each one of the great creatures bore a rider, some in the armor of the Magekind, others in that of the Two Kingdoms.

Noticing the harnesses the dragons wore, Nineva hid a tight, slightly malicious grin. *I'll bet they loved that.*

Those not mounted on dragons rode armored Sidhe horses. "They must be under one hell of a spell," Kel commented in a low voice. "Horses generally don't like dragons very much. We eat 'em."

Nineva barely heard. Her attention had fallen on a group of towering, muscled figures with long lupine muzzles, wolf-pointed ears, and claws like knives. Thick fur covered them—deep red, black, brown, gray, white, and blond in a range of shades that matched normal human hair color. "What the hell are they?" she whispered, forgetting for the moment that she was furious at him.

"Dire Wolves." Kel shrugged. "Or werewolves, take your pick. Merlin created them to keep an eye on the Magekind. We only recently found out about them."

"Werewolves? Like the queen? But she turned into a regular wolf after her baby was born."

"Dire Wolves can assume more than one form."

"There you are." They looked around as Arthur strode toward them in a gleaming suit of golden armor, intricately engraved in magical symbols. He wore Excalibur sheathed across his back tonight, the gems of the great blade's hilt catching the light of the magical torches. For the first time, Nineva could believe he was the king the legends spoke of.

Llyr walked at his side in iridescent dragon-scale armor. One of the huge werewolves followed. It was odd to see familiar silver eyes looking out of that savage wolf face.

Nineva dared step closer to the werewolf as Llyr, Arthur, and Kel conferred. "Where's Prince Dearg?"

Diana smiled, flashing white and intimidating teeth. "Back at the palace with his great-grandma Oriana and every guard we've got. Anybody tries anything, Oriana will turn 'em into a frog." She sighed. "I hated to leave him, but I've got a feeling we're going to need every Dire Wolf we can get." Her gaze shifted to her husband's face. "Besides, I was damned if I was going to let Llyr ride into battle without me to watch his back."

Nineva nodded, her own gaze drifting to Kel. Pissed as she was at him, she felt exactly the same.

Every instinct she had whispered that this was about to get ugly.

Piaras howled in rage, his golden body lashing in the spell that held him. Even Varza found herself taking a step back from his fury. He roared Draconian curses and threats, demanding that they return the stolen Egg even as he swore he'd take his revenge for what they'd done to him.

He'd flown right into the trap without hesitation. It apparently never occurred to the Dragon Lord that the Sidhe could be a real threat.

It had taken more than a hundred warriors—fifteen of whom lost their lives—but at the end of the day, Piaras had been bound in chains of magic. With Arralt's magic holding the dragons contained, Varza was able to possess the beast just as she had her Sidhe victims. This time, though, she'd let her victim's spirit live. The better to use him later.

After that, stealing Cachamwri's Egg had been child's play—though admittedly nerve-wracking child's play. Keeping the Dragon Lords from sensing her possession of their leader had taken every bit of skill and magic Varza had.

But she'd done it. Now they had Semira's Sword, Merlin's Grimoire, Cachamwri's Egg—and the sacrifice that would power the first stages of the spell.

Good thing, too. Even through the wards, she could almost sense her master's impatience.

She turned from Piaras just as Arralt strode toward her, radiating a raw excitement. That didn't surprise her. He was one of those who was intoxicated by risk.

But then, he'd never had the Dark Ones teach him the price of losing.

"My forces are ready to gate," he announced.

"Good. My master's warriors wait as well," Varza told him. "Prepare the sacrifice." She turned and moved to the altar she'd conjured in the center of the great chamber. Around it lay the twisted lines of the death spell she'd drawn, waiting only the last rune to complete its magic.

Her master's orb hovered over the altar, casting its yellow light over sword, book, and egg. Death magic hung in the air, heavy and black with potential.

"Sacrifice?" Piaras demanded, sinking back on his haunches as Arralt's men surrounded his spell cage.

No one bothered to answer as the rebel general walked over to the altar and accepted the dragon spear she handed him. Over fifteen feet of thick Sidhe wood, it was heavily worked with runes to strengthen it. Its razor-sharp head was the length of his forearm.

Fear flickered in the Dragon Lord's eyes as Arralt moved toward him with the weapon in both hands. "You would not dare, ape!"

Arralt gave him a faint, cold smile. "I would dare a great deal, lizard." To the ten warriors who surrounded the dragon, he added, "Ready yourselves."

The men, his most experienced fighters, gave short, tight nods. He dropped the spell cage that held the dragon.

Instantly, the great beast lunged for him, jaws opening in preparation for a blast of magical fire. The nearest warrior cast a spell line that snapped around the creature's muzzle like a rope, jerking his mouth closed. Piaras reared, dragging the warrior off his feet. The dragon jerked his head, trying to dash the Sidhe against the far wall, but the other fighters were already casting their own lines.

Everywhere they touched him, the spells immobilized his body, freezing legs and wings until he was finally left sprawled on the stone floor, panting in defeated rage.

"Turn him on his side," Arralt ordered.

Other warriors ran forward to lend their strength on the lines. With grunts of effort, they managed to roll the struggling beast until his chest lay exposed.

Arralt radiated icy pleasure as he approached the Dragon Lord. Piaras's muscles twitched with effort to fight, only to subside into helplessness under the weight of the binding spell.

The general drew back the spear and drove it into the beast's chest. Piaras grunted in agony and convulsed as the point penetrated his heart.

Quickly, Varza hurried forward and grabbed the spear as Arralt stepped away. She jerked it from the dragon's chest and used its bloody point to draw the last crucial rune on the floor.

As the dragon died, the stink of released death magic made even Arralt gag. Varza barely noticed, all her attention on the magic rising around her like a storm.

She lifted the point again and turned to the altar where the Grimoire lay open. Using the dripping spear, she scrawled a symbol across the tome's pages. Throwing the weapon aside, she picked up the Sword of Semira and nodded at Arralt.

He stepped forward and lifted the Egg high over the Grimoire. Without hesitation, Varza rammed the sword right through it. Blood poured from the cracked shell and fell on the open book.

And the spell exploded in a soundless burst of light. Raw energy lanced up from the altar, shooting toward the ceiling of the cavern and knifing right through the thick stone.

When the glare faded, the book was gone.

Breath held, Varza extended her senses upward, reaching

for the wards that surrounded the planet thousands of feet above. She saw the spell strike the barrier and sizzle along the lines of force. Everywhere it touched, the wards faded and went out.

In a heartbeat, all of them had vanished.

Varza smiled, but it was more snarl than anything else. "It's done."

Arralt and his men, the fools, cheered. Evidently the general hadn't noticed the life she'd lived back on Odra, or realized he'd just delivered himself and his people to the same fate.

Rakatvira's voice blasted from the orb, clear now that the wards were gone. "The conquest begins now. We move on Avalon."

SEVENTEEN

One minute she was talking to Diana. The next, light exploded in her head with a white-hot burst of agony, and she was on her knees, gasping and blind.

"Nineva!" Fear rang in Kel's voice. He caught her and drew her into his lap. "What is it?"

"Semira . . . ," she rasped. In the depths of her mind, she could hear the goddess screaming. "Something's happened to Semira . . ."

Diana's voice rang somewhere off to the left, tight with panic. "Llyr! What the hell is going on?"

"Cachamwri. They . . . attacked him . . ." Llyr sounded as weak as Nineva felt. He must be down, too.

A woman cursed with impressive inventiveness. "The wards are gone. That's what's hit the Avatars—they did something to the sword and the Egg."

"Not to mention Grim," Arthur snarled. "Well, that's torn it. We're fucked."

"Gates!" a man shouted. "Somebody's gating in!"

"Dark Ones!" The roar of warning went up, followed

almost instantly by battle cries and blood-chilling, inhuman howls. Around the hillside, dragons leaped skyward in
a thundering wind of beating wings.

"Magekind!" Arthur bellowed over the wind as he began to run. "Attack!" With a roar, his people charged in his
wake.

Aware of countless armored feet rushing past, Nineva
struggled to drag herself out of Kel's lap, despite her debilitating weakness. "Help me up!" she grated through her
teeth. "We've got to go fight!"

"I know." Kel rose and pulled her upright with one
hand. "Well, you warned me," he said grimly. "And you
were right."

"I don't think it would have mattered." Nineva braced
her legs and fought a wave of dizziness. She felt gutted,
and the familiar heat of Semira's Mark was gone from her
chest. "We wouldn't have had time to finish the spell before they hit us."

"Could we do it now?"

"There's no point. I can't feel Semira at all. I think she's
dead." Nineva knew better than to let herself think about
that now. Guilt would cripple her, and she needed to be
able to fight.

Llyr was up now, too, though his face was white and
grim as he made for the dancing roan stallion another
Sidhe held for him. Diana hovered anxiously as he swung
aboard the huge animal. "Are you sure you're up to this?"

"I have to be," he told his wife grimly, driving his
spurred heels into the horse's muscular ribs. "I'm king!"
He galloped toward the sound of battle, Diana loping at his
heels. The other werewolves followed her, lifting their
voices in chilling howls that rang across the battlefield.

"I've got to change, too," Kel shouted to Nineva. "We'll
do more good if I'm in dragon form."

"Go!" she cried, stepping back. The rest of the army

had already disappeared down the hill to engage the Dark Ones, so he had plenty of room to transform.

She felt his magic flood over her skin, and he was a dragon again. Given the howls and screams coming from the battlefield, Nineva was damned glad of it.

She ran forward, grabbed the harness he wore, and managed to haul herself up and onto his neck. He leaped skyward before she was even settled. Nineva grabbed at the straps, kicked her feet into the stirrups, and held on for dear life.

Kel's huge wings carried them up and over the battle into a sky full of darting, fire-breathing dragons and their warrior passengers. Unfortunately, it was also full of magical blasts, boiling with energy and zipping through the air like antiaircraft fire.

The blasts were huge, easily the size of boulders, and a seething blood red.

And they stank of death magic.

One ate through a dragon's shield even as he twisted and fought to escape. A heartbeat later, he and his rider burst into flame and fell screaming from the sky.

"Holy fuck," Nineva whispered, chilled to the marrow as she looked away from the impact.

Kel jolted under her. "Arthur!" She had to grab for the harness as he suddenly went into a dive, plummeting toward the ground. She managed not to scream and conjured a crossbow with a magical bolt nocked in it.

They found Arthur squared off with an enormous Dark One. The alien looked surprisingly like a medieval woodcut of a demon, standing a good nine feet tall on two hooves, its lower body covered with thick black fur. The rest of it was bright red, with huge clawed hands, tusklike teeth jutting from its lower jaw, and a pair of curving black horns. It hacked at Arthur with a huge axe it held in both hands. The axe rang against Excalibur as the alien tried to batter its way through Arthur's guard.

It had apparently landed at least one good blow. A river

of scarlet spilled down the vampire's armored chest as he danced around his foe. It looked like far too much blood to Nineva's healer's eye.

The Dark One looked up and saw Kel plummeting toward him. The creature fired off a spell blast, forcing Kel to jerk to one side. Even as the dragon steadied under her, Nineva took careful aim with her crossbow and fired. Her bolt lodged in the Dark One's massive shoulder, but he brushed it off like a mosquito.

Oh, she thought, *that's not good at all.*

Kel slammed into the Dark One like a freight train, knocking the alien off his feet. There was a sickening crunch, and the dragon roared in pain. Nineva conjured another bolt and stood up in her stirrups, trying to see over Kel's massive body. She saw nothing but a blurring impression of a lashing dragon neck and the flash of the Dark One's magical axe. There was no way to get a shot at all.

"Kel!" she screamed over the howls of combat. "Dammit!" She vaulted from the harness. Landing on her feet, she scuttled around the dragon, narrowly avoiding his swinging tail.

Blood ran down Kel's muzzle from a wound over his eye as he breathed a gout of flame at the Dark One. The blast boiled off the creature's shield with such heat and power, Nineva could feel it from where she stood.

As the flames died, the Dark One charged, drawing back his axe as he aimed for Kel's head.

Nineva fired her crossbow right into the alien's eye. The creature toppled, its body bursting into flame as her spell tore through it.

Stunned, she dropped her bow and stared. She hadn't expected that to actually work.

"'Ware right!" Arthur roared in her ear. She jerked around as Excalibur flashed, parrying a sword swung at her head by a Sidhe in black rebellion armor. An instant later,

Kel's flame rolled over the rebel, who fell from his saddle, shrieking as he died.

"Sweet Semira . . . ," she whispered, shaken by her close call. If Arthur hadn't blocked that swing . . . "Thanks, Arthur!"

"What the fuck are you doing on the ground?" Kel roared. "Do you want to get killed? Mount up!"

"What part of me saving your life did you miss?" But she ran for his offered scaled hand and let him boost her astride his neck.

"Thank you! Now stay in that damned harness before you get stepped on."

"That's why I've got Gwen on a dragon," Arthur shouted. "These bastards are a little too fuckin' powerful, Kel. I hope to hell we can take them." He took a deep breath and charged the nearest alien, bringing up Excalibur for a blurring swing. The creature bellowed as it whirled to engage him with a massive sword of its own.

Nineva scanned the battlefield as she conjured another crossbow bolt. Her heart sank. Here and there were dead demon bodies, true, along with a great many fallen rebels.

But there were entirely too many lying dead in Magekind or Two Kingdoms armor, alongside the bodies of their horses and dragon allies. Many of the corpses were so badly mauled and burned it was impossible to tell whose side they'd been on. But it looked uncomfortably as if the allies were losing.

"This doesn't look good!" Nineva shouted as Kel took to the sky again. She aimed her crossbow and fired off a blast at a rebel. It bounced off his spell shield, and he kept hacking at the vampire he was fighting.

"I know." Kel flew toward a group of rebels and blew a plume of fire down at them. Fireballs splashed against his shield as he climbed away.

She stared down over one beating wing. It looked as if a couple of the rebels had fallen, but the Dark One who led them didn't even break step. He flung himself at a Dire Wolf, and the two huge monsters started tearing at one another with claws and fangs. The Dark One tried to burn the werewolf with a spell, but the beast simply shrugged off the blast and kept trying to rip out his opponent's throat.

"We could use a few more werewolves," Nineva shouted.

"We could use a few more everybody," Kel called back grimly. "The odds suck."

Abruptly, flame flashed just above them. Nineva ducked instinctively, then straightened at the sound of a familiar mental voice.

Kel . . .

"Cachamwri!" The dragon almost tumbled out of the sky in his surprise as he stared up at the god. "You live!"

Barely. I need you, boy. I need you to help me recover from what they did to me. And it was apparent just looking at him that whatever spell the rebels had worked had cost Cachamwri dearly. Where before he'd blazed with colorful flames, now he appeared almost ghostly, his outline transparent.

"Whatever I have is yours," Kel told him.

"What about Semira?" Nineva demanded. "Do you know if she lives?"

Aye, but greatly weakened. She still clings to existence within her sword, but if she is not freed soon, she will be lost.

For the first time since the battle had begun, Nineva felt a flicker of hope. "At least she's alive."

From the corner of one eye, she saw something shoot at her head. She hastily flattened herself over Kel's neck as the fireball whizzed over her.

We need a moment's quiet to do this, boy, Cachamwri told them, and pointed his muzzle toward the crest of the hill. *Head over there.*

Obediently, Kel flew over the battlefield, dodging blasts and arrow attacks as he went. "It's not going well," he told Cachamwri.

That's putting it mildly. You're losing. The Dark Ones are preparing to gate in more reinforcements.

Kel cursed as Nineva's heart sank to her booted toes. "We're screwed."

Not quite yet, Cachamwri said. *Not if we act quickly.*

"We'll do whatever we have to," Nineva told him.

"Yes," Kel agreed grimly. "Whatever it takes."

They landed on the hill a moment later. Nineva swung down from the harness, her gaze straying to the battlefield. There was, thank the Goddess, no sign of more gates yet.

But even without fresh Dark One forces, it was apparent the allies' losses were too great. Many lay dead or wounded, while those still standing were locked in desperate battle with the Dark Ones and the rebels.

Behind her, she heard Kel ask, "What must I do?"

Open your mind to me, the Dragon God said.

Guilt stabbed Kel again at the sight of Cachamwri's pale, ghostly outlines. Despite what Nineva had said, he knew he was responsible for what had happened to the Dragon God, not to mention the imminent destruction of them all at the Dark Ones' hands.

He'd been so sure there was a way to avoid sacrificing Nineva. And he'd been wrong.

Now he had to make it right.

Kel dropped the mental barriers that he'd always maintained to protect his magic and his thoughts. He opened himself completely to whatever the Dragon God cared to do to him, forced every muscle to relax in surrender. "I'm ready."

Pale fire flashed as Cachamwri shot toward him. For an instant, the god seemed to take up his entire field of vision.

And then Cachamwri hit him.

It was like being thrust into the heart of a sun—a blinding wave of heat and energy. Then came the alien memories, the mind so impossibly vast and ancient he could scarcely comprehend it at all. Kel found himself shrinking away from that massive consciousness in awe and dread.

Cachamwri may have been a dragon once, but he was something entirely different now. Something that might snuff Kel out like a candle.

Buck up, boy. I did not choose you as my host by accident. Relax and let it come, and you'll find the strength you need.

Yes, Burning One. Despite his instinctive fear, Kel reached out to the great, glowing presence that filled his mind. Touched it.

And in that moment of contact, he sensed the surprising depths of Cachamwri's love.

Then the god wrapped him gently in great, glowing wings. Understanding flooded Kel like a tsunami of light. He saw what Cachamwri needed from him, just as he saw how to save both Semira and Nineva. And he realized that his guilt was pointless, because this couldn't have happened any other way than it had.

And instantly, everything became clear.

You had to allow the theft of the Egg, Kel realized.

Yes. Otherwise the Dark Ones would only have found another way to invade in another five years, the Dragon God told him. *And I would have been unable to prevent them from succeeding. Billions would have been enslaved, and Semira and I would have been destroyed. By luring them here now, I may be able to kill their leader, Rakatvira, preventing his next attempt.*

May?

Nothing is ever certain.

The Dragon God had taken quite a risk to save them, and it had almost cost him his life. The destruction of his Egg had gutted his power. To rebuild it, Cachamwri had to take physical form again in order to reconstruct his connection with the Mageverse. He was far too weak to create a body of his own, so he needed to borrow an ally's.

Llyr had been an option, but his Sidhe form was too

frail to survive the union. Kel alone had both a dragon's sheer strength and power—and, most importantly, the love of Nineva Morrow, Avatar of Semira. Because it was that love that would enable them all to survive.

Unfortunately, they'd all have to go through hell to do it. Literally.

"Kel!" Nineva stretched out a shaking hand to touch her dragon's head. When Cachamwri had rushed into him, he'd gone down like a felled ox. She'd feared for a moment he was dead, until she'd felt the breath puffing from his nose.

Suddenly those great ruby eyes sprang open and met hers, fierce with demand and determination. Magic burst around him, and he was human again. He rolled to his feet and reached out to take her cold hands in his warm ones. "Truebond with me."

Thoroughly confused, Nineva gaped up at him. "What? Now? What happened to Cachamwri? I thought . . ."

"This is part of that." Kel drew her closer, his gaze intent on her face. "We have to work the prophecy spell. It's the only way to save Semira and power Cachamwri enough to repair the wards before the next wave of Dark Ones arrive."

A shaft of cold dread struck her. For a wild moment, Nineva wanted to refuse—but in that instant's hesitation, she heard the screams of agony and death from the battlefield. She took a deep breath. "I'm ready."

"Not yet. The Truebond first."

"But isn't that like the Magekind version of marriage? Do we really have time?"

"We've got to make time, because it's the only way any of us will survive it. I have to lend you my strength."

"While I burn?" The implications were obvious. She drew back in horror. "You'd feel it, Kel. You'd feel everything."

"Yes." His ruby gaze was steady. "But I'll also make sure you survive."

"No. No way in hell." The idea that he'd share the agony she'd known in her dreams was appalling. "I don't want you suffering like that."

"Do you think I want you to?" He released her hands and caught her by her shoulders. "Nineva, the spell will kill you if we don't Truebond, and then *none* of this will work."

"But . . ."

"Trust me."

Gazing up at him, she smiled slightly. "Of course." She took a deep breath. "How do we do this?"

"As Cachamwri said—open your mind to me." He lowered his head.

Nineva rose onto her toes and gave him her mouth, letting her eyes slip closed. For a moment, it was nothing more than the familiar touch of lip on lip, exquisite and tender. Then she carefully lowered the mental barriers she'd learned to build as a child.

Kel's thoughts brushed hers. She sensed his power, smelled the familiar wild musk of dragon scales . . . And something more than that. Something even older, even more powerful.

Cachamwri.

Uncounted centuries flashed over her. Faces, dragon and human, snarling and smiling and roaring in pain, voices howling and laughing. The clash of steel on steel reverberating through her body. Aching loneliness, the panic of being trapped and tiny in a cage of steel. Then the secure knowledge of Gawain's steady friendship as he shared his soul to keep Kel sane.

Finally her own face, looking surprisingly fragile, illuminated in the pure light of his love.

Realization took her breath and made her eyes sting.

Kel truly loved her. Loved the sweet lines of her body and the unwavering sense of duty in her soul. He admired her intelligence and enjoyed her humor. Adored the hot skill of her mouth on his body and the tight clasp of her sex.

And he was absolutely determined that he would not lose her. He'd do anything to save her. Anything at all.

She only hoped she was worthy of him.

Oh, you are. And for a moment, he caught her up in a swirl of hot passion.

And Nineva gave it all back to him—the love she had for his courage, for his kindness, for that beautiful, powerful body. She showed him how she admired his strength and his skill, his unflinching loyalty to his friends no matter what it cost him. The curiosity and fearlessness that led him to reach out when the rest of his people shrank away.

He was everything she'd ever dreamed of in her secret girl's heart and her cautious woman's soul.

And so for a moment they were one, curled together in their glowing cocoon of peace, sharing the love between them like a fine, sweet wine.

Until Cachamwri's ringing voice pierced that instant like a chiming clock. *There's no more time. Shift, boy. Call the magic now.*

Reluctantly, Nineva opened her eyes and found herself wrapped in his powerful arms. He looked down at her, and she saw the longing and regret in his gaze.

And the fear of what the next moments would be like for both of them.

She forced a smile and backed away, knowing exactly how much room he'd need to change. Oddly enough, the terror that had dogged her was gone. She knew he'd do everything he could to protect her—just as she knew he'd succeed.

Magic flared. The next instant, he loomed over her, blue scales glinting, his eyes glowing red. But she could still feel his mind, just as human, just as Kel.

Now, Cachamwri ordered, his voice rumbling in their joined thoughts.

Nineva felt Kel tremble as he took a deep breath and closed his glowing eyes. Through the Truebond, she sensed him reach into the Mageverse deeper than he ever had before, drawing power into his being. She felt it fill him, flooding his cells, foaming in his blood. More and more of it, more than he'd ever known how to tap before, more than he would have dared even if he had known. So much she felt it splash into her, until every inch of her skin tingled and Semira's dead Mark came back to life on her breast.

Then Kel drew in even more.

He was glowing now, a shining brilliant blue that cast light across the frosty grass. Watching him blaze against the sky, Nineva thought he was the most magnificent thing she'd ever seen.

Varza swung her magical axe with ruthless strength. The Sidhe loyalist tried to duck aside, but he was too slow. The huge blade bit into his enchanted cuirass as if it were no more than thin paper. Blood showered Varza's face as he screamed. Teeth gritted at the savage pleasure, she drew the life force from his dying body and added it to her store of magic, then jerked her axe from his chest. He fell in a bloody heap as she turned away in search of new prey.

Smiling in satisfaction, she surveyed the battlefield. It was going well, but that went without saying. Every death on either side became fodder for the Dark Ones' magic, making them still stronger. Even the dragons would eventually fall before them.

Slave! Rakatvira's mental snap made her flinch in the anticipation of pain.

She whirled and hurried toward him, sketching a careful bow. "Yes, Master?"

"There's something going on atop that hill." The Dark One glowered. His eyes glittered yellow against the mask of blood that covered his misshapen face. More of it dripped from his clawed hands and smeared his massive chest. "Find out what it is and stop it. I like it not."

She bowed again. "As you command, Master." Turning, she caught sight of the hilltop in question. Rakatvira was right. Something was glowing up there, bright and blue, waves of living power building steadily. Whatever it was, it was obviously a threat.

Varza started toward the hill at a jog. Spotting Arralt and a group of his men finishing off a dragon and its rider, she raised her voice in a shout. "General! With me!"

He whirled and snarled like a wolf, obviously in no mood to take orders. Wordlessly, she pointed at the hill. Arralt followed her finger and lost the snarl. Shouting a command at his men, he headed after her as Varza began to run.

"Nineva." Kel's voice seemed to ring in her head like the sound of chimes.

Nineva drew herself proudly to her full height and faced him steadily, though he glowed so bright now, he made her eyes tear. She watched his jaws open. There, down in the darkness of his throat, she watched the hot shimmer of a flame ignite.

It was the last thing she saw.

Kel's breath boiled over her in a savage sheet of fire like the blast of a flamethrower. The agony was worse even than her nightmares, a hell of white-hot pain, crisping skin, burning hair. Nineva shrieked, the sound blending with Kel's roar of anguish. She shrieked again, flailing, blind, her eyeballs bursting, flaming flesh peeling from charring bone.

Dying . . .

Varza stopped dead at the top of the hill. Centuries of torment among the Dark Ones had made her virtually immune to horror, yet even she took a step back.

The woman was blazing like a torch, performing a macabre dance of agony on the burning grass. She could not possibly be alive, yet she continued to move, continued to scream.

The dragon whose breath had seared her lunged to grab her flaming body—and he ignited, too. Their shrieks of anguish rose in a horrific chorus that went on and on as they burned long past the time they should have been dead. Until, blessedly, the two figures collapsed, the fire winking out. Smoke rose from the blackened corpses.

Varza backed away as the hair rose on her neck. "I don't know what in Rakatvira's black name they were trying to do, but whatever it was failed," she told Arralt. "They're no threat to us."

Together they started back down the hill.

Nineva! Kel flooded her consciousness like a blast of cool water.

Too late. The thought was weak, dim. Nineva could feel herself beginning to float. Somewhere overhead shone a pearly, calming light. She tilted her seared face back to look up at it and sensed the sweet promise of peace. No more endless battle, no more pain. No grief or duty or failure. Just peace, drawing her upward.

No! Kel's voice was distant, dreamlike, yet she could still hear the fear and desperation in it. *Don't leave me, Nineva. Please. Not when I've finally found you . . .*

She looked down and met those crimson eyes that were somehow looking down at her as though he held her in his arms.

You can't die. She knew he was trying to play on her sense of duty. *How will we beat the Dark Ones without you?*

Semira can do it. She's got her power back. Nineva could sense the goddess through the bond that connected them even now.

She's free. I've done my job. I can go home. I can see Daddy.

But what about me? The pain in the thought stabbed through the pleasant numbness of death. *There's nothing for me without you.*

She could feel his grief, his pain and failure. He'd done everything he could, but it meant nothing to her. She hadn't loved him after all.

His heart stuttered in his chest. *What are you doing?*

It seems, he said distantly, *that I'm dying.*

And his heart stopped.

No! She kicked away from the light. *No! We live together. Come back, Kel!* Desperate, she reached for him through the Truebond, reached for her magic, and sent it flooding into him.

Instantly she realized it wouldn't be enough. She was no longer even alive herself. They were both too far gone . . .

No, my brave girl. I'll not let you die. Not when you sacrificed so much. It was Semira, her voice stronger than Nineva had ever heard it.

Power flooded her, sweet and clean and bright, washing through her poor, seared body. Spreading healing like the purest water sinking into parched, dead earth.

Her heart lurched and began to beat. Nineva convulsed, coughing, choking on ash. Then suddenly the obstruction was gone, and she dragged pure air into her lungs. "Kel?" Her voice emerged as a cracked wheeze.

Lifting her head, she realized she was lying on her back. She rolled over onto her hands and knees, ash crackling and raining around her, and staggered to her feet.

Something huge and black and misshapen lay in the center of a circle of burned grass. Something that looked like it might have been a dragon.

He couldn't possibly be alive.

"Kel!" she wailed it. Had she endured all this, only to lose the one thing that mattered?

A great red eye opened, bright against the surrounding char. He snorted convulsively and scrambled to his feet, shaking himself like a wet dog. Ash flew from his body, revealing clean, whole, scaled skin.

Would I have let him die when he gave me back my power? Cachamwri asked in the Truebond, sounding amused. *That would have been a poor reward for such generosity and sacrifice.*

Then would you do something about the nightmares I'm going to be having for the next six centuries? Nineva asked tartly, brushing at the ash on her arms. The skin beneath it glowed. She stared down at it, startled.

He laughed. *I think that can be arranged. Semira, my love?*

I'm here. Free. Semira's voice spoke in Nineva's mind, reverberating like the sound of silver bells. *I'm free at last.*

And we have a great deal to do, if you're to stay that way, Cachamwri told her. *Let's get to it while our children tend to their enemies.*

He burst from Kel's chest, blazing bright as a star as he flew skyward, sparks flying from his wings. Kel gasped in surprise.

Nineva felt something vast stir within her, then pull free. A lush female figure emerged from her body and darted skyward, shining like moonlight, her hair dancing around her naked body as she flew. *Wait for me, my love!*

Semira. Free. Nineva felt tears sting her eyes. She'd done it. She'd succeeded.

"What. Have. You. *Done?*" The female voice roared in fury.

Startled, Nineva whirled. A group of armored warriors stalked toward her, Arralt in the lead. Ahead of them walked a woman, green hair matted with blood, yellow eyes narrow with rage, a massive battleaxe in her hand.

Varza.

EIGHTEEN

Kel was still feeling battered and dazed from the horror of the death he'd shared with Nineva, but rest obviously wasn't an option. He roared and charged the knot of rebels. The female spun aside from his path. He heard her axe ring against Nineva's conjured shield, but before he could turn back, he had his clawed hands full with rebel Sidhe.

Even so, through the Truebond he could feel Nineva's steady determination as she went to battle with the witch.

The team of rebels circled Kel as he turned, trying to determine which one to pick off first. He could tell by the way they moved that they were veterans, skilled with the lances, axes, and swords they held. They didn't even flinch at the prospect of taking on forty feet of pissed-off dragon. And they knew how to do it, too, as they closed in on him like wolves around a bear.

But the bear in question was hardly a wimp either. Kel darted his head at a warrior who'd come too close with his spear. Clamping his jaws down on the man's thigh, he jerked him into the air and gave him a vicious terrier shake.

There was a scream and a snap, and the man went limp, dead of a broken neck. Kel tossed him aside.

Before he could savor the triumph, pain sliced into his right rear leg. Kel twisted and sent his tail whipping around. It caught the warrior who'd driven the spear into his haunch, batting him skyward like a pop-fly ball.

The spear, however, did not disappear, so the bastard wasn't dead.

And neither were his friends, because they closed in on Kel with roars of rage, swinging axes and jabbing lances into any part of him they could reach. He leaped skyward and beat his wings hard enough to blow them back, catching another of their number with his tail while he was at it.

The remaining five warriors scuttled to a more respectful distance, cool-eyed and calculating.

Unfortunately, they'd done as much damage to him as he had to them. Two lances protruded from his body now, someone having caught him behind the right shoulder. Worse, he bled from half a dozen sword and axe wounds.

He breathed a fire blast at them, mostly to give himself time to think while they scattered.

Unfortunately, he was more adept at fighting battles like this in human form, where he presented his opponents with less target to hit. Too, shape-shifting would heal his injuries, one of which was bleeding too damn fast.

Kel let his magic pour through him. The next moment, he stood on two feet again, the familiar weight of a sword in his hand and armor protecting his body.

"Now," he growled, "let's try that again."

Nineva circled with the yellow-eyed Sidhe, keeping a wary eye on the witch's axe. Despite her near-death experience, Semira had returned Nineva's body to its full strength, or maybe even better. She felt fresh and strong, her sword and shield solid and familiar in her hands.

And she was more than in the mood to kick some alien ass.

"You're the one who engineered all this," Nineva snarled. "You stole Grim and the Egg and tried to kidnap the queen."

"Your grasp of the obvious is stunning." Varza lunged, swinging the axe in a hard, flat arc.

Nineva barely caught the blow on her steel shield, which bucked with the impact. She thrust her sword at the witch's gut, but her opponent danced away.

"You should have stayed dead, bitch." Varza spun, using the momentum of her body to add force to her axe blow.

Nineva jumped back, avoiding the diagonal slice that would have cut her in two. She immediately swung her own blade, but Varza ducked and kept her head.

"Your death will only feed my magic," the alien sneered.

"Gotta kill me first, skank."

Just beyond her opponent, she saw Kel pivoting with that inhuman grace of his to catch one of the rebels with a vicious slash. The man went down and didn't get up. She could feel Kel's grim satisfaction as he went after the next warrior.

She just hoped she'd have as much luck with Varza.

Semira spread her arms, glorying in the magic that flowed through her now that she had escaped the sword. *Ahhh, my love,* she purred, *freedom is so sweet!*

Cachamwri circled her, multicolored sparks shooting from his wings. His tail curled around her thighs. *I have dreamed of your freedom.*

He'd first touched Semira's glowing, trapped mind centuries before—and fallen helplessly in love. He'd wanted to free her from her sword then, but she wouldn't allow it. She had, she said, a duty to fulfill the prophecy and protect her people from the Dark Ones.

Now all those millennia of lonely patience were finally at an end. Semira was free. Goddess to his god, the eternal immortal lover he'd always dreamed of . . .

What joy they would know.

Soon, Semira told him. *But first, we must re-create the wards before the second wave of Dark Ones arrives.*

True enough. He cocked his head back and contemplated the planetary ley lines that crisscrossed the sky. *It should not be too difficult if we work together.*

She glanced downward, absently checking on her Avatar and Kel. Death magic roiled over the battlefield like black smoke, thickening with every warrior who fell—and making the Dark Ones even stronger. *It occurs to me,* she said slowly, *perhaps we need not be content with merely rebuilding the wards.*

The dragon's flaming head turned to study her. *What do you have in mind?*

Semira smiled and told him.

Kel blocked the sword thrust at his chest as the warrior spun by him. He disengaged his blade before the other could tear it from his hand, then drove his own point through the rebel's chest. The man grunted in pain. Kel watched his eyes widen through the slit in his visor before they rolled back. The rebel fell dead, his body falling off Kel's sword.

A blade flashed at his head, and Kel leaped back, landing nimbly as the final fighter studied him with narrow, hate-filled eyes. He grinned tightly, recognizing the man's gaudy fang-decorated horsehair crest.

It was Arralt himself.

"Freeing those gods accomplished nothing. I'm going to gut you," Arralt snarled, "and then I'm going to hunt down that milksop Llyr Galatyn and rip out his heart."

Kel smirked at him, sensing the rise of mystical energy

far over their heads. "I beg to differ. Feel that? Semira and Cachamwri are up there now, casting new wards. Your Dark One reinforcements won't be able to get through. And then we'll pick off the leftovers. Including you."

"You—!" Arralt broke off his snarled curse, eyes widening in surprise. "The magic! That's not just the wards—what are they doing to the death magic?"

Kel rocked back in surprise, realizing his opponent was right. The stench of alien magic was thinning like lifting fog. His eyes widened in delight. "I'll be damned. They're putting up some kind of dampening field."

Concentrating, Kel summoned a fireball. It blazed as hot and bright as ever. "Doesn't seem to affect ours, though." He gave Arralt a feral grin. "Oops."

Sick realization filled the rebel's eyes before he roared in fury. "You! You did this! You've destroyed everything!"

Kel laughed in his face. "Oh, not yet. But I'm going to."

Arralt lunged at him, his face twisted with insane rage as he swung his sword in great arcs back and forth. Kel retreated, parrying each swing, his blade jolting in his hands with each ringing contact, while he watched for the opening that would let him take the general's head.

Nineva was bleeding from a dozen wounds. They burned along her thighs, arms, and hands, across her rib cage and belly. She ignored the blood and ache. After what she'd been through, they scarcely registered.

All that mattered was taking down the bitch who'd done this to her, to Kel and Semira and Cachamwri, not to mention to all the dead and wounded who littered the battlefield.

And she was close to doing it, too. Varza had switched her axe to a sword, then conjured a lighter blade to replace that. She was moving more and more slowly, as if the blows Nineva had landed were also beginning to tell on her.

"Getting a little weak, Varza?"

The witch sneered. "Not as long as there's a dying man on this . . ." She broke off, her eyes widening. "What?"

Nineva grinned. "Took you long enough to notice it, bitch. My goddess has been busy with the ley lines." She'd felt the death magic fading a good fifteen minutes before. Apparently Varza had been too intent on killing her to notice. "No wonder you're getting weaker."

"Not too weak to kill *you!*" The alien bared her teeth and swung her sword. Nineva knocked her point aside, then drove her own weapon through Varza's chest in one ruthless thrust.

The alien's gaze fell, taking in the blade that pierced her. "No . . ."

Nineva bared her teeth. "Oh, yeah."

Varza darted a hand out, her gauntlet simultaneously disappearing from it. Before Nineva could flinch, the alien jammed her fingers through the eye slit of Nineva's visor to touch bare skin.

Something malevolent and powerful rolled from those fingers—the touch of an alien mind, an alien soul. Streaming into Nineva's being. Attempting to wipe her spirit from her body.

She's trying to possess me! Nineva realized in horror.

I don't think so. Kel snarled in the Truebond, sending a wave of strength and magic to reinforce hers. Varza's attack faltered.

Nineva drove one hand against the witch's chest and blew a fireball right through her. The alien mind winked out as Varza fell dead on the grass.

Nineva dropped to one knee, panting, spots dancing before her vision.

"Varza!" Arralt shouted as he saw the witch fall. Anguish and despair rang in his voice.

Kel drew back his sword. For an instant, the rebel's eyes

met his, and he knew the bastard would parry. Yet the blade never came up as Kel followed through with every ounce of his considerable strength.

Arralt's head spun away.

"I'll be damned," Kel murmured, lowering his sword as he watched the general's body tumble to the ground.

"He knew he'd lost," Nineva said.

He followed her gaze to the battlefield. From this vantage point, it was easy to see that the tide had turned. The rest of the rebels were even now going down before Llyr and his men, while the Magekind, the dragons, and the Dire Wolves were wiping out the Dark Ones.

"Without their death magic, the aliens are just big guys with swords," Nineva said, pulling her own blade out of Varza's corpse.

Kel grinned savagely. "And Arthur knows just what to do to big guys with swords."

Kel and Nineva spent the next three hours flying back and forth over the battlefield, breathing fire and throwing spell blasts to help in the mopping up.

The Sidhe rebels started surrendering as soon as word went out Arralt was dead. Llyr and his men rounded them up and took them prisoner.

But nobody offered any quarter to the Dark Ones, who fought with the single-minded viciousness of cornered rats. Killing them all off was a bloody, exhausting business, but finally the last demon was dead.

Nineva walked the battlefield at Kel's side, scanning for wounded among the fallen. Anyone she found still living, she worked to heal.

With the exception of the Dark Ones. Those, Kel took care of with a swift stroke of his sword.

Nineva and Kel weren't the only ones circulating across the battlefield. It seemed every Sidhe, Maja, and dragon was also at work, healing those they could and sorting the dead for burial.

There were far too many dead. More than three hundred Magekind had fallen, along with thirty werewolves and several thousand Sidhe, most of them rebels.

One hundred and fifty dragons had also died in the battle.

"Kel." Nineva stopped short, her gaze falling on one massive body. It lay sprawled and broken, its skin horribly burned, but she sensed a faint trace of life within it. Beside it lay a bipedal figure, too badly burned to identify, and quite dead. "Think we can save that dragon?"

"If we work fast," Kel said grimly, breaking into a run toward the fallen dragon. Nineva sprinted after him.

But as they came around its shoulder, they found someone already kneeling by the huge head. Nineva drew up in surprise.

It was a boy. He looked no more than fifteen or so, his chin as smooth as a girl's, his body long and narrow in the plain wool robe he wore.

The dragon moaned in pain, one brilliant blue eye slitting open, startling against the burns that marred its white scales.

With a sense of horror, Nineva recognized her. It was the pretty white dragon who'd flirted with Kel. "Eithne?" She hurried over and dropped beside the boy as she cast a quick translation spell. "Oh, Eithne . . ."

"It hurts!" the white dragon moaned. "I can't heal . . . It's too bad! Tried, but . . ."

"Shhh." The boy rested his hand on her neck. Nineva gave him a startled look. He spoke the Draconian language without the use of a translation spell, something she wouldn't have even believed possible to a human throat. "See? Your pain fades."

"Oh," Eithne said, sounding weakly surprised. "That *is* . . . better."

"I can take it from here," Nineva told the boy in Cachamwrian Sidhe. He had to be one of her people, given the spell he'd just cast. "This is no place for you. Your parents are probably . . ."

"Nineva," Kel interrupted, his voice very low. "That's not a boy."

Her mouth dropped open as he told her through the Truebond exactly who it was. She sat back on her heels and stared.

Magic poured from Merlin's long, slender hand, flooding over the dragon's body in a glittering wave. Everywhere it touched, the burns faded and disappeared, replaced by healthy white scales.

Finally the alien wizard took his hand away. Eithne sat up with a heave of effort and looked around, worry on her dragon face. "Aevar? Where's Aevar?" Her blue gaze fell on the blackened figure lying a short distance away. "Oh, Aevar . . ."

And softly at first, she began to keen in a Draconian cry of grief.

It was almost dawn when they gathered in the Magekind's council chambers—Arthur, Llyr, Diana, the Majae, and the Knights of the Round Table, including Kel and Nineva.

And of course, Merlin, who presented Arthur with the Grimoire. He'd reconstructed the magical tome from the remnants of it he'd found among the ley lines.

"You returned." Arthur accepted the book, staring at his mentor with dazed eyes. "Or—had you ever left?"

Merlin laughed, a surprisingly deep and masculine sound coming from a face so young. "Oh, I left. Nimue and

I have been very busy, spiking the Dark Ones' guns." He sobered. "But when I sensed my Grimoire's destruction in a death magic spell, I knew you needed me."

"And you weren't wrong," Arthur admitted.

"I don't know." There was a trace of pride in Merlin's infinite eyes. "You seemed to have things well in hand when I arrived."

"If you hadn't raised the wards again and nullified the Dark Ones' death magic . . . ," Morgana began.

"I had nothing to do with that." Merlin gestured gracefully, pointing out Nineva and Kel. "You'll have to ask those two about what happened to the wards."

"Damn, Gecko," Gawain said, staring at them. "What did you do this time?"

Kel shrugged. "Freed Semira from her sword and helped her and Cachamwri regain their powers."

Gawain blinked. "How the hell did you do that?"

He met Nineva's eyes and took her hand in his. His fingers felt warm and strong. "Together."

Sunrise and the coming Daysleep sent the vampires grumbling to their beds, though only after Merlin promised to stay the week.

Nimue, it seemed, was back on whichever planet Merlin had come from, busy testing champions among the intelligent race they'd found there. Merlin wanted to get back to his lover, but decided that he'd catch up with his Magekind and Dire Wolf creations first. He went home with Arthur and Gwen, who were almost ridiculously delighted with the prospect of Merlin as a houseguest.

The sun was coming up by the time Nineva and Kel left the capitol building and started the long walk toward his hillside home. They could have gated, but she wanted to breathe air that didn't smell of smoke and death.

They weren't even halfway home when they heard Draconian voices lifted in a shout.

Nineva's head snapped up as the sound echoed over the city. She shot Kel a troubled look. "I thought they were going home."

He frowned. "Apparently not. We'd better go check it out."

They found the dragons gathered on the rolling countryside that lay beyond the battlefield. Sitting in a huge concentric circle, the great beasts lifted their voices in a thunderous song of praise.

In the center of the circle lay Cachamwri, glowing like a star, with Semira lounging on his back like a lazy cat.

"Look," the Dragon God called as Nineva and Kel circled overhead, staring down at them in surprise. "It's our brave heroes!"

As one, the dragons raised their heads and roared. "Kel! Nineva!"

It was unmistakably a cheer of approval. Kel almost fell out of the sky.

Cachamwri laughed, a great, booming sound. "Come down, you two. I was telling them how you saved us all."

The dragons responded with another deafening howl of approval.

Holy hell, Kel said through the Truebond, sounding stunned.

Nineva poked him in the neck. *Land, would you? I want to hear this.*

They spent the next hours being feted and praised by the same creatures who'd tried to kill them the day before.

Kel told her later that he doubted they were entirely sincere—especially not the Dragon Lords.

As for the collective Dragonkind opinion of humanity, he predicted that would be even slower to change. Still, the courage and skill the Magekind and Sidhe had shown had indeed altered perceptions among the younger generation. And so had Cachamwri's obvious love for Semira, whom he seemed to see as the only being remotely like himself.

True love, Nineva murmured in their mental link as they finally flew home. *Ain't it grand?*

Kel snorted.

"Look," Nineva said, pointing a slender finger as her voice rose in exaggerated joy. "Is that . . . ? Why yes, I do believe it is! It's a bed!" Naked, conjured clean of both armor and blood, she fell face-first across Kel's huge mattress. "Hello, bed. I've missed you so."

"You," Kel told her, "are a twit."

"I'm also seriously sleep-deprived." She sat up long enough to fling back the covers, then squirmed underneath. "And I feel like I've been run over by a train." Yawning hugely, she added, "Or an entire flock of dragons."

"Dragons do not travel in flocks."

"Gaggles?"

"That's geese."

"Herds?"

"Horses."

"Big, flappy bunches?"

He lifted the covers and crawled in next to her, then hauled her against his side. "Sleep."

"That's what I'm trying to do, if you'd just shut the hell up."

Kel snorted and wrapped his naked body around hers. With a sigh of satisfaction, she cuddled back into him.

In seconds, they were both asleep.

NINETEEN

Nineva woke to kisses. Slow, openmouthed, hungry. She smiled sleepily. "You taste like apples and honey."

"That's why they call it magic." Kel cupped her bare breast, his thumb stroking her nipple to full erection.

She stretched against him like a cat, loving the feel of that clever hand, the mouth pressing gentle nibbles beneath her jaw. He found her ear and licked it until she giggled. Sliding a hand down, she located his cock, brawny against her belly, and stroked it gently. It felt like warm satin over a core of stone. Her fingers discovered his pulse, beating strong and steady.

A giddy joy suddenly rose in her. They'd survived. Against all odds—hell, they'd both died—they lived. Dark Ones defeated, Semira freed, wards back up and protecting both planets against another invasion.

"I can't believe we made it," Nineva murmured against Kel's mouth.

"I can." He gave her a deliberately arrogant smile. "I'm good."

"Yeah?" She pushed him over onto his back and rolled on top of him, straddling his thighs. "Prove it."

"Okay." He grabbed her backside in both hands and lifted her like a feather pillow. Before she knew what hit her, he'd spread her across his face and was giving her a long, wicked lick.

She gasped and squirmed. "Kel!"

He made a muffled sound with a distinctly satisfied note. Both hands reached up her torso and found her breasts. His fingers discovered the eager jut of her nipples and began to squeeze and tug. A long, juicy curl of pleasure made her sigh and catch the headboard.

Although . . . Nineva pulled off him.

"Hey, wait a minute . . ." He grabbed for her again, but she was already rearranging herself, head-down along his body. She grabbed his cock and angled it upward for a long, teasing lick of her own.

"Well," Kel said, his voice muffled by her straddling thighs, "if you insist."

"Less talking, more nibbling," she suggested, and swirled her tongue over the fat plum head of his cock.

He laughed and obeyed, licking with wicked enthusiasm. Suddenly he paused, and she sensed the rise of magic through the Truebond. The next stroke of his tongue made her jerk in delighted surprise.

"Is that *forked*?"

"How kinky do you think I am?" he lisped.

She giggled helplessly, squirming as he demonstrated. Until he finally paused again and said, "Less laughing, more licking."

Prodded, she leaned forward with a final snort of laugher and engulfed the head of his cock. Slowly, she started working it deeper into her mouth, suckling him hard. He stiffened, arching under her with a gasp of delight.

Then he deepened the Truebond link, and suddenly she could feel exactly how her mouth felt hot and wet around his most sensitive flesh. She gasped, intrigued, then drew off him and gave him a testing swirl of her tongue. Cupping his balls with one hand, she stroked, adding another luscious layer of sensation.

Kel, however, was not one to take pleasure passively. The next lick of that long forked tongue had her jerking. He rumbled in satisfaction at her reaction.

To retaliate, she bent her head and nibbled around the cap of his cock, enjoying the sensation of her own teeth through the bond.

So they played with each other, teasing, licking, slow gentle bites, the stroke and brush of fingers. And each touch made their building orgasms tighten a bit harder, a bit closer.

"Don't come," he warned against her sex. "I'll go over if you do."

Nineva smirked. "That sounds like a challenge."

"Better not, wench. Not if you want that cock somewhere other than your mouth."

Laughing softly, she lowered her head and sucked one of his balls into her mouth, then played her tongue over it. The sensations coming through the Truebond made her squirm. Any minute now, he'd . . .

"All right," he growled, "you asked for it."

He tumbled her onto her back as she shouted in laugher, then sat up and rolled between her thighs. Lifting her backside in both hands, he drove his cock into her wet, ready sex. That first lunge made both of them groan.

Kel drew out slowly, his eyes slitted in delight, then started working back in again. She panted, loving the thick satin feel of him, the strength and heat.

Grabbing his powerful biceps, she stared up into his starkly handsome face, the swing of his cobalt hair, the flex of his great shoulders. "I love you," she managed.

* * *

Those words were almost enough to make him come all by themselves. Kel managed to fight off the storm of pleasure with pure willpower as he gasped, "I love you, too!"

What a fucking understatement.

Nineva laughed, hearing the thought in the Truebond. Her lush inner muscles tightened on him, and he felt the first hard pulse deep in his core.

Or maybe it was hers. With the Truebond, it was hard to tell.

Kel let go, driving hard, glorying in the sweet, slick heat. She met him thrust for thrust, rolling her hips in time to his, straining for the hot explosion that danced just beyond their reach.

When it burst free, orgasm triggered orgasm in a luscious feedback loop more intense than anything either of them had ever felt before. The long jets were endless, blinding.

When he finally collapsed beside her, it took the last of his strength to pull her on top of his chest. They lay like that, boneless as rag dolls, wanting nothing more than to breathe.

The happiness Kel felt was so huge, it felt like a second climax. A thought occurred to him, but he hesitated, trying to come up with a suitable way to voice it.

Nineva lifted her head and grinned at him. "Yes."

Pretending offense, he glowered at her. "You could have the decency to let me ask."

"So ask."

"No. I've changed my mind."

"You lying lizard, you have not."

He lifted an aloof brow and stared, daring her.

She gave up in disgust. "Okay, then. *I'll* ask." The mock offense faded from her face, leaving behind a soft, lovely glow. "Marry me."

Kel smiled in pure, sweet joy. "Yes. Cachamwri's Egg, yes."

But there was the funeral to get through first, a memorial service that saddened them both despite their glowing joy.

The Sidhe and the Direkind had returned their dead to their families for separate services, but the Magekind had a different tradition. Kel told her Avalonian funerals were usually held in the central square, but there was no room for so many biers there. Instead it was held on what had been the battlefield.

So they gathered again—the Magekind, many of the Sidhe, a surprising number of Direkind, even a few dragons. All but the dragons wore full court mourning, black velvet heavy with embroidery and muted gems.

Nineva, her hand in Kel's, looked around with a kind of sad approval; the Majae had been busy with their magic. There was no sign of blood and death here anymore, no scorched earth or magical burns. The Magekind had turned the entire area into a vast summer garden, blooming and warm in the moonlight despite the winter that lay all around. Here and there were huge bronze statues—a dragon in the act of taking off with his Maja rider, a mounted loyalist Sidhe warrior, an armored vampire swinging his sword.

And in the center of it all stood the biers, arranged in circles. Men and women lay in armor or elaborate gowns, the injuries that had killed them gone, their faces calm as if in sleep. Flowers were mounded around them—roses, orchids, exotic Mageverse blooms Nineva knew no name for. The scent of them had a kind of sad beauty.

Then the ceremony began, first with prayers from representatives of each religion the fallen had followed. After that, friends and loved ones spoke of those they'd lost, some speaking simply, some with soaring oratory.

Nineva was crying long before it was finished. Even Kel wiped tears without shame.

At last Arthur stepped into the center of the garden. Looking regal, every inch a king no matter what office he held now, he lifted his voice. "We have known such grief the last year, so many losses. This is the worst of all. So many brave men and women gone, Sidhe and Magekind, so many gallant dragons fallen. So many who gave up immortal lives in battle against a vicious foe, that their people might live in peace. It is a debt we can never repay—except by what we do with the lives they paid for. Make the best of them, my friends." He let his voice ring. "And never forget."

Arthur drew Excalibur as all the vampires followed suit. "Magi, present arms!" A forest of swords pointed skyward, Kel's among them.

Merlin stepped out of the crowd to Arthur's side, beardless and oddly beautiful in black velvet robes that fell around his slim body. "Majae!" he called. "Join with me in sending our lost ones home."

Power lanced from his fingers and struck the biers, his magic blending with that the Majae obediently fired. The biers exploded into a globe of blinding light that shot skyward and detonated to shower the garden in a rain of sparks.

Blinking back tears, Nineva leaned into Kel's shoulder as a reverent silence fell.

After such sadness, Nineva would have expected their hasty wedding to be a dark affair, but she'd underestimated the Magekind's love of a good party.

It was held two days later in the central square, which was decorated with huge urns of shimmering red Mageverse roses for the occasion. The impressive crowd included all the guests who'd attended the funeral. Even the dragons wandered around in human form, apparently having been taught to shift by Soren. Most of them looked uncomfortable, but gamely determined to honor Kel. It almost seemed they were trying to make up for how they'd treated him.

The exception was Eithne, who made an exquisite platinum blonde and seemed to be having the time of her life flirting with every Magekind and Sidhe she encountered. Including some of the women; evidently she didn't have a firm grasp on how to determine human gender.

Nineva, however, had her own concerns to worry about. She'd dithered over what to wear, conjuring half a dozen court gowns. Finally she went with the one she'd always secretly dreamed of, regardless of whether it was appropriate for a Sidhe royal or not.

So it was that she walked down the aisle on the arm of Llyr Galatyn wearing a traditional white wedding gown, complete with seed pearls and yards of white lace. Her veil was so long, it brushed the pearl-strewn silk of her train.

To her delight, Kel looked as stunned as any mortal bridegroom as he stood waiting with Gawain under a rose-covered arch. Merlin stood with them, a great silver cup in his hand. The alien wizard wore yet another robe, this one white and strewn with emeralds, rubies, and intricate runes embroidered in gold.

Evidently, the Magekind came by their flair for the dramatic from Merlin.

Still, Nineva was only barely aware of him. Her groom held her full attention.

Kel looked incredibly handsome in a blue velvet tunic, its slashed sleeves revealing the white linen of his shirt. Blue hose clung to the powerful muscle of his thighs. A knight's golden spurs adorned his boots, a match for the belt knotted around his lean waist. His sword swung by his side, its gold and gems glinting.

His bow was reverent as Llyr extended her hand in his.

Kel straightened and accepted her fingers into his warm ones. Nineva couldn't take her eyes from him as they knelt together.

Later, she could not for the life of her remember the words Merlin spoke over them.

Apparently she made the correct responses, because Kel never flinched. His deep voice rang over the listening crowd as he swore to take her for his wife and hold her close to his heart.

Finally Merlin lifted the cup high over their heads. "Just as they share this wine, may Nineva and Kel drink deep of life's joys, finding strength in one another for those times of challenge."

He offered the cup to her, and she took it carefully. The metal felt surprisingly warm in her hands as she bent to sip of the frothing liquid inside. It tasted of sunlight and spring. Her mouth curled up in delight as she turned to Kel. "Drink deep of this, my husband. It is indeed sweet."

As he accepted and drank, symbolizing their union, the crowd lifted their voices in a shout of approval.

Nineva watched Kel hand the cup to Merlin again, scarcely noticing the tears of happiness that ran down her cheeks. When he hauled her into his arms, his kiss tasted like alien wine, exotic and shimmering with power.

The Magekind celebrated as fiercely as they grieved. There were tables loaded with food for the Majae and those guests who, unlike the vampires, actually ate. Nineva sampled delicious dishes she didn't know the name of, drank intoxicating drinks, and danced until her feet ached.

She was staggering from the dance floor with her new husband when a tall man she at first mistook for a Sidhe stepped into her path.

Then she noticed that his skin was tinted with blue, and his glowing blue eyes had slit pupils. The iridescence falling around his shoulders was not hair, but feathers. At his side stood a woman so lovely, she took Nineva's breath.

Nineva recognized Semira at the same moment Kel gasped and dropped to one knee, dragging Nineva down with him. He bowed his head. Around them, Sidhe and Dragonkind dropped to their knees, too, while the humans simply looked a bit confused. "Cachamwri, you honor us."

"Semira, my goddess," Nineva managed as her heart began to pound.

"Oh, up, children," the Dragon God said impatiently. "I have a wedding gift for you."

Nineva and Kel exchanged a slightly panic-stricken look as they quickly stood again. Kel cleared his throat. "We are honored yet again, though it is not necessary, Burning One."

"Well, of course not, but we wish to do it anyway. Come here, girl." Cachamwri caught Nineva's hand and drew her toward him. His mouth touched her cheek. Power surged through her with a little jolt that made her eyes go wide.

Nineva stared at him. "Oh." She blinked, as his gift burst full upon her. "Oh!"

Cachamwri smiled slightly and nodded. "Go then. I know you want to."

Her eyes flicked to Semira, who made a little shooing gesture. "You earned it, child."

Kel watched in bewilderment as his bride abruptly floated off her slippered feet, the train of her wedding gown swaying as she rose higher and higher. "Nineva, where are you . . ."

Light flared all around her, and she vanished. In her place was a lovely golden dragon, wings spreading wide to catch the wind. She looked down at him with a Draconian laugh. "What are you waiting for? Come on!"

Kel didn't have to be asked twice. He leaped after her,

letting his magic carry him upward until it was safe to transform.

As the crowd below broke into cheers, he followed the woman he loved toward the horizon.

Below them, Morgana Le Fay tucked her arm into Soren's and whispered, "I wondered how long it would take her to figure out that trick."

"She's not going to *stay* a dragon, is she?" Eithne demanded from his other side, sounding a bit horrified.

Soren only laughed. "Now, why would she do that, child, when it's so much fun both ways?"